WHAT READERS ARE SAYING ABOUT KAREN KINGSBURY'S BOOKS

"I've never been so moved by a novel in all my life."

—Val B.

"Karen Kingsbury's books are changing the world—one reader at a time."

—Lauren W.

"I literally cannot get enough of Karen Kingsbury's fiction. Her stories grab hold of my heart and don't let go until the very last page. Write faster, Karen!"

—Sharon A.

"Whenever I pick up a new KK book, two things are consistent: tissues and finishing the whole book in one day."

—Nel L.

"The best author in the country."

—Mary H.

"Karen's books remind me that God is real. I need that."

—Carrie F.

"Every time I read one of Karen's books I think, 'It's the best one yet.' Then the next one comes out and I think, 'No, this is the best one.'"

—April B. M.

"Novels are mini-vacations, and Karen's are my favorite destination."

—Rachel S.

Other Life-Changing Fiction™ by Karen Kingsbury

Stand-Alone Titles
Fifteen Minutes
The Chance
The Bridge
Oceans Apart
Between Sundays
When Joy Came to Stay
On Every Side
Divine
Like Dandelion Dust
Where Yesterday Lives
Shades of Blue
Unlocked
Coming Home—The Baxter Family

Angels Walking Series
Angels Walking
Chasing Sunsets
Brush of Wings

The Baxters–Redemption Series
Redemption
Remember
Return
Rejoice
Reunion

The Baxters–Firstborn Series
Fame
Forgiven
Found
Family
Forever

The Baxters–Sunrise Series
Sunrise
Summer
Someday
Sunset

The Baxters–Above the Line Series
Above the Line: Take One
Above the Line: Take Two
Above the Line: Take Three
Above the Line: Take Four

The Baxters–Bailey Flanigan Series
Leaving
Learning
Longing
Loving

Baxter Family Collection
A Baxter Family Christmas
Love Story
To the Moon and Back
In This Moment
When We Were Young
Two Weeks

9/11 Series
One Tuesday Morning
Beyond Tuesday Morning
Remember Tuesday Morning

Lost Love Series
Even Now
Ever After

Red Glove Series

Gideon's Gift
Maggie's Miracle
Sarah's Song
Hannah's Hope

e-Short Stories

The Beginning
I Can Only Imagine
Elizabeth Baxter's 10 Secrets to a Happy Marriage
Once Upon a Campus

Forever Faithful Series

Waiting for Morning
Moment of Weakness
Halfway to Forever

Women of Faith Fiction Series

A Time to Dance
A Time to Embrace

Cody Gunner Series

A Thousand Tomorrows
Just Beyond the Clouds
This Side of Heaven

Life-Changing Bible Story Collections

Family of Jesus
Friends of Jesus

Children's Titles

Let Me Hold You Longer
Let's Go on a Mommy Date
We Believe in Christmas
Let's Have a Daddy Day
The Princess and the Three Knights
The Brave Young Knight
Far Flutterby
Go Ahead and Dream with Quarterback Alex Smith
Whatever You Grow Up to Be
Always Daddy's Princess
Best Family Ever: A Baxter Family Children Story

Miracle Collections

A Treasury of Christmas Miracles
A Treasury of Miracles for Women
A Treasury of Miracles for Teens
A Treasury of Miracles for Friends
A Treasury of Adoption Miracles
Miracles—a Devotional

Gift Books

Forever Young: Ten Gifts of Faith for the Graduate
Forever My Little Boy
Forever My Little Girl
Stay Close Little Girl
Be Safe Little Boy

www.KarenKingsbury.com

KAREN KINGSBURY

WHEN WE WERE YOUNG

A Novel

HOWARD BOOKS
New York London Toronto Sydney New Delhi

Howard Books
An Imprint of Simon & Schuster, Inc.
1230 Avenue of the Americas
New York, NY 10020

This book is a work of fiction. Any references to historical events, real people, or real places are used fictitiously. Other names, characters, places, and events are products of the author's imagination, and any resemblance to actual events or places or persons, living or dead, is entirely coincidental.

First Howard Books trade paperback edition July 2019

HOWARD and colophon are trademarks of Simon & Schuster, Inc.

For information about special discounts for bulk purchases, please contact Simon & Schuster Special Sales at 1-866-506-1949 or business@simonandschuster.com.

The Simon & Schuster Speakers Bureau can bring authors to your live event. For more information or to book an event, contact the Simon & Schuster Speakers Bureau at 1-866-248-3049 or visit our website at www.simonspeakers.com.

Interior design by Davina Mock-Maniscalco

Manufactured in the United States of America

10 9 8 7 6 5 4 3

Library of Congress Cataloging-in-Publication Data is available.

ISBN 978-1-5011-7001-0
ISBN 978-1-5011-7002-7 (pbk)
ISBN 978-1-5011-7003-4 (ebook)

To Donald:

Well . . . we are starting our third school year as empty-nesters. I never liked that term. And I can tell you now with all my heart that there's been nothing empty about the last few years. They've been full of beautiful walks and meaningful talks, nights when we randomly jump into the car and spend an evening with Kelsey and Kyle, and our grandbabies Hudson and Nolan. We play tennis and Ping-Pong and hang out with our wonderful friends. And yes, we miss having our family all together every day. But when they all come home the celebrating never ends. What I mean is, I've loved raising our kids with you, and now I love this season, too. God has brought us through so many pages in our story. The Baxter family came to life while our children were growing up. When the Baxters told stories around the family dinner table, we were doing the same. And when their kids auditioned for Christian theater, our kids were singing the same songs. Our family is—and always will be—inexorably linked with the Baxters. So thank you for creating a world where our love and life and family and faith were so beautiful I could do nothing but write about it. So that come some far-off day when we're old and the voices of our many grandchildren fill the house, we can pull out books like this one and remember. Every single beautiful moment. I love you.

To Kyle:

You will always be the young man we prayed for, the one we believed God for when it came to our precious only daughter. You love Kelsey so well, and you are such a great daddy to Hudson and Nolan. I literally thank God every day for you and for the friendship we all share. Thank you for bringing us constant joy. We pray and believe that all the world will one day be changed for the better because of your music, your love and your life.

To Kelsey:

What an amazing season this has been, watching you be the best mommy ever for Hudson and Nolan. Your little boys are happy and healthy and strong, and most of all they love Jesus. I love when Dad and I hang out at your house. It is so full of love and joy, peace and patience and God's Holy Spirit. Because you and Kyle have intentionally welcomed the Lord into your home. What a beautiful time for all of us! Hudson is deep and kind and joyful, with a heart that hints at the powerful ways God will use him in the years to come. And Nolan is a little sponge, learning everything he can from Hudson and you and Kyle. He's such a joy to be around! I believe God will continue to use your precious family as a very bright light, and that one day all the world will look to you and Kyle as an example of how to love well. Love you with all my heart, honey.

To Tyler:

I remember that long-ago day when you were a ten-year-old and you said, "Mom, someday I'm going to write music and make movies. But I think I'm also going to write books in my spare time. Like *you* do!" And now, that's exactly what you're doing. How amazing is it that we have the privilege of writing together? Already we've had one screenplay—*Maggie's Christmas Miracle*—show up on the Hallmark Channel, and now a series of books about the Baxter children! I never could've imagined the ways God would work all this together. You're still songwriting, still writing original screenplays and dreaming up movies. But now you're writing books in your spare time, too. I love it! God has great things ahead, Son, and as always I am most thankful for this front-row seat. Oh, and for the occasional evening when you stop by for dinner and finish the night at the piano. You are a very great blessing, Ty. Love you always.

To Sean:

I will always believe that God has great plans for you. Like your dad and me, you are using your mid-twenties to find your way, to figure out your journey of faith and the future ahead. And to become the kind of person you want to be—in faith, in work, and in your relationships. You are a beloved son, Sean. I can't wait to celebrate all that your life will be in the years to come. Stay in His word. I love you always and forever.

To Josh:

Way back when you were little, we always knew you'd grow up to be a hard worker, and you absolutely are! As our much-loved son, always remember that having a relationship with Jesus is the most important gift you will ever give your family. In the years to come, as you walk out your faith together, just know how much we love you. We always have. We believe in you. We are here for you always!

To EJ:

What a tremendous time this is for you, EJ. You are doing so well at Liberty University, so excited about a career in filmmaking. Just one more semester and you'll have your degree! We are so very proud of you, Son. Isn't it something how God knew—even all those years ago when you first entered our family—that you would need to be with people who loved God and loved each other. But also people who loved the power of storytelling. I'm so excited about the future, and the ways God will use your gifts, and the gifts of your siblings, to make movies that will impact the world for the good. Maybe we should start our own studio—making movies that will give people hope. Whatever the future holds, remember that your most powerful hour of the day is the one you give to Jesus. Stay in His word. Pray always. I love you.

To Austin:

I'm so grateful I can see you when I travel to Liberty University to teach. You are tall and strong and a godly presence on that campus, Son. But not only that. You are a loyal friend with a very deep heart. During breaks we will continue to have many happy times together as you still have three semesters left! But even now, more than halfway through your college education, I still miss you in the everydayness, Austin. You have been such a light in our home, our miracle boy. Our overcomer. You are my youngest, and no question the hardest to let go. At times the quiet here is so . . . quiet. Even with your dad's jokes and your two little nephews in our lives. So, while you're at Liberty, on nights when you lie awake in your dorm, just know that we have cherished every moment of raising you. And we are still here. We always will be. Love you forever, Aus.

And to God Almighty, the Author of Life,

who has—for now—blessed me with these.

Jessie
RJ
KARI ∞ TIM (deceased)
∞
RYAN
Annie
Maddie
Hayley
BROOKE ∞ PETER
Sophie
Egan
DAYNE ∞ KATY
Blaise
THE BAXTER FAMILY

Cole
Devin
Sarah Marie (deceased)
ASHLEY ∞ LANDON
Janessa
Amy
Heidi Jo (deceased)
ERIN ∞ SAM
(deceased) (deceased)
Clarissa (deceased)
Chloe (deceased)
Tommy
LUKE ∞ REAGAN
Malin
Johnny
JOHN BAXTER ∞ ELIZABETH (deceased)
∞
ELAINE

THIS BOOK IS part of the Baxter family collection, but it can be read as a stand-alone novel. Find out more about the Baxter family at the back of this book. Whether you've loved the Baxters for a decade, or you're finding them for the first time—*When We Were Young* is for you.

WHEN WE WERE YOUNG

1

Noah Carter's paramedic uniform felt like it was made of lead. His black work boots, too. Like gravity had doubled down on him. Or maybe it was something else. Maybe his heart was trying to kill him.

He deserved it.

The rolling green grass of Bloomington's Rose Hill Cemetery came into view. Already Noah could feel the serenity of the place. He parked his old gray pickup in the back lot and cut the engine. It was the second day of November.

The last day of his marriage.

Clouds gathered in the distance. Big storms forecast for Indiana. No surprise. There wasn't a single sunny thing about this chilly afternoon. How could it have come to this? What had gotten so bad that he would walk away from Emily Andrews?

He loved her. He still loved her.

Just not when they were together.

Noah pressed his back muscles into the worn cloth seat and stared out over a sea of tombstones. This was where he needed to be. Perspective ruled supreme in a cemetery.

Especially this one.

His heart had led him here, to this place of death and defeat. The reason was obvious. For a long time now he could feel his heart turning on him. In the last two years, though it kept him alive, it had become a separate being, pulling away from the rest of his body. So that with every beat he could feel the struggle, the fight. His heart digging its claws into him and dragging him down, pressing against him. Spreading destruction and discouragement like arsenic through his veins.

If his heart was going to kill him, the job was almost done. He was moving across town tomorrow.

Noah climbed out of his truck and zipped up his blue paramedic jacket. *Breathe, Noah. Just breathe.* His shift at the firehouse had been longer today, and on the way out he'd run into the new fire chief, Landon Blake.

Last day of his marriage. He runs into Landon Blake, of all people.

The guy was the poster child for a perfect marriage. He had a slew of kids, including a niece they were raising. But every time Noah saw Landon and his family at a picnic or party, the man looked head over heels in love with his wife.

The chief was a Christian, Noah knew that much. Bible verses hung on the walls of his office. His faith showed in his actions. The man was intentional about his staff, always asking the guys about their home life.

This afternoon was no different.

"You doing well?" Landon had asked him. "Everything okay with the family?"

Why the chief would ask that today, Noah would never know. Unless God, Himself, put the question in the man's mind. Whatever the reason, Noah wasn't about to open up there at the station. What could he say? Everyone's favorite Internet couple was calling it quits?

Noah hadn't breathed a word about the pending split. He certainly wasn't going to talk about it with Landon Blake. "All's well, Chief." Noah hadn't even slowed his pace. Just waved at the man and walked right on past.

Conviction tightened its hold on Noah.

Never mind, he told himself. *What's done is done*. Everyone would know soon enough. Emily didn't look up to him. Didn't respect him or believe in him. She was jealous of the fans Noah talked to online, and she no longer felt loved. End of story.

He glanced at the swirling clouds over the cemetery. The news would surprise everyone, of course. It would make headlines. Most of their followers would be devastated by the breakup. Especially people who found a reason to stay married because of what they saw in Noah and Emily.

But the person it would've hurt most of all would never know.

Sweet Clara.

A cold wind blew across the rows of tombstones and

washed over Noah. He turned up the collar on his jacket and pushed into it. He didn't come here much anymore, but today a visit seemed only right. Because Noah wasn't just leaving Emily and their two kids. He was leaving Clara, too.

Even if she wasn't alive to know it.

Three inches of rain had fallen in the last few days, so the ground was soft as Noah moved into the plotted field. Four rows in, six gravestones over and there it was. Noah stooped down and brushed off the marker.

Clara Andrews. 1990–2016

Tears stung at the corners of his eyes. *Dear Clara.* He leaned back on his heels and stared at her name. *You're whole now. Your body is perfect, the way your spirit always was.* Noah breathed deep and turned his gaze to the sky again. "You take good care of her, God." His whisper blended with another gust of wind. "No one ever loved You more."

Clara had been Emily's younger sister. Just as beautiful, but born with cerebral palsy. She walked with braces and crutches and struggled to speak a clear sentence. But she was golden through and through. Everyone loved Clara, but Emily most of all. Their father left home when Emily was ten, and eight years later their mom died when her car got trapped in a flash flood.

After that, Emily raised her sister. Clara was always happy, always well loved because Emily took care of her with a fierce sort of protection. As if her own life depended on it.

It was why Noah had fallen in love with Emily in the first place, there in the cafeteria at Indiana University.

Those were big-time football days for Noah, back when he was a star quarterback for the Hoosiers. His world revolved around his teammates, his NFL dreams and his personal successes. He might never have noticed Emily if it weren't for Clara.

Noah turned his attention back to the tombstone. "This isn't how it was supposed to go, Clara, girl." He sighed. Gravity pulled hard at him again. "You tried to warn me."

She did. A year before the seizure that took her life, Clara had come to him with her iPad. In her own endearing way, she had struggled to ask her question. Just a couple words. "Too . . . much?"

Clara lived with them. She had from the time Noah and Emily married. And that day her words were not a complaint or a criticism. They were simply a question formed from the innocence of her soul.

On the iPad was Noah's Instagram account. @When_We_Were_Young. The account that had blown up when the two of them got engaged. The one that allowed them to buy their house. The one that paid the bills.

Clara had held up the device and looked from the smattering of stunning photos to Noah. Then she'd said the clearest sentence Noah had ever heard her say. Standing a little taller, leaning on her crutches, she spoke straight to him. "Noah . . . Emily . . . needs you."

The implication was clear. Clara believed that her sister didn't need one more perfect social media post or another thousand people following them, obsessed with their life. Emily needed Noah. At the time he only smiled at Clara and nodded. "Of course she needs me." He didn't blink. "We all need each other!"

Noah felt then the way he still felt today. He had never set out to become Internet famous. None of them had. But from the day he asked Emily to marry him, the world had been drawn to them. A million people on Instagram alone looked forward to every update. What they were doing that day, what they might say to each other, the way they parented their kids, the flowers that lined the walkway to their front door.

Every single detail about their life and love.

From the beginning Noah had been in charge of posting. It was his Facebook page people followed, his Twitter account, his Instagram. He was responsible for keeping the posts inspirational. Engaging. Beautiful.

How many people had Noah and Emily's story helped along the way? How many followers had found their way back to faith and family? Their social media presence was important. The world needed people like them.

Noah gritted his teeth. Emily used to feel the same, thankful for a platform to share Bible verses or encouragement. But sometime after Clara died, Emily changed. Posting about their lives no longer felt fun and meaningful. She didn't care how many likes or retweets they got, or whether their numbers were growing.

As if their story was no longer worth sharing.

Noah took a heavy breath and stood, his eyes still on Clara's grave. Never mind that their social media accounts netted them six figures a year. Or that Noah could work far fewer hours at the fire station on a good month of Internet income.

They *were* making a difference. Which was why Noah wouldn't give it up. Their story was touching hearts and changing lives. Wasn't that the point? Wasn't it worth the effort? Noah still thought so.

Even now.

Not Emily, though. She thought their whole platform had become one big farce. Nothing but smoke and mirrors. That the faces they wore for the public were not the faces they wore around the dining room table.

Or in the bedroom.

Ever since Emily's change of mind, tension grew like weeds where love had once flourished. And there was nothing either of them could do to change the fact. The more Noah tried to convince Emily to smile for the camera, the more closed off she became. She accused him of being more concerned with their mostly female followers than with the life the two of them were really living.

He could still hear her frustrated criticism as far back as two years ago. "We used to post about our happy life. Now we're forcing life for the happy posts."

The temperature was dropping. Noah exhaled. "I don't know, Clara." His words came in a broken whisper. "Maybe I should've listened to you." He still wasn't sure. What was wrong with sharing their love with the world?

And how come Emily was jealous of the fans? Of course he needed to respond to their followers.

Noah could still think of a hundred reasons why their social media presence was a good thing. Emily couldn't think of one.

"But that's just a part of why we're splitting." He moved his toe along the edge of Clara's gravestone. "It's so much worse than that, Clara."

For months now their differences about posting on social media had paled in comparison to something else. These days, Emily no longer thought Noah was real.

"You only need me for one reason," she had told him a week ago. "So that you can stay in the public eye. @When_We_Were_Young." She looked mean. Like she hated him. "Well, Noah, we aren't so young anymore. And this isn't love. It hasn't been for a long time."

He had tried to reason with her, tried to keep his cool. "That's not true, Emily." His voice betrayed his frustration. "Think about where we started. It's still that way with us. At least it could be."

But she wouldn't let up. "It doesn't matter where we started. It matters where we are now." Her eyes were flat. "We're a show. Nothing more."

Noah clenched his jaw. If that were true then maybe they were doing the best thing: taking a bow before things got truly ugly. Before the kids suffered.

The kids. Gravity doubled down.

Aiden was four and Olivia, two. Neither would remember the show, as Emily called it. They would also never know the joy and security of having both parents under the same roof. Which was maybe also a good thing. Better not to know their parents fighting and scratching and clawing at each other.

Better to see a more beautiful picture of their mommy and daddy after the divorce. When they had separate addresses. Noah squinted toward the distant trees. Kids rebounded. At first they'd notice that Noah wasn't around as much, or that they had to go to a different place to see him.

But time would heal even that. Another gust of wind blew over him. Yes. The kids would be fine. He was convinced. As for their social media, he would take a break, of course. And then he'd start it up again. Focus more on the followers and ways to encourage them. Less about him. Nothing about Emily.

The clouds were darker now, the next storm almost overhead. Time to go home and do the one thing he never thought he'd do. Pack up his bags and leave the girl of his dreams.

Noah stooped down once more and spread his hand over his sister-in-law's name. "I'm sorry, Clara." His eyes welled up again. "If I could have found a way, I would've loved Emily forever." He blinked a few times so he could see. "I'm sorry."

Clara once had a game she liked to play with Noah. She'd limp toward him, her eyes lit up. That big one-in-a-million grin stretched across her pretty face. Then she'd tilt her head. "Forever, right?"

"Forever and ever," Noah would say.

"Daddies don't . . . always . . . leave." She had said it a thousand times since the day Noah and Emily married. They knew their lines by heart, he and Clara.

"Not this daddy." Noah would put his hand alongside Clara's cheek. "Not ever."

It was Clara's game because deep down she needed reassurance. Needed it every day. Seeing her own father leave had altered her life. Never mind her limited abilities, she understood the loss. And because of that there was one thing she desperately wanted for her beloved sister.

That Noah Carter would never, ever leave.

His heart wrestled within him. *Clara, forgive me.* He ran his fingertips over the granite letters in her name, and as he did he could see her again, the sparkle in her blue eyes, the innocent crooked smile. Clara never believed she had special needs. Never let cerebral palsy stop her from caring about people. She couldn't do a lot of things, but Clara definitely knew how to love.

She did it so well that back then Noah couldn't imagine their home or their lives ever being anything but beautiful. Couldn't imagine love running dry. The way it had now.

Once more he stood, and with a final look at Clara's grave, he turned his back to the wind and walked toward his truck. He had rented an apartment across town, his new home starting tomorrow. The third day of November. Four days before their eighth anniversary.

So far he had no furniture, which suited him. He'd

sleep on the floor—penance for finding a way to fail Emily. Then when his new reality became something he could live and breathe under, he'd haul himself to a furniture store and get the basics.

All while wishing God had shown them a different way, a way to save their marriage. For Emily to stop snapping at him and for him to find a way to reach her. But that prayer had gone unanswered like so many others in the last year. Noah stared at the stormy sky once more. Clara wouldn't be here beneath the cold wet merciless dirt if God had answered their prayers.

A quick step up into his truck and Noah set out for their house in Clear Creek, where they still lived as a family. Where they were still a they. The four of them, for one more night. After he moved out, Emily and the kids would live there. But *they* wouldn't live there. Never again.

The house was three blocks south of their friends Ryan and Kari Taylor. The Taylors were maybe in their early forties, and every Wednesday night they led a Bible study. A year ago it was something Emily looked forward to every week. Noah tagged along because that was what Emily wanted.

Now the two of them hadn't been to the study in over a month. Once they decided to end things, when they were sure there was no going back, no saving their marriage, they stopped attending. No point hanging out with people committed to staying together.

Yes, Ryan and Kari Taylor were two more people he was about to let down. Two more on a growing list. Kari was the sister of Ashley Baxter Blake, his fire chief's wife. So in no time everyone at the Bible study and at the firehouse was bound to know what had happened. How @When_We_Were_Young had fallen apart.

Noah kept his eyes on the road. Rain began to pound against his windshield and he could hear words in the rhythm. *You don't have to do it . . . don't have to do it . . . don't have to . . .*

As if all of heaven were crying because this was the very last night Noah Carter would live under the same roof as his family.

Three bolts of lightning shot down around him like so many well-aimed spears. Noah slowed his truck in the deluge and flipped his windshield wipers up a notch. Was God trying to tell him something? Sending lightning to get his attention? However bad this storm, it was nothing compared to the one raging inside him.

At home, Noah pulled into the garage and walked through the back door. He took off his boots and stood there, listening for their voices. Emily and Aiden and Olivia. In another life he would've called out to them, anxious to see their faces. Ready to hug their necks.

But not today.

His family wasn't home. They were spending the evening with Ryan and Kari.

"Anywhere but here," Emily had told him last night. "Watching you pack."

The memory of her broken voice twisted Noah's heart again. He didn't blame her.

A month ago he had been called out to a wicked car crash. Four girls flying down Highway 37 south toward Bloomington. The driver must've gotten a text, because she crossed the centerline and hit a semitruck. Head-on.

Only a handful of times had Noah responded to a call as horrific as that one. The driver died with her phone still in her hand. The girls in the backseat, too. Just the female in the front passenger seat lived long enough to be taken to the hospital.

Noah remembered removing her broken, battered body from the wreckage. As they loaded her into the ambulance he had one thought: the girl was never going to make it. And she didn't. Died halfway to the emergency room. But he would never forget the way her body felt in his arms. Gasping for breath, heart barely beating, death minutes away.

The same way Noah's marriage felt tonight.

No wonder Emily didn't want to watch.

He walked through the kitchen and down the hall toward the bedroom. Emily hadn't slept here for a long time, though Noah had offered. Her spot was in the den now, on the sofa. Better than trying to sleep in their bed, she had told him. With or without him. At least until he moved out. The kids had never noticed, and the arrangement was easier on everyone.

The silence between them was too loud for either of them to get much rest.

When Noah reached their room he grabbed on to the doorframe and stared at the bed, the place where their love had once been the center of their universe. Some mornings he would wake and watch her sleep, her long, blond hair, the way it fell in waves past her shoulders, her flawless profile and pretty cheekbones.

He'd lie there like that, just watching her, waiting for her to open her pale blue eyes. People said Emily looked like Kate Hudson. Noah thought they were wrong. Emily Andrews was far more beautiful. The most beautiful girl Noah had ever seen.

Once upon a yesterday, he would take her hands in the morning and pray for her, asking God to protect her and bless her day. He exhaled. When was the last time he'd done that? The last time they'd prayed together about anything?

Noah couldn't remember.

Deep breath. You can do this. His suitcases were on the floor, empty and ready. He picked up one, then the other and set them on the bed. Sadness pressed in around him again. For a long moment he stared at the comforter, the pillows. He ran his fingers over the familiar softness.

Here was where they had loved and laughed and cuddled their babies on long nights. Noah straightened and blinked a few times. *Now it's just a place to pack my bags.*

Already he had packed up his home office—all except his computer. And a few boxes he had in his closet. The rest of his things were in the garage waiting for him to toss them into the bed of his truck tomorrow. All he had left were his clothes.

Noah walked to his dresser and opened his top drawer. He pulled out two handfuls of socks and tossed them in one of the suitcases. Then he returned for his T-shirts, but as he reached toward the rear of the drawer something sharp pierced his finger. He pulled his hand back and rubbed at a tiny spot of blood.

"What in the world . . ." He pulled the drawer out further.

Only then, as the light hit that spot, did he see what it was. A sinking feeling churned at Noah's stomach. He stepped back and shook his head. No way. The room began to spin, and Noah grabbed the dresser to steady himself. Really? Now, when he only had hours left in his own home, when all that remained was to pack up the essentials? Now, he would find this?

The pin was part of a boutonniere. The one he had worn on their wedding day.

Noah picked it up and looked at it, studied it. Crazy, because he had searched for this a year ago and couldn't find it. He had thought it would make a good social media post for their seventh anniversary.

Now it was nothing more than a marker. Like the stone over Clara's grave. *Here lie the remains of Noah and Emily's marriage.* Thunder shook the house, but it was nothing compared to the silence. Nothing compared to the flower in his hand.

Dried and crumbled, sharp enough to cut him. And long since dead.

Just like their marriage.

2

Up until now, Emily Carter hadn't told anyone Noah was leaving. She rarely talked to her dad, and Noah's family lived in London. Conversations with them didn't go deep and were every few months at best.

But for all the ways she'd held the sadness inside and hidden it from her private and public worlds, today it would all come to the surface. Because in an hour, Emily and the kids would go to Ryan and Kari Taylor's house. Kari was onto them. She knew something was wrong with Noah and Emily.

Of course the other reason their breakup was about to be public was more obvious.

Noah was moving out tomorrow. He was headed home to finish packing.

Which was why at five o'clock that evening Emily buckled Aiden and Olivia into their car seats and took them to Chick-fil-A for dinner. Two boxes of chicken tenders later, and the three of them pulled into Jackson Creek Park. The rain was holding off for now. So for the next half hour she pushed the kids on the swings.

Anything but head back home.

"Higher, Mommy!" Aiden's cheerful singsong voice cut through her sad thoughts. "All the way to the moon!"

"You got it, buddy." Emily didn't have to pretend with the kids. They made her happy even now. When her world was falling apart. "To the moon and stars!"

"Yes!" Aiden kicked his feet toward the sky.

"Me, too." Olivia was in the baby swing beside her brother. She grinned at Emily. "Swing, Mama. Swing high."

Emily stood between the two, pushing Aiden, then Olivia. They chattered with each other, Aiden asking Olivia if she ever wanted to fly like a bird and Olivia giggling. Like Aiden was the funniest person in the world.

The sky was darker now. Emily lifted her eyes to a break in the clouds. *If only we could stay here. Lost in the innocence of a swing set and playground. If only time could freeze, here and now.*

While she and Noah were still married.

"Higher, Mommy! Please." Aiden grinned at her.

"Good manners, buddy."

Emily kept pushing, kept answering like she was hanging on every word. But all she could feel was the past swirling around her, washing over her like a rogue wave, consuming her. One thing was sure. The storm about to move over the park was nothing like the one they'd been walking through for more than a year.

The crazy thing was even now, no one knew. Not until tonight.

So many people would be shocked.

The online world would be, of course. None of their

followers would've seen this coming. But more than that, the people who actually cared about them. The ones they did life with. They would be stunned. Emily glanced at the adjacent jungle gym.

The playgroup moms hung out here twice a week. Just a dozen mothers from Clear Creek Community Church with kids the same age as Aiden and Olivia. Emily talked to a few of them on a regular basis. Every couple days at least. For the last four weeks she had ordered herself to tell them the truth. But the words simply wouldn't come.

Their social media following meant that even those friends saw Emily as the other half of everyone's favorite former football player, Noah Carter. No, her friends didn't talk about her public persona at coffee dates or playtimes with the kids. Only one of them had ever even brought it up.

But they all knew.

Emily was Internet famous. A term she had never liked and now hated.

In the virtual world beneath the glass of every laptop, computer, iPad, and smartphone, people felt like they knew Noah and Emily. Masses had followed them from the day they got engaged. They loved them with heart emojis and commented that Noah and Emily were #goals for the rest of them. They retweeted and reposted and shared everything Noah ever uploaded on their various social media formats.

Because like other social media stars, up until now

Emily made her living helping Noah create pictures and pretty words about their practically perfect family. Their enviable love.

So how was she supposed to tell her friends that the perfection was only in pictures? That Noah was no longer the guy he'd once been. Or maybe he'd never been that guy at all. He didn't love her anymore. That much was for sure. All they ever did anymore was fight.

Yes, at home things had fallen apart and . . . well, now she and Noah were calling it quits. No more picture-perfect love. No more social media.

Aiden's voice broke the moment. "The clouds are scary." He stretched his legs, gathering speed on his way up to the sky.

"Yes." Emily's heart felt every word. "They are scary, baby. But we'll be okay. We will."

Emily checked her watch. Five-thirty. By now Noah would be home, packing his clothes. Since yesterday, his two large bags had been sitting against the wall in their bedroom. Right about now he'd be grabbing stacks of jeans and sweaters and dress shirts and tossing them into his suitcases. Like he was about to take a fall vacation.

Instead of undoing every bit of love they'd ever shared.

"I'm ready for the slides." Aiden looked back at her from the swing.

Olivia nodded. "Slides, Mama!"

She helped them down and watched as they ran to the structure in the middle of the playground. Usually she stayed close to them on the slides and bridges and monkey bars. Not today. The equipment was safe.

Emily took a spot on the nearest bench. "I'm right here." She waved at them.

Both kids waved back.

If only she could get a grip on her thoughts. What was happening and what was she doing here? When her whole life was falling apart? Kari Taylor was the only one who suspected trouble between them. Emily and Noah's involvement in the Taylors' weekly group started a year ago, when Kari had approached her one Sunday after church. Something about the woman reminded Emily of her mother.

"You should join us," Kari had said. Then she had told Emily how the meetings worked. An informal conversation first and sometimes a dinner. Then the six or eight couples would sit around the Taylors' living room and open the Bible.

"The focus is marriage. How we can love better and why marriage is worth the fight." Kari had looked deep into Emily's eyes. "I think you and Noah would love it."

The truth was they needed it.

Olivia waved at her from the top of the slide. "Hi, Mama!"

Aiden was right behind her. "Don't worry, Mommy. I've got her."

Emily smiled. "You're a good boy, Aiden. Such a nice brother."

The memory from a year ago was still right in front of her. Clearer than the kids.

Back then Emily and Noah had thought they could save their marriage. They were sure of it. The two of them dated every week or so and always tried to find common ground. More often than not, though, their evenings ended with a social media post for the public and silent tension for the two of them.

A deadly combination.

So when Emily had jumped at the offer of a Bible study group focused on marriage, Noah had been less excited.

"It's too personal." Noah had looked alarmed from the minute Emily brought it up. "People will study us. They'll think we're in trouble."

Emily had stared at him a few beats before stating the obvious. "We *are* in trouble, Noah."

"Exactly." He had paced the kitchen that Sunday night. "The other couples will figure it out. And then . . . everything we've worked for . . ." He shrugged. His voice sounded weary, like that of someone three times his age. "Look . . . I don't want people in our business."

"You *what*?" Emily's laugh had dripped with sarcasm. She had taken a step closer, narrowing her eyes. He couldn't be serious. "You don't want to lose what we've worked for? Fame? An imaginary illusion? Is that all I mean to you?" She had wanted to leave, take a drive and figure out what she was supposed to do next. But the kids were asleep upstairs. So she had tried to reason with him. "You don't want people in our business? Are you kidding me, Noah?"

She had turned her back on him and then after a few seconds she'd spun around and faced him, glaring. "People are *always* in our business. That *is* our business, right? Inviting people *into* our business and giving all the world—"

"Okay!" He had yelled loud enough to wake the kids. "I get it." Upstairs Olivia had begun to cry.

"Nice, Noah." Emily had leaned on the kitchen counter. "Wake the baby."

"Stop!" He'd lowered his voice, but his anger had filled the room. "Enough!" He was seething, his face red. Like a sea of fighting words were pushing to escape his lips.

"What does that mean? *Enough?*" She had still been angry, too, but she found a quieter voice. Upstairs, Olivia had settled back down. "Enough what?"

"Enough of you trying to convince me." He had exhaled and taken a step closer. As he did the fight began to leave him. "We can go to the Bible study."

She had stared at him, at the flash of darkness in his eyes and the tight line of his lips. She had a lot more to say. Like the fact that going to a Bible study for married couples shouldn't be this hard. Or that if the invite caused him to be so angry, maybe it was too late already.

But Emily had kept quiet.

"Will you do me a favor?" Instead of rage, Noah's expression went flat. His shoulders sank as his request came. "Can you hide it?"

"Hide what?" She couldn't tell where the hurt stopped and the anger began.

"This." Frustration filled his eyes and he waved his hand around in the air. As if he were trying to clear away the poison between them. "Hide . . . this. Whatever *this* is. Please."

And so they had.

The memory stopped short as Aiden ran up to her. "Is the storm coming, Mommy?" Olivia was close behind. Aiden looked around, clearly nervous. "Or can we keep playing?"

Emily studied the clouds. It was getting darker, but so far no rain. "You have time. A few more minutes."

"Yay!" Aiden took his sister's hand and they ran back to the slide.

Like coming to the park, the weekly Bible studies had become their routine. Ryan and Kari Taylor's seventeen-year-old daughter, Jessie, would come to the house each Wednesday to watch the kids so Emily and Noah could fake it. Hide it.

Week after week after week for the past year.

They would spend those two hours chatting with the other couples about their workdays and deadlines and kids and houses. They would eat dinner with the appropriate laughter and speak kind words for Kari Taylor's cooking. Kari was part of the Baxter family. Everyone in Bloomington knew and loved the Baxters. It was easy to find nice things to say.

Then when their Bibles were open, Emily and Noah

would take turns reading right along with everyone else. Once on the short way home, Noah had stopped the car. "Just two things that really matter, right?" He had looked so handsome, so much like the Noah she had fallen in love with. His eyes had held a glimmer of hope. "Love God? Love people? Right?"

"Right." Emily had watched him. Wishing things were different.

"Then why . . ." Noah's look had gotten deeper. A look of heartbreak and defeat. His voice fell to a broken whisper. "Why can't we love each other? The way we used to?"

Emily had no answers. Not then and not now. She could hardly remember why they had fallen in love in the first place. As if their suffocating marriage had changed her. The way it had long since changed him.

Some Wednesdays after meeting at the Taylors' house Emily would sense progress. Even a little. Times when he would take her face in his hands and brush his cheek against hers. He would whisper words he hadn't said in forever. "I love you, Emily. We can do this. We can."

But the trying and failing and hiding it from their friends all came to an end last month. They stopped going to Bible study and about that time Noah sat her down after the kids were in bed. Then he spoke words she never thought she'd hear. "Emily . . . I rented an apartment."

The ground turned to quicksand, and Emily wondered if she might slip between the tiles and die right then and there. It took a minute to find her voice. "You . . . what?"

"I'll move out the third of November." His tone was gentle. "We both know it's our only option. For the kids."

For the kids? Emily hated that phrase. Did Noah really think divorce would be good for their babies? How could that even be possible?

The broken moments of their recent past stopped replaying for a minute. Emily watched the kids taking turns on the slide.

Noah had explained himself a dozen times since then. Aiden and Olivia were young. They would never know what they'd lost. Never remember the family they once had, or what it was like living together in the same home. That had to be better than raising them together in a world of fighting and bickering. Better to be apart, Noah had said a dozen times. Where their lives could be full of light and love. In two separate happy homes.

A chill ran down Emily's arms. Thunder sounded in the distance. Light and love? Two separate happy homes? How could Noah think this divorce would lead to that?

Her response had been the same every time Noah brought it up. The only way for the kids to win was for them to win. Pure and simple. They needed to find a way back to what used to be. That long-ago time when love was real and they were real. When everything didn't have to be an opportunity for a viral post on Instagram.

Emily thought about their social media name. The

one that was famous. @When_We_Were_Young. If only they could remember what that felt like. The two of them and only the two of them. Another rumble of thunder. "Okay, kids. Time to go."

"One more time, please!" Aiden was at the top of the slide. Olivia, too.

She smiled at them. Aiden looked so much like Noah. "Okay. One more."

Her breath felt heavy as she exhaled. Deep down, Emily knew this suffocating ending was killing Noah, same as it was killing her. Neither of them wanted their marriage to die. But here they were.

And tomorrow Noah Carter, the only man she'd ever loved, would leave and start a new life. Because the bridge between them had long since been shattered, and they had no way to the other side.

Emily imagined the scene in the morning. When Noah Carter drove out of her life. If her heart was still beating tomorrow at this time it would be a miracle.

Rain started to fall as Emily slung her bag over her shoulder and lifted Olivia into her arms. Aiden stayed close beside her as they headed to the car. On the way they passed the four plastic dinosaurs. The ones Olivia liked best.

"Dinoars, Mama!" She pointed as they hurried by. A whimper came from her. "Dinoars!"

"Not now, sweetie." Emily sped up her pace as another clap of thunder hit. "It's about to pour rain."

The wind picked up, but Aiden didn't seem bothered. "You know what I did, Mommy?" He grinned up at her. "I pretended the swing was a spaceship! And the slide was a planet far, far away." He skipped a few times and held his hands up toward the rain. His laughter eased the pain in her heart. "You know why, Mommy? Cause I'm good at pretending."

Me, too, she thought. They reached the car and she buckled Olivia in first. Aiden climbed into his car seat on his own, then Emily walked to the other side of the SUV and made sure he was buckled tight. She looked straight into her little boy's eyes. "I *thought* you were in a spaceship." Emily found her smile. "You looked like a big, strong astronaut."

"Thanks, Mommy." He giggled again and pointed to his sister. "Livi really wanted to play on the dinosaurs. That was going to be her best part."

"Dinoars." Olivia shrugged her shoulders. "Dinoars . . . night-night."

Emily hurried to the driver's seat and slid behind the wheel. "Yes, Olivia. Dinosaurs had to go night-night."

"Mommy." Aiden looked at Emily's eyes in the rearview mirror. "Livi's still working on saying *dinosaur*. We can give her some time."

A genuine smile filled Emily's soul. After tomorrow, these two were going to give her a reason to get up each morning. "We can definitely give her some time."

Another clap of thunder shook the parking lot. Aiden caught her reflection again, eyes wide. "Good thing we're safe in here. Because Jesus is keeping us safe, right?"

"Right." Emily started the car and pulled out of the parking lot. With everything in her she wanted to believe that what Aiden said was true. That Jesus was keeping them safe. She chose her next words carefully. "We're going to see the Taylors, okay? They invited us over."

From the mirror, Emily watched Aiden give her a curious look. "Is Daddy going?"

"Dada?" Olivia raised both hands, palms up. The adorable way she had of asking any question.

Emily's heart ached. *No one told me it would hurt like this,* she thought. *And tonight is just the beginning.* Deep breath. "No, honey." She shot a happy smile over her shoulder at Aiden. "Just us this time."

Aiden stared out the window for a moment. The rain pounded the car in earnest now, washing over the windshield and roof of their Subaru. Finally her little boy released an anxious sound. A whimper, almost. Then he looked at Emily again. "I want Daddy to come. I miss him."

"Yeah, baby." She needed to get past this moment. Another glance in the mirror. "I miss him, too."

After that, Emily kept her eyes on the road. She did miss Noah, absolutely. With every heartbeat, some days. The way he used to be. Fall of 2006 and 2007 . . . 2008 and 2009.

That was the Noah Carter she missed.

Emily gripped the steering wheel and held the vehicle steady against the storm. Kari Taylor had called last Thursday, after Noah and Emily had missed another

Wednesday. "I can't get past it," Kari had said. "This feeling . . . like something isn't right with you and Noah."

"Us?" The room had started to spin, but Emily had only forced a laugh. "We're good. Really." The lie came easily. She was used to this. "It's just that we're—"

And that's where her ridiculous explanation died.

In the silence that followed, Kari's words came like a gentle breeze. "Come over, Emily. Please. I'll listen, that's all. Whatever it is."

Since then Emily had been dreading the meeting, but now it was here. Ten minutes later she and the kids hurried from the car to the Taylors' front porch. The storm raged all around them.

As soon as Kari opened the door, Emily could see the truth. Whether God had told her, or Noah had called, this much was obvious. Kari knew how bad things were.

The proof was in Kari's eyes.

3

Emily and Aiden and Olivia walked inside and took off their wet shoes and jackets. Ryan Taylor met them in the entryway. "I hear I have a couple kids who like to play the dinosaur game!"

Ryan was the head football coach at nearby Clear Creek High School. "Dinosaur!" Aiden's eyes lit up. "You know how to play that?" He jumped a few times in place.

"You bet." Ryan roared and held his hands up like claws. His laughter kept things light. "I'm a goofy dinosaur. My kids could tell you that."

"Yes! This is going to be the biggest fun!" Aiden clapped his hands. "My daddy taught me how to be a dinosaur." He pumped his fist in the air. "I'm really good."

Emily looked at Olivia. Her little girl didn't seem to know exactly what was happening. But she jumped around a bit, too. "Dinoar!" When Aiden was excited, she was excited. Always.

Heartbreak was bound to work the same way.

The Taylors' daughter Jessie joined them. "Come on, Olivia. We'll be the girl dinosaurs."

"Be good, Livi." Emily kissed her daughter's soft

cheek. Then she looked from Jessie to Ryan and mouthed the only thing she could say. "Thank you."

Whatever had happened to make them come together as a family tonight to help her, Emily didn't know. But she desperately needed this. Time to sit with Kari at her kitchen table and talk.

Just the two of them.

Ryan and Jessie and the kids started up the stairs, roaring and laughing.

"Let's go in here." Kari led the way to the kitchen. She poured them each a cup of coffee and they sat, face-to-face. Emily looked down for the first minute, staring at the swirls of steam coming off her drink. What was she supposed to say? How could any of this be happening?

"That bad, huh?" Kari's voice was calm again. So soft Emily could barely hear it. "I've been feeling that was the case. I knew God wanted me to reach out to you."

Emily lifted her eyes to her friend. "Noah hasn't called you?"

"Not at all." Kari took a sip of her coffee, her attention never leaving Emily. "You come up every time I pray. We haven't seen you for five Wednesdays." Concern filled her voice. "Noah won't return Ryan's phone calls." She paused. "We knew something had to be wrong."

Emily took a slow, deep breath. There was no easy way to say it. She could start back a year ago, when things first began falling apart. But maybe it was better just to get to the point. Today was all that mattered. Where they were now.

She let her eyes lock onto Kari's. "Noah's leaving tomorrow." The words felt like so many rocks in her mouth. Would they ever get easier to say?

At first Kari seemed not to fully understand. "He's . . . taking a trip? For work?"

"No." Emily shook her head. "He's moving out." She felt the start of tears. "He's at home packing right now."

"Oh, Emily." Kari set her cup on the table. Her face became a few shades paler. "No." Her voice fell to a whisper. For a long while she sat there, like she was processing how this could have happened. "Are you saying he needs a few days away? Is that what this is?"

Exhaustion pressed in around Emily. Suffocating her.

Would it be like this every time she tried to explain how their marriage fell apart? How she let Noah Carter walk away? Emily stared at her coffee. No one would believe it. Not even someone like Kari.

The thought of years of conversations like this made Emily feel tired and sad. She inhaled and lifted her eyes to Kari. "Noah has an apartment across town." She put her hands around her drink. The warmth worked its way through her, but it stopped short of her freezing heart. Emily shook her head. "It's over between us. I'm . . . I'm sorry I didn't tell you sooner."

Kari let the news sit between them for a moment. Then she reached across the table. "I'm sorry." She sighed. "I don't know what to . . ." Her pause seemed to help her collect her thoughts. "Can we pray? Before we talk?"

"Sure. I guess." Prayer. Something Emily hadn't done

in days. What was the point? Noah was leaving anyway. The only man she had ever loved—would ever love—was walking out of her life. Tears blurred her eyes. She couldn't talk even if she knew what to say.

Kari took the lead. For the next few minutes she spoke the most beautiful words to God, calling Him the Healer and One who gives hope. She asked Him to comfort Emily and walk with her through this. Then she praised God for being the Wonderful Counselor and she ended the prayer with a single request. "God, we ask for a miracle—whatever that looks like. That Noah would come to his senses and find a way to make this marriage work. Because that's what You want, Lord. It's what Emily and Noah want deep down. We ask believing, in Jesus' name. Amen."

Emily wanted to say amen, but she could only mouth the word. Kari might as well have prayed that pigs could fly. Noah was leaving.

His mind was set.

"Emily. Tell me what happened." Kari sat back and picked up her coffee. "I can't believe it. You two are . . ."

"The couple everyone wants to be." Emily looked at her wedding ring. "I know." The sound of her children's laughter came from upstairs. She wasn't sure she had the energy to tell the whole story now. But she didn't want to go home, either. "The social media . . . it's been killing us for a long time."

And like that the story came. Emily didn't spare any details.

For twenty minutes Kari listened. When Emily reached the end, she felt fresh tears. "We don't know how to be us anymore. How to be real." She sighed. "He used to be my hero. Now I don't even know if the guy back then was real." She swirled the coffee in her cup. Then she lifted her eyes to Kari's. "Like . . . was it all a big act? To get more followers? To build our public image?"

Kari nodded. "I can see that." She seemed to measure her words. "But, Emily . . . if what you and Noah had wasn't real, no one would've followed you." Her pause felt heavy. "Have you thought of that?"

Emily bristled. This was the last thing she had expected. For Kari Taylor to take Noah's side. She leaned back and crossed her arms. "It *was* real." She let that settle for a few seconds. "But it isn't now. Somewhere along the way it stopped being real. He started craving the attention from . . . from a million beautiful strangers." She put her hand over her heart. "After that, *we* stopped being real. I look at him now and . . . I don't know who I'm seeing. He cares more about the virtual world than me."

"Okay." Kari sounded confident. Like she was sure her advice was going to make a difference. Even now. "So stop the social media. Pull the plug." Kari's eyes held hers. "Take a few weeks away and remember how to hear God's voice again. Then throw out your computers and find your way back to real."

Emily loved how that sounded. Find their way back

to real. She searched for a way to make Kari understand. "Noah doesn't want that. He thinks I'm the problem. Not our online presence. Plus it's our income. He'd do anything for the advertisers."

"Advertisers?" Kari looked confused.

"Yes." Emily felt sick explaining the situation. Like they'd bartered their marriage to the highest bidder. She sighed. "We make quite a lot of money with every social media post."

The reality seemed to land on Kari. She nodded. "I see."

Emily uttered a sound that was more cry than laugh. "He plans to pick back up with posting sometime after the divorce." She shook her head. "If you can believe that."

Kari looked shocked. "He isn't thinking straight." She hesitated. "I mean, he knows things have to change." Kari looked confused. "Right?"

"Of course." Emily felt overwhelmed again. "But he thinks I'm the one who needs to give in. That I stopped wanting to smile for the camera because I stopped respecting him. But him? No, he still loves it. It's become one big egofest for Noah." She exhaled. "And he can't see any of that."

For a while there was quiet between them. "Is that what happened?" Kari was quick to complete her thought. "I mean, at first you smiled for the camera. Why *did* you stop?"

Emily looked at her coffee cup. The first memory

that came to her was on her lips before she could stop it. "It's the fans. The other girls." She looked up. "Over time he started, I don't know . . . talking with them more often." She paused, hating the way her heart hurt. "I walked into the office one night about a year ago and he was chatting with some blonde. Back and forth. Like they were friends."

"Got it." A shadow fell over Kari's face. "I can see why you aren't so quick to smile."

"Exactly." Emily wasn't sure she was explaining it right. "I mean, I know he's not really into these girls." She felt the tears again. "I don't think so, anyway." A sick feeling started in her stomach. "But he loves being a celebrity to them. Loves the attention and the enormous following. The fame." She hated putting this into words. "He isn't *that* shallow. Really. He can't be." She closed her eyes for a moment. When she opened them she looked right at Kari. "He had the deepest heart before."

"So . . . he talks to these girls because they're fans . . . of the two of you?"

"Right." Emily exhaled. "But I think a lot of the girls might have wrong motives. Half of them comment on his looks. How I'm so lucky to have a guy like him. How he's so hot. That sort of thing." She shrugged one shoulder. "I think he likes it because he keeps chatting online with them. When me and the kids are right there in the other room." Her tone grew more intense. "Like, get off the computer and come be with your family."

"Yes. You're right." Kindness filled Kari's tone. "A couple times when I went on your profile I saw women saying things like that. Those flirty comments." She paused. "And he's been spending more and more time talking with them?"

"So much time." Emily waved her hand in the air. "He's missing out on me and the kids because he's on the computer. Constantly." She leaned back. "He sees nothing wrong with it. He says all he ever talks about with these fans is me. Us. How they should turn to God. They're just followers. Fans." Tears stung her eyes again. "Meanwhile I'm putting the kids to bed by myself. Going to bed by myself. And waking up in the morning to Noah staging some photo shoot around the breakfast table."

This time Kari looked down for a moment. When she lifted her eyes her expression was filled with sorrow. "So . . . You've lost what's real."

"Yes." Finally someone understood. "Over what's virtual."

"I'd be upset, too." Kari reached out and took her hands again. Her next words did not come quickly. "Emily . . . God is a God of miracles, you know that."

Emily was beginning to wonder. First her mother, then Clara. Now losing Noah. The sound of Aiden's and Olivia's laughter came again from upstairs. Emily whispered, "I guess." Her tone wasn't convincing.

"It's true. Your marriage isn't over yet." Kari hesitated. "God can do anything. Even now."

Tears threatened once more, but Emily held them back. She had said all she could say. A half hour later she had gathered her kids and thanked the Taylors for caring. On the drive home she thought about the details she'd shared with Kari. She could've gone into greater depth, but why? No sense talking about each fight or angry night or the moments when Emily was certain they were headed for divorce. Noah was moving out in the morning.

That said it all.

• • •

KARI WAS STILL reeling an hour after Emily and the kids left. Ryan had been busy helping RJ with a science experiment, but now—with dinner and homework behind them, Kari asked Ryan to take a walk. The storms had rolled through and the night was calm. A cool breeze hung in the evening air.

When they were alone, the gentle wind on their faces, Kari gave Ryan the details. How Emily no longer wanted to be part of their social media fame, how she had come to believe their public persona was all that mattered to Noah. And how he spent all of his time online, talking to his female fans.

"Emily is hurt, and it seems like Noah no longer feels loved and respected by Emily . . ."

"I can see that." Ryan gave a side nod, like he was considering the sad situation. "If Emily's always frustrated with him and disapproving—for good reason—then Noah's going to feel shot down. Not a good situation for either of them."

"Exactly. They've reached an impasse." She sighed. "Noah's leaving tomorrow." Kari glanced at her husband as they walked toward the park at the end of their street.

"What?" Ryan looked shocked. "I can't believe it. Why didn't they tell us sooner?"

"I guess they didn't know what to say." Kari lifted her eyes to the night sky. "What would that be like, documenting every moment and outing, every emotion and thought for all the world to see?"

Ryan shuddered. "Miserable." He took hold of her hand and slipped it into his jacket pocket.

For a while they walked with just the rustle of the wet fallen leaves on the ground and the occasional barking dog. Kari took a long breath. "We need to pray, Ryan. I mean, they can still make this work." She loved the feel of Ryan's fingers between hers. Lately things had been a little tense between them, too. "With God all things are possible, right?"

"Definitely." Ryan had the same look as when he tried to help Jessie with trigonometry. Like the answer had to be out there somewhere. "They need to pull the plug on the social media. That's for sure."

"Noah won't consider that." Kari almost hated to say it. "They make money on it. Advertisers pay them for their posts." She slowed her pace. "Did you know that?"

"No." Ryan looked discouraged. Again they walked in quiet for a few minutes. "Remember . . ." Ryan's voice was softer, "when it felt like we didn't have a chance?"

A swirl of memories filled Kari's heart. "We were so

young. So many misunderstandings." She ran her thumb along Ryan's. "There you were lying in a hospital bed with a neck injury . . ."

"And all you could hear was that nurse telling you my girlfriend had been by." Ryan stopped walking and faced her. The love in his eyes was the same as it had been all those years ago.

If only Kari had been paying attention.

"The girlfriend was me." She smiled. "And I didn't even know it."

A soft sad chuckle came from deep in his chest and they started walking again. "All of life changed in that moment."

He was right. Kari let the pieces form in her mind. After that she had written Ryan off and married Indiana University Professor Tim Jacobs. They were expecting their first baby—Jessie—when Tim's affair came to light. He'd been seeing one of his students, and at the same time that girl's former boyfriend had been stalking Tim.

The crazy guy shot and killed Tim a few weeks before Jessie was born.

Kari and Ryan reached the park and started on the lit path. This was their routine, their favorite way to spend an hour together each night. Kari caught his eye again. "You saved my life after that."

"Hmm." Ryan released her hand and put his arm around her. "I'll never forget the look on your face when I moved back to Bloomington. When I showed up at church in the middle of all the madness."

"And how you were there at the hospital after Jessie was born." Kari looked through the darkness to the trees above. "I can't imagine if all that was documented on social media. The way we came back together . . . your love for Jessie—like she was your own." Kari shook her head. "Our wedding." She stopped again and faced him. "If all that was splashed over the Internet."

"We would've survived it." Ryan's eyes shone with a love that never dimmed. "You and I would've survived anything, Kari, girl."

"We would've." Her voice dropped to a whisper and the rest of the world fell away.

Suddenly the bad news Ryan had told her a week ago was right there between them again. Like a physical object. Kari pushed the reality from her mind. That could wait. She wanted to keep the focus on the crisis with Noah and Emily.

Ryan put his hands on either side of her face and stepped closer, so their bodies were touching. His kiss put an exclamation mark on all they'd just shared, all that made up their own love story. "Nothing could ever make me leave you."

Kari wanted to believe that. She had to. Even with the news.

Tears stung her eyes. Ryan was a successful football coach at Clear Creek High, and Kari stayed busy with the kids and her interior design work. But no busyness or passing of the years could touch what she and Ryan Taylor shared. Not even the bad news.

They were still living out their own second-chance love.

Ryan kissed her again and put his arm around her like before. As they started back toward the house he breathed deep. "Noah and Emily still have a chance. I have to believe that."

Later that night, when they were about to climb into bed, Ryan took her hand once more. "Let's get on our knees. For Noah and Emily."

It was something they'd done often throughout their marriage. When one of their kids was in a difficult place or when they faced unimaginable losses. Kneeling together to pray wasn't something they merely talked about in theory or figuratively.

Kari and Ryan actually believed in it. Even now.

She nodded and followed him to a spot near the foot of their bed. In the back of her mind she told herself maybe they should pray for their own marriage as well. But that could come later. Tonight was about their young friends.

And so together they dropped to their knees and in urgent, whispered words they asked God for a miracle. That God would get Noah Carter's attention now. This very night.

Whatever it took.

4

His family had been home for an hour, and still none of them had come in to see him. Noah wasn't surprised. There were no rules for this, no playbook to tell them how to walk out their last day together.

Still, Noah figured at some point the kids would come find him. It wasn't normal for them to stay to themselves. To not even wonder where he was. Was Emily already turning them against him? Five years from now would they forget to call him when they got chosen for a Little League team or named student of the week? Would he become a figure from the past?

Noah couldn't stand the thought.

He should go out there, of course. But that would mean looking into Emily's blue eyes, asking her about the day as if everything were normal. Pretending this wasn't their last night together.

Something Noah wasn't about to do.

So he let the hour slip by. Every few minutes he'd stop folding or filling his suitcases and listen to their little voices, their laughter. Just listen. Surely they would run down the hall any minute. But they never did.

Now he was sorting through the last boxes from his closet, old yearbooks and college newspapers detailing his every success, every touchdown. An article from September 2006 lay at the top of a pile of papers. All of them in the box because Emily had saved them.

His eyes found the beginning of the story.

> Noah Carter turned in a stunning three-touchdown performance Saturday in a 21–7 win over Western Michigan. Carter, a freshman . . .

That's as far as he got before it hit him.

The house had gotten quiet. Aiden and Olivia weren't making any noise in the kitchen. He couldn't hear Emily's voice, either. A quick look at his phone told him what had happened. Emily must've put them to bed. Without telling him.

Noah set the box on the floor and burst through the bedroom door. "Emily?" Was she serious? How could she do this? Didn't she think he'd want this final piece of normal? The chance to help them brush their teeth and climb into their pajamas? A last time to pray with them and kiss them good night?

Anger stirred Noah's hurting soul as he walked through the empty kitchen and down the hallway to the kids' part of the house. First door on the left was the playroom.

Noah shot a look inside. Nothing. The place was empty, toys cleaned up, stacked in their bins and on the shelves. *Come on, Emily. Are you serious?* He clenched his jaw and walked toward the bedroom. Sure Emily could blame this on him, and maybe it was his fault. But it was hers, too. She hadn't smiled at him in months. And now this?

A few feet from the doorway, Noah heard Emily's voice. He stopped. His heart beat so hard he could barely hear her.

"I already told you, Aiden." She sounded patient. Like her world wasn't falling apart. "Daddy's busy. He's packing."

"Why is he packing?" Their son's voice was tight with fear. "Where is he going?"

Olivia began to whimper. "Where Dada?"

"Kids, it's going to be okay." Again Emily sounded fine. Like she was explaining why they had to clean the playroom. "Daddy has to go away."

"No!" Aiden raised his voice. "No, Mommy, please. I don't want Daddy to go away." He was crying now. "Tell him to stay! Please!"

Noah felt his anger triple. What was she doing? He grabbed a quick breath and burst into the room. He ignored Emily. Couldn't look at her.

Instead he went straight to Aiden.

Their little boy was out of bed and running to him. "Daddy!" He held out both arms. "Hold me, Daddy. Please, hold me."

Noah swept him up and cradled him. Like he used to do when Aiden was a baby. The child buried his head in Noah's shoulder. He spoke in muffled words that

Noah could understand for one reason alone. Aiden was his.

"Mommy . . . she said you're packing. You're going away!"

"I'm sorry, Aiden, buddy. Mommy didn't explain it very well." He looked over his shoulder and glared at Emily. She was sitting on the edge of Olivia's bed, but she wouldn't make eye contact. Just stared at her folded hands.

Noah shook his head. When had she become his adversary?

"Dada?" Olivia sat near her pillow. Her eyes welled up with tears. She held both hands up. "Go?"

How was he supposed to deal with this? He kept Aiden tight in his arms and sat on the edge of the boy's bed. "First . . . Daddy is never leaving you and Livi." He could feel Aiden's tears soaking through his paramedic shirt. Noah stroked his son's hair and his little back. "Never, ever, ever."

The child's sobs still shook his body. But gradually he lifted his tearstained face to Noah. "Wh-why are you packing?" He rubbed his fists over his cheeks. "Why?"

What was he supposed to say to that? How could he tell his little boy that Mommy and Daddy could no longer live together? Or that Emily had stopped respecting him months ago?

Noah felt the pressure on his heart double. Gravity weighed against him, mocking him. He searched for the right words. But he settled for the only thing he could think to say. "Daddy is going to live in another house. But that doesn't mean we won't be together." Noah kissed the top of Aiden's head. How many times had he done this, held his son and comforted him?

And how could he do this at the end of a hard day if he didn't live here?

Noah's words seem to land on Aiden. "So . . . you're moving to another house?" He leaned back and studied Noah's face. "Why would you do that? You're a'pposed to live here."

For a brief few seconds, Emily looked up. Noah could feel her accusing eyes on him. As if she was interested in the answer, too. Like somehow she really thought this was all his fault.

He kept his focus on Aiden. *Don't cry,* he told himself. *Stay strong.* "It's just something I have to do, buddy. So everyone will be happier." His words sounded ridiculous. Something he had to do? Leave his family? "But I'll still see you." He looked past Aiden to Olivia. "I'll still see you, too, baby girl."

Olivia didn't say anything. Tears still made her eyes wet, but she wasn't crying. She had no real idea what was happening. Emily held her hand, and for a minute the room was quiet. Just the occasional quick breaths from Aiden.

Their son was calmer now, the tears slowing. "But, Daddy . . ." He put his hands on Noah's cheeks and looked straight at him. Straight to the deepest part of his soul. "I'm happy now. With you living here. So we can wrestle before bedtime."

Knives through Noah's heart couldn't have hurt this bad. "I want that, too, Aiden." He smoothed his son's blond hair from his eyes. "I really do."

There was nothing to say. No understanding the situation. Not for Aiden or Olivia. Not for Emily or him. Who could make sense of a couple that once loved each other with every breath, now standing by while love died? Taking part in choking the life out of it?

"It's time to sleep." Noah set Aiden down on his bed and helped position the pillow beneath his head.

Aiden yawned. "When are you leaving?"

"Tomorrow." There was no soft way to say that. It simply was.

"No." His cry wasn't as loud as earlier. Aiden sat up and wrapped his arms around Noah's neck.

Noah had to remind himself to breathe. This was worse than anything he had imagined. Finally Aiden loosened his grip and settled back onto his pillow. "I'm going with you, Daddy." A slight smile lifted his lips, but the sobs were back. Racking his body, shaking his little heart. "Please? Can I go with you?"

"Aiden." Noah had to get out of here. He couldn't hold back his tears another minute. "You can come see me whenever you want. Mommy and me already decided that."

It was time to pray, something they did together

every night. But Noah couldn't bring himself to say a word to God. "You sleep well, buddy. Okay?"

Aiden's eyes were sleepy. But he blinked them wide open at that. "What about our prayers?"

"Pray!" Olivia was lying down now, too. Emily still sitting near her, holding her hand.

Noah heard Emily exhale. Like she didn't want to do this any more than he did. Noah worked the muscles in his jaw. *Forgive me, God. There is no greater hypocrite than me.* "Sure. Yeah. Go ahead, buddy."

Aiden nodded.

For a quick second Noah caught Emily looking at him. Probably wondering how he was going to pull this off.

Breathe, he told himself. *The words won't come unless you breathe.* Noah reached for Aiden's little hand. His warm fingers felt familiar, like home. Because he had held his little boy's hand every night like this . . . as far back as Noah could remember.

But he wouldn't expose his kids to a lie. And that's what Emily and he had become.

Noah closed his eyes. Then he summoned every ounce of strength he had left and let the words come. "Dear Jesus, thank You for Aiden and Olivia. Thank You for Mommy and Daddy." It was the same every night. He inhaled. Every word like a hammer to his heart. "Thank You for our house and our family. And thank You for loving us so much."

It was Aiden's turn. "Thank You, Jesus, for our puppy, Indy, and our kitty, Benji. Thank You for my fast feet when I beat Jack in our race at preschool today." He grabbed a few quick breaths. The normalcy of their nighttime routine was clearly calming his troubled soul. "Thank You for big trucks across from church and for dinosaurs at the park and for Olivia. Thank You for Mr. Ryan playing with us tonight. Thank You for mashed potatoes and macaroni and cheese. And . . ."

He stopped, and Noah opened his eyes. "You done, Aiden?"

His son shook his head. "Something more." He swallowed a few times. Fresh tears filled his eyes. "Please, Jesus, make Daddy stay home. Because he lives here. And we live here. And who will I wrestle with at night if Daddy's gone?" He did a little sob. "And please bless Mommy and Daddy. Amen."

This was where everyone was supposed to say amen. But the word only came from Aiden and Olivia.

"Daddy?" Aiden looked crushed. "You didn't say amen."

"Right. Sorry." Noah couldn't believe this. Couldn't exhale. "Amen."

"Mommy?" Aiden sat up again and stared at Emily.

Emily didn't hesitate. "Amen."

Aiden settled back into his pillow. His eyebrows were still low over his eyes, his hurt and frustration easy to see. "You always have to say amen." He looked from Noah to Emily and back again. "Else you don't even mean what you prayed."

That was all Noah could take. He bent down and

kissed Aiden's cheek. "You're right, buddy." He smiled at his son. He couldn't think of anything harder than saying goodbye to Aiden and Olivia. Now and again tomorrow. He ran his thumb along his son's brow. "I love you, Aiden."

The child stared at him for a long moment. His eyes told the story. He wasn't okay. Fear and uncertainty had never been part of his life. Not ever. Not until tonight. And Aiden didn't want any of it. "I love you, too, Daddy."

Noah smiled again and then he let go of Aiden's hand and moved to Olivia's bed. Emily went to Aiden's at the same time. Again they didn't look at each other. Noah stared into the innocent eyes of his baby girl. "Good night, Livi." He kissed her cheek and held her hand for a long moment. "Daddy loves you."

Olivia might've only been two. But she understood something was wrong. No question about that. She angled her head and in the sweetest voice she said the only thing she could say. "Where, Dada? Where going?"

His stomach was a mass of knots. What was he supposed to say? He found the same smile and patted her head. "Daddy will always be with you, Livi. Always and always."

It was enough to settle Olivia into her pillow. Her eyelids looked heavier. "Hold you, Dada." Even in her sleepiness she sat up and put her baby arms around his neck. "Hold you."

There wouldn't be anything left of Noah's heart by the time he got out of here. He held on to her and tried to avoid the accusing thoughts slamming at his brain.

Little girls paid big prices when their daddies left. A lack of trust for men, bad relationships down the road. The price was high for little boys, too. If Dad wasn't around, then Aiden's friends would be. Too often the worst kinds of friends.

Would they both grow up to hate him?

Noah couldn't think about it. It was up to him. If he stayed involved in their lives, there would be nothing to worry about. It had to be better than watching Emily and him destroy each other.

Olivia was still clinging to him. Noah held her tight and kissed her cheek again. Then he gently laid her down on her pillow. "Love you, baby girl."

Her eyes held his for a few seconds. "Wuv you, Dada." She yawned. "Night-night."

"Night, honey."

Emily beat him to the light switch. Once the room was dark, the two of them slipped into the hallway and Noah closed the door behind them. As soon as he did, he stared at her. His voice was part seething anger, part whisper. "Are you kidding me, Emily?"

"What?" She was clearly just as angry.

They couldn't talk here. Aiden would be out in the hall in a heartbeat wanting to know why Mommy and Daddy were mad at each other. At four he was still sweetly naïve enough not to connect the dots. Daddy moving out didn't mean there was a problem with his parents. Not in Aiden's mind. Because up until now Aiden and Olivia had never seen their parents fight.

Noah pointed to the other side of the house. "We need to talk." He mouthed the words. He had never been angrier.

"Agreed." Emily spat the word like it was poison on her tongue. She followed him to their room and slammed the door behind them. "Go ahead. What are you going to say, Noah? That I shouldn't tell them the truth? That you'd rather spend time talking to strangers on the Internet than with us?"

"We had an agreement." He stared at her. The person she had become. Her hands on her hips, her face a twist of disgust. She looked nothing like the Emily he had fallen in love with.

"*You* had an agreement." She threw her hands in the air. Her tone cut deep. "I didn't want any of this. What did you expect me to do? Lie to him? Tell him that after tomorrow you just happen to be living in another house?" She released a short breath. "You don't want us."

"And you don't want me."

"Not the way you are. Spending half your time at home on the Internet. Talking to girls you don't know rather than being with us." Her response was quick. "You're right, I don't want that. Not another day."

"Is that right?" He laughed, but he could hear nothing funny about the sound. "You blame me for making money with our posts." He motioned to the bedroom furniture and closet of clothes beyond it. "But I don't see you struggling to *spend* the money. How's that Subaru working out? Huh, Emily?"

A rapid series of shock waves seemed to come over her. "Really, Noah? You're going there?" She crossed her arms. "Sell it all. I can take the bus if it means having you back. The man I married."

He stared at her and shook his head. "I give up." Another harsh-sounding laugh. "You wanted this, too, Emily. Don't forget that. I can't just undo it."

"Yes you can." Her scowl was as unattractive as her voice.

"That's another thing." He took a step closer. "You never smile anymore. Like you've forgotten how."

Fire sparked in her eyes. "I smile plenty." She dropped her voice. "When you're not around."

He studied her, searched her angry eyes. After a few seconds he shook his head. "I can't take it, Emily. I'm done."

"Me, too." She glared at him. "Just leave now, Noah. Why wait?"

"I would if I could." Without hanging around for another dig, Noah turned and stormed past her. Deep inside, he could feel how hard his heart had grown toward her. This time tomorrow he'd be finished with conversations like this. Finished with these awful moments of hatred. "Never mind." He waved his hand at her, brushing her off. He never even looked back. "I have nothing else to say."

He pushed himself down the hall and toward the foyer. One more night. That was all he had to get through. Just one more night. He wanted to take her up on her offer and walk out the front door now. Sleep on the lawn, if it took that to avoid her toxic hatred. But he couldn't do that to Aiden and Olivia.

Instead he went to his empty office. Before he could close the door, he saw her. Emily was marching toward him, clearly still upset. As she came closer, Noah took a few steps back. As much distance between them as possible. That was the goal. The reason he was moving.

"I wasn't finished so don't walk out on me." Her arms hung at her sides, fists clenched. "Save that for tomorrow, will you?"

Noah had no desire to fight her. What was the point? He felt his shoulders sink a few inches. "What do you want, Emily?" He was still mad, but he was tired of fighting. Tired of her. "We had a deal. Whether you admit it or not." His pause wasn't long enough for her to make a rebuttal. "The deal was we'd protect the kids. Which means you shouldn't take Aiden and Olivia to bed by yourself on my last night here. And you shouldn't have told him I was leaving. That was my job. That was the deal."

Her voice was louder than his. "That wasn't the deal." She looked right through him. "The deal was till death do us part." Tears shone in her eyes, but they didn't touch the anger in her face. "Remember that, Noah?"

"Just go." He turned toward the far wall and then back to her. "What's the point of yelling at me? It isn't going to change things."

Emily looked like she could break something.

"What's the real reason, Noah?" She looked at the computer on the desk, the place where he made most of his social media posts. Those two items and a chair were all that remained in the office. In a blur Emily shoved the screen, knocking it on its back. "One of your fans got your attention? Is that what this is really about?" She looked him up and down. "And why do you have *mud* on your knees?" Her eyes found his again. "What are you hiding?"

"Nothing!" His voice was loud again. If the kids heard him, so be it. He gritted his teeth and fired the words like so many bullets. "I was at the cemetery, okay? Visiting Clara's grave. Because losing Clara didn't just happen to you. All right?" He was breathing hard, like he might explode from the pain and rage whirling within him. "It happened to me, too."

The mention of Clara's name seemed to have an instant effect on Emily. She straightened, and the lines in her face eased. Like she didn't know what to make of his explanation. "Good night, Noah. I'm going to bed."

She didn't wait for him to say anything, just turned around and left him standing there. Like a tombstone from the cemetery earlier. Marking the death of their marriage. He exhaled and set his computer screen upright. She would be in the den by now, making up the sofa bed. Noah didn't move, didn't dare leave the office. Not until she was asleep.

The last thing he wanted was another exchange with her.

He sat down at his computer and opened their Instagram account. There were hundreds of private messages, questions and comments he hadn't looked at yet. Usually he checked in on the fans every few hours. He opened the window and spotted a few of the regulars. A blonde who went by @UpforAnything had the most comments lately.

> Noah, where are you?? I'm dying here! Post something about you and your beautiful wife. I'm waiting!

She was waiting. Noah stared at the comment and then shifted his eyes to the girl's profile picture. Heavy makeup, flirty eyes. Low-cut top. Noah had talked back and forth with her a number of times. A few of her comments stayed with him.

> Makes my day when you answer me, Noah.

> You're the hottest guy on Instagram. Emily is so lucky!

He closed Instagram and stared out the window. Tonight the black sky mirrored his soul. Why had he answered girls like her, anyway? Was Emily right? Had he forgotten the purpose of their social media accounts? No question, in the past year there were times when he couldn't wait to come here, escape to the office. Away from Emily's chilly tone of voice.

Her accusing eyes.

A few touches to the keyboard and the computer powered down. What would his parents say if they knew he was leaving Emily and the kids tomorrow? They had moved to London when Noah left home for college. They still lived there, near Noah's brother and his family. With so many miles between them it was easy not to talk at all.

Noah couldn't remember the last time they'd done more than say hello through text. FaceTime with the kids used to be a regular occurrence. Every few weeks at least. Now it had been months. His mom had texted him a few days ago asking if they could schedule a call. She missed him, missed Emily. Definitely missed Aiden and Olivia.

Like always, Noah promised they'd find a time. Eventually. As soon as they had a spare hour. But hours for his family weren't a priority anymore. Noah felt guilty and he knew why. His parents had raised him to believe just one thing about marriage.

It was forever.

If things got tough, it was time to step up. A Christian marriage was about putting your spouse first. Noah used to believe that. Before Emily made the whole thing feel impossible. He sighed. Gravity was having its way with him again. Yes, if his parents knew about his decision to leave they'd be on the next plane from London to Indianapolis.

Whatever it took. They'd be there to help. Even if they needed to take leaves of absence from their jobs.

They had no idea how desperate things had gotten.

Noah pushed back from the computer and stood. His

feet felt like they were dragging through wet cement as he walked from the office back to the bedroom. The light was on in the den, but Emily was in for the night. No more fighting or questioning or accusing. It was all behind him except the sad, slow drive from here to his new apartment.

A desperate sort of sigh came from the deepest part of him. He had to finish packing. The morning would be here before he knew it.

As he reached his suitcases the thought hit him like a truck. Tomorrow at this time he'd be alone. As terrible as that sounded, a glimmer of hope shone a light on the situation. At least he'd be free. Free of Emily's oppressive disappointment and rude voice and mean eyes. Her disrespect.

His life with Emily was over. It really was. And as hard as the scene with the kids had been, as painful as all of this was, a part of Noah wasn't sad at all. He had to get out. Things would be better for all of them. The kids would understand in time. In fact, he wasn't just okay with the decision ahead.

He could hardly wait.

5

Emily was ready for bed, but she wasn't tired. Her whole life was caving in around her. Another storm was hitting outside. Gale-force winds battered the windows and it sounded like the very walls of the house were being ripped away.

Who could sleep through a storm like this?

She padded down the hall to the kids' room. With practiced quiet she opened the door and looked at them. They were both asleep, unaware of the terrible weather, the fear from earlier gone. Emily felt the sting of her own tears again. Watching Aiden and Olivia tonight had been the saddest thing she'd ever done.

And Noah hadn't even left yet.

What was the future going to be like for these two? For the three of them? She looked from Aiden to Olivia. *Lord, we've made a mess of this family. It's Noah's fault, but it's mine, too. I should've told him I needed a break from social media after Clara died. I can't accuse Noah of pretending, when I did the same thing.* The prayer got stuck there. It had been a while since she had prayed on her own like this.

Emily narrowed her eyes and looked through the dark room to her babies' faces. *Despite Noah and me, even with our failure, please, God, would You protect these two? None of this is their fault. Please, God. We all need a miracle.*

Without making a sound she shut the door.

Outside the rain was settling down again, the way storms in early November often did. The humidity from early autumn was long gone, so the air was crisp. A preview of winter. Emily walked to the coat closet, grabbed her longest, warmest jacket and slipped it on. She headed out the back door and took a seat on the porch swing. It was far enough under the roof that it hadn't gotten wet in the storm.

She pulled her coat close to her body. Noah had installed this swing the week they moved in. She could still hear him, still see the smile on his face. "Most people have a swing on their *front* porch." He laughed. "Not us. Know why?" He walked up to her and took her hand.

Their eyes held as if time had stopped.

"Because our front porch is too small?" Laughter had come easily for both of them back then.

"Not at all!" Noah spread his hand toward the swing and then the fenced grassy yard where Aiden was running in circles, chasing a butterfly. "This"—he grinned at her—"is the view I want when I'm on a porch swing." He came close to her and kissed her. Slow and with a passion that they had taken for granted back then. "You're the only view I ever want, Emily."

His long-ago words died on the chilly night breeze.

Emily set the swing in motion, slow and easy. She never meant to fall in love with Noah Carter. Never meant to fall in love, at all. She and her sister, Clara. That was all she needed. Love would only hurt and cut and leave. Emily had been through enough of that.

The sky was still dark, not a star anywhere. More storms were forecast. Emily looked deep into the night and suddenly it all came back to her. Life as she'd lived it before Noah. Emily was a toddler when Clara was born, too young to remember. Too young to know why her mom looked sad so often or why her daddy was gone all the time.

Too small to understand that Clara had cerebral palsy, that she wouldn't be like other little sisters. Not ever. Emily didn't mind. She didn't know anything else. Clara was her best friend as far back as she could remember.

Emily filled her lungs with the cold lonely air. Children had an uncanny ability to love, to look past the flaws grown-ups so easily noticed. Usually before they saw anything else. Emily wasn't sure when she understood that Clara was different. That it wasn't normal for a little girl to walk with braces on her legs and crutches in her hands.

All Emily knew was that she loved Clara. Loved her with a fierce protective kind of love that lasted every day of Clara's life.

She blinked and the memories in her heart came alive.

Emily running slow on purpose, so Clara could keep up with her. Clara laughing, her eyes bright, as they sat on either side of the teeter-totter at the park. And the swings. Clara's favorite part.

There she was, so close Emily could almost touch her. Little Clara, swinging high, her damaged legs dangling, very different from the way other kids looked. But no little girl ever smiled so big. "More, Emily. More!"

And Emily would push her again and again and again. Because when Clara was at the park she seemed so happy. "You're flying, Clara," Emily would cry out, celebrating with her sister. "Look at you!"

Their mom would always be nearby. On a park bench or right beside Emily taking turns pushing Clara. The three of them would laugh and talk about Peter Pan and Tinker Bell and how Clara was on an adventure every time she climbed in a swing.

An adventure to Neverland.

Those were Emily's first memories. Clara and her, together all day, every day.

But at some point school interrupted those days. Clara was special, that's what their mother said. So she had to go to a different school. Ride a different bus. Emily could remember climbing out of bed one night and finding their mother alone at the kitchen table.

Always alone.

"Where's Daddy?" Emily sat in the closest chair, the hem of her white flannel nightgown low around her ankles.

"He's out, honey." Her mother smiled, but even as a child Emily could see how it didn't quite reach her eyes. "He'll be back soon."

Her dad was always out, so Emily hadn't worried too much about that. Instead she had gathered her thoughts, the reason she had left her bed that night. "I want to go to school with Clara."

"What?" Her mother was kind, gentle. She put her arm around Emily's shoulders. "Honey, you can't do that. You're doing so well." Concern seemed to fill her eyes."Mrs. Baker says you're the smartest child in class."

That didn't matter to Emily. She shook her head. "I can be less smart, Mommy." No words from a seven-year-old were ever more sincere. "Please. I want to be with Clara. She's my best friend."

Tears had filled her mother's eyes, but she didn't cry. She never cried. "Clara goes to a school for special children, Emily. It has to be that way."

Emily's voice got louder. "Please, Mommy." She stood and looked right at her mother. "I'm special, too. We can be special together."

But no amount of convincing could change her mother's mind. Emily was too young to understand what *special* meant, or to voice her real concerns. If she wasn't with Clara at school, who would look out for her? What child would run slow beside her so Clara didn't get left behind? Who would push her on the swings? Who would help Clara find her way to Neverland?

Since Emily couldn't be in class with Clara, she made

up for it when they got home. If they were best friends before, they were even closer after that. Clara's school got out later than Emily's. So by the time the bus dropped Clara off in front of their house, Emily was outside waiting. Blond ponytail dancing behind her as she ran to meet her sister.

Clara's face would light up and the driver would hand Clara's crutches to Emily. "You need help?"

"No, sir," Emily would say. "I've got her." And she would help Clara to the sidewalk. Then she would position the crutches in Clara's hands and Emily would put her arm around her.

Every single day.

As they made their way back to the house, Emily would ask the same question. "How was your day, Clara?"

"Good." Clara never talked much. Only a few words at a time. Words that were hard to understand. And her smile wasn't quite normal. But it was the best one Emily had ever seen.

Clara would usually work to say the next words. "How . . . your day?"

And Emily would light up because finally, finally all was right with the world. She and Clara were together again. "It's perfect now," Emily would say.

That's how the days and months and seasons went.

Right up until their father left home.

Emily was ten when one day after school she found her parents yelling at each other on the front porch. Even now Emily could remember how she felt. She had been walking home from the bus stop and the sound of her father's angry words had stopped her cold. His car was parked along the curb, the engine running, door open. Like he was going somewhere.

"I can't do this, Judy. I can't." He threw his hands up. "I have someone else. It's over."

He had someone else? What did that mean? Who else could he possibly want other than Emily's mother and Emily and Clara?

Her dad turned to leave and at the same time he caught Emily's eyes. And like Emily, he stopped. For a moment etched in her mind ever since then, her daddy stared at her. His eyes seemed to say he was sorry and guilty and frustrated. Also that he loved her. But no words came.

Instead he grabbed a duffel bag from the grass, climbed in his car and drove away. "Daddy?" Emily yelled after him. She was old enough to not cry about everything. But she couldn't stop the tears that day. She ran after his car for the entire block before she tripped and fell to the sidewalk. "Daddy." She reached out toward his car as it moved farther away from her. "Daddy, don't go!"

But the car didn't turn around and her father never came back. She didn't see him again for eight years. And by then it was too late for the two of them. Too late for her to trust him or love him or want time with him. It didn't take Emily long to realize that at least one reason their daddy left home was Clara. Because he didn't know how to help her or love her, and because of something even uglier.

He didn't want to be a father to someone with cerebral palsy.

If Emily had been protective of Clara before their dad left home, it was nothing to how she became around her sister after that. One good thing came of their father's leaving. They could no longer afford Clara's special school. There was a class for kids like Clara at Emily's school. Not with the services and instruction and therapy of the other school. But it was better than nothing.

That's what their mother had said. The new class for Clara was better than nothing.

Emily disagreed. She thought it was the best thing in the world. She insisted on riding with Clara on the special-needs bus, so their mother got permission for her to do just that. Once Emily overheard her teacher talking to her mother.

"Mrs. Andrews, Emily really should ride the regular bus, with students like her."

Her mother stood a little straighter, her eyes suddenly hard. "Clara is like Emily. More than you know."

A smile spread across Emily's face. She had never loved her mother more. And so Emily was allowed to keep riding Clara's bus with the kids who weren't quite like other kids. Emily felt like she belonged. After all, she didn't have a daddy, and plus the nicest students at school were the ones on that bus.

Clara most of all.

Emily set the porch swing into motion again and crossed her arms. The night was colder now. Thunder rumbled in the distance as the memories kept coming.

Every Sunday the three of them would go to church. Emily and Clara and their mama. Church was a small building with mostly older people. They would sit together and Emily would help Clara turn the hymnal pages. Clara would do her best to sing along. Sometimes her voice would be too loud and usually she wasn't on key.

But she was happy. They were happy.

Sometimes Emily wondered why Clara's legs didn't work right. Why her words were jumbled and why her mind seemed slow. "What happened to her?" Emily found her mother doing dishes in the kitchen one night after Clara was in bed. "Why is she like that?"

"She has cerebral palsy." Her mom looked sad as she said the words. "That's the reason."

"Cerebral . . ." Emily couldn't remember exactly what her mom had said. "Why does she have it? And when will she get better?"

Her mom did her best to explain the situation. She sighed and dried her hands. Then she faced Emily. "When Clara was born, she didn't get air soon enough. A part of her brain died as a result."

"So she's not getting better?" Emily couldn't believe it. She always thought one day Clara would be healed. That she'd run and talk and sing like Emily.

"No, honey." Her mama pulled her close and hugged

her. "Clara is just a little easier to love, that's all." Her mother looked deep into her eyes. "Sometimes I think we're the ones with special needs. Not Clara."

Their mother was right about that. No one trusted people like Clara did. Their father had left them, but Clara didn't hold a single bad thought for the man. She talked about him like he still lived with their mother in the room at the end of the hall. "Daddy asleep," she would say. And when she drew a picture of a tree or a house or a family, she would include him in the drawing. Then she would hold it up and grin. "For Daddy."

Clara was the kindest person Emily knew. No one loved deeper, no one cared more completely than Clara.

No one ever would.

6

Emily breathed deep. It was time to go in, time to try to sleep.

But she wasn't finished remembering. She moved the swing again, felt the gentle sway beneath her. Nights like this she missed Clara so much. Her sister would've blocked the door before she would've let Noah walk out on them. She would've been devastated by what was about to happen.

Absolutely crushed.

Emily thought about what Noah had said. How he'd been by the cemetery earlier, because losing Clara hadn't just happened to Emily. It had happened to both of them. She squinted into the dark night. Nothing about that statement fit the narrative of the man Noah Carter had become.

He was selfish and self-centered now. He cared more about his public persona than his family. Yet somehow, the day before he moved out, he had taken time to visit Clara's grave. Something the old Noah might've done.

Don't think about it, she told herself. It would only

make tomorrow's goodbye that much harder. Emily settled into the swing and pulled her coat even tighter around her shoulders. As she did, the story of her life came back again. Right where she'd left off.

The part about church.

Emily was thirteen when she began to let her mind wander during Sunday services. *God is love,* the pastor would say. He loved the world so much He sent His Son Jesus to die for them. So they could go to heaven.

What did all that mean? Emily would long for the chance to debate the pastor. God loved them? If that was true, why would God allow Clara to have a brain injury at birth? Clara was eleven then, and at times the boys her age made fun of her. Once Emily caught a few of them limping along, imitating Clara.

Clara noticed and her smile faded. She looked to the ground as she struggled to keep moving.

Emily dropped her backpack and ran to the boys. "Don't you ever"—she shoved one of them to the ground and then the other—"make fun of my sister again." She stood over them, staring at them. She couldn't have been eighty pounds back then. A wisp of a girl with long pale blond hair.

But no one was going to hurt Clara. Not ever again.

After that the meanness from other kids probably continued. But it didn't happen in front of Emily. Still, it made her wonder about God. How could He let mean kids say things about her special sister? Why didn't He just do a miracle and let her be whole and well?

When Emily was a sophomore in high school she began to study her mother. The way she worked hard and came home at three each day to make dinner. Her smile was always a little sad, but it was there. Their mother never complained about having to raise the girls by herself, never looked discouraged or defeated.

All three of them did the dishes each night, and their mom made it fun. She would put on music like Steven Curtis Chapman's *The Great Adventure* and Michael W. Smith's *Go West Young Man*. They would sing and dance and get the work done together. Clara would sit at the counter and dry pans.

Then they would settle down to homework. Their mom would sit beside Clara, helping her add numbers or spell words. Things that were easy for other kids. Once in a while Emily would look up and watch her mom. Just watch her. The patient tone when she talked to Clara, the gentle way she would put her hand over Clara's and help her form letters.

Even knowing that Clara might never form them on her own.

Despite all the ways God had let Clara down, and even with their dad gone for good, their mom had kept her faith in God. "Jesus loves us," she would tell the girls each night. "Be sure to thank Him before you go to bed."

Amazing, Emily used to think. How could she believe so completely? Meanwhile, with each year, Emily's own faith had been fading. She doubted God and His good plans for their lives. But their mom never did. She always trusted, always loved, always stayed. She never gave up.

By the time Emily was a junior, she had one wish for her life. That she might grow up to be just like her mom. Except for the faith part, of course.

In the inventory of Emily's childhood, the next piece was the toughest of all. She looked over her shoulder, in case maybe the kitchen lights were on. In case Noah was sitting at the table waiting for her. Ready to change his mind.

He wasn't.

And since she was more heartsick than tired, Emily let the rest of the story come. The three of them had finally found a rhythm, finally reached a place where Emily didn't go to sleep each night angry at her father. Clara was still the same. She still talked of their father with fondness. She still hadn't learned to walk or run or talk like the other kids.

And she was still Emily's best friend.

Together with their mother they had a beautiful life. Even if Emily didn't exactly believe in God the way her mama did. Then two months before Emily's high school graduation, their mother left for a weekend trip to Texas. Her sister lived there, and she'd just moved into a new house.

"I'll help her set up and be back Monday morning," their mother told them. The girls were old enough to stay by themselves. Their mom hugged them that Friday before she left and they went to school. "I love you girls so much." She looked at Emily. "Take Clara to church, okay?" She shifted her smile to Clara. "You love going to church, right?"

"Yes, Mama." Clara's words came quickly. More clear than usual. "I love Jesus."

Emily did as she was asked. Not just to honor her mother, but because Clara truly did love being in church. The sermon that week was about the brevity of life. So short, so uncertain. "You never know when you'll wake up for the last time," the pastor told them. "There's never a guarantee about tomorrow."

His point was clear. "Be ready," he told them. "Stay on the narrow path that leads to life."

Emily thought about that. Was God just a taskmaster? Someone forcing people into acts of obedience under the threat of certain death? A mean boss who stood by while kids like Clara were born broken, an unseen force who hovered nearby while people lived in fear of not waking up one day?

Halfway through the sermon, Emily looked at Clara. She wore a simple smile and every now and then she nodded along. Like she'd never believed so fully in a Bible message as she did that one. And she understood, no doubt. Clara's difficulties were more physical than cognitive.

But that moment Emily remembered feeling like she was the one with special needs. Because for the life of her, she couldn't understand God. Or how people could worship Him and serve Him when someone they loved could be gone in the blink of an eye.

It was with those thoughts still in her mind that she came home from school the next day to find her father sitting on the front porch. Emily's heart fell to the ground. Why was he here? What could've made him come?

She wanted to run ahead and ask him. But she wouldn't go faster than Clara. It wasn't until they were halfway up the sidewalk that Clara realized their father was sitting there. The sight of him made her stop and after only a few seconds, Clara broke out in a smile. "Daddy! You . . . home!"

As if he'd only been gone a day or so.

Emily felt anger fill her from head to toe. She didn't want him here, not for any reason. But even more than the rage she felt, was a fear like she'd never known in all her life.

Why in the world was he here?

Clara leaned into Emily as they made it up the front steps. She hobbled up to their father and stopped close to him. Clara couldn't hug him, couldn't release the grip on her crutches. So she kissed his cheek instead. "How you been?"

Their father looked uncomfortable. More than that he seemed upset. "I'm fine, Clara. It's nice to see you." He stared at Emily. "Why don't you get your sister situated inside? I need to talk to you."

Emily couldn't breathe, couldn't speak. Her heart

was pounding in her chest, filling her senses. She didn't want to get Clara situated. She wanted him to leave. But she had no choice. She tried to find her voice. "Clara . . . come on. Let's go inside."

Clara nodded. She grinned at their father once more. "Good . . . see you!"

"Yes." Their dad stared at the ground. Like it was too painful to look into Clara's sweet eyes. When he lifted his head, he couldn't maintain eye contact with her. "You, too. Good to see you."

Emily helped her sister into the house and to the kitchen table. Her mind raced. Shouldn't their mom be home by now? Her flight would've gotten in that morning, right? So what was happening? It had been eight years since she'd seen her dad. He hadn't contacted them even once. So why would he just show up?

And what was that look in his eyes?

Emily set Clara up with a stack of construction paper and some crayons, a glass of water and a plate of apple slices. All Clara's favorites. Then she got down on Clara's level. "I'll be right back, okay? I'm going outside to talk to Dad for a few minutes."

Clara didn't seem alarmed. She picked up the blue crayon and started to draw.

A desperate prayer formed in Emily's heart in that moment. *Whatever this is, let me be strong for Clara. If You're there, God, get me through this for her. Don't let her see how scared I am.*

The prayer must've worked. Emily's sister was busy

coloring in a perfect blue sky. Like she had no idea anything might be wrong, no sense that seeing their father on the front porch was an ominous sign. She stopped and looked up. "Love you, Emily."

They were words Clara didn't struggle with. She said them so often, they came out sounding almost normal. Emily smiled at her. "You're perfect, Clara."

Her sister grinned. Then she turned back to the crayons.

As Emily walked away, she felt like she was going to throw up. She thought about going to the bathroom first, but she couldn't hide from whatever her father wanted to tell her. He must have bad news. Why else would he be here? He was married to another woman and living in Michigan.

Five hours away.

There was no way he was here on a Monday afternoon unless something terrible had happened. Emily forced herself to walk out the front door. She could barely move. Her heart was beating so hard by the time she reached him, her chest was heaving. She could feel herself gasping for air, feel the pounding against her ribs. She found her dad brushing tears off his cheeks.

His face was red now, as if he'd been holding his breath. "Emily . . ." He looked up at her. "Something happened to your mother."

"No!" Emily was eighteen, old enough to know better than to argue such a statement. But she couldn't believe it, couldn't stand to let him keep talking. "She's fine!

She's coming home today." Emily pointed at his car parked in the driveway. Her voice was shrill and loud. "Leave. I don't want you here. Go! My mom is fine!"

"Emily . . ." He stood. His own eyes were dry now. Filled more with fear than sorrow. As if his need to tell her the truth was greater than his own sadness.

"Don't say it!" Emily ran down the steps and to the edge of the front yard. She pointed to his car again. "Leave, Dad! Go!"

Instead he followed her. He came to her and gently took hold of her shoulders. "Emily, your mother is dead. I got word early this morning."

He was saying something else, something about how he couldn't let Emily and Clara hear the news from anyone but him. How there had been too much rain this weekend in Texas and a flood had washed away the rental car her mother was driving. How her mama hadn't had time to get out and how they'd found her body late last night.

There were other details, too. But Emily couldn't allow herself to hear them. She pulled away from her father and fell to the ground, clutching at the sidewalk and the grass around it. The place where her mother had walked out to the airport taxi just three days ago.

The specifics of that day and the ones that followed were a blur for Emily. Somehow she had found the strength to get up and go inside, to tell Clara what had happened and to hold her weeping sister long into the night.

Her father had stayed for a week, handling her mother's bank affairs and making sure Emily had an understanding of the family bills and finances. A life insurance policy paid almost immediately, giving the girls enough to live on for several years. Enough for college even.

Emily hated spending that time with her father. What could he possibly have cared about Emily and Clara's mother or the loss the girls were feeling? He had walked out. Enough said. But they needed help, and so Emily tolerated his stay.

At the end of the week, he asked Emily to talk to him on the front porch again. "I'd like you girls to come live with me. In Michigan." He looked at the house and then at Emily. "This is too much for you to handle on your own."

Emily felt her resolve harden. Her father knew nothing of what she could handle. She lifted her chin and said the next words with a strength she didn't quite feel. "We're staying here. I can look after Clara. Like I always have."

There was nothing her father could say to change her mind. Emily was an adult, after all, and already planning to attend Indiana University. In the end their father agreed to make Emily legal guardian over Clara. Not long after, Emily graduated summa cum laude and spent the summer helping Clara remember how to smile again.

The loss of their mother was harder than anything they'd been through, but they survived it together.

Sometimes before they turned in for the night, Emily would sit in the chair in Clara's room and tell her stories of the old days. Every wonderful thing about their mother.

Stories neither of them ever tired of.

One week into summer, on a Saturday night at dinner, Clara set her fork down. "Emily?" Clara had to have a special fork and plate, large enough to catch the pieces that didn't quite make it into her mouth.

"Yes?" Emily played all the roles by then. She took care of Clara, did the shopping and paid the bills. She made sure Clara was enrolled in the good school again for the coming fall. The one closer to their house with the special training for kids like her. Money from their mother's life insurance took care of that.

But in that moment, over dinner, Emily was allowed to just be a high school graduate trying to figure out her future. And Clara was simply her best friend.

"Church, Emily?" Clara took another bite and thought for a minute. "Can we? Please?"

Emily hesitated. Going to church again was the last thing she wanted to do. But for Clara . . . Emily clenched her jaw and forced a smile. "Yes, Clara. We can go."

Never mind that Emily had struggled to understand why God would allow Clara to have a brain injury at birth, or the fact that she would never grasp the reason God had taken their mother.

When they both needed her so desperately.

But if Clara wanted to be at church, they would go.

And so they did. That Sunday dozens of people welcomed them and hugged them, they talked about Emily and Clara's mother and invited them for dinner. Some of the people had reached out before. But now it was like they could see for themselves how it really was just the two of them.

Two sisters against the world.

The pastor's sermon wasn't what stayed with Emily that day. A Bible verse wasn't what changed Emily's mind about God. Rather it was something one of her mother's friends said on the way out. She put her hand on Emily's shoulder. "You're an amazing young woman, Emily Andrews."

Emily didn't want pity. She nodded and managed a slight smile. "Thank you."

"Not because of how you love that sister of yours. That's easy for you, your mama told me that a long time ago. You two are best friends." The woman paused. "But because you're here today."

At first Emily wasn't sure what the woman meant. "Ma'am?"

"A week before your mama's accident, she called me. She told me she had learned to live without your daddy. And she had figured out how to make a life for you girls without him." She looked deep into Emily's eyes. "But she knew you were struggling in your faith."

The truth cut Emily to the core. "She did?" All that time she had tried to pretend. So she wouldn't trouble her mother with her doubts.

"She knew." The woman seemed in no hurry. As if this were the most important thing she had to say all day. All year, even. "On our last phone call, she told me she had just one prayer. That you and Clara would stay close to Jesus all your lives. Not just go to church because she went to church. But really love the Lord. So the three of you would have eternity together."

The woman's words came like so many bursts of icy cold air. Her mother had said that? Her final wish was that Emily would love Jesus with all her heart? That Emily and Clara wouldn't just go through the motions? Emily thanked the woman, but the news changed her.

There had been no final words with her mother, no last conversation or sweet goodbyes. No one had known that she'd hop in the rental car to run to the store for milk and get swept away in floodwaters. She hadn't had time to call for help, let alone call her girls.

So the conversation with the woman at church became all Emily had, the only thing left of her mother. As if her mom had given her a final message after all. That night after Clara was in bed, Emily stepped onto the front porch and looked at the moon. And in the next hour she told God everything she wanted to say.

She asked Him why He hadn't given Clara a healthy body and how He could stand by and watch while Clara limped and struggled through life. And she asked how her father could be so callous and then somehow think she and Clara would move in with him after all these years.

Even now she could hear herself, speaking her questions out loud into the summer night air. "I'm mad at you, God. I have a right to be mad. Clara deserves so much more. What's going to become of her? What will her future be? And what about the people who are mean to her?"

One question after another, but finally . . . finally Emily ran out of questions. Or she ran out of breath. Whatever it was she sank to the lone chair and she hung her head. An ocean of tears came, and in the next hour she heard God. Felt Him right there beside her. His hands on her shoulders, holding her so she wouldn't fall to the ground in sorrow.

The world was a mess, that was true.

But God . . . God was there. He loved her mother and He loved Emily and Clara. She would never get through the years ahead without Him. Her mother must've known that.

And now Emily knew for herself.

Whatever reason God had for taking their mother home so soon, Emily was certain where she was. Alive and whole and praying for her and Clara from heaven. Praying with one hope, one wish.

That Emily and Clara would love Jesus, too.

They didn't miss a Sunday service after that. Not only did Emily find her way to a believing faith in God but she loved Him. More every week. Clara seemed to notice, because she was happier. Almost as happy as she'd been before their mother died.

Summer ended and Clara started back at the better school. Emily took a dance scholarship at Indiana University and somehow their schedules worked. Life was hard. But it was sweet and it was good. She and Clara had each other, and they were working toward their future.

Emily had no idea that three weeks later she was going to meet Noah Carter.

And that nothing would ever be the same again.

7

Noah's head was killing him.

He had finished packing, and his bags both stood in the corner. But he could barely see them through his blurry vision. *Concussion headache,* he told himself. One too many hits back when he was a football player. Every now and then they struck again. The way they had in the days and weeks after his last injury.

Rub the temples, he reminded himself. He dropped to the edge of the bed and pressed his fingers into the sides of his head. Slow circles. Firm and steady. Anything to relieve the pressure. But it didn't work. It had to be the concussions.

Or maybe not.

Maybe his brain was screaming at him to find some other way, any other way. He couldn't stand being around Emily. But he couldn't stand himself for leaving her. How could both be true? His outbreath filled his cheeks and leaked slowly through his lips.

One more look at the kids. That's what he needed.

He opened his eyes and tried to focus on the suitcases. The edges of everything he looked at were still blurry.

Nights like this he could feel that final hit again, feel the crush of the linebacker's helmet against his. The way his head snapped back and slammed against the ground.

A clean knockout. That's what the papers said later. Like they were in the ring for a heavyweight fight instead of playing college football. He remembered waking up and the whole room spinning. Not just a little, but fast. Round and round and round. He hadn't made it to his side of the field before he threw up.

And that was just the beginning.

There were times in the weeks after that vicious blow when Noah wondered if he'd ever get through a day without the dizziness that made it impossible to open his eyes for more than a few minutes. His brain had been that bruised, that damaged.

For some guys, life really never would be the same again. Noah might've been one of them. A statistic in the world of football injuries. He might never have recovered fully if not for one person.

Emily Andrews.

Noah pushed aside his pounding headache. He had to see the kids, had to watch them sleeping in their beds one more time. Their quiet breathing and peaceful innocence. After tonight there would be visits, when the kids came to his apartment for the night. But there wouldn't be another chance to see them sleeping here. In their own beds.

His brain banged against his skull with every step. The light was still on in the den. Emily must be awake.

But she certainly wasn't going to come find him. Not after the argument they'd had earlier. He didn't blame her. At this point neither of them could stand being together.

For a long moment he gathered himself outside the kids' room, and willed his headache to lighten up. Finally he opened their door just a crack. In the glow of the hallway light, he saw Olivia first. She had her blanket tucked up close to her face, her gold curls spread across the pillow. In her other arm she held her teddy bear. As if tonight she needed all the security she could get.

Failure added to his hurting head. He looked at Aiden. His son was in a ball on his side, not moving. But he didn't quite look asleep, either. Just then he shifted a little, adjusted his hand up closer to his face.

"Aiden?" Noah's whisper was barely audible. "You awake, buddy?"

Aiden rolled onto his other side, eyes closed. Noah waited. He must be asleep. Just dreaming probably. Trying to figure out why his father was moving out in the morning. How was a four-year-old supposed to understand something like that?

Noah didn't move, didn't say another word. But he couldn't turn away just yet. How were his kids going to survive without him here every night? How would they be okay after he left? What was going to happen to them? He felt nauseous. The headache and the reality of the moment. Aiden and Olivia would probably talk about tomorrow as long as they lived.

"I was four," Aiden would tell his friends and teachers, his wife and kids one day. "My dad and mom were this Internet famous couple. Everyone loved them. But it was all an act." Then Aiden would pause for a minute, really let that sink in. "I remember the night before my dad left. How he told me he was leaving. I cried myself to sleep and I guess in some ways I was never the same again."

Something like that.

Olivia would have her story, too. Maybe she'd have a litany of boyfriends, one after another. With each one she would say the same thing. "My dad left when I was two. I never really had a male role model in my life."

And then what? Would she be one of *those* girls? Always looking for affection in the wrong places because she felt rejected by her daddy?

He had to stop. Quit doing this to himself. Otherwise he was going to lose his dinner right here on their bedroom floor. He breathed in. If only his headache weren't so bad. A few blinks and he peered at them again, struggled to see his Aiden and Olivia clearly once more. He couldn't remember the last time he'd prayed over them. Sure he said bedtime prayers with them. But he couldn't remember when he really took a minute and prayed over his sleeping babies.

But here—when it was his last chance to do so in their own bedroom—it was the only option. He steadied himself against the doorframe. *My God, I have no right to talk to You. None at all. But I have to ask You something. Before it's too late.*

The pain in his head was screaming now. He could barely focus.

Please, protect Aiden and Olivia, Father. Protect them from my selfishness and Emily's hard heart. We're a mess, Lord. It's too late for us. I know that. Nothing can save my kids from this broken home. It'll always be part of their story.

He breathed deep, and even that made the pain worse.

I guess I'm asking You for a miracle. You know, that the statistics won't have the last word for my kids. Divorce doesn't destroy every kid who goes through it, right? Anyway, I love them so much, God. More than they'll ever know. Will You help them? Please?

That was it, all he could pray. He couldn't stand to be here another minute. One final glance at Aiden and Livi. The peaceful in and out of their breathing. The way they still looked so little when they were asleep. Then he stepped back and let that chapter close.

The chapter where Noah and Emily lived in the same house and shared the same name. The part of his kids' story when Mommy and Daddy still loved each other.

Noah's dizziness was twice as bad as before. He struggled to make it back to his room and brush his teeth. His vision was blurry and a halo shone around everything he looked at. A concussion migraine. That's what his doctor called it. Every now and then someone with Noah's history of head injuries was bound to get a migraine.

But Noah had researched head injuries and concussions. This wasn't a migraine. It was much worse. It was scar tissue and brain damage making itself known, reminding him that he'd suffered at least some permanent damage with his first head injury out on that football field.

And the second time he'd almost died.

Stress or illness, severe anxiety. There were a handful of triggers for these kinds of debilitating headaches. No surprise he would get one tonight.

He climbed under their covers for the last time, flipped off the bedside lamp and lay back on the pillow. It had been years since he'd had a headache like this. He expected he might end up in the bathroom, vomiting.

Every heartbeat sounded in his throat and temples. The aching grew worse with every few breaths. He should get up and take something for the pain. But he didn't have the energy. And slowly, in a haze of pain and heartbreak, Noah began to fall asleep until there was only a cloudy, dizzying emptiness.

A preview of his future.

• • •

AIDEN OPENED HIS eyes as soon as his daddy closed the door. He was kind of asleep. Kind of not. But he didn't want to talk right now. He was still trying to figure things out. Why his daddy was packing and where he would be sleeping tomorrow.

Another house?

What did that mean?

He sat up and swung his legs over the edge of the bed. He had to be quiet. If Olivia woke up he'd be in trouble. He blinked a few times. But maybe he was already in trouble.

Always when there was a storm and the thunder was loud against the house, when lightning made the sky bright or the rain and wind came too hard, Aiden knew just where to go.

To his daddy.

When he thought he saw things moving in his closet at night or when he had a dream that he fell off his Big Wheel. When the other boys made a running game at preschool and forgot to ask him to be part of their group.

Every time he would go to his daddy.

Then he remembered. That had happened just yesterday. A long time after he and Olivia had gone to sleep a superbad storm came over their house. Thunder sounded like monsters making the windows shake, like someone was trying to get into his room.

Olivia kept sleeping, but Aiden was finally too scared to stay.

So last night he ran as fast as he could down the hallway to his mommy and daddy's room. Mommy must've been in the bathroom, because only Daddy was in bed.

Aiden jumped in and crawled under the covers. Quick as he could he snuggled up next to his dad. The storm got louder, but it didn't matter. He was safe because he was with his daddy.

A little while later his dad woke up. He rolled over and looked at him. "Buddy, what are you doing in here?"

"The storm." It was all Aiden needed to say.

His daddy smiled and rubbed his head and closed his eyes. Aiden was always allowed to come sleep with his mommy and daddy if a storm was bad. He'd thought there was going to be a bad storm tonight. Thunder had started at the park when they were on the swings.

But now the sky was quiet.

Even if the windows weren't shaking and the lights from lightning weren't slamming down from heaven, still he was scared.

Scared about his dad moving.

And where was he going? Aiden tried to remember. A different house. Yes, that was it. His dad was moving to a new house. His feet were cold outside the blankets. But he couldn't lie down. Not with so many thoughts in his head. Aiden had a friend at preschool, Jamal, whose daddy didn't live with him.

At first when Jamal told Aiden, it sounded kind of exciting. Two houses. Sleepovers. But Jamal said it wasn't exciting at all. It was terrible, because he never saw his dad 'cept on weekends. And sometimes Jamal sat on the grass at recess and cried.

And there was nothing Aiden could say to make him stop. No running games or monkey bars or swings. Because all Jamal wanted was his daddy.

Which was how Aiden felt right now. Because right now his daddy was still here in the same house. His bed was still down the hall right where it was supposed to be. Right now Daddy still took care of him. If a storm came he still knew exactly where to run.

Aiden blinked his eyes a few more times.

A long breath came from him. A sad breath. He needed someone to help him. Someone who would come right into the house and tell his daddy not to leave. But who would that be?

Aiden thought hard. His teacher wouldn't do it. She didn't live nearby. Maybe his mommy. But she seemed too sad. She hadn't said any words at all when everyone was here in the bedroom earlier.

Then all of the sudden it hit him.

God!

He could ask God to help him! Wasn't that what Mommy and Daddy had always told him and Olivia? Whenever they were in trouble, God was right there. Just waiting for them to talk to Him. It was called praying. You could ask God for anything.

Because God was always listening.

Aiden looked through the window at the dark night. So very dark. Somewhere past the sky was where God lived. In a place called heaven. That's what Mommy had told him a few days ago. What he had to say was very important, so he needed to be as close to God as he could get.

With steady feet, he stood on his bed and held his arms and hands straight up. High as he could get them. "Do you see me, God?" He whispered the words.

He stretched a little higher. "I know You're up there. Mommy and Daddy say so." His balance was a little bad because the bed was soft and his covers weren't that even. But he stayed as tall as he could. "Do You see what's happening, God? My daddy is moving out tomorrow."

Aiden waited in case God wanted to say something.

But there were no words from God, and Aiden's arms were getting tired. So he finished his prayer. "Will You do something to make him stay here? At home? Because . . . well, because this is home. For all of us."

He thought for a few seconds. "Amen."

His shoulders were sore when he lowered his hands. Then he lay down in bed, pulled the covers up and closed his eyes. He felt much better now.

Aiden took a deep breath and smiled.

He could hardly wait to see what God was going to do next.

8

Kari couldn't sleep.

After they prayed, she and Ryan had turned in and for a few minutes they'd talked about the kids, their upcoming projects and sports camps. Then Ryan had fallen asleep. That was a while ago, and now Kari lay there staring at the ceiling.

At first it was Ryan's news that kept her awake. Did he really think she wasn't bothered by what was about to happen? Her whole world was about to be rocked. And Ryan didn't seem to care.

But their own troubles would have to wait. The more pressing issue tonight was Noah and Emily. She took her phone from her bedside table and opened Instagram. Without thinking she went to @When_We_Were_Young. Before she could open the account, her phone buzzed and a text message appeared. It was from Ashley.

I can't close my eyes. You awake?

A smile started in Kari's heart and lifted her lips. Ashley had always been a night owl. Back when they shared a room and still today. She climbed out of bed and tiptoed into the hall, down the stairs and into the sunroom off the back of the house. Once the door was shut behind her, she sat in the old rocking chair and called Ashley.

"Hi." Ashley laughed, her voice quiet. "I had a feeling you might be awake."

"What are you doing up?" Kari loved her sister, loved that they could have moments like this. "It's eleven o'clock."

"Folding laundry." Ashley sighed. "Landon's been asleep for three hours. Long day."

"Got it." Kari could picture her sister, working through a mountain of clean jeans and T-shirts, towels and socks. "I couldn't sleep, either."

"Laundry?" Ashley was in a good mood.

"Not tonight." Kari didn't want to go into detail. "One of the couples in our group is going through some hard times. Social media is involved. Just praying for them."

Ashley didn't know anyone in their group. The mention of social media wouldn't tip her off to who it was. And Kari didn't say more than that. Noah and Emily deserved their privacy. Besides, Kari hated gossip. She was intentional about avoiding it.

"Social media? Ugh . . . I hate that. So many couples are struggling because of that." Ashley's tone was genuine. "Too much time on Instagram or Facebook. Missing the person right across from you. So many reasons to struggle in a marriage. I guess we've all been there. One time or another."

"Yes. Speaking of that . . . whatever happened to the firefighter? Brady, right?" Kari leaned over her knees and looked into their backyard. "Did he ever marry that girl?"

"They're planning a Christmas wedding." Ashley's smile was evident in her voice. "Landon's so glad I reached out to him."

"It took him a bit to get there." Kari remembered how upset Landon had been when Ashley started visiting the Facebook account of a stranger, trying to find a way to help the guy locate his long-lost love. She was glad her sister and her husband had worked things out.

"Like I said"—Ashley sounded at peace over the situation—"we've all been there. Love is hard work."

"Yes." Kari shifted back in the rocking chair. Before the recent news, her only struggle with Ryan hadn't been because of social media. It had happened before they were married. When Kari felt terrible turning to him after the death of her first husband. Like there had to be more time before she could allow herself the chance to love again.

In the midst of that time, Ryan had taken a job with the New York Giants and moved to Manhattan. Not until Kari finally drove to New York and surprised Ryan at his apartment did he understand how sorry she was for shutting him out. How she was ready to try if he was.

Ashley was right. Love was never easy. Relationships were complicated. For a moment Kari thought about telling Ashley the news. The thing Ryan had sprung on her a few weeks ago and how her heart was breaking over the changes ahead. But she stopped herself. Ryan wanted her to wait until the plans were final. Telling Ashley would come later.

Kari steadied herself. "How are the kids?" Kari hadn't talked to her sister in a few days. It was good to hear her voice, good to take her mind off the situation with Noah and Emily.

"All I can think about is Cole." Ashley's voice was more wistful. "I can't believe he's a senior. He's made his decision on a school."

"Oh, I didn't know." Jessie was going to attend Indiana University and live at home. Something Kari was grateful for. Cole, though, had looked at a handful of schools all across the country. Last time their families were together, he'd been trying to narrow it down. Kari ran her hands along her arms. The night was colder than she'd thought. "Where's he going?"

"He's following Connor Flanigan and his younger brother, Shawn."

"Liberty University!" Kari was happy for Cole. "I always thought that was his first choice."

"Yes." Ashley sighed. "A full day's drive from here." She sounded like she was trying her best to be positive. "I know it's the right place. I really do. But I looked at the calendar and figured out what day he'll leave in August. Now that's all I can think about."

Kari's heart hurt at the thought. "Did you ever think our kids would grow up so fast?"

"Never." She paused for a minute. "Even Amy's little survivor sapling is growing up."

"Mmmm." Kari pictured the little tree, a seedling of the real Survivor Tree in Oklahoma City. It was the one thing her niece Amy had wanted last spring. And now it was planted behind the original Baxter house, in Ashley and Landon's backyard. "That's beautiful. How's she doing?"

"Great. She stays around home more than most kids her age. But I love that about her. And I think it's normal. Given what she's been through."

It was true. Kari pictured their sister Erin and her husband, Sam, the way they had loved their four girls before the car accident that took their lives. Three of the girls were in heaven with them. Only Amy had survived. She was twelve now and she lived with Ashley and Landon. "She loves being with you." Kari felt her heart melt. "Sweet girl."

"She told me the other day that I remind her of her mother." Ashley's voice was heavier now. "What she remembers of her." Ashley hesitated. "It made me realize I need to talk to her more about Erin. Make sure she doesn't forget what kind of mother she was, how deeply Amy was loved by her. The fun things they used to do, the songs they used to sing."

Kari set the rocker in motion. "I hadn't thought about that."

"It's up to me." Ashley sounded committed to the task. "All of us need to keep Erin's memory alive for her."

The conversation bounced to Kari's children. How Annie had an upcoming dance recital and how RJ was playing middle school football. "His next game is Saturday."

"Perfect. We were talking about what to do this weekend." Ashley's voice was happier now. "I'll talk to Landon, but I'm pretty sure we'll be there."

Kari thought about her son, and how at eleven he loved football as much as his father had back then. He was a quarterback like his daddy, and last week he'd taken a hit to his knee that left him on the ground for nearly a minute. Kari took a slow breath. "Sometimes I wish he liked tennis or golf. Something that didn't involve torn knee ligaments . . . or head injuries."

"I get that." Ashley's son Cole had played and her younger son, Devin, was on a flag team this fall. "Football's scary. Especially for us moms."

They talked about Ashley's husband, how Landon was enjoying his promotion. "I'm so proud of him." Ashley sounded like she was beaming. "I always knew he'd be chief one day."

"When you think about all he's been through as a firefighter." Kari shook her head. "If anyone deserves the promotion it's Landon."

"True." Ashley hesitated. "Sometimes I think about how he nearly died rescuing that little boy from the house fire. And after that his days at Ground Zero in New York City, looking for his firefighter friend in the rubble of 9/11." She sighed. "And his lung illness, of course."

"I remember it all." Kari and the rest of the family had stood by Ashley and prayed often for Landon. "After that he couldn't fight fires."

Ashley drew a long breath. "Which nearly killed him in a different way."

"Well, I know this." Kari smiled. "He'll be the best fire chief Bloomington has ever had."

"He will." Ashley yawned. "This was just what I needed. The laundry's done, so I'm going to turn in."

"Okay." Kari still wasn't tired. "Me, too."

"And that couple from your group, I hope they work things out. I'll pray for them. God knows what they need."

"Yes, He does." Kari stood and walked back into the house. "That's exactly what we're praying for." They said goodbye and Kari dropped into the nearest chair. She stared at her phone and pulled up Instagram. In a few clicks she was on the Carters' profile. At a glance she could see twenty or so pictures and posts, beautiful shots of Noah and Emily and the kids. Photos of them at breakfast and on a walk, images of their dinner table and backyard garden.

Some photos had Bible verses laid over them. But always the theme was love. That was the goal of the account according to the description at the top. Kari read the words Noah had written.

This is the story of Noah and Emily Carter and how once upon a time we fell in love. Since then God has taken us on a journey that we hope will inspire you and encourage you. In case you wonder what love looked like for us . . . when we were young.

A sick feeling worked its way through Kari. She clicked on the last update Noah had posted. It was from a week ago. Little Aiden holding a bouquet of dandelions. The words beneath the picture read:

Life is full of weeds. It takes love to see them as something beautiful. Something God will use one day to make you smile.

Who even wrote that? Kari couldn't believe Noah had typed those words knowing that he was about to leave Emily and the kids. Weeds could be beautiful? Was he serious? Had he grown so attached to his virtual world and so disconnected from reality that he didn't even realize what he was saying to the public?

Kari looked at the likes beneath the post. There were more than ten thousand. She tried to picture that many people. Ten thousand had attended a women's event she went to a few months ago. An entire arena, every row packed.

That many people.

Kari pulled up the comments. There were eight hundred. She scrolled through the most recent and scanned the things people had said.

What a cutie . . . just like you, Noah.

Mini-me, Noah . . . he'll be just as handsome as you when he grows up.

Where's the pics of you and Emily . . . we need more, more, more!

I learned everything I know about love from you and Emily. God bless you both!

Hottest dad. Cutest family. Ever. #futuregoals.

I have one wish in all the world—that I would wake up and be Emily Carter.

The comments went on and on. More than half were from females. They weren't exactly suggestive, at least not most of them. But some were definitely flirty.

Kari clicked off her phone and closed her eyes. No wonder Emily was struggling. In some ways Noah was having a very public affair with thousands of girls. They adored him, openly complimented him on his looks and his romance and the way he loved Emily.

Some were clearly outspoken about wishing they were in her shoes.

Like the last comment.

She stood and went to her room. Whether she fell asleep or not, it was time to get to bed. Time to settle her mind, give her troubled heart to God and ask Him again for a miracle. The way she and Ryan had prayed for one earlier.

Maybe not just for Noah and Emily, but for Ryan and her, also.

Why did her husband feel the need to change things now, just when life was so good for all of them?

When she was finished praying, she thought again about the Carters' social media profile. She didn't know Noah's motives or exactly what might have happened between him and some of the female fans. But she definitely understood Emily's anger, her heartache. And something else. The one thing she absolutely knew for sure about Noah's social media status. No matter what he said about their public persona, it wasn't love.

Not even close.

9

Emily still wasn't ready to sleep, didn't want to move from her spot on the back porch swing. The spot where Noah had promised they would watch their kids grow up. She couldn't stop thinking about one thing:

She would never sit here with him again.

The breeze had tapered off, and in the still of the night between storms, Emily could feel her heart beat. Hard and fast. Proof that the stress of this season was constant. Even here in this quiet spot. She breathed in slow through her nose and set the seat in motion ever so slightly back again.

No, she had never intended to marry Noah Carter. Never thought about marrying anyone. She had Clara, and that was enough. Her full-time purpose. Clara had no one on earth except Emily. How could there be room for a man in her life?

At first it was easy to live the single life. Emily's days at Indiana University were crazy busy. Emily arranged her classes and dance practice so she could drive to Clara's school each day, pick her up and bring her to the university. Clara loved watching Emily dance.

Sometimes Emily would smile at her sister during practice, and the look of joy and excitement in her eyes was easy to read. As if Clara were living vicariously through her, cheering her on. Finding just as much joy watching as she would if her own legs worked.

Three hours of dance, and then Emily would take Clara to the university cafeteria. A quick dinner and they'd head home to study. Finally Emily would make sure Clara got her shower and that she had clean clothes laid out for the next day. In the morning Emily would make breakfast for the two of them, and then she'd drive Clara to school and the routine would start all over again. It was a full schedule, and sometimes Emily would catch a look of guilt from Clara.

"I'm too much," Clara told her once as they ate dinner in those first few weeks of the semester. "Not fair."

Emily stood and put her hands on Clara's shoulders. She looked right into her eyes and prayed her sister would fully grasp every word. "I want to do this, Clara. I wouldn't want it any other way." Emily smiled. "You're my best friend. And you're all the family I have. Don't forget that."

Clara's smile had warmed Emily to the deepest part of her soul. Her sister believed every word. After that Clara didn't bring it up again. They functioned the only way they knew how, and that meant they were together all the time.

Whenever they weren't in school.

It was the third Tuesday that fall and for the first

time Clara had gone home with a friend from school. Emily had talked to the girl's mother and worked out the details. It felt strange after dance practice, being at the cafeteria without Clara. As she grabbed a salad and some grilled chicken, Emily took a table. She was thinking about calling and checking in on Clara.

But at that exact time a dark-haired guy wearing a football jersey and jeans walked up and joined her. Just sat right down across from her like they were old friends. "I'm Karl." He held out his hand. "You're the most beautiful girl on campus, so I thought I'd come say hello."

The guy was good-looking, but his brash attitude and mannerisms made Emily want to choke on her lettuce. She shook the guy's hand and stared at her dinner. How was she supposed to get him to leave?

"I'm on the football team. Karl Harvey. Tight end." He raised his brow, like she must certainly know who he was. "Caught the winning touchdown last Saturday?"

Emily looked up. She shook her head. "I haven't been to a game." She smiled, but it felt weak even to her. Maybe the guy was in one of her classes. "Do I . . . know you?"

"That's the thing." Karl leaned over the table so his face was closer to hers. "Not yet. But you will. Very soon if I have it my way." He sat back and grinned at her. "Which I usually do."

Right at that minute, when Emily was about to bolt from the table and never come back to the cafeteria again, a tall blond guy with broad shoulders and kind blue eyes walked up. He didn't look at Emily. Rather he gave Karl a light shove. "Move over."

Karl looked up. His too-friendly face twisted into a scowl. "Hey . . . I'm busy here."

"I see that." The blond looked from Karl to Emily, then back again. "Looks like you're bothering my girlfriend." He turned to Emily. "Is that right, love? He bothering you?"

Emily felt dizzy. "Um . . . well, I . . . I was trying to eat. So, yeah."

"See?" He gave Karl another shove. "Go sit with the rest of the team. This is my spot."

Karl looked doubtful. "Come on, Carter. You don't even know her."

"Look." The blond slid Karl off the bench little by little. "I might be your teammate, Harvey. But that doesn't mean you know everything about me." He pointed. "Now go! Get!"

Clearly disappointed, Karl stood and turned to Emily once more. "You don't know what you're missing, sweetheart." He gave the blond guy what looked like a reluctant smile. "Quarterbacks always get the girl. I'm telling you."

And with that he was off for the back of the cafeteria. The spot where the football players usually ate. The blond guy watched him go, then he looked at Emily. "Hey. I'm Noah Carter."

"Mmmm." Emily couldn't help but smile. "Quarterback, I take it."

"Not today." He punctuated the air with his finger. "At this very moment I'm rescuer and chief distracter for . . ." He waved his hand toward her. "I don't even know your name."

Emily remembered thinking that whoever this Noah guy was, he had smooth down to a science. She held out her hand. "Emily Andrews." She glanced to the spot where Karl had relocated. "I didn't know what to say to him. So . . . yeah, thanks."

"You're welcome." He shook her hand and did a slight bow. "Just another day in the life. Rescuing fair maidens being hit on by my teammates."

"Oh." Emily heard her voice turn flirty. She couldn't help herself. "So you do this often. Rescuing girls?"

"Well." He leaned his forearms on the table and lowered his voice. "Truth be told, you're the first one." He grinned. "I couldn't stand to see Karl hit on you."

"When you could do a better job yourself?" She laughed, her eyebrows raised.

"Me?" Noah feigned a shocked sort of hurt. "Not at all." He relaxed back into the bench. "Seriously. You just looked like you could use a little help."

Emily liked that, and for some reason she believed him. Maybe because he was the cutest boy she'd ever seen, or because he made her laugh. Whatever it was, she didn't want him to leave.

All her life she'd been too busy with Clara to think about boys. She'd attended just a handful of high school dances, and then only with groups of friends. But when

Noah glanced at his watch and suggested the two of them get coffee across the street, Emily's yes was out of her mouth before she could stop it.

From the beginning he had that effect on her.

Clara wouldn't be home for another few hours, so what would it hurt? They walked to the café and took a booth at the back. She ordered coffee with cream and he got a decaf cappuccino. "Coach doesn't like us having caffeine."

She smiled. "You must be pretty good."

"Why do you say that?" He leaned back, an easy grin at the corners of his mouth.

Emily felt herself relax. Noah seemed to have an uncanny ability to read her, to tell that she was playing with him a little. "You mean . . . because I'm the starting quarterback?"

"No." She heard the teasing in her voice. "Because you care enough to skip caffeine."

He laughed. "Yeah, I wish that's all it took."

She pointed to a bruise on his forearm. "Like that, you mean?"

"Right." He pushed back his shirtsleeve to reveal another two black and blue areas. "It's a commitment."

"So why do it, Mr. Rescuer?" She was serious now, though the air between them was still easy. "You love it that much?"

"I do." He angled his head, like he was trying to see deeper into her heart. "Surely there must be something you love that much. Or someone."

"Touché." She returned the look, staring into his eyes. Who was Noah Carter and why did he have such a pull on her?

"Okay." He raised his eyebrows. "Maybe I'll hear about that later." Another smile. "As for me, yes, I do love the game. Since I was two." He shrugged. "Now I'm shooting for the stars. Trying for the next level."

The next level. Emily blinked a few times. "Pro football?"

He laughed. "You're not a fan, are you?"

"Well." She wrinkled her nose. "Not really. Sorry." Football had been her mom's sport. Something she loved to watch. Emily had never gotten into it. "I guess I never had time to understand the game. Tight pants. Big shoulders. Huge helmets. Everyone crashing into each other."

"Wow." He raised his brow, his eyes still teasing her. "Sounds barbaric."

"Isn't it?" Her laugh caught her by surprise. She couldn't remember the last time she'd enjoyed a moment like this with someone other than Clara.

"Okay, yeah. You're right." Noah angled his head. "Definitely barbaric. I'll give you that."

They both laughed then, like they'd known each other all their lives. And in slight shifts and bits, Emily felt the walls around her heart and soul start to wobble. The time with Noah had been like water to her very existence. Like God had been showing her what she'd been missing by never letting anyone new into her life.

While she and Noah talked, Emily reminded herself

that she absolutely loved being with Clara. She would choose her sister every day. But she'd never had a date like this. Not ever.

She told him general details about her life. How she'd always lived in Bloomington and how Clara was everything to her. But no matter how charming Noah was, Emily didn't mention Clara's disability, didn't feel the need to talk about it. Didn't tell him about her mother, either. Noah asked questions as she talked, and Emily's answers came easily. She was on a dance scholarship. No she wasn't into the Greek life and no she didn't have a boyfriend. Her only reason for being there was to get a degree.

So I can take care of Clara forever.

Halfway through her coffee, Emily sat back and set her cup down. "So what about you, Noah Carter? Where are you from?"

"Nashville." His eyes sparkled. "Can't carry a tune in a bucket, though."

"I was going to ask." She giggled. "Now that I think about it, you do seem like a country western kinda guy. Big hat. Boots."

"I do?" It took him a minute to figure out she was kidding. When he did he chuckled and pointed at her. "I like you, Emily Andrews. I think we're going to be good friends."

And that's exactly what happened.

Especially after the scene that played out the next evening.

Emily had Clara with her and like usual, after dance

practice the two walked to the cafeteria. Same seat. Same time. Karl nodded at Emily as he walked by, but he didn't stop. Emily smiled to herself. Noah had put an end to that. But Clara noticed the exchange. The slightly nervous way Emily looked at her salad plate.

People usually took Clara for being more mentally slow than she really was. Because of her crutches and the crooked way she moved, because she had trouble forming words or sentences, or because her mouth hung at an unnatural angle, even when she smiled.

But Clara wasn't as slow as people thought. The truth was, most details didn't get by her. Like when their dad left home or when their mother didn't come back from Texas.

Clara understood. She cried and felt and hurt and laughed. The difference was, Clara had a high pain tolerance. Physical pain, yes. But emotional, too. When the arrows of life hit Emily, they often took up residence in her soul, where they festered and stung for months or years. Forever, sometimes. Not so with Clara. The arrows hit her and she felt them. But then she let the arrows fall away. As if the sunshine of a new morning was more than enough to clean the slate.

Clara lived with a simplicity, an abandonment that Emily had never mastered. And something more. Clara had a sixth sense of sorts. An ability to feel shifts in the wind and subtle unspoken feelings. Like God had given Clara that to make up for what she didn't have.

Clara put down her special fork, the one Emily carried in her backpack. Then she watched Karl move on, and she turned to Emily, her eyes big.

"Emily?" She reached her hand across the table and put her fingers over Emily's. "Who?"

"Him?" Emily shrugged. "Just a football player. It's nothing."

"You know him?" Her words were pointed, no matter how long it took her to say them. "Foot player?"

"Okay." Emily smiled at her sister. "He tried to sit with me last night. When you were at your friend's."

Clara narrowed her eyes. "No . . . like him?"

"No." A quick laugh came from Emily. "Too pushy."

Before Clara could respond, Noah walked up with his tray. He looked from Emily to Clara. "Care if I join you?"

Emily had never seen Clara blush before, but beneath the gaze of Noah Carter, her cheeks turned a bright shade of red. She nodded and slid her tray over, so he'd have somewhere to sit.

Panic coursed through Emily. She hadn't told Clara about Noah or their coffee and conversation. He was just a friend, she had told herself. Someone she might not even see again. After all, he was busy and popular. Big man on campus.

And she never wanted to worry Clara. Because if some far-off day Emily fell in love, Clara might wonder where that would leave her. Who would care for her and love her? She had nothing to fear, so Emily had spared Clara the story.

But now . . . she willed Noah not to talk about their time together. So Clara wouldn't feel hurt that Emily hadn't told her about it. She held her breath. *Let it feel like a beginning.* She watched him and waited.

Noah took the seat next to Clara and gave Emily a quick grin. Then as if he could read Emily's mind he turned to Clara. "Every day I go sit with those loud, crazy football players." He smiled. "And I see you two sitting here." He picked up his fork, his eyes never leaving Clara's. "I always wonder the same thing. Why aren't there more people sitting with the two prettiest girls on campus?"

Clara beamed, coming to life under the warmth of his attention. She lifted her chin and giggled—in her special Clara way. "Thank . . . you."

Emily was about to interpret, not everyone understood Clara at first, but Noah nodded, his eyes still on Clara's. "You're welcome." He smiled. "I mean it." He shot a sincere glance in Emily's direction and then he ate a few bites of his dinner.

The whole time Emily was too stunned to move, too shocked to say anything. Only Emily and her mom had ever been this genuine to Clara. Chills ran down her arms. Clara must've felt incredibly comfortable around Noah. Because she put her hand on her chest. "I'm Clara." She motioned to Emily, her hand more jerky than smooth. "Sisters."

Again Noah seemed to understand Clara without any trouble. "I figured you were sisters. Same blond hair and blue eyes." He winked at her. "Nice to meet you, Clara."

Emily could only watch, mesmerized. Noah had the easiest way about him. Like he hung out with people like Clara every day.

Next Noah turned to her. "Oh . . . and you." He snapped his fingers lightly, like he was trying to remember. "You're . . . Emily, isn't it?" He pointed at her again, like he'd done the night before. Only this time it was as if he was trying to place her. "I feel like I've seen you around school."

"Maybe." Emily felt her eyes sparkling under his gaze, but she kept up the act. "Noah, right?"

"Yes." He set his fork down and held out his hand. "Nice to meet you."

"And you." Emily reached out and their fingers touched for a beat or two longer than necessary. That was all it took. The shaky walls around her heart crumbled under the feel of his skin against hers.

This time the blush was hers. And for some reason Clara didn't notice. She was too busy grinning at Noah.

It was the beginning of an even greater friendship than Noah had talked about last night over coffee. Because from that moment on it involved Clara. When Noah didn't have football he came to the dance hall and sat with Clara through Emily's practice. The small set of bleachers was situated behind glass, so that visitors wouldn't interrupt the dancers.

But it didn't matter.

Noah's presence was always the best kind of interruption. Through the glass and throughout practice, Emily could see him talking to Clara, see the way he poured into her and made her feel special. It was all Emily could think about—the way Noah had loved Clara from the beginning.

Emily squinted into the stormy night sky. It was darker than before. Like all of earth knew Emily and Noah were ending things. Clara's sweet face filled Emily's mind. Her kind, childlike eyes and the smile that never quite left her mouth. Tears gathered again and Emily let them come. Maybe it was a good thing God had taken Clara home early.

Because it would've killed her to see Noah Carter walk out that door in the morning.

10

Noah had to be dreaming. Because all he could see was Emily, young and beautiful and smiling. The smile that had captured his heart, the one he hadn't seen in a year.

At least not directed at him.

If it was a dream, Noah figured he might as well let it come. Especially since it kept drawing him like a riptide back to the beginning. The time when he and Emily first met. Noah could feel the pillow under his head, but all he could hear was Emily's sweet voice.

From the first day of the semester, Noah had noticed them, Emily and Clara getting their meals together. The gorgeous blond-haired girl walking close to the one with crutches, clearing random chairs and sliding tables out of her way. It was like she didn't care about anything but the special-needs girl with her.

Noah figured the blonde must be the caretaker for the girl with crutches. Maybe she was getting her degree in special education. Something like that. But after a few days Noah could suddenly see what he hadn't realized before.

The girls looked alike.

Not in their mannerisms or their facial expressions. But in every other way possible. Same hair, same skin tone. Same kind way with each other. And it hit Noah—the girls must be sisters. If that were the case, the blonde helping the other one along was doing all she could because she cared for her sister.

And if they weren't sisters, Noah figured they had to be best friends.

Every night they sat at the same cafeteria table, the kind blonde and the sweet girl with the crutches. Sometimes over dinner, while his teammates talked in loud bursts and boasting voices about the blows of practice, Noah could feel himself tune out.

All he wanted to do was watch the beautiful girl across the way.

So when the day came that she was by herself, Noah spotted the situation immediately. Saw her from his place in line waiting for a cheeseburger. And then—just when he could imagine himself walking up and sitting across from her—he watched Karl Harvey take his spot.

Noah didn't take his eyes off the two of them even after he got his food. He could tell a lot from the way the blonde held herself, the way she leaned back from the table a few inches.

She wasn't into Harvey.

So he created a plan on the spot, and at just the right time he walked up and took a seat at the table. Like he belonged there, as if the two of them had been dating for a month. He said something clever to Harvey, something about leaving his girlfriend alone.

Whatever his words, the trick worked. Harvey slumped off to the football tables, and Noah had his first conversation with Emily Andrews. He could still see her pale blue eyes, the way they tried to stay distant and aloof. It hadn't worked. Instead they had sparkled just enough to keep him there. Enough to give him the courage to suggest a walk to the café across the street.

That night, sitting across from her in a corner booth, he fell in love with her. With the spunk she showed when she told him he looked like a Nashville guy—the type to wear cowboy boots and a ten-gallon hat. He loved the way she laughed and how she played with her pretty hair when she didn't seem sure how to answer his questions.

She was a dancer who had lived in Bloomington all her life. Close to her sister and close to God. She didn't care about the Greek life and thought of herself as sort of an outcast. "I'm here for one reason." Her smile warmed the air between them. "I need a degree."

But there was something she never talked about, and Noah wasn't going to ask. Not yet. She never talked about the girl with the crutches. And so as the hour passed, a story began to form in Noah's heart.

The girl with the crutches had to be Emily's sister. Which was maybe why Emily came across guarded, the reason she didn't talk much about her home life or her family. Halfway through their time together that night, Noah was almost certain.

Emily was trying to protect her sister.

Either way, Noah had never met any girl like Emily. With every passing minute, he became more enamored, more taken by her presence, her laugh. By the end of the hour he made a commitment to himself, something he absolutely intended to see through, whatever it took.

One day, he was going to marry Emily Andrews.

It was all he could think of that night and through the next day. So that night, when he saw Emily with the girl at dinner, he made another plan. He was going to act like last night hadn't happened. Let that be Emily's call.

The move turned out to be exactly what Emily wanted. And yes, the girl was Emily's sister. Clara. One of the kindest, most pure humans Noah had ever known. One of his favorite people in all the world.

Dinner that night lasted long after the rest of the football team left the cafeteria. By then he loved Clara as much as she loved him. Before they parted ways, Clara invited him to watch Emily's dance practice with her.

That was all the encouragement Noah needed. And so he waited until the following afternoon—and when the football team finished early, he showered and headed straight for the dance hall. He found his way to the right studio and took a seat next to Clara. She beamed at him. "Like you, Noah."

That's all she said. *Like you*. But it was all she needed to say. The friendship between him and Clara was fast and certain from the beginning. Clara pointed to the dancers out on the floor and Noah turned his attention to Emily. For the rest of the rehearsal, Noah had to remind himself to breathe.

Emily danced like the wind, with the grace and beauty of a fiery leaf floating to the ground on an autumn breeze. She was the music to his song, and every movement was a note that filled Noah's heart.

It became a routine for the next few weeks. Whenever Noah finished practice early enough, he'd go sit with Clara and watch Emily dance. Then the three of them would go to the cafeteria and make their way to Emily and Clara's table. The guys on the team gave him a hard time, but Noah didn't care. He sat with the players at lunch. Dinners were for Emily and Clara.

The first weekend after Noah met Emily, the football team had an away game at Ball State. Noah played the game of his life, but only because he wanted Emily to hear about it. So he could impress her. At least that's how he remembered it. A home game against Southern Illinois was set for the following Saturday.

Noah came up with a plan to get Emily and Clara there.

Over their cafeteria dinner Friday night, Noah turned to Clara. "I have a football game tomorrow. Right here." He grinned at Emily and then back to Clara. "I'd really love you to go."

Emily shook her head and gave him a wary look. But she couldn't keep from smiling. Especially as Clara's eyes lit up. "Yes! Yes . . . please!" She turned to Emily. "Please!"

There wasn't any choice after that. Noah winked at Emily, and her cheeks darkened just a little. The next day Noah reserved seats on the fifty-yard line for Emily and Clara.

He would always owe Clara an assist for helping him win Emily over. Because Clara loved football from the first drive of the game. Knowing Emily and Clara were in the stands watching, Noah played even better than he had the week before. He threw for more than four hundred yards and three touchdowns to beat Southern Illinois by one point.

After the game, he didn't get to see them, so he texted Emily and asked if he could stop by her house. He was shocked when she responded with her address and a smiley face. Up until then she'd repeatedly kept her home life a mystery.

When he arrived at her small house, she answered the door and stepped out onto the porch. "Clara's asleep." Her voice stayed at a whisper. She looked up at him. Her eyes were even more beautiful in the moonlight. She pointed to a couple chairs. "Let's sit for a minute."

When they were side by side, their knees almost touching, Emily turned to him, her face all lit up. "Must've been the decaf."

"What?" Noah didn't track at first.

"No caffeine. Your coach asked you to stay away from regular coffee, remember? And I'm glad you did." She smiled big. "Because, Noah, you are a very good football player."

"Hmm." He rubbed at a bruise on his right arm and surveyed her. "You think so? Did someone explain the game to you?"

She laughed out loud. "You crossed that white line a bunch of times and everybody cheered. So, yeah. I didn't need a lot of explaining."

Noah nodded. "Thanks." He let his eyes hold hers for a while. "That means a lot. Coming from a non-fan like you."

"You never know." She was teasing him again, allowing just enough flirting to take his breath away. "You play like that, I might have to come back."

"Well, that might just make my whole season." He grinned. "But mainly"—he felt the shine in his own eyes—"what did Clara think?"

"Clara?" Emily laughed again. "She is your new number one fan. No question." Emily brought her voice back down to a whisper. "If I don't take her next time, she'll find another way there. I'm sure of that."

The conversation seemed to stall there, and Noah gripped the arms of his chair. He had no idea what was coming. He looked at the closed front door. "Your parents sleeping, too?"

A half minute passed before Emily took a deep breath and settled back into her chair. "That's what I want to talk to you about, Noah. It's sort of a secret. About my family."

In the next ten minutes she told him a story he had never expected and could hardly believe. Both her parents were gone, and at eighteen, Emily was the head of the household.

"So . . . you take care of Clara full-time?" Noah couldn't get his mind around the responsibility. Until then he had never guessed that the two girls lived alone. "Who takes her to school?"

"Me." Emily didn't look troubled. "The summer was the hardest. Right after our mom died." She hesitated and looked into the night sky. "What choice did I have?"

He had to agree. "Now I get it."

"Get what?" She faced him, calm and sure of herself. Like someone twice her age. Her eyes were wide and full of trust. Noah had the feeling she was starting to care for him, too. Maybe more than he knew.

"Why you are the way you are . . . with Clara." He narrowed his eyes. "You care so much." He paused. "I have a secret, too. But it's not as big a deal as yours."

She angled her face, flirting with him. "I'm listening, Nashville." There she was, the same Emily from coffee that first day. Teasing, having fun with him. "Let me guess. You really do have that big ol' hat at home."

"Maybe." He looked at her for a long moment. "Before I met you, I was . . . watching you."

"What?" A laugh slipped from between her lips. "Watching me? Like where?"

Her laughter was a good sign. He added a weak chuckle. Then he looked at his tennis shoes for a few seconds and back at her eyes. "Actually, I'm serious. At the cafeteria."

He explained the situation, not quite sure what she'd think. But as soon as his words were out, compassion came over her. "Because you wondered about Clara? That's why you watched us?"

"Well . . ." He winced. "I sort of thought you were the most beautiful girl I'd ever seen. So there was that." His smile fell off. "But it was something more. The way you cared for Clara. I figured she might be your sister."

"You did?" Emily looked happy about this.

"The two of you could be twins if Clara wasn't—" He caught himself. There was no easy way to finish the sentence.

"I get it." Emily's eyes were gentle. "I know what you mean." The corners of her lips lifted a little. "Clara's very pretty. That's a compliment, being compared to her."

Noah nodded. "Anyway, I mean . . . you never left her side." He didn't blink, didn't look away. "Which was even more beautiful. Honestly. It was something I looked forward to every day, watching the two of you."

Understanding dawned on Emily's face. "I like that, Noah. That you noticed the two of us, not just me." She put her hand over his for a few seconds. "Thanks for sharing your secret."

"You, too." He wanted to take her in his arms and hold her, shelter her from a big, bad world where she was completely in charge of her special-needs sister. But it was too soon. He stayed in his seat and let himself get lost in her eyes. "Let's make a deal."

She laughed. "A deal?"

"Yes." He took hold of her hand and gave it a couple light squeezes. "No more secrets. Because friends don't hide things from each other."

"Okay." She eased her hand from his and crossed her arms. A shiver seemed to pass over her. "Friends. No secrets."

Her emphasis on the word *friends* was clearly intentional. Noah hid his disappointment. He had time, however long it took. He'd do whatever he could to help her see she could trust him with her heart. But for now he only nodded and smiled. "We have another home game next Saturday. Against Connecticut."

She stood. "Clara will be there." Her shoulders lifted in the sweetest shrug. "I guess that means I'll be there, too."

"Don't feel forced or anything." Noah grinned. "I can get an escort for Clara."

Her expression turned playful again. "Actually, Noah Carter, I think I like watching you score touchdowns. The whole stadium cheering your name. Makes me happy for you."

"Good. I like you being there." Noah felt his heart melt. So much that he wondered if it might seep out his pores and spill onto the porch. But he worked to keep things light. "I'm guessing it's time to go?"

"Yeah." She looked over her shoulder. "Clara and I have church tomorrow. Early."

"Okay." He stood and moved closer. Then he gave her the quickest, most friend-zone hug he knew how to give.

He stepped back and slid his hands into the pockets of his jeans. "I played better today. With you there." He smiled. "See you Monday."

Her cheeks darkened again, just a little. "See you, Noah."

As he walked away, Noah thought about all that had happened that day. Victories on a number of levels. She had opened up to him about her home life and admitted she enjoyed his football game. Their friendship had taken root and now she and Clara would be at his game next weekend.

Noah turned onto his side. The dream was so real, so vivid. Like he was reliving those days, walking through them and breathing the same air all over again. His head still pounded and he couldn't wake up if he wanted to.

But he didn't want to. As long as he was back in the past with the Emily he'd fallen in love with, he didn't care if he never woke up. Sleep dragged him back to the beautiful past.

After that night on Emily's porch, the next week flew by. More dance rehearsals, more dinners in the cafeteria. And then it was football Saturday. Noah couldn't imagine what personal records he might break against Connecticut. Emily was so good for him; just knowing she and Clara were in the stands was enough to give Noah a confidence he'd never quite felt before.

Sure enough, he scored three touchdowns in the first half. And he fully expected to score as many over the last two quarters. Instead, he lined up on the first play of the second half and then . . . then everything about the memory happened in slow motion.

He took three steps back, one eye on the pocket created by his offensive lineman. Then without warning he was hit with a blitzing, terrible force from the right side. He could barely remember slamming to the ground and hitting the left side of his helmet on the field. His head's collision with the turf made a deafening sound in his ears and ricocheted through his brain. The one thought Noah had was this: he had never been hit so hard in all his life.

Then there was nothing but darkness.

11

Noah blinked his eyes open and sat straight up in bed. *Breathe,* he ordered himself. *You have to breathe*. His body was shaking and his arms and legs were sweaty. He gasped for air.

What had happened? He squeezed his eyes shut and then opened them, and the memory returned. He had dreamed about the hit again. Why did he have to re-create it in his sleep? He massaged his left temple and sat up.

His head hurt so bad, almost like the tackle had just happened. He looked around the room. Where was Emily? She would help talk him down from this. Soothe the way his heart raced and his brain pounded every time this happened. Every time his nightmares forced him to relive the hit.

The one that nearly ended his football career.

"Emily?" He looked at her side of the bed. Strange. It didn't look slept in. Had she fallen asleep on the couch, maybe? Or did she have something this morning? He gripped the edge of the mattress and stared toward the bedroom door. "Emily? Are you here?"

He didn't hear the sounds of the kids, either. A quick look at his nightstand and the pieces came together. His alarm clock read eight o'clock. Which meant he hadn't set it because he didn't work today. It was Saturday. Of course. Emily and the kids were at the park with the moms' group from church. Once a month.

Today was that day.

He rubbed his head again and worked his fingers into the back of his neck. Good thing he didn't have to work until Monday. It would take most of the weekend for his headache to wear off. Advil would help—though he had to be careful with that, too. His kidneys couldn't take much more painkiller. Not even ibuprofen.

His lungs were still working double time. *Exhale, Noah. Come on. Help me exhale, God. Please.* He forced his body to relax. What was the verse? Philippians 4:6–7. *Do not be anxious about anything, but in every situation, by prayer and petition, with thanksgiving, present your requests to God. And the peace of God, which transcends all understanding, will guard your hearts and your minds in Christ Jesus.*

Yes, that was it. He let the words run over in his mind a few more times. With each repetition he felt his body relax a little more until finally his breathing was almost normal. He looked from side to side, stretching his neck until he could feel some of the tension waning.

A few deep breaths and Noah felt a little better. Time to get up and change the lightbulbs in the hallway. Emily had been asking him to do that for two weeks. He needed to check it off the list. He yawned and swung his legs over the edge of the bed.

As soon as his feet hit the ground a lightning bolt of alarm shot through his body. What was this feeling? Scratchy fibers? He lifted one foot, then the other. Then he stared at the floor. What he saw made the room start to spin.

Carpet? What in the world?

This wasn't his bedroom. It couldn't be. He and Emily had wood floors in their room. Not this . . . this cheap worn-gray shag carpet. Noah began to shake again, his shoulders and arms and face trembling. The bed they shared sat on a dark wood floor with wide planks. They were a gift. One from Noah to Emily on their first anniversary. All new hardwood throughout the house. They could afford it because their social media platform was taking off. Emily had loved those floors. She talked about them all the time.

So where were they?

He braced himself on the wall and closed his eyes. What was happening? Where was he? He blinked his eyes open again and walked to the bedroom window. The trees and the front yard, they were gone, too. Instead there was a parking lot and a series of apartment buildings.

Had he fallen asleep at someone's house? Was his headache so bad that he hadn't made it home? Was he forgetting things? The pounding was still there, as strong as it had been yesterday. He pressed his thumbs and forefingers into his eyebrows and willed the pain away. *Please, God, make it go away. I have to get home.*

This definitely wasn't his house. He took in the details of the room. He was fully awake now, so he could see more clearly. Everything was wrong. This bedroom was much smaller than the one he shared with Emily. Small nightstand, pressed-wood dresser. Clothes in a heap on the floor.

Clothes on the floor? Noah squinted at the pile and with slow shaky steps he moved toward it. He picked up a pair of jeans and then another. And another. Then he dropped them like they were burning his fingers. Every shirt, every pair of pants and socks were his.

All of them.

A sick feeling started in his gut. Why were so many of his clothes here, in the house of a stranger? He swallowed hard. Full-blown panic was closing in on him. He walked toward the door. "Hello?" His voice trembled. "Is . . . is anyone here?"

Before his hand could touch the doorknob, he noticed something that caught his breath. A framed photo on the wall. Noah stared at the images. Two children. A boy and a girl. Maybe seven and five years old. Noah heard his teeth begin to chatter. At the same time chills ran down his arms and legs.

Who were these children? He didn't know them, but they had an uncanny resemblance to Aiden and Olivia. A foot away was another framed photo. Noah moved closer and studied it. As he did, he felt his breathing grow steady again.

Finally. Something he recognized. The picture was of the four of them. Emily and him, Aiden and Olivia. A professional portrait they'd had taken a few months ago. Noah touched the faces beneath the glass. Sweet Emily, her blue eyes full of love and hope. He ran his finger over Aiden's face next. The mouth and chin so like Noah's. His little-boy confidence that with Mommy and Daddy holding him, all things were good and wonderful.

Noah smiled. Then there was Livi. He ran his thumb over her pretty face. She was still a baby, still happiest when she was cuddling with Emily and him. But every day she was becoming more independent. Olivia had Emily's eyes, but somehow she looked more like Clara. Like Clara would've looked if she hadn't been born with cerebral palsy.

He was still smiling at the photo when another shock ran through him.

Why would these pictures be hanging on the wall of someone else's room? Noah took a few steps back, his heart pounding again. Where was he? Had he been sick? Had his parents flown home from England? Was he at the house of some other family friend?

None of it made sense. He slid into a pair of sweats and a sweatshirt. With shaky steps he moved to the bathroom, but nothing about it looked even a little familiar. He looked in the mirror. Again he took a step back. What was this? He looked terrible. Lines at the corners of his eyes and a week of stubble on his face. A shudder came over him. "Come on, Noah. Get it together." How sick had he been?

He found a washcloth on the towel rack and doused it in cold water. Then he pressed it to his face and worked it around the edges of his eyes. Even then his head hurt. Every movement made it worse.

With the cloth against his face, Noah took another deep breath. Was this because of his concussions? It had to be. Whatever it was, there had to be an explanation. He must be at the house of a close friend, someone they knew very well. Well enough that they would have photos of him and his family. Yes, that had to be it.

Noah steadied himself. He would figure things out as soon as he got into the main room. After that maybe he should see a doctor. His headaches had never been this bad. He dried his face and fixed his hair. Was it his imagination, or was the color darker than before? Probably just the usual for late fall. His hair was blondest during summer.

He found a pair of socks and shoes near the bed and slipped them on.

Okay. He stood and breathed deep again. Time to figure this out. He left the room and walked down the hall like someone with a purpose. First things first. He needed to know where he was. The main room didn't look familiar, either. Outside. He gritted his teeth. *I need to get outside.* Yes, that was it. A quick few minutes outside and he should recognize the neighborhood. That would help.

The front door was bolted shut. Whoever's house he was at, they were concerned for their safety. Couldn't be anyone in the Clear Creek neighborhood where they lived. No one locked their doors there. At least not that he knew about.

He undid the latch and stepped onto the stoop. Immediately he was staring at the door of another dwelling. Just ten feet away. And it hit him then. He wasn't in a house. This was an apartment, which was why he could only see other similar buildings from the bedroom window. He was in a big complex, and the unit he was in was just part of the development.

Okay, so that was a clue. He had gone to visit a friend in an apartment complex.

Noah went back inside and shut the door. Turned the lock, too. He leaned his back against the closed door and surveyed the room. The place was smaller than most apartments he'd ever been in. Tiny living room with just a sofa and a single armchair. Small television on a plain metal stand.

His eyes wandered to the kitchen. Like something in a hotel room. Barely big enough to turn around in, boxy with a small round table at one end. Four folding chairs hugged the edges. He shifted his gaze to the living room and something else caught his attention: a plaque hanging on the wall.

It was a wooden piece with lettering across it. Word

art. Noah smiled. Something familiar. Emily had always loved word art. He moved closer and read the message.

Life gives you two choices. Regret the past or change the present. You can never go back, so make the change. Start today. Life is not a dress rehearsal.

Noah squinted. The words were strangely familiar, but he couldn't place them. Couldn't remember seeing this wall hanging before today. He read the words again and shook his head. They were beautiful. A good message for anyone, anytime.

A knock sounded at the door and Noah jumped. Who could it be? He blinked, his heart racing. Whoever it was could maybe help clear everything up. It was probably one of his close friends or someone from the fire department. Maybe Kari and Ryan from church.

He opened the door and stared. He was wrong.

There on the other side stood Aiden and Olivia. Only they weren't four and two anymore. They were the kids from the photograph hanging in the bedroom.

"Daddy!" Aiden ran to him and wrapped his arms around his waist. "I missed you so much! Happy October!"

Aiden missed him? And it was October already? How much time had passed? A sickening fear breathed on the back of Noah's neck. "Hey, buddy. I'm right here." He pulled his son close and ran his hand over the back of his dark hair. Wasn't it blond just yesterday? Noah grabbed at something to say. "You . . . you look bigger!"

By then Olivia was clinging to him, too. "Hi, Daddy. I'm so glad it's Saturday! I missed you, too."

His legs began to shake again. "You don't have to miss me!"

"This is our big day!" Aiden walked around the place like he knew it. He took off his jacket and threw it on the sofa. "You really think I look bigger?" He puffed out his chest. "My flag football coach says I'm the tallest seven-year-old on the team."

Seven? Aiden was seven?

That was impossible. Just yesterday he was four and in preschool. And why was Olivia so tall? Panic filled his veins and Noah felt his body freaking out. Something was terribly wrong. How had he lost three years? He couldn't breathe, couldn't talk. Adrenaline coursed through every inch of him. He needed a doctor. He gasped for air. *Enough, Noah. Calm down.*

Whatever this was, he couldn't let the kids see how afraid he was.

What had his son said? Something about his coach telling him he was tall? "That's . . . that's amazing, buddy. You're the tallest seven-year-old I know, too." Noah smiled at his son. He was still shaking. "Right." He swallowed again and looked toward the door. "Where's Mommy?"

The smiles on both kids' faces fell a little. Aiden was the first to speak up. "Mommy went shopping. She'll be back in four hours." He narrowed his eyes, like he was concerned for Noah. "Like always, Daddy. Remember? First we do breakfast."

Remember? *No*. A terrifying question dawned on

Noah. Was this the brain damage doctors had warned him of? The possible amnesia he'd read about? That must be it, the concussions were finally taking their terrible toll. Not only that, but maybe his memory was going. The headaches must've gotten worse and he must've slipped into cognitive decline. Early onset dementia. How many times had his doctor warned him about this?

He gulped a few big breaths and smiled at Aiden, then Olivia. "Right. So what's for breakfast?"

Olivia giggled. "You're silly, Daddy. You know!"

But he didn't. And now fear was paralyzing him, making it impossible for him to move or speak or think of what to do next.

Aiden grabbed the remote and flipped on the TV. "Is it okay if we watch the game during breakfast? It's the big one!"

Noah stared at his son and a small bit of what he said made sense. "Indiana football!"

"Yep. Today's the game against Michigan." Aiden grinned at him. "We're going to do this, Dad. We have to beat 'em."

"Right." Noah wondered if the kids could tell he was falling apart, that his breathing was coming in short, ragged bursts. Whatever was happening, he had no choice but to play along. If his memory was going, he could at least stay in this moment. He took hold of Olivia's hand and walked to the kitchen. "Now about breakfast."

"Pancakes, Daddy. Remember? We always have pancakes." Olivia skipped ahead of him and opened the fridge. "We need eggs and milk first."

"And pancake mix." Noah could do this. His head was still pounding and nothing made sense. Like why Aiden and Olivia were so old. Maybe if he pretended to understand, eventually his memory would return. And he'd know how he had lost three entire years.

He found a baking mix in the cupboard and Aiden joined them. Noah worked with both kids to make a platter of pancakes and a pan of scrambled eggs. The football game played in the background while the three set their plates at the table and sat down.

Aiden and Olivia picked up their forks and started to eat. Noah raised his eyebrows at his kids. "Hey, hey." He shook his head. "We need to pray."

First Aiden dropped his fork, then Olivia released hers. They stared at him. "Daddy?" Aiden's voice sounded confused and a little worried. "We . . . don't pray when we have breakfast with you."

The sick feeling was back. Noah had no idea what that meant, but he didn't press the issue. "We do now." He smiled from Aiden to Olivia. "Bow your heads."

Despite his headache and foggy brain, regardless of the details he couldn't remember or the fact that he still didn't know whose apartment they were in, Noah prayed. And for the first time that morning something made sense. He still knew how to talk to God. "Lord, bless today and this breakfast with Aiden and Olivia. Let us have a day where You are glorified and where love comes first. For all of us. In Jesus' name, amen."

The kids said their amens, too, but more like they were in a daze. Like they couldn't believe what had just happened. When Noah opened his eyes the kids were staring at him. He laughed and nodded to their plates. "Eat up. Cold pancakes are never good."

Breakfast gave Noah a chance to think, really focus on what was happening around him. He clearly needed a doctor, but that would have to come later. When Emily got home. While he ate his pancakes an idea hit him. He looked from Aiden to Olivia and back again. "So." He waved his fork toward the living room. "What do you think of this place?"

Olivia shrugged her slim shoulders. "Same as always."

But Aiden knew something was wrong. Noah could tell by the look in his eyes. "Daddy . . . we love it. You know that." He took a bite of his eggs and chewed slowly, his eyes fixed on Noah the whole time. "We don't care if it's small."

"Or that we share a room." Olivia smiled at her brother. "It's an adventure here."

"Right." Noah felt the room spinning again. Why had they downsized to an apartment? Excruciating headaches. Memory loss. Yes, that was it. His concussions had finally caught up to him. He must've taken a medical disability from work and the resulting pay cut would've sent them here.

Things were beginning to make sense. As they did,

Noah felt a wave of peace and normalcy return to him—even while his headache continued to rage. Aiden and Olivia were the same as always. Just three years older.

Then the answers hit him. If his memory was broken, he could go to the right doctor and get it fixed. Then he'd have every beautiful moment he'd missed. All three years' worth. He had read about that back when he was in college after the first blow to his head, how concussions could cause memory loss but that specialists were finding ways to restore what was missing.

So what about Emily? No doubt this had affected her. Toward the end of breakfast, Noah lowered his fork and looked straight into Aiden's eyes. "How's your mom? She's okay? She's doing good?"

"She's great." Aiden smiled big. "She likes having Saturday mornings for errands and shopping and stuff. That's what she always says."

Noah nodded and stared at the cold pancake pieces still on his plate. Emily was doing great. Those were his son's words. Noah moved his fork through the syrup. Good. Good that Emily was happy and that she loved Saturdays for errands. She was always efficient that way. Everything was fine.

Maybe it was better than fine, because whatever memory issues he was having, right now he felt fully aware of himself and his surroundings.

They finished eating and were watching the Indiana game when Aiden had an idea. It was halftime—the score tied 7–7. "Let's go throw the football!" His eyes lit up. "The kids in my class still can't believe Noah Carter's my dad. Best quarterback in Indiana history. That's what everyone says."

A sense of pride worked its way past Noah's headache. He smiled. "Great idea. Let's go play." He looked at Olivia. "Sound good, honey?"

"I brought a coloring book." She laughed a little. "I usually color, Daddy. That's better."

She usually colors. Noah blinked again as he cleared the dishes and put them in the sink. The place didn't have a dishwasher, so he'd have to wash them by hand later. Olivia grabbed one of the small folding chairs from the table and some crayons from the kitchen cupboard, and Aiden found a football. All here at what was obviously their home.

They found a stretch of grass between the buildings. Olivia set up her chair and began to color, and Noah and Aiden played catch for an hour. Everything else might feel foggy and crazy and out of place. He might've lost three years, but he could still throw a ball. The leather against his fingers still felt like an extension of his arm.

When Aiden tired of playing, they all went back inside and watched the second half of the game until it was clear Indiana wasn't going to win. Then they returned outside and tossed the ball a few more times. Now whenever Aiden caught the ball he pretended to dodge tacklers and break free and run untouched past an invisible goal line. Olivia had finished coloring and now she was acting the part of the cheerleader, shouting encouragement to her brother and celebrating every imaginary touchdown.

And that's what they were still doing when Emily pulled up.

Noah saw her first. She looked gorgeous, her blond hair longer than the last time Noah could remember. He started to jog her way, but then she got out of the car and yelled over the roof, "Come on, kids! We have Sofia's party at the park in fifteen minutes."

Just like that Aiden threw the ball back to Noah and then the kids ran inside. Noah barely noticed. His eyes were on Emily alone. She sat back behind the wheel and pulled out her phone.

As if Noah wasn't standing fifteen feet away, watching her. As if he didn't need her to right whatever was wrong, to help him get to the doctor. He took a few steps closer. "Hey!" He smiled at her and waved. "How was your morning?"

Either she didn't hear him or she was too distracted to answer, because she never looked up from her phone. Behind him, Noah heard the kids. They both had their things as they ran to him, and one at a time they hugged him. Olivia turned her soft blue eyes to his. "Pancakes next week, too?"

Noah smiled. "Of course." Why was she talking about next week already?

Aiden waved at him, and he and Olivia hurried to the car and climbed inside. Olivia was still in a booster seat, but she buckled herself in with no trouble.

"Ready, Mommy," Aiden called out.

Emily put the car in gear.

What was happening? "Emily!" Noah jogged a few steps toward the car. "Wait!" He hadn't hugged his wife, hadn't kissed her lips. And right now—with his head still killing him—that was all he wanted. All he needed. "Emily, hold on!" Noah ached to have her in his arms.

But she pulled the car away from the curb and started to go. "Emily!" he yelled after her, but she didn't stop. He raised his voice. "When will you be back?" The car was leaving with all his family inside it. "I love you!" He took a few more steps and stopped. "Hurry home!"

Noah watched the car disappear. As if Emily was no longer his wife, but the image of someone he used to know.

In a single uneven heartbeat the fear was back, breathing hot against his neck and face. Threatening to suffocate him. He shook it off. Everything would be fine. Emily just didn't hear him. That was it. She was probably in a hurry. The party at the park and all. They'd be home before dinnertime and everything would be okay.

Suddenly Noah's headache was worse. Every movement killed him. He walked back to their bedroom, changed out of his clothes and climbed into bed. At least that much was familiar. The bed. Same one he and Emily had shared since they got married.

Noah closed his eyes and let sleep come. Maybe a nap would eliminate the headache or bring back his memory. He still hadn't taken any Advil, which was probably a good thing. If he could shake it on his own, his memory might return. All three years of it. Yes, that was what would happen. A good nap and everything would make sense. It would all line up.

In a few hours everything would be back to normal.

He rolled over and fell asleep before he could give it another thought.

12

Emily was still on the back porch, still wide awake when her phone buzzed. Was this Noah asking her to come back inside, wanting to make things right? Ready to give their marriage another chance?

She grabbed her phone and looked at it. Kari Taylor. Emily sighed and opened up the message.

Are you awake? I can't sleep. Just keep thinking of you and Noah.

Emily's heart warmed at the thought. It was good to have a friend in the middle of the heartbreak. Yes, I'm awake. I'm thinking of us, too. She thought for a moment. Maybe if we'd paid more attention at your Bible study. Back when the two of us attended.

After a few seconds, Kari responded. It's not too late.

Yes, it is. Emily had to be honest. Her fingers flew across her phone's keyboard. But back then . . . wow, I mean the lessons were so powerful. Week after week all those couples talked about how after God, marriage had to come first. Over careers or hobbies or even a person's own interests.

Emily waited. It was true. Kari and her husband had done an amazing job bringing up topics from the Bible and applying them to the art of marriage. But she and Noah never seemed to notice the lessons. They were too busy pretending to be fine.

Kari texted her again. *Putting each other first, that's a decision. The two of you could still do that now. Think of others better than yourselves.*

Frustration worked through Emily's heart. Kari didn't understand. She read her friend's text again: *Think of others better than yourselves.* The admonition ran through Emily's heart. Ryan and Kari had said those six words more times than Emily could count.

But that wasn't what Noah and she had done. Not at all.

She texted her response. *I wish we would've listened the first time we heard you say that. It's too late now. He's leaving in the morning.*

Other teachings from the couple came to life again. Keep short accounts. Don't go to bed angry. Expect the best of each other. All things that were easy for the Taylors. But for Emily and Noah? They had failed each of those nice-sounding teachings, one after another. Over and over and over again. Until now it really was too late.

Another text appeared. *I'll let you go. But please, Emily, you have to believe. Even now God can work a miracle.*

There was nothing Emily could say to that. *Thanks, Kari.* She hesitated and finished her text. *Good night.*

Emily closed down her phone and set it on the table beside her. Enough talk about what was and wasn't possible. Kari didn't understand. Anyway, it was easier to think of the past. She closed her eyes and let the memories come again until there was nothing she could do to stop them.

And suddenly she could smell the hint of a distant bonfire, feel the crisp fall air on her face. She was there in the stadium seats with Clara and she was actually having fun. At a football game. The first time she had ever watched Noah play. She could hear the band and see the cheerleaders. The fight song filled the air around her and she was watching Noah run the ball into the end zone for the Hoosiers.

Clara had struggled to her feet, her face the picture of pure exuberance. So it went with every play, every first down all four quarters of the game. She didn't understand all the rules, but Emily loved every minute. More than that, she had learned something about Clara that day.

Clara understood football. Like she'd been a lifelong fan.

Which maybe she had been.

Then Emily realized the reason. When her mom was still alive, she would watch football with Clara on Saturdays in the fall. While Emily took dance lessons. Not until that game of Noah's did Emily connect the dots. Of course Clara loved football. It was a connection to their mama.

But if Emily loved the game at first, she hated it a week later. She was watching Noah take the snap and raise the ball over his head like he was going to throw it. The whole stadium saw what Noah couldn't see. The linebacker barreling toward him like a freight train. Emily could see the hit before it actually happened. But she couldn't stop it and then . . . the violent blow was sickening. Helmet to helmet.

The horrific sound silenced the crowd into a collective gasp.

Noah crumpled to the ground and lay there, not moving. Emily had her hands over her mouth. Beside her, Clara kept shaking her head and muttering under her breath. "No . . . no . . . no."

Emily couldn't feel her heartbeat, couldn't breathe. "Noah," she whispered. "Wake up. Please, God, let him open his eyes."

It took five minutes before he came to, before his fingers made even the slightest movement. Paramedics ran onto the field with a stretcher and ten minutes later Noah was whisked away in an ambulance. Emily didn't know what to do. The second-string quarterback took Noah's place and the game resumed, though the atmosphere was still and somber.

She couldn't stay, couldn't sit here with Clara wondering what had happened to Noah. Emily put her arm around her sister. "Let's go to the hospital and check on Noah. How does that sound?"

By then Clara was crying, quiet tears streaming down her face. She didn't answer, didn't ask any questions. She just nodded and struggled to her feet.

At the hospital Emily and Clara identified themselves as Noah's friends and they were told to stay in the waiting room with two team trainers and three assistant coaches. All of them waiting on word about Noah.

An hour later a doctor came to talk to them. He had gray hair and he looked gravely serious. He introduced himself as Dr. John Baxter. Kari Taylor's father, Emily would learn later. Dr. Baxter was kind, but he spoke with an urgency. "I need to get hold of Noah's parents. Do you know . . . are they still in London? That's what his school file says."

"Yes." Emily was on her feet before any of the Hoosier personnel could say anything. Her knees shook. "They live near Noah's brother and his wife and family."

Dr. Baxter nodded. "I called the number the school had on file. No one answered." He hesitated. "Does he have any other family in town?"

"No." With every word the doctor spoke, Emily grew more afraid. Was Noah even alive? She forced herself to respond like an adult. To take this on. "He has his team and he has me."

One of the coaches stepped up. "We're fully responsible for him. How is he?"

Dr. Baxter hesitated. He explained that since Emily's name was listed as his emergency contact, she could stay there to hear the news.

For a moment Emily rejoiced in the fact. Noah had listed her as his emergency contact just a few days ago. When one of the coaches had pressed him to provide at least one person not in England. She was thrilled to be asked. That meant he cared deeply for her. Like a best friend or a sister, even. Emily helped Clara take a seat at the far end of the waiting room. Then she joined the men from the team. Clara was watching, but Emily didn't want her to hear the news. Even if she were allowed. Not yet.

"So how is he?" Emily reminded herself to breathe. The five guys from the team were waiting, too.

Dr. Baxter gave a slight shake of his head. "He's going to make it. There were a few minutes there where we weren't sure. His head took a very, very serious hit."

He didn't have to tell Emily. She watched it happen. "How is he now?"

"He's breathing on his own. But his MRI shows a severe concussion. He'll be out the rest of the season. If he ever plays again." He gave the coaches and trainers a knowing look. "My recommendation is that he hang up his cleats."

When Noah was well enough to leave the hospital a few days later, that was Emily's recommendation, too. By then both of them knew the prognosis. Noah's brain had taken such a devastating blow that any additional injury to that part of his head could be fatal or life-altering. Not only that, but he still had weeks of concussion rehab ahead.

Emily had never met Noah's parents, but she became their point person, too. They called daily from London, but since Noah was recovering well enough they chose not to fly home. Funds were tight and they wanted to make a longer visit the following summer.

His mother begged Emily to let them know if anything changed or if Noah got worse. She was trying not to cry one of the last times they talked that semester. "Please, can you look after him, make sure he's going through the rehab he needs?"

And Emily promised.

One thing was certain. Noah wouldn't get the care he needed living in the dorm with the other football players. Since he had no family in the area, Emily did the only thing she could think to do. She took his recovery on herself.

So Noah moved into Emily's mother's old room. While he was still in the hospital, Emily sold her mother's mattress and box spring on Craigslist and rented a hospital bed. She and Clara also went to the local fabric store and bought dark heavy material to make drapes for the window. Dr. Baxter had been clear. Noah needed as much darkness as possible, day and night. It was part of the healing process for his brain.

At first Noah fought the idea of moving in with Emily and Clara. "You need to study. You two have your life," he told her before he was discharged. "I'll be fine. In the dorm with the guys."

But Emily wouldn't hear of such a thing. "You're staying with us till you're well. I promised your doctor and your parents."

After that there was no further discussion. Noah truly had no option. He needed to get well and Emily was willing.

She would never forget the look on Noah's face when he first shuffled into his temporary bedroom. His head still hurt but at least he could walk and talk. He wore dark glasses, even indoors. At the doorway he stopped, like he was taking it all in. The elevated hospital bed, the adjacent tables and the dark curtains that hung over the window.

Then he turned to her. "You . . . did this for me?"

"It's nothing. This is what friends do." Emily led him to the bed and helped him sit on the edge. "You'd do it for me. If I ever took a hit like that in dance."

"Sure." He caught the humor in her voice and he chuckled. Just the slightest chuckle. But it made him wince all the same. "Mmmm. My head's killing me."

From behind them Clara stood in the doorway. "Sleep. He . . . needs sleep."

She was right. Since that first moment in the hospital waiting room, Emily had kept Clara in the loop about how Noah was doing. The two of them prayed for him every night before they went to sleep and every morning before heading to school.

Noah smiled at Clara. "She has a point."

"Yes." Emily gave a solid nod. "That settles it. Get some sleep, mister. I'll bring you lunch in a few hours."

Dr. Baxter had given her a list of foods he could eat, proteins and healthy fats and green vegetables that would help his brain fully reboot. Absolutely no sugars or grains. Emily was up for the task. Three hours later she brought him a lunch of scrambled eggs and spinach and avocado. And so a new routine began.

Emily still took Clara to school every weekday, and she still drove to Indiana University and attended her classes. Still picked up Clara and took her to dance practice. Only now they would stop at their house on the way, make Noah a late lunch and check on his pain level.

Then, instead of dinner at the cafeteria after dance, Emily would stop at the football office and get Noah's classwork. She and Clara would drive home and Emily would make food for Noah. The three of them would sit in his room, the lights barely bright enough to see by. And they would work on homework. Emily would take turns helping Clara and then Noah—reading to each of them and walking them through basic assignments.

Every day Noah got a little better, a little more like himself. At his two-week checkup at Dr. Baxter's office, Noah was cleared to step into the light. His headache was very dim now, definitely bearable. He wore his dark glasses on the drive back to Emily and Clara's house, but once inside he took them off.

Clara was in her room changing, so for that moment Noah and Emily were alone.

Emily could still see the emotions playing across Noah's face. Gratitude and indebtedness, but something else. Something deeper. A passion that hadn't been there before. "Emily." He put his hands on her shoulders. "What would I have done without you?"

"You'd probably hate your roommates." She loved the feel of his hands on her shoulders, but she hated it at the same time. This was a friendship, not a relationship. She didn't want to fall in love with him. She found a light bit of laughter. "You know . . . because they're so loud and all."

He wasn't laughing. He touched his fingers to her cheeks and the feeling made her dizzy. "I have to tell you something." His eyes never looked away, never left hers. "I love you, Emily Andrews. I'm in love with you."

She shook her head and felt fear creep into her eyes. "No, you can't."

"Why?" He took a step closer. "I'll never love anyone the way I love you, Emily. What's wrong with that?" He still didn't blink, didn't look away. "You feel it, too. I know you do."

They could hear Clara in her room. The time was still theirs. With everything in her Emily wanted to deny it, to tell Noah he was wrong. She cared about him only as a friend. But it would be a lie. They both knew it.

When she didn't respond, Noah drew her close, inch by inch, breathless second by second. And in what might've been the sweetest moment in Emily's life, Noah kissed her.

Like she was born to love him, Emily did the only thing she could do. She kissed him back. Emily had no idea how long they stood there, lost in each other. She moved into his embrace and they kissed again. Emily had never felt so wonderful.

Even so, while she was still kissing him, she forced herself to stop, to find her senses. "I . . . can't." She tried to remember a single voice of reason, but she could no longer hear anything but his breathing. "Noah . . ." She took two steps back, her cheeks hot, tears in her eyes. "I can't be more than your friend."

Noah's eyes were dark with desire. "Look what we have, Emily. Why?" He was breathing hard. He took a step closer, clearly wanting to kiss her again. "Why would you refuse something like this?" He exhaled, like he was trying to find a modicum of self-control. "Is it because you're afraid we'll . . ."

He let the sentence dangle there. She knew what he meant. Her whole body knew. If she kept kissing him like that, she'd definitely be afraid of that. But there was more on Emily's mind. "No. I mean . . . It's not only that." She led him to the living room and sat next to him on the sofa. The touch of his hand in hers made her want to be in his arms again. She released his fingers and tried to focus. Clara absolutely could not hear her next words, so Emily kept her voice low. "It's my sister."

"Clara?" Noah looked confused. "I don't understand."

Emily felt tears spring to her eyes. She pressed her hand to her chest. "I am *all* she has. I'm everything to her."

"I know." He clearly didn't understand where this was going. "How does that affect us?"

"Because there's no point in dating, when I'll never get married." A single tear spilled onto her cheek. "Do you understand?"

Noah reached out and dried her face with his fingertip. Then he took hold of her hand again and searched her eyes. "You'll never get married?" He kept his voice low, too. "Because of Clara? Is that what you're saying?"

"Yes." Emily nodded. "She needs me. Where I go, she goes." Her tears came harder now. "What would I do, get married and move off to a new house? Leave her here by herself?" She shook her head. "I won't do that. Never."

The pieces seemed to come together then. Noah still had hold of her hand as he studied her. "Listen to me, Emily."

She sniffed a few times and dried her face with the back of her other hand. "What?"

"Someone who loves you would never make you leave Clara." He stood and helped her to her feet. "I'll be your friend if that's what you want. But just remember that." He looked at her for a few seconds and then gave her a sad smile and turned toward his bedroom.

At Clara's door, Emily watched Noah stop and give a few light knocks. "Clara? You cleaning up?"

"Yes." Her answer was slow and drawn out. "Come in."

Noah looked back at Emily and then, leaving the door open, he joined Clara in the bedroom. Emily heard his voice turn cheerful. "Hey there. I still want to hear about your day."

"Yes." Clara didn't need a lot of words to express her love for Noah Carter. Her tone said everything.

Emily stood there in the living room like her feet were stuck in cement, replaying what had just happened.

The kiss that had her still catching her breath, and the intent of Noah's words. That if someone loved her, they would have to love Clara, too. The two sisters could never be separated. Noah understood.

After that Noah seemed careful to keep his distance. Emily hated every minute of it. All she could think about was his kiss, his arms around her. Instead, Noah spent more of his time at home with Clara. The two of them would sit together at the dining room table doing schoolwork.

Sometimes Emily felt like an outsider, like Noah preferred Clara's company to hers. One night after Clara went to bed, she asked Noah to come sit by her. "What's happening?" She looked into his eyes, searching for answers. "You're acting so different."

It took him a minute to reply. Like he was choosing his words with great care. "I'm in love with you, Emily." His eyes were bright with kindness and understanding. "You want only a friendship." He took hold of her hand, but only for a brief moment. "I'm trying to figure out what that looks like."

She nodded. "Fair enough." What else could she say? She stared at her hand, the one he had just been holding. The feel of his skin against hers was still working its way through her body. "I'm sorry." She lifted her eyes to his. "I . . . I don't know any other way."

"It's okay." His smile was the saddest thing she'd seen in a long time. "I'm trying to find my way to being just friends."

Two weeks later Noah moved back into the dorm. He wasn't cleared to play football, of course, but he was doing exceptionally well. His vision and memory were back to normal. No sensitivity to light and no more headaches. The first night he was gone, Clara didn't eat her dinner. "I . . . wish he . . . was here."

Emily could only agree. "I wish that, too."

Everywhere she looked there were reminders of the days when Noah had lived there. The sofa where they sat and watched TV some nights, the table where they did homework. His bedroom. And the place in the living room where they'd stood when Noah kissed her.

That most of all.

Their friendship remained and grew deeper. Noah was on the injured list the rest of the football season, but that meant he had more time with Emily and Clara. He shared Thanksgiving and Christmas with them and the whole time he never again tried to kiss her. Brief hugs. Nothing more. Emily understood. His way of figuring it out. Like he had told her.

In January, Noah attended her dance recital and for just a moment from stage, Emily caught his eyes. And in that single instant she knew. He didn't really see her as a friend, he never would. Noah was in love with her, through and through.

But Emily didn't know how deeply she'd fallen for Noah until the end of February, when he made a decision that rocked her world. One she didn't see coming.

He was going to play football again.

Despite the doctor's warning, and even a serious discussion with his head coach and parents, Noah's mind was made up. He'd been on a scholarship to Indiana, the only way his family could've afforded for him to attend school there. By playing again, he would keep his financial assistance. Not only that, but he had been at the top of his game when he got hit. He tried to explain it to Emily one evening at her house. Clara sat nearby, doing her homework.

"What if someone told you dance was over. Finished." He leaned closer to her, his elbows on his knees. "And you fought and prayed and got stronger. Then you woke up one day and realized maybe it wasn't over. Maybe there was still a way." He paused. "Wouldn't you take that chance, Emily?"

Their faces inches apart, all Emily wanted was for him to kiss her again. She wanted to tell him not to do it, that she loved him and couldn't bear to see him hurt again. But the look in his eyes told her he was convinced about his decision. If she was going to be his friend, Emily needed to support him.

"I would." She remembered to smile. "I'd want to dance again."

"Good." He sat back and exhaled. "So you understand this? Please . . . tell me you understand?"

"I do." She pushed away the fear inside her. Where he wouldn't see it. "Football is what you do. If . . . the doctor says it's okay and if your headaches are gone, then . . ."

"I have clearance." He chuckled. "From the team doctor. He didn't like it, but he gave it." Noah took hold of Emily's hand, the way he still sometimes did. "My coach gave me a test to see my reaction time, to see if the concussion did any lasting damage. Emily, I'm fine. Better than fine." He laughed again. "Or at least I will be when I get back to the gym."

He explained his reasons in more detail. The team doctor had studied his MRI tests and told Noah that his concussion hadn't been as serious as he'd originally thought. Besides, guys came back from serious hits to the head all the time. It was part of the game. Especially when they recovered as well as Noah had.

So that was exactly what Noah did. He worked out like his life depended on it, pushing himself further and harder than at any other time in his life. And the work paid off. He played well during spring practice and when summer camp started he was in the best shape he'd ever been in.

When Emily asked him how things were going, Noah's answer was the same every time. Football season couldn't get there fast enough.

Emily and Clara would go watch his scrimmages in the heat of those July afternoons. Always Emily caught herself holding her breath, reminding herself to exhale. She had read up on concussions and she knew what Noah had never told her. No matter how well he performed on reaction tests, regardless of how strong he got, another hit to the same spot of his head could do permanent damage or worse. It could kill him.

But Noah was determined, and since they'd found their way to a lasting friendship, Emily could do nothing but support him. Clara, too. They prayed for Noah before every practice. And they prayed before every game all summer and into the regular season, when Noah made headlines for leading the team to its best record in a decade.

Noah Carter was back.

But in his limited off time he still belonged to Emily and Clara. He'd come to their house after practice, spend time with them on campus, and whenever he could, Noah would find his way to Emily's dance rehearsals. His entire sophomore year Noah didn't have even the slightest injury. He was healthy and strong and he played so well Emily actually forgot to worry about him. Stopped thinking he was even vulnerable to another hit like the one he'd taken his freshman year.

He was that good, that strong.

But in his junior year, halfway through the second quarter of the fourth game, Emily and Clara were watching Noah run the ball when the unthinkable happened again. Flying at him from the left side was a linebacker Noah didn't see coming until . . . the horrible, terrible blow.

The hit that made a sickening sound through the entire stadium. Again.

And just like that, Noah was on the ground. And all at once, life and time and existence stopped for Emily. Because Noah was in trouble. Deep trouble. He wasn't moving, and ten minutes later he still hadn't moved. All Emily could think was: what if this was it? What if Noah was dying out there on the field?

"Wait here," she told Clara.

Tears ran down her sister's face like before, and Clara only pointed to the field. "Go!"

Emily didn't hesitate. She scrambled down the stairs and onto the sidelines until a security guard stopped her from running onto the field. "Please . . . let me see him!" Emily cried out. She couldn't help herself. "He needs me. I have to see him."

The man wouldn't let her pass by, but somehow Noah must've heard her. Because through the crowd of coaches and paramedics circled around him, Emily saw Noah do something he hadn't done until that moment.

He moved.

13

Kari rolled onto her side and checked her phone for the tenth time in an hour. Emily was done texting her. And now it was just after midnight. She sighed and flipped onto her back. Trying to sleep was a waste of time.

She sat up and looked at Ryan. He was completely out, like none of the recent news was weighing on him at all. She studied him a minute longer. The changes ahead were so big Kari couldn't get her mind around them. Couldn't imagine life in the next six months.

And not a bit of it seemed to bother Ryan.

Kari scooted out of bed and eased into her robe. More thunder sounded in the distance. Kari shivered. The house was chilly. Or maybe it was just the cool draft deep inside her heart. The cold air of uncertainty and sorrow borrowed from a time soon to come.

A sigh came from her aching soul. Today the pain of what was ahead felt heavier, sadder than she could bear. She pulled her robe tighter around her and found her slippers.

With the light of her phone, Kari took quiet steps into the hallway and upstairs to Jessie's room. Their daughter had been up late studying. One more semester and she'd be off to college. Kari watched her sleep. Poor girl thought she was going to live at home.

Ryan's changes ahead were bound to affect Jessie more than RJ and Annie. The youngest two would have time to build a new world, time to make new friends. But Jessie would feel like she'd lost her place. Like she had nowhere familiar to return to on college breaks or summers.

Jessie's room was dark, her door open. Kari peered inside and looked for a long time at her oldest. *Beautiful girl,* Kari thought.

Ryan wasn't her biological father, of course. But he had come back into their lives when Jessie was a newborn. He was the only daddy their daughter had ever known. And always Ryan had gone out of his way to love Jessie, to look out for her needs and emotions.

Which made his news even harder to understand.

Kari leaned on the doorframe and closed her eyes. They would tell the kids in the next few weeks, but even now Kari was sure no one would believe it. The truth was this:

Last week Ryan had accepted a job coaching football at University of Arizona in Tucson.

Kari remembered the night he found her in the study to tell her about the offer. His face looked pale, his expression tight. But even then his eyes sparkled with excitement.

"Kari, girl . . . love. I have something to tell you."

Her very heartbeat worked in rhythm with his, so Kari knew immediately that whatever it was, the ramifications were significant. She swallowed hard and closed down her computer. Email could clearly wait.

Ryan held out his hand. "Come on. Let's go out front."

That night had been warmer than usual. But a chill had worked its way through Kari all the same. She found a jacket in the front closet and followed him onto the porch. They sat in the swing and for a long moment Ryan didn't say anything.

Finally he took a deep breath and turned to her. "It happened."

"What?" Her heart beat so loud she wondered if he could hear it. "Something at work?"

Ryan had taken hold of her hands. "Remember in August when I heard from University of Arizona? They talked to me about joining their football staff?"

Kari's mind raced. "You . . . you let it go." She hesitated. "And we decided we didn't want to move." Her eyes met his. "Right? Wasn't that what we said?"

"It was. But I told you, I'd already sent them my résumé." He seemed to try to keep his thrill of the moment at bay. But there was no hiding the fact that he was happy about something. "I didn't hear back, so I thought they'd gone in a different direction." He searched her face. "Until earlier today."

Suddenly it was all Kari could do to exhale. "They called?"

"The head coach. And, the athletic director was on the line." Ryan held her hands a little tighter. "Kari, they want me on staff. I'd be the first assistant. Answering directly to the head coach."

"The season is almost over." Her voice grew quiet beneath the sound of her own breathing. Fast breaths that came one on top of the other. "Why now? And you mean . . . they want you in . . . Arizona?"

"The head coach is retiring next year, Kari. No one knows yet." Ryan hadn't been able to keep from smiling. Even just a little. "With my NFL coaching experience, they want me to run the program a year from now."

As long as Kari had loved Ryan she had never seen him look so hopeful. Like all his life he'd waited for this opportunity. The news swirled in her mind and finally she asked just one question. "When?"

Ryan sat straighter in the swing. "Soon." His smile faded. "They want me in a few months. February, probably." He hurried on to the details, as if even in his excitement he knew this part of the news wasn't good. "You and the kids could take a while longer to join me. So they could finish the school year. Maybe move in late May or early June."

The swing felt like it was giving way, breaking free from the porch ceiling and floating into space. Late May or early June? Their family was moving to Arizona at the end of the school year?

Everything Kari had known to be right and true about marriage, all the things she had ever taught about looking out for your spouse rather than yourself came over her all at once. Gradually she caught her breath and settled her racing heart.

With all the love she had for Ryan Taylor, she looked deep to the place in his heart that belonged only to her. "I don't want to go. You know that."

"Yes. I . . . I haven't accepted the offer, Kari." He searched her eyes. "I won't take it if you don't want to move." He ran his thumbs over her hands. "We're a team. Always."

Kari nodded. And in that moment she found the words she never thought she'd say. "If you think we should move to Arizona, Ryan, then we'll move." Tears filled her eyes.

Since then they'd had half a dozen conversations about when they might tell the kids, and how Jessie would feel finishing high school and then moving to Arizona, more than 1,500 miles away. Immediately after graduation. They talked then about the long-term future for Ryan in Arizona. Kari was surprised they were interested in him, honestly. He had no college experience. Yes, he'd been an assistant for the Giants before they married, but that was nearly two decades ago. Since then he'd led the program at Clear Creek High.

Mostly so he could be with Kari and start their family.

Ryan's reputation as a coach must've been greater than Kari realized. Sure, the idea of being a head coach at a major university had crossed Ryan's mind every few years. But he'd always decided that their life in Bloomington was more important than taking a college coaching job.

And Kari had always loved him for it.

The more they'd talked, the more Ryan's enthusiasm for the Arizona job had grown. As it did, Kari did a little research. What about Indiana University, a few miles from their home? What about the Colts, where their friend Jim Flanigan coached?

The Internet turned up no obvious job openings on either staff. So a few days ago after the kids were in bed, Kari found Ryan in the TV room watching *SportsCenter*. He muted the sound as she sat beside him.

"Hi." She smiled and faced him.

"Hey." He leaned in and kissed her. Just long enough to underline how happy he still was. "What's up?"

Kari kept an easy tone. She wasn't coming against his job offer, just looking for options. Ways they might stay in Bloomington. "This might sound obvious." She paused but only for a few seconds. "What about Indiana University? Or the Colts?" Now that she had broached the subject she couldn't stop herself. "It just seems since everyone around here knows you and those teams are local, maybe you could see if there's an opening there?"

His smile dropped off a little. "You don't think I've looked?" Hurt filled his eyes. "You think I *want* to move us across country?"

"It's your choice." Kari couldn't stop herself. "You're the one who wants something new. No one else wants to live in Arizona, I can promise you that." She regretted her words as soon as she'd said them. But she couldn't take them back. Besides, they were the truth. Her feelings—no matter how they came across.

"Wow." He stood and for a long moment he just stared at her. "So that's how you really feel?"

Be honest, Kari, she told herself. "Yes." Her eyes locked on his. "That's how I feel."

Ryan's shoulders sank. He returned to his spot next to her. A dazed look came over him. "Why didn't you say so? When I first told you?"

She shrugged, and tears blurred her eyes. "I told you I didn't want to go. But I wanted to support you, Ryan. I still do." She shook her head. "But Arizona? In just a few months? Like, is it a done deal?"

"Yes." The slight lines at the corners of his eyes steeled and his voice grew more resigned. He drew a slow breath. "I accepted the position." He hesitated. "I'm sorry. I . . . I should've told you." He rubbed the back of his neck. "I don't know what else to say."

"Wait . . . what?" Kari stood. She walked a few feet toward the television and then spun around and stared at him. "You said we'd talk it over, that you'd tell me before you accepted it."

Ryan grabbed the remote and flicked off the TV. "Sit down, Kari. Please."

"No." She kept her voice in check. The kids were sleeping. "You said you'd tell me first."

He stood then, too. "You said you'd support me. No matter what." He raised his hands. "So when the athletic director called, and I just . . . I felt the freedom to tell him yes."

A loud outbreath came from her. "And when were you going to tell me?"

"Later tonight." He glanced at the dark TV and back at her. As if *SportsCenter* might've been more important somehow. He closed the distance between them. "I'm sorry . . . I should've found you sooner."

"I mean, I'm in shock here, Ryan." She shook her head. "I guess there's nothing to discuss." She gave him a sad look and walked toward their bedroom without looking back.

They hadn't really talked about it in the days since. Kari still felt hurt. If they weren't supposed to think of themselves first, how come Ryan hadn't talked with her before agreeing to the move? A sick feeling worked its way through her. The kids were going to be so upset.

Even still, with all of that, she meant what she'd told him when he first brought it up. She would go if he wanted her to go. Obviously.

She would think of him before herself. That's what she believed about marriage and she would follow through with her actions. A part of her was actually happy for him. Even now. But Arizona? When the school year ended?

She opened her eyes and looked at her sleeping older daughter again. After they told the kids, there would be no going back. Everything would be different. The tone in their home would be forever changed. Kari felt the weight of the situation like a wet blanket on her shoulders. Since finding out about Ryan's new position, she had gradually gotten used to the idea. Every day she had accepted the move a little more. She wanted to be supportive. The kids would understand, too.

But it would take time. Because everything they loved about living in Bloomington, near sisters and cousins and parents and grandparents, was about to become part of the past. The reality took Kari's breath.

Two tears slid onto her cheeks. She dabbed at them with the palm of her hand. As terrible as the move would be, and as much as telling the kids was going to kill her, the worst part was something simmering deep in Kari's soul. Because of the way Ryan had handled all this, she'd lost a little faith in him. Like she and Ryan weren't on the same team anymore. And now she felt distant from him. More so every day. Even tonight, when the focus was on Noah and Emily.

Like the two of them were oceans apart.

• • •

ASHLEY BAXTER BLAKE sat up in bed, eyes wide open, and stared out the window. The lightning in the distance was beautiful tonight. She sighed. Ever since her sister Kari had called earlier and asked her to pray for the couple in their Bible study, she hadn't been able to sleep. Ashley had been caught up in the one detail her sister gave her.

Social media.

She breathed deep and sighed again. As she did, her husband, Landon, rolled onto his side and faced her. "You can't sleep?"

"Sorry." She put her hand on his shoulder. "I didn't mean to keep you up. I'll go downstairs."

"It's okay." He smiled at her. "I have an idea." He reached out and touched her face, her cheek. "Let's take a walk and watch the storm as it comes in. Nothing better than a thunderstorm approaching the old Baxter house."

This was just one more reason why Ashley loved him so much. "Really?" She checked the clock on her nightstand. "It's one in the morning."

"Perfect. The storm should be here in half an hour. At least according to the Weather Channel."

They both stepped out of bed and got dressed. Then they quietly tiptoed past the kids' rooms, downstairs and out the back door. For a few seconds they stood there, listening to the low rumble of thunder, and watching the distant sky light up every few seconds.

"I love a good storm." Landon put his arm around her shoulders and eased her against his body. "This lifetime could never have enough moments like this." He kissed her head. "Not if we live a hundred years."

The wind in the bare trees overhead was picking up. Ashley felt dizzy from his words soft against her cheek, the poetry in his soul. She turned and faced him. "I love you, Landon. If I haven't said so lately."

"I love you, too." He ran his hands through her hair.

"You have the most beautiful hair. Has anyone ever told you that?"

Their eyes held, and they both smiled. They were the same words that dear Irvel had once said to Ashley. Irvel, the oldest resident at the Sunset Hills Adult Care Home. The place where Ashley had worked back at the beginning, when she and Landon were trying to figure out their feelings for each other.

"Sweet Irvel." Ashley's voice was a whisper. The storm was getting closer. The light piercing the sky made everything about the moment feel otherworldly. "I still miss her."

"Sweet *you*." Landon leaned in and kissed her. The sort of kiss that took Ashley's breath. The storm rolling in was only part of the magic of the night.

After another long kiss, Landon stepped back. "Let's take that walk." He put his arm around her shoulders again and they started out. "So what's on your mind?"

Ashley had to think a bit to put it into words. "Kari told me something about a couple in their Bible study. They're having trouble in their marriage." She glanced at Landon and then back at the ground ahead of them. "I guess social media is putting a wedge between them."

"Hmm." Landon nodded. "That's a big problem for a lot of people."

"Kids, too." They lived on ten acres, and they were taking a familiar path. The one that led to the stream behind the house. "I think I know why it was keeping me up."

"Tell me." Landon removed his arm and took her hand instead. He worked his fingers between hers.

And like that the story spilled out, one that Ashley had been carrying since earlier that week. "Cole and I talked about his generation, and how everyone's caught up in comparison." She slowed down and looked at Landon. "It's terrible. The way things are."

"It is." Landon led her past their niece's new tree. It had grown a foot since they planted it. They continued on the path until they reached the stream.

Ashley knew where he was taking her. To the huge rock that sat on the edge of the creek, the place where Ashley and her siblings would gather when they were kids, when they needed time alone or time together. Their secret place.

When they reached the rock, Ashley and Landon both climbed up and sat side by side. It was still damp from the rain, but not enough to soak through their clothes. The moon was directly overhead, just like Landon had said. Thunder rolled, maybe a few miles away by the sound of it. But here, the moving creek water and surrounding trees made the storm seem a million miles away.

"It's crazy." Ashley pulled her knees up and stared at the creek. "Cole's friends are on Twitter and Instagram and Snapchat. Some of them still have Facebook accounts." She sighed. "They're so busy making sure everyone knows what's great about their life, they don't have time to live it."

"True." Landon sounded troubled. "We had a suicide call last week. The girl survived, but she told the doctor and her parents that she couldn't keep up. It didn't matter that she had four hundred followers on Instagram, she had never been more lonely." He paused. "Finally she couldn't take it anymore."

Ashley took a slow breath. "I read the saddest thing the other day about kids Cole's age." She shifted so she could see Landon better. "It was an article that said fewer people believe in Jesus and why He came to earth. That He died for them."

"I read that, too." Landon took her hand and smoothed his thumb over hers. "How since the 1960s the United States has conducted this great experiment: life without God."

"Yes." Ashley nodded. She felt the hurt in her heart again, the way she had when she read the story. "Clearly that experiment has failed."

"Right." Landon nodded. "This generation is asking questions. They get hundreds of likes in a week, but no one likes them in real life. They love dozens of posts every day, but they don't love themselves. They put on a picture-perfect face for social media, but they're terrified of the truth: None of them has a clue about their futures. Why they're here. The purpose of life."

Ashley thought about Cole's friends. "Kids need to help each other. Get off social media. Limit it to one day a week. Something."

Landon leaned back on his free hand and stared at

the night sky. "It's like Pastor Mike said last week. People are slaves to the tyranny of the trivial."

"Exactly." Ashley slid a little closer to her husband so their arms touched. Overhead, thunder clapped a little closer than before. "All that time on social media. What does it even matter? Real life. That's what counts. Time with God and the people you love." She looked up and kissed him. "Moments like this."

"Mmmm." He took gentle hold of her face and touched his lips to hers again. "A virtual life could never compare."

For a long time they were quiet, leaning against each other, watching the moonlight on the gentle water below. It felt like a scene from heaven, like all of time had stopped so they could share these minutes together.

Ashley was first to break the beautiful silence. "I'm glad you and I aren't slaves to the Internet." She smiled up at him. "I'm not willing to give up this . . . for emptiness like that."

"However . . ." His eyes sparkled. He kissed her again. "I wouldn't mind ending a moment like this for a different kind of moment back in the house."

"True." Ashley never broke eye contact with him. "Lead me home, baby."

Landon smiled and helped her down from the rock. On the way back to the house, Ashley was keenly aware of every detail. The sound of the creek behind them, the autumn wind in the trees overhead. The approaching storm and the feel of Landon's arm around her. The way

Amy's little elm tree had taken root in the backyard like it had been there forever.

What was this generation missing, spending so much time on smartphones and iPads and computers? Comparing themselves to other people and getting crushed a little more each day? Before they reached the house, an idea hit Ashley. She stopped and faced Landon. "I just thought of something."

A quiet chuckle came from his lips. "Of course you did."

She wrinkled her nose a little. "I guess I do that a lot." She uttered a soft laugh.

"I wouldn't have it any other way." Landon drew her close and kissed her once more. "Tell me your idea."

"Let's make a family challenge. From now through New Year's Day, let's stay off social media. Our kids don't have to compare Christmas gifts and vacations with hundreds of people. Let's just live our life."

Landon thought about it. Then he smiled. "I like it. We can spend more time talking or playing board games."

"Right. And less time on our phones, in general." The more she thought about the idea the more she liked it. "We can live like the old days." She grinned. "Like when we were young. When there were no cell phones and no Internet."

"Yes." Landon ran his hand along her back and searched her eyes. "We can make it fun. So everyone gets behind it."

"Maybe even Cole's friends." She felt the heaviness again of the conversation earlier in the week. "They need a break from that garbage. So they can live again."

The wind was picking up, the storm nearly on top of them. Landon smiled at her. "You have any idea how much I love you?"

"I think so." She grinned. "But you know what they say." She touched her lips to his. "Actions speak louder."

And as the rain broke open above them, they made their way back into the house to celebrate life and love and all the very real things God had given them. Here and now. In the real world.

14

Noah must've needed the nap because he was dreaming again, his head still throbbing.

In the story that was his life with Emily, the next piece was coming into view. Noah was grateful. He still hated that Emily hadn't gotten out of the car and come to him. The kids had seemed happy enough, Emily, too. But he wanted to hold her and kiss her. Tell her how thankful he was to be married to her. How grateful that she had chosen him, after all.

Even now Noah ached to feel her in his arms. But she'd been in too much of a hurry. He sighed and rolled onto his other side. At least he had his dreams. Until she came home again.

College seemed like a blur of football and finding his way back from injuries. His first concussion had happened his freshman year. He wouldn't have made a full recovery if it wasn't for Emily. Clara, too. She helped whatever way she could.

Bottom line, Emily and Clara became his family. His own parents visited from London that summer and tried to talk him out of playing football again. But Noah had made up his mind. Football meant a free ride through school. Besides, he still had dreams of the NFL and he wasn't willing to give them up yet.

But then he got another concussion his junior year and it was the same thing all over again.

Noah moved into Emily and Clara's house and Emily nursed him back to health a second time. He could see her in his dream, sitting on the edge of his bed putting a cold cloth on his head. Anything to keep the headaches at bay. This time he had a different doctor, and the man had prescribed oxycodone to battle the pain. But Emily didn't like the idea.

After he'd taken four pills, she started to cut him off. One afternoon he took firm hold of her wrist. A little too firm, and his voice held a tone he didn't recognize. "I need those pills, Emily. Get them for me."

She shook her head. "I won't." She was on her feet, staring at him, glaring. "I will not be party to your death, Noah Carter. A concussion is awful. But those pills will kill you."

Deep down Noah knew she was right. Days later, when the pain had subsided, he found her in the kitchen and took her hand. "I'm sorry." He searched her eyes. "For how I treated you that day. I wanted those pills so bad."

She touched the side of his face. "I did what I had to do."

"Why?" He eased her closer, so their bodies were almost touching. "Why do you care so much?" His heart pounded being so close to her. "Look at me, Emily. I'm a wreck."

"No, you're not." Her fingers were still on his cheek, velvet against his skin. Her expression grew more serious. Desperate, almost. "You're the best guy I know and . . . and I almost lost you."

For two years they had kept things platonic. If Emily wanted to be friends only, then Noah would make sure the relationship stayed that way. Not just because it was what she asked for, but because it was the only guarantee to keeping her around. To staying in her life.

But in that moment, in the quiet of the kitchen, it was Emily who didn't follow the rules. She brushed his hair to the side and he got lost in her eyes.

Then before he knew what was happening, she leaned up and kissed him. "Noah . . ." Her voice dropped to a shaky whisper. "I've wanted to kiss you again ever since . . . since that time."

"Me, too." He took the lead now, kissing her until they both knew they had to step back or cross lines. "Emily . . ." He tried to steady himself. "I can't . . . we can't be like this and still be just friends." He raked his fingers through his hair. Where was the cold cloth when he needed it?

"I'm sorry." She leaned back against the kitchen counter. "I don't know what to do, Noah. I don't."

"All I know is . . . we can't kiss like that." He paced into the living room and back to her. "One day I want to marry you, Emily, but if you plan to stay single forever . . . for Clara . . . then . . . then I just can't." Tears welled in his eyes as he finished. "I can't do this."

"I know." She stared at the floor. He'd never seen her look so embarrassed. "I just . . . I want you. I want this. But . . ." She lifted her face to his again, her eyes dark. "You deserve someone who's not tied down."

"Not tied down?" He squinted at her. "Are you serious, Emily? You think I see Clara as a burden?" He mumbled something under his breath. "No, Emily. She is not a burden. Not at all." He took a step back. "The burden is you . . . thinking you can't love me. That you only have room in your heart to love Clara. Like if you find love and you're happy, then somehow that means you care less for her."

He paced again, and let out a single laugh. There was nothing funny about it. "You're wrong, Emily. Completely wrong."

That was all he could take, so he walked away. Went to his room at the back of the house, turned off the lights and went to sleep.

In the morning he found a minute alone with Emily while Clara was gathering her things for school. "Hey." He touched her elbow. "I'm sorry. About last night."

She was filling her backpack with homework and notebooks. At the feel of his touch, she turned and looked at him. Her eyes were cloudy with remorse. "It was my fault. I . . . I shouldn't have kissed you."

He wanted to scream at her, tell her of course it wasn't her fault. They both had been dying to kiss each other for two whole years. But that would get them nowhere, so he only smiled and nodded. "Okay, then." He moved to the door. "Let's just keep it at that."

Which was what they did for the next few weeks, until Noah got clearance once more to return to his dorm. This time all the world knew for sure that Noah Carter was finished with football. He had to be. But there was a blessing that came with his second concussion.

It was on the opposite side of his brain.

That meant he was no worse off than he'd been before. The only difference was that now both sides of his brain were more vulnerable than they'd been before the concussions. His new doctor called it a stroke of luck.

Noah called it an answer to prayer.

All along he had known Emily and Clara were talking to God about him. It wasn't something they shared about much. But Noah knew. And after surviving his second concussion, he started to wonder if there might be something to the whole idea of praying.

Noah had certainly been raised with the idea, living in Nashville. Tennessee wasn't just in the Bible Belt. It was the buckle. Christian music played in the post office and while he sat in the dentist's chair. There was literally a church on every corner. The joke among his friends had always been that if you gave directions you could never say, "Near the church on the corner." You had to specify which church.

Because most busy corners had more than one.

Noah had even attended a private Christian school—

Christ Presbyterian Academy. The administration and teachers at CPA loved God and they definitely loved the kids. Noah was a standout student athlete, lettering in football, track and baseball. But believing in God didn't really matter to him. Yes, he sang the songs at chapel and knew the answers in Bible class. Maybe he believed. He wasn't sure. So Noah went along with the routine, thinking nothing of it. But one chapel stood out in Noah's memory. The idea that Jesus calls His followers to let go of self and live for Him. He didn't mind the *idea* of God, but *living* for God?

That was the last thing Noah Carter intended to do.

After graduation, Noah took a final look at the football field and his old high school, and then he drove off. As soon as he left campus and made the right turn on Old Hickory Boulevard, he put thoughts about God behind him. His parents moved to London the next week and he was on his own.

Living for Noah Carter. Not God.

Noah had his own plans, his own ideas. He was headed to Indiana University on a full-ride scholarship. There he would tear up in football and one day get drafted by the NFL.

Still, flash forward two years, after that second concussion, when he had been lying in Emily and Clara's darkened back bedroom trying to remember what day it was, and thoughts of God came back to him. He could picture himself—that confident kid leaving CPA, so sure he would live life on his own terms.

But there he was, his future hanging in the balance.

One evening Clara had come to him. She opened the door and used her crutches to make her way to his bed. Then she smiled down at him and said just two words. "I prayed."

Noah looked at her. "Thank you." Every word still hurt his head at that point. But long after she left the room, he couldn't stop thinking about what she'd said. So did that mean God was looking out for him, that maybe He was waiting for Noah to think about Him again? About whether He was real and if He was, what that might mean for Noah?

Not until he had moved back into his dorm did he meet Emily one afternoon. By then it had been two weeks since their kiss. Noah looked intently at her. "I have a question."

Emily seemed unsure about what was coming, but the two of them found a picnic table in a shady corner. They sat down on the same side and faced each other. She looked deep into his eyes. "I'm listening."

"You and Clara, you believe in God."

"Yes." She raised her brow, like she was surprised this was what he wanted to talk about. "You know that."

He felt restless, like he wouldn't be at peace until he could make sense of this. "Tell me something, Emily." His gaze grew more intense. "Why?" He stood and walked to a nearby tree. Then he turned and looked at her again. "Why believe?" He tossed his hands and let them fall again. "Your dad walked out when you were ten. And then your mother dies in a flash flood." He hesitated. "Does that seem like the work of a loving God?"

Emily's face grew more patient and kind with every few words Noah spoke. She waited until he was finished. "God didn't do those things to my parents."

No question she believed what she was saying. He crossed his arms. "You don't think He could've made your dad stay . . . or kept your mom alive?" He thought for a moment. "He definitely could've kept Clara from having cerebral palsy."

His statements sounded harsh, even to him, but he couldn't help it. He had to know what she thought, why she still believed in God after all she'd been through. All Clara had been through.

Emily didn't say anything at first, just patted the spot beside her. "Come here, Noah. So you can hear me." She put her hand over her heart. "Really hear me."

He did as she asked, and when she took hold of his hand, he didn't pull away. "This is a fallen world." She looked to the depths of his soul. "Everything's broken. Everyone." She took her time, as if she really wanted him to hear this part. "Jesus is not the reason that bad things happen. He's the Comforter. The One who comes alongside us in the most difficult times."

The Comforter. Noah let the words settle in his mind. "Couldn't he just fix things? Like that's His job, right? Rescuing people. Making miracles happen." Noah shrugged. "So how can you be okay when He lets bad things happen?"

"My mom loved God before I did." Emily stared off, as if she were seeing her parents together again. "After my dad left I watched how she handled it. How she ran the house by herself and got by with little."

"Little love?" Noah was listening, savoring how she was revealing her heart to him, a bit more all the time.

"Little from a man, anyway. And little in the way of material things." Emily smiled. "Yet every morning I found my mom sitting at the kitchen table reading her Bible." She looked back at him. "She used to say, 'A chapter a day keeps the darkness away.'" Emily nodded. "After she died I started to believe her."

Emily explained that she'd had doubts about her faith before her mother died, but after the funeral, there was nowhere else to turn, no one to help her but God. "For the past few years God has become my . . . everything. Jesus walks with me wherever I go. He's my Father, my Savior, my Comforter, my Friend."

Every one of those titles seemed like someone Noah could use in his life. His parents still lived in England, and with his football dreams shattered, and Emily still refusing to be in a relationship with him, he definitely wanted something more than himself.

Over the next few months, God turned out to be just what Noah needed. He and Emily started a Bible study, reading about the family of Jesus. With every new story, every section of Scripture, Noah came a little closer to the Lord. By January of his junior year, with his concussion completely healed, Noah made a decision.

He wanted to be baptized.

A few dozen people were gathered at their church that day and when he came up through the surface of the baptismal water, Noah hugged Clara first, then Emily. All of them burst into applause.

Once Noah had a real and lasting friendship with God, his whole life felt better. Strong and more ordered. As if it didn't matter what happened next because God was leading him. God was in control.

Emily told him that praying was just like talking to a best friend. The more he did it, the easier it would get. And so it was. Noah talked to God about school and his purpose in life, football and Emily. Her most of all.

But the more Noah prayed about football, the more he could sense God telling him the same thing. *Noah, My son, I have great plans for you. Very great plans.* Noah began to connect the dots. If God was telling him about great plans ahead every time Noah prayed about football, then the answer was obvious.

God wanted him to play again!

And so Noah became convinced of something that sounded crazy to everyone else. He was going to try. One more time, for his senior year. That way he could see if there might be an open door for him to play in the NFL. The great plans God kept laying on his heart.

When he told Emily one night at her house between homework assignments, she turned pale. Noah wondered if she might collapse to the floor. "You can't be hearing that from God." Emily shook her head. "Noah, you almost died with that last hit. And now . . . now your head can't take another injury. You know what the doctor said."

It was true that the team physician didn't like the risk. But if Noah could pass the reaction tests and analytical tests, the man had promised to clear him. Concussion protocol was very specific. A player either passed or failed the various tests. And a pass meant clearance to play. Like before, Noah began eating better and working out twice a day. And once more, by spring of his junior year, Noah passed every test with flying colors.

The doctor and his coaches all signed off. His parents even reluctantly agreed. He was physically able to play for his senior year if that was what he wanted to do.

Like before, his dedication to the game took its toll on the time he could spend with Emily and Clara. But still he ate dinner with them at the cafeteria, and made it to their house after practice a few nights each week.

But something changed between Emily and him. She seemed colder, more aloof. Like the walls that were there in the beginning had grown back up around her heart again. One night he knocked on her door and as soon as she let him inside he could tell something was wrong.

She'd been crying.

Sure, she tried to hide it, tried to dry her eyes before he stepped inside. But he knew her too well. They sat down on the sofa and he took both her hands in his. "What's wrong? Emily, tell me."

The anniversary of her mother's death had been the week before, so Noah figured it might've been that. But instead of answering him, she looked at the place where their hands were joined. And in small subtle ways she began to tremble.

"Are you sick?" He kept his voice low, since Clara was asleep by then. "Please, Emily, talk to me."

Finally she lifted her eyes to his. By then she was shivering, her teeth chattering a little. "I'm afraid, Noah." For the first time in months, the walls were down again and it was just the two of them, the way they had been before. "I'm so afraid."

He pulled her close and held her, rocked her until she wasn't shaking anymore. Then he pulled back a few inches and searched her eyes. "What are you afraid of? Everything's fine."

For a long time she only stared at him, her eyes brimming with fresh tears. "I . . . I don't want anything to happen to you."

The reality of her fears hit Noah hard. Between God's affirmation and the doctors and coaches clearing him, he had forgotten that she still worried about him. "Emily, it'll be fine." He held her again, running his hand along the length of her pretty blond hair. "God is with me. He'll keep me safe."

Emily put her hand alongside his face, her skin gentle and warm against his. "I can't lose you, Noah. I . . . didn't know how much I cared until you decided . . ."

Suddenly it hit him. "Is that why you've been different? Because you're afraid?"

She leaned closer and rested her forehead on his, her

arms around his neck. "Yes." The word was only a whisper. "I never wanted to fall in love with you. But . . ." Her eyes found his again and something in the air around them changed.

A desperation came over them, the result of denying what they felt for far too long. Her face was in his hands and his lips were on hers. The kiss started fast, marked by a passion that was finished with waiting.

But gradually it slowed and Emily's tears slid down her cheeks. She pulled back and dried them. "What if . . . something happens to you, Noah. I couldn't . . ."

"Shh, baby. No. Nothing's going to happen. God's already told me." He kissed her again and another time. And gradually he could feel her sadness leave. After a minute she started laughing. The sort of laugh that came from sheer exhilaration.

He slid back enough to look at her, and sure enough, she was beaming. She ran her hand over his hair and down his arm. "You called me baby."

"Is that okay?" Noah wasn't sure what to expect. He certainly had not planned on any of this.

"Yes." She giggled and kissed him again. "Please, Noah. Please, call me baby." She traced his cheekbone with her thumb. "That's all I want. With every breath, it's all I've ever wanted since you got hit the last time."

Noah felt a crazy mix of joy and sorrow. She was his. Finally. And nothing would ever separate them. But she could've told him so much sooner. "I thought you still wanted to be friends."

"Sometimes I do." She looked sheepish, and she shrugged one shoulder. "But not really. I was talking to God about you, and I realized that if I lost you . . . and you never knew . . ."

"How you really feel?" Noah drank in the sensation of her breath against his face, the touch of her fingers intertwined with his.

"Yes." She smiled and it reached all the way to her tearstained eyes. "I had to tell you." She stood and he did the same. Was she kicking him out already? Then she asked him the craziest thing. "Dance with me, Noah. Will you?"

She didn't have to ask him twice. "I've wanted to dance with you from the first time I saw you in rehearsal."

"Really?" She stepped easily into his arms. "You should've said so."

"I should've—" He stopped himself. She was kidding again. Back to the Emily he had fallen in love with.

She started to laugh, letting her head tip back, her hair spilling down almost to her waist. "I'm a crazy fool, Noah Carter." Her eyes found his again. "Hold on." She used her phone to start a song on the living room speaker. It was Adele's "Make You Feel My Love." Emily kept the music low.

As soon as the song started, Noah began to waltz with her across the room. Every single note felt like a dream, like all the years of wanting her and waiting for her had finally led to this.

He sang along with the words, "I could make you happy, make your dreams come true . . ."

Even before the song ended, their dance slowed and Noah kissed her again, their bodies still swaying to the music. "I love you, Emily." He whispered near her ear. "I have from the first day I met you."

"Me, too." She pulled back and grinned at him. "I just . . . I didn't want anything to change with Clara."

"I know." He kissed her once more. "Baby, nothing ever will. I promise."

"Okay." She had her arms around his neck. "And nothing can happen to you."

"Never." His cheek brushed against hers. A question rose to the surface of his heart, and when the song stopped he stepped back and looked into her eyes again. "Will you be my girlfriend, Emily? Please?"

She went to him, her head on his chest for a long minute. Then she looked up at him. "Noah . . . don't you see?" She smiled. "I already am." They swayed a minute longer and she locked eyes with him again. "I want to remember this forever, even a million years from now. The days when we were young."

On the drive back to his dorm that night, Noah remembered thinking she'd better never break up with him. Because no matter what happened from here, one thing was definitely true.

He would only, ever and always love Emily Andrews.

Till he drew his last breath.

15

Noah woke up slowly, his legs tangled in the bedsheets. A cold breeze drifted across the room and he looked at the window. Why was it open? And how had it gotten so cold?

It had to be in the twenties.

He set his feet down and . . . there it was again. The cold, scratchy carpet. His feet jerked back like before. Where were the wood floors? And how could he have agreed to this cheap carpet? His memory was jumbled, but in the recesses of his mind he remembered something.

They lived in an apartment now. That was it.

He crossed the room and slammed the window shut. November wasn't usually this cold. Especially when thunderstorms were in the forecast. Not only was the air outside freezing, but it was bright and sunny, and the apartment was quiet. His head was pounding again, and his vision, blurry like before.

Emily and the kids should definitely be home by now. The party at the park couldn't possibly have gone this long. He stepped into a pair of jeans near his bed and walked bare-chested into the cramped living room. There on the small end table near the ratty sofa was a three-foot drugstore Christmas tree.

Noah felt the room begin to spin. A Christmas tree? What was happening? Who had come by their apartment and set up a tree? They never decorated till after Thanksgiving. And if it was Christmastime already, then why didn't they have a real tree?

They always had a real tree.

He walked to the small plastic shrub and looked hard at it. Eight red and green bulbs hung from the fake branches. That was it. Even the green of it wasn't realistic. More like the color of an old Army Jeep.

Something was wrong: his family should be home and it wasn't Christmas. He glanced at the counter, saw his phone and grabbed it. Fine. This would give him some answers. The code to unlock it worked on the first try.

At last. Noah exhaled. Something that made sense. It was five-thirty in the morning and in a few clicks he figured out that he was mistaken. It was December, already. The first Saturday in the month.

In the calendar square it said, "Aiden's soccer game—9:00 A.M." Today. December the fifth. Aiden had a soccer game? When did Aiden start playing soccer?

Noah dropped to the nearest chair and let his head fall into his hands. After his beautiful dream, all he wanted was Emily. This confusion and headache . . . the amnesia . . . nothing made sense. Whatever was happening to his mind, he needed help. Clearly. The concussions were stealing his very life and he couldn't remember a thing.

Entire months were slipping away. Years.

He needed to see a doctor as soon as possible. Maybe check himself into the emergency room. Noah looked around. He had to get his bearings first. He sat on his sofa and watched the sun come up, watched the morning light reflect on the ugly little Christmas tree. Or maybe the fake tree was a joke, something Emily had brought home to make him laugh.

He was always teasing her that she had too many Christmas decorations. Garlands across the windows, a nativity on the fireplace mantel, Mr. and Mrs. Frosty anchored by the front door. Noah sat up a little straighter. Wait.

Where were all Emily's decorations? She might've brought the little tree home as a joke, but she wouldn't have kept her other Christmas things in boxes. Even here in the tiny apartment. She would've at least wanted a happy atmosphere.

A shiver ran the length of his arms. Where was everyone, anyway? He walked down the hall again and peered into the kids' room and then back at his own. In case Emily was still in bed and he'd only missed her. But the rooms were empty. He was here alone.

Maybe Emily had gone with the kids to her aunt's house in Texas. Once in a while she would do that. But if she'd taken that kind of drive, why hadn't he gone with her?

Noah had no answers. He returned to the sofa and when his phone told him it was eight o'clock he got dressed. Added a shirt and sweatshirt, thick socks and work boots. According to his weather app it was seventeen degrees outside. Which made sense now that he knew it was December.

When he was ready, he grabbed his keys off the counter and went outside to look for his truck. It would normally be in the garage, but this wasn't his usual place. Where did he park it here at the apartment? He used the clicker a few times, but instead of the truck, an old Volkswagen parked twenty feet from his front door beeped in response.

Okay, so he drove a VW now. One more thing he had to get used to. Behind the wheel Noah felt things returning to normal. Landmarks began to look familiar. The Chick-fil-A was where it was supposed to be, the Hobby Lobby was across the street where it belonged.

Christmas garlands were wrapped around every post along Main Street. That was normal, too. Since it was Christmastime. He drove past the Texaco station and the car wash and then he pulled into the parking lot adjacent to the field. The place where youth soccer was played.

Noah was glad this was familiar, because he'd never had a reason to come here before. He'd only driven by.

The parking lot was full, but Noah found a spot near the back. Despite the freezing morning, the sun was bright. He shaded his eyes and tried to see which field might contain seven-year-old boys.

But they all looked like older kids.

Noah took a deep breath and held up his phone. He could call Emily. Wherever she was, she had to know where their son played soccer. After all, he didn't even know Aiden was interested in the game. Her phone rang twice, then three times before she answered.

"Hello?" She sounded tired. Like she was frustrated with him. "Noah?"

"Hi." He paused. "Is everything okay?"

"What's that supposed to mean?" She let out a heavy breath. "Are you coming to Aiden's game or not? He's expecting you."

"Of course." Noah didn't know what to say. "I'm here." He rubbed his temples. If only his head would stop hurting. "Where are you? Which field?"

"Six. The one in the northwest corner. Where he always plays." She didn't sound quite as mad. "He'll be glad you came."

Noah had a hundred questions, but he couldn't put a single one of them into words. "Emily . . . I think something's wrong with me."

She didn't say anything. Just waited.

"I mean . . . I went to bed yesterday afternoon and it was October." He realized he sounded crazy. "I woke up today and it's December. And it feels like . . . like entire years have disappeared. And there's this small plastic Christmas tree in our living room."

"*Our* living room?" She made a laughing sound, but it was more mean than funny. "Really, Noah?" Her patience was clearly gone. "You need to see a doctor. I've been saying that. Anyway . . . hurry. The game's about to start."

"Okay." He walked toward Field Six. "See ya." He hung up the phone. Even from the parking lot the boys looked far too old. Maybe Aiden was really good. Maybe he was playing up a few years. Yes, that had to be it.

Noah slid his hands into his pockets and kept walking. What was wrong with Emily? Was she mad at him? Maybe he'd done something to upset her. And what did she mean about *our* living room? She had no patience for him, and he had no idea why. Whatever the reason, he was almost to the bleachers when he saw something that stopped him cold.

Emily was sitting next to another man.

From where Noah stood, Emily couldn't see him. But he could easily see that his wife and the man shared something special.

They were talking, their faces close to each other. And every now and then Emily would laugh the way she used to laugh with him. Her head tipped back, hair spilling across her shoulders. That was something else. Her hair was shorter now.

Then he saw the thing that nearly killed him, nearly stopped his heart for good. The man took hold of Emily's hand. Right there in front of all the parents and families and kids, his wife was holding hands with another man.

What could possibly be happening here? Was this part of his concussion, too? Was he hallucinating?

He walked to the front of the bleachers and marched straight up to her. As he did, Emily released the man's hand. Guilt colored her face. Noah couldn't believe this was happening. For a few seconds he only stared at her and then at the man. "Hey, buddy, get lost. Leave my wife alone."

"Noah." Emily was on her feet. Her eyes were wide, like she was shocked. "What are you doing?"

What was *he* doing? He took hold of her hand and led her to an empty spot in the bleachers a few rows up. He lowered his voice and spoke straight at her. "What am I doing?" His mind was racing; the wood planks beneath his feet felt like they were made of rubber. "How dare you ask that, Emily? When you're openly flirting with another man right here. In front of everyone."

"Flirting?" The guilt faded to concern, and almost at the same time to outright fear. "Something is very wrong with you, Noah. After the game I want you to drive to the hospital and get checked." She jerked her hand free. "Maybe you have a brain tumor. Something."

Why was she talking like this? So harsh and . . . disapproving. "I'll go. But come with me. Please, Emily."

"No." She stood her ground. "Go by yourself." A glance over her shoulder at the other guy, and her look hardened. "We have plans today."

He wanted to kiss her in the worst way. Even now, when she was treating him like he'd done something wrong. So in a move as familiar as breathing he took her hands again and tried to pull her into his arms. But again she jerked back.

"Noah. Stop!" She was shaking now. "This is . . . it's completely inappropriate. Especially in front of the other parents."

She was worried about them seeing him hold his wife? Noah's headache felt worse, the pounding louder. He had to collect himself, so he gave Emily a sad look and sat down. She scowled at him and returned to her spot next to the other guy. Of all things.

From where he sat, Emily looked nothing like the girl he'd married. Like she was only a ghost of the girl he used to love.

Maybe if he focused on Aiden, things would slip back to normal. His head would clear and he would see her sitting there by herself, looking for him. Of course she'd be looking for him. The two of them loved each other.

He squinted out at the soccer field and pulled his sunglasses from his sweatshirt pocket. Once they were on he could finally see the kids' faces. It was a time-out, and the players stood huddled around the coach. He could see each of the boys clearly.

But where was Aiden?

This had to be his group of players. Emily wouldn't have sat on this side if this wasn't their son's team. He searched from one boy to the next until finally his eyes landed on a tall kid at the end of the row. The boy's eyes and face and hair looked familiar. But one thing was sure.

If it was Aiden, he wasn't seven. More like ten.

Just then the boy noticed him and gave him a nod. Not a wave or a smile or a whispered hello. Only a nod. Noah's heart ached in a way he'd never felt before. What was wrong with his son? He always smiled when he saw his daddy. Even yesterday, when it was fall and Noah was seven. Aiden had still run to him and grabbed hold of his legs.

But here . . . it was almost like . . . like Aiden was embarrassed by him.

Noah waved, but Aiden had already looked away. Noah looked down at his jeans and work boots. Was he dressed weird? He used his sunglasses to check his look. His hair was neat, nothing standing on end. So then what was the problem? How could Aiden be acting like this? Was his brain this messed up?

Noah was still sorting through all that when two girls ran up the bleachers. One of them was clearly Olivia. She looked at him and hesitated. Then—like she had become suddenly shy—she gave him a weak sort of wave and continued toward Emily.

Without hesitating, she cuddled up next to her mother. The other little girl found her spot between her parents a few rows in front of Emily.

Why was Olivia ignoring him? Noah felt like he was sinking, like the ground below had opened up and he was slowly but surely slipping into a river of quicksand. He wanted to talk to his daughter, ask her how she was doing. But maybe it was better to sit here and wait for his headache to let up. Aiden and Olivia were completely different kids than they'd been last time he'd seen them.

Were they afraid of him? Did they know about his head injuries, from playing football and taking that second hit? Noah leaned back and tried to imagine what that would be like for his children, not knowing whether their father would remember the times they were having.

For the entire first half, Noah didn't say a word. He went from watching Aiden to Olivia and finally to Emily. Every few minutes Aiden kicked a goal. So that answered that question. Yes, their son was a great athlete. Just like Noah.

But so what?

The guy sitting by Emily never left. Once when Noah looked their way, the man had his arm around her. This had to be part of his brain injury, collateral damage. The man probably wasn't even real. But why would he imagine another man with his wife?

He and Emily were crazy about each other. She was the only girl he'd ever loved, the one he couldn't wait to kiss and hold and dance with across the living room floor. Even now, with her sitting far away from him, he couldn't wait to hold her.

Whenever all this got worked out.

Halftime came, and the players ran up the bleachers to be with their families. Again Aiden cast him a quick look, and this time a glimpse of a smile. But nothing more. He and Olivia stayed with Emily and the other man until the second half started.

Noah thought about walking over and telling the stranger to leave. Maybe a little more forcefully. Because enough already. He needed time with his wife. But he was sure once his head cleared the guy would be gone. Part of this crazy aberration.

Just then one of the women sitting a few feet away approached him and took the spot at his right side. She was a brunette, a little younger than Noah. Pretty green eyes.

"It's hard, isn't it?" She smiled at Noah. "It's the same for me."

Noah had no idea what she was talking about. He stared at the action on the field. Aiden was about to score another goal.

"I know." The woman wouldn't let up. She sighed. "Sometimes I don't want to talk about it, either." She shook her head. "It doesn't get any easier. I know that."

The situation was uncomfortable and getting worse. Noah turned to her and narrowed his eyes. "I'm sorry, do I know you?"

She laughed. "Late night?" Between her hands she held a paper cup of what looked like hot coffee. She held it up and laughed again. "I know all about late nights. I'm not here at Quinn's soccer game without my coffee. Not after a Friday night."

Noah stared at her for another few seconds, and then back to the game.

"I mean, don't judge, right?" She took a sip of her drink. "If Mark's going to play the field, I can, too. It's the single life all over again."

Okay, so the woman was divorced. That much was clear. Noah still didn't know her, didn't have a clue what she was talking about or why she'd moved over to sit next to him.

Now she held her gloved hand in his direction. "I'm Rebecca." She laughed again, but it was quieter this time. "We met the first week of the season."

Noah took the woman's hand and gave it a light shake. Then he dropped it. Like it was poisonous. What was she doing? Didn't she know he was married? He glanced at Emily. His beautiful, perfect Emily. Why was she still over there? More than the ache of his throbbing head, another reality consumed him: he missed her. Missed her more with every breath.

The woman was talking again. "Anyway, I was thinking . . . I mean, you're that big former quarterback. Everyone knows you." She lifted her coffee again, like she was toasting him. "Noah Carter. Everyone's hero."

What in the world was she talking about? If she knew Noah it must be because of @When_We_Were_Young. He was about to ask her when she brought it up.

"I used to follow you and Emily." She shook her head. "Everyone thought you'd last forever. Both of you blond and beautiful. Aiden and Olivia little mirror images of the two of you."

Noah's heart started to pound and at the same time

the pain in his head doubled. What did she mean, everyone *thought* they'd last forever? He looked straight in the woman's eyes. "Look, Rebecca. I'm in love with my wife." He smiled. Kindness was always the best go to. "I'm not sure what you've heard, but we're actually doing great. We really are going to last forever."

Rebecca stared at him for half a minute. "Whatever you drank last night, don't have it again. You sound a little wacky." She took another sip of her coffee. "You and Emily have been divorced for six years. Everyone knows that." She uttered a single laugh. "In case you forgot."

The world around him began to spin. He grabbed the edge of the bleacher and steadied himself. "No!" Why was this happening? Who was this crazy woman? "Whatever you heard . . . it's a lie." He didn't want to talk to this person, didn't want this conversation. He might be sick and seeing things. His memory might be bad. But there was no way he and Emily were divorced. He loved her with all his heart. All he wanted was to walk over to Emily, grab her hand and take her home. Ask her about the fake little Christmas tree and pull the other boxes from the attic. Or wherever they were.

They would decorate the house while the kids played in their room, and then they would put on Adele and dance across the carpeted floor. And they would kiss, the way they had that first time, his freshman year. The way they had in the kitchen after the hit in his junior season.

Or the time on the sofa when she finally told him how she felt.

He'd had enough of Rebecca. "I'm sorry." He stood and gave the woman a smile that felt as plastic as his Christmas tree. "I need to go."

Whatever his mind was doing, whatever tricks his eyes were playing on him, Noah was over it. He and Emily needed to go home. He walked across the bleachers, ignoring his dizziness and the pain still exploding between his temples.

When he reached Emily, both she and Olivia looked at him. The guy gave him a smirk but then turned his attention to the field. "Go, Aiden, attaboy!" he yelled toward the action.

"Look." Noah couldn't take another minute. He moved directly in front of the man. "I don't know who you are, but you need to go. I'm taking my wife home and my family home."

Emily's eyes darkened. "Noah! I told you . . . that's enough!" She stood and faced him. "Don't make a scene."

He took a few steps to the side and she stood and followed him. "I'm not making a scene." His eyes found the guy, still sitting by Olivia. "That . . . *guy* is making a scene." Noah lowered his voice, but it didn't hide the anger in his words. "Emily, you are a married woman. I can't believe you'd let that jerk have his arm around you."

She blinked a few times. "Noah, you need help. You really do."

"That's for sure." He turned away from her for a few seconds, and then looked straight back at her. "My kids barely talk to me and my wife's flirting with some stranger. I think maybe we all need help."

"Noah." She crossed her arms. "When's the last time you saw a doctor?"

"I don't know." He felt his anger fall away. "Yesterday it was fall and . . . and the kids were seven and five. And today it's December, and they're ten and eight. My life is passing before my eyes, Emily. And I don't remember it." He reached for her hand, but she pulled it away. "I don't remember anything but you."

"Noah . . ."

"I mean it." He felt tears in his eyes. "I love you, Emily. I'm dying to hold you, to kiss you. It feels like it's been forever."

Again Emily just stared at him. "I can't tell if you're messing with me." She angled her head. "But if you're not . . . you should know the two of us have been divorced for six years."

Everything was spinning again. The words hit him like so many bullets. "No." He shook his head. "Please, Emily. That's impossible. I love you more than ever. You're my everything."

She shook her head. "You see that man over there?"

Noah didn't want to look, but he couldn't help himself. "He's a stranger. He needs to leave."

"He's not a stranger." She took a deep breath. "He's my boyfriend. And one day soon he'll probably be my husband, Noah." She distanced herself from him. "You need to accept the fact. Please. For all of us. And you need to see a doctor." With that, she turned and left. Walked off to the man and took her spot beside him.

Noah wanted to shout at her to come back, run across the bleachers and grab the guy, throw him off the edge of the stands. Beat him up so he would never dream of showing his face again. But all he could do was stumble down the steps and drag himself to the car.

There was nothing he could say to Aiden or Olivia, no way to convince Emily to make the guy leave. She didn't want Noah, not right now. As he pulled his brokenhearted body across the parking lot, only two things echoed through his aching head.

One very much a lie, and the other, very much a truth.

The lie was that Emily thought they were divorced. And she wasn't the only one. The strange woman, Rebecca, thought so, too. As if this . . . split between Emily and him were public.

Why would he ever end things with his beautiful Emily?

But whatever had created that confusion, or the strange visions, whatever was happening to his brain to make him forget whole sections of his life, that terrible lie was nowhere near as powerful as the truth. The one truth that completely consumed him.

He had never loved Emily Andrews, never ached for her, more than he did right now.

16

The hours passed slowly as Emily kept her spot on the backyard swing. She still wasn't tired, but that wasn't the reason she stayed. It was the story. Their story. The one she might not have the chance or desire to play out again.

Not after they were divorced.

If only they could've found a way to make love last. Like Ryan and Kari Taylor. Emily leaned back in the swing and let the next part of her memories come.

Once they were an official couple, Emily couldn't wait for the times when she could be with Noah. His senior football season came, and she and Clara sat in the stands again. And like before they prayed for his safety.

Every down, every play Emily would hold her breath, and every time Noah got back up again. Once in a while he would flash her a thumbs-up. Just so she would know he was okay. And instead of getting hurt, the most amazing thing started to happen. At least for Noah.

He began to play better than at any time in his life. Like maybe he really had heard from God about the good plans He had for Noah. His stats were proof.

With every game, Clara relaxed a little more and returned to enjoying the games the way she had his sophomore year. By then she had finished high school and she was taking classes at an occupational center. Learning how to ring up sales and clean floors and take orders at a fast-food restaurant.

The only sorts of jobs Clara would ever work.

She'd gained an understanding by then, a realization that she wasn't like other kids her age. Of course she knew that. But after graduation, when she asked about going to Indiana University, she didn't wait for Emily's response.

"I can't go." She dragged the words out. "Right? I can't."

Emily wanted to wrap her sister in her arms and protect her from anything that would hurt her. From people who weren't kind or the harsh reality that college was out of the question for her.

But if there was one thing that made Clara happy, it was watching Noah play football. And as the weeks went by and Noah kept winning, Clara remained his biggest fan. On Sundays they would go to church and lunch together, the three of them. And afterward, they'd wind up back at Emily and Clara's house, and Noah would focus his attention on Emily's sister.

Emily could see him talking to her still, even now.

Noah would sit across from her at the dining room table and ask about her week at occupational school. "We learned . . . how to mop." Clara struggled with every word.

"Now that"—Noah grinned at her—"is something I've always wanted to learn."

And for the next half hour, Clara gave Noah lessons on how to use a mop. For her to do the task, she had to set one of her crutches down. Which meant she was making progress, learning to be more independent.

Emily sat back and watched the two of them, Noah struggling to grasp even the basics of how to move the mop across the floor. Clara may have known that Noah was playing with her a little. But if so, she didn't seem to care. The attention from him was everything to her.

And for that reason it was everything to Emily.

Later that night, when Clara had turned in, Noah took Emily in his arms and kissed her. Minutes passed and neither of them could stop. They were crazy about each other. But they were careful not to let things go too far.

When he finally did pull away, Noah's heart seemed heavy. "I know why you care so much for her, for Clara."

"She's amazing. The sweetest person on earth." Emily was still in his arms, swaying to the rhythm of his heartbeat.

"But learning to mop . . . that was the highlight this week." He shook his head. "It just breaks me, Emily. I would do anything to help her. Anything."

Emily smiled at him, tears blurring her eyes. "You already have." She hesitated. If only she could memorize the love and concern on his face. "Every time you throw a touchdown, Clara forgets anything else. And for that minute she doesn't have cerebral palsy and her greatest accomplishment is not pushing a mop." Another pause and she pressed her lips against his. "It's watching you play."

After that, the fears Emily had been plagued with before the season started to fall away a little more each week. God really did have Noah, and He blessed him one game after another.

Every now and then Noah would post something on social media about Emily. A selfie of the two of them walking across campus, or a photo of their hands linked together. The message was clear.

Handsome Noah Carter was off the market.

Emily didn't care about what the public thought, but still when he'd post about her it felt nice. Even better were the times when he included Bible verses or something about his faith, how God was leading him to success.

Throughout his senior season at Indiana, Noah only brought up the NFL a couple times. He was sure he wouldn't be drafted, that's what he told Emily. Someone like him, with two previous concussions, would be too great a liability for any pro team. He would graduate college, thankful for his football days.

Then he'd apply to the local fire department. Noah wanted to be a paramedic. The two of them could practically see the years ahead. As long as they were together, Clara had a place in their midst. Noah had already said that. Even better, he had proven it. He loved Clara almost as much as Emily did.

Life looked like a story whose ending was already written. And it was an ending Emily could hardly wait to live out. Noah and Emily, forever and ever.

But a few days after his last game, the buzz started. No quarterback in NCAA Division I football had ever thrown for more touchdowns or had a better rating. Whatever that meant. Newspapers suddenly wanted to interview Noah and ESPN did a feature on him. How could he have come back from two concussions to play so well his senior year?

Noah had one answer.

Prayer.

"The people I love most were praying for me." He would smile for the camera. "I was praying, too. I felt God calling me to play again, and that He had great plans for me. Now it makes sense. He gave me the perfect season. God and a bunch of amazing linemen!"

At first Emily didn't understand the media interest. But one night Noah sat her down and explained what was happening. "The NFL draft is in the spring." He searched her eyes, looking all the way to the center of her soul. "You know that, right?"

"The draft?" She shook her head. "Is that like when the pros pick teams?"

"Sort of." Noah smiled at her. He took her hand and worked his fingers between hers. He explained how the NFL owners would go several rounds, choosing college players they wanted on their rosters.

"They can take anyone, huh?" Emily wasn't sure

where he was going with this. "So it's like a surprise when the draft comes."

Noah looked at her for a long beat. "Not completely." He swallowed a few times, never looking away even for a second. "Emily, I've been contacted by the Colts and the Bears. And a few others." He paused. "It looks like I'll be drafted after all. That's what the coaches are telling me."

That Friday, Noah had a battery of tests, routine exams for someone who might qualify for the NFL. For their money, any pro team would want to know they were getting a healthy quarterback and not damaged goods. They wanted to be sure that a blow to his head wouldn't send him to the sidelines.

Or worse.

Noah passed his physical exams with high marks and great ease. He was in the best shape of his life, no question. The whole time Emily didn't know what to think. Was he really going to play in the NFL? And how could any doctor know exactly what his risk of a head injury would be?

But then came the cognitive assessments. Dr. Dan Roberts from the NFL met with Noah in a medical conference room and handed him a stack of quizzes. Noah told Emily later that the exam was half the size of an old phone book. When Noah asked if the doctor was serious, the man didn't crack a smile.

Noah said the doctor went on to tell him the exams were important. After two serious concussions, some football players began to show cognitive decline as early as a year or two later.

The fact made Emily sick. A year or two later? That was ridiculous. Noah was perfectly fine. But since the tests were mandatory Noah had no choice but to work through them. He told Emily how Dr. Roberts had left him in the room by himself. He had two hours to complete the questions. There were sections on memorization, analytical application and deductive reasoning.

When the time was up Noah had a headache. But when Dr. Roberts walked back into the room, he had completed every page. Then the doctor said something that seemed to worry even Noah. At least that's what Noah told her later. The doctor said that the testing wasn't a joke. He wanted to make sure Noah understood.

"Of course," Noah told the man. "I did my best. My head's fine."

Before he left that day, the doctor had given Noah the results of the exam. Noah said the doctor held the document and sat in the chair next to him. He folded his hands on the heavy test packet and looked hard at Noah. Yes, Noah had passed it. But barely. Which worried his doctor. Noah told Emily the man's eyes had looked heavy with concern. "I have to permit you, Noah. You fall in the range of normal, and that's all the NFL wants to know. It clears you with the league." Dr. Roberts had hesitated. "But you have the right to a second opinion, Noah. Your life could depend on it. If I were you I'd get two clearances. For peace of mind. So the people you love don't have to bury you early."

Emily gasped out loud when Noah told her that part. What a terrible thing to say. The people he loved wouldn't have to bury him early. God, Himself, had given Noah the green light to play. Besides, it had been eighteen months since Noah's last hit and he'd had the best season of his life. It was the reason everyone thought he'd be drafted in the first round.

His head injuries were behind him.

Before Noah left the office, the doctor had given him the number of an expert neurosurgeon in the area, Dr. Larry Porter. A man who specialized in head injuries.

Noah told Emily how he wanted to be angry at Dr. Roberts. In Noah's mind, if he passed the tests, he passed. End of story. God had great things ahead, right? But Noah also had the sense the man was truly trying to help him. So he took the details and left the office.

Later Noah told her he had wrestled with the information. He was weeks from realizing his dreams. So on the way to the car he threw the specialist's number in the trash. What would it matter if another doctor recommended against him playing in the NFL? Wouldn't most doctors steer patients away from the game? Even perfectly healthy people? Football was brutal. Everyone knew that.

He had been approved by a doctor for the NFL.

What more proof did he need?

Emily told herself the facts over and over again. Anything not to be consumed with worry for Noah and his health. Anything to shut out the doctor's terrible warning. Emily did, though, agree with the doctor about one thing.

"You really should get a second opinion, Noah," she told him that night after his test. "He's right about that."

The next Monday, while Clara was at occupational school, Emily and Noah walked around the track at the university stadium.

"It's everything I ever dreamed." He took Emily's hand and pressed his fingers between hers. "It looks like I'll be playing in the pros! Can you believe it?"

And Emily could feel her heart slip to her knees. She didn't want him to see her fear, but she couldn't help it. Even just hearing him talk about the doctor's warning had made her terrified.

Still, the last thing Emily was going to do was make Noah feel bad here, in the light of his good news. She walked a little closer to him and found her smile. "That's wonderful, Noah. I . . . I'm so excited for you."

"Who would've thought?" He laughed, but it was more the sound of disbelief. "A few agents have been calling. My coach recommended one of them. Joel Walker." Noah raised his eyebrows. "So I actually talked to him earlier today."

Emily's head began to spin. She had never been more relieved than when Noah had walked off the Indiana University football field for the last time. Sure, she and Clara would miss seeing him play. But they'd get over it.

Noah was safe and whole and all theirs again.

But everything had changed now. They kept walking,

their arms brushing against each other. She lifted her eyes to his. "So . . . like you could go first round? Or first drawer? Something like that." She tried to laugh, but the sound fell short.

"Top drawer?" He had never looked happier. "You crack me up, Emily Andrews. First round. You had it right."

"Thank you." This felt comfortable, teasing him, playing with him. "So first round. That's amazing."

"It could mean millions of dollars. The chance to be starting quarterback for a pro team next fall. It's everything God told me. The good plans He had for me. They're still playing out." Noah acted like he was ready to burst. He was that excited. "You're the first person I've told."

Emily didn't know what else to say. "I'm happy for you, Noah. Really." It was the least she could say. The best way to celebrate his good news—no matter what it meant for her. She had to remind herself to draw a breath. "When will you know?"

He told her the date, and that became the only thing Emily could think about. The Colts seemed the most likely team to take him, at least according to his new agent. Noah talked to Emily about it all the time. "Think about it, me playing less than an hour away. Everything could stay just the way it is for all three of us."

She would nod and smile and try to sound enthused. But the idea of him being drafted left her with nothing but uncertainty. Once in a while Clara would ask why

Noah didn't come around as often as before. "He's training," Emily would tell her. "Getting ready for the NFL."

Clara didn't need to be told twice what was happening. Deep down, she understood. One of the pro teams was likely going to hire Noah. And then, well . . . then things would change.

"I want him here." Clara couldn't discuss the situation, but she could say that much. And she did several times in the weeks leading up to the draft.

Once when Noah was at their house, Clara told him, too. "Stay here, Noah. Please."

He smiled and took hold of Clara's hand. "I'll still be here. Whatever happens." He glanced at Emily, who was sitting across the room. "I'll always be here."

Finally Draft Day came. Noah was invited to New York City to attend the live event along with the other expected first-round picks. His parents and his brother and sister-in-law and their two kids all flew in for the occasion.

The agent sprang for airfare for Noah and Emily and Clara, and everyone met up at Radio City Music Hall for the big moment. The entire scene felt surreal to Emily. The group of them dressed in their finest clothes, sitting with Noah to watch his future play out for all the world to see.

Emily sat on one side of him, and Clara on the other. Behind them Noah's parents sat with his agent as they waited through one selection after another. Noah had been so sure that Indianapolis would pick him that he wore a Colts hat the entire week leading up to the draft.

But now he wore a suit and a look of peace. After every round he would lean close to Emily. "It might not even happen. Keep praying."

She was, with every breath. Clara, too. Emily could tell by the serious look on her face. Her eyes narrowed and intense, taking in the events on the stage, clearly aware that whatever went down today it would affect the future. For all three of them.

Finally it was Indy's turn to make a pick. The NFL commissioner stepped up to the microphone and announced that the Colts were taking Jed Brown from Ohio State University. A linebacker.

Emily could feel Noah sink back in his seat. Joel leaned over and patted Noah's shoulder. "It's okay. It's coming." He grinned. Of course he grinned. This was a win-win situation for an agent. He stood to make a lot of money on Noah in the coming years regardless of what round he was drafted in.

Two names later, the commissioner stepped up to make another announcement. "And with the tenth pick, the San Diego Chargers select Noah Carter, quarterback from Indiana University."

Emily felt time grind to a halt. Noah leaned in and kissed her, and then he was on his feet, shaking the hand of his agent and hugging his family. Then leaning in to hug Clara. She grinned and returned the hug, but only because she loved Noah.

Sweet Clara had only a hint of how their world had suddenly shifted off its axis.

Noah made his way to the stairs and then up onto the stage. He shook the hand of the commissioner and the man put a Chargers cap on Noah's head. They posed for a picture and someone ushered Noah off the stage.

Joel leaned in close to Emily. "We'll go meet him in the back after a few minutes. He'll do interviews with the press first, then we can join him in the reception area."

The whole place was buzzing. Emily smiled and nodded. "Sounds great."

Sounds great? Even now she wasn't sure how she had mouthed those words. In a blur his family, along with Emily, Clara and Joel, met up with Noah, just like the agent had said.

His parents were over the moon excited. "You've waited all your life for this, Son." His father shook his hand and then gave him a hearty hug. "Way to work hard. I'm proud of you."

Not even a mention of the concussions.

Emily had spent time with Noah's parents before, when they came to Indiana for a summer trip. But tonight was about Noah and only Noah. She and Clara seemed to be invisible to everyone in the room. Everyone but Noah. He caught Emily's eye constantly. His smile was equal parts hope and concern.

For the next few days, Emily did all she could to play along with Noah's thrilling news. The Chargers were set to pay him eight figures, with a $5 million signing bonus. A deal Joel Walker had worked out.

At Indiana University, the student body was beyond proud of Noah. When Emily and Noah walked across campus they were stopped every minute or so. "Way to go, Noah!" or "Make the Hoosiers proud, Carter."

One after another.

Emily was happy for him, truly she was. But not long after they returned from New York she sat down on her front porch one night and prayed about her next move. Like before, the most important part of her life was Clara.

Her sister had no one else.

If Noah had been drafted by the Colts, that might have been one thing. There could've been a way for them to stay together. But San Diego? Emily watched Clara over the next few days. One afternoon she even skipped class to sit in on Clara's occupational work.

Her sister had friends there, people she'd gone to high school with. Teachers who cared. The small center might not have seemed like much to most people, but to Clara it was everything. Her entire existence outside their little home.

A week after the draft, Emily made up her mind. It was a decision that would just about kill her. She was certain of that. But she had to stay in Indianapolis with Clara. Which told her what she needed to do next. She asked Noah to meet her at the house that night, after Clara was asleep. Then she did the one thing she never expected to do.

She broke up with Noah Carter.

17

Somehow Noah made his way from the soccer field back to his bed. Their bed. The bed he still shared with his wife, Emily. Because he refused to believe anything else. He couldn't exactly remember driving back to the apartment or getting out of his jeans. But he must have, because here he was. In bed again.

The pain in his head wouldn't let up, even as he drifted off to sleep. He was thankful for his pillow, thankful for the way his heavy eyelids closed. Sleep was the best thing for a head injury, Noah had been told that dozens of times. But it was good for another reason, too.

Because in his dreams his past with Emily made perfect sense.

Typically when he had a headache, Noah's sleep came in fits and starts. But not this time. As soon as he closed his eyes, he was back again. His senior year at Indiana University, just days after being drafted by the San Diego Chargers.

From the moment the NFL commissioner announced that San Diego was taking him with the tenth pick, Noah felt the ground beneath his feet turn liquid.

Sure he walked up onto the stage and shook the man's hand and smiled for the photographer.

In the reception room he did everything he was supposed to do. He wore the San Diego cap and chatted with the news anchors and a dozen cameras. Hugged his family and his agent and of course Emily and Clara.

But inside he was burning with just one question.

How was he going to move to San Diego when Emily and Clara lived in Bloomington?

The short answer was easy. Now that he was a Charger, Noah suddenly had more money than he could imagine. Enough to buy a house for Emily and Clara minutes from the San Diego stadium. Whatever they wanted would be theirs.

But he knew from the moment his name was called, Emily wouldn't see it that way. Clara loved Indiana. It was her home, and Emily wouldn't want to change things. Not at the risk of upsetting her sister.

He was at Emily and Clara's one afternoon when Emily stepped outside for a phone call. Noah watched her go and realized this was his chance. He moved to the table where Clara was doing her homework, simple steps for the lesson on operating a cash register.

Noah sat across from her. "I have an idea, Clara." He took hold of her hand and looked deep into her eyes. *Lord, let her understand me. Let her be open to the idea.* "How would you like to move to San Diego, California? Sunshine and palm trees. The ocean a few blocks away?" He held out both hands. "Wouldn't that be something?"

Clara had always been so easygoing. Emily might think her sister wouldn't want this change, still Noah had to find out for himself. But she didn't give him a lighthearted smile and a simple nod of her head; instead Clara's arms began to shake. Her eyes started to twitch and she shook her head in rapid, short bursts. "No. No California." Her words would have been totally indiscernible to someone else, but Noah understood every one of them.

"Clara, it's beautiful there."

"This . . . is home." She started to cry, started breathing erratically. In a matter of minutes she went from perfectly happy to a full-blown panic attack.

Emily would be back in a few minutes, so Noah had to hurry. He went to Clara and put his arm around her shoulders. "It's okay." He ran his hand down her arm. "You don't have to go anywhere. You can stay right here."

Understanding seemed to dawn on Clara. Her eyes grew wide and even more fearful. "Emily stay? Emily here?" She stared right at him, desperate for everything to stay the same. "Noah stay here?"

"It's okay. No one's going to leave, Clara." He didn't know what else to tell her. He was scheduled to report to the Chargers' spring camp just after graduation. Of course he had to go. "I'm right here, sweetie. No one's moving."

A few minutes passed before Clara stopped crying and settled down again, until she clearly felt safe once more. When she did, Noah returned to his spot at the table and watched her, working on her skills, proud of herself and her accomplishments.

In that moment he understood. As if her life depended on it, Clara did not want change. She didn't want to move down the street, let alone to California. This was the house she and Emily had shared with their mother, after all. In her perfect world, Clara wanted to stay here with Emily and him and keep living the idyllic life she had grown to love.

Forever.

When Emily returned from outside, she sensed immediately that something was wrong. She hurried to Clara and put her hand on her sister's back. "Everything okay?" Emily stooped down so she could see Clara's face. "You all right?"

"Emily stay." Clara seemed to search Emily's face. "Noah stay."

"Yes, of course, honey. We're right here." Emily cast Noah a quick look. "No one's leaving."

Then Emily motioned for Noah to follow her to the back of the house. They stepped into the spare room, the one where Noah had recuperated after both concussions. Emily didn't look angry, just unsettled. She kept her voice quiet. "What was that?" She looked hard at his eyes. "Why did she say that?"

Noah chose each word with care. "I was talking to her about San Diego, whether she might want to go there. Palm trees, the ocean. That sort of thing." He was sure he looked as helpless as he felt. "I had no idea that just asking her would . . . would be so hard."

"It's not your fault." A sigh filtered up from Emily's chest. "She hates change. It can trigger a meltdown in someone with cerebral palsy." She stared at the shag carpet beneath her feet and shook her head. "That's why I work so hard, Noah. To keep her routine the same. Day after day."

"I didn't know she'd react like that." He took her hand. "Emily, look at me." He waited until their eyes found each other. "I'm sorry. I won't bring it up again."

She said something next that would stay with him. "I'm never taking Clara away from here. This is her home." Her look lingered, as if she didn't want to spell out exactly what she meant. "Please . . . don't talk to her about it again."

The conversation sent Noah into a tailspin worse than either of his concussions. This was what he'd worked for all his life, right? A trip to the NFL. But if Emily and Clara wouldn't go with him, then what choice did he have?

Four days later Emily invited him to her house after his workout. It was past nine o'clock by the time he got there, so Clara was in bed. Noah knew something was terribly wrong the minute he saw Emily.

She invited him in and led him to the sofa, the place where they'd had so many conversations before. Only this time Noah could tell something was different. Emily clearly had been crying, but her eyes were dry now.

When they were seated, facing each other, their knees touching, Emily took his hands. There was nothing subtle about the reason he was there, no breaking it to him over a series of minutes. He knew what this was about before she opened her mouth. Finally she looked into his eyes and said the words he never thought he'd hear. "We have to end this, Noah. It's over."

He felt sick to his stomach and all sound shut down. For the next few seconds he couldn't hear anything she said. Like he had been sucked into a vacuum with no way out. But eventually her words started landing on him again.

"The NFL is your dream, Noah. You need to go." Her tone was gentle, but firm. Obviously she'd thought this through. "I refuse to hold you back, but . . . it's like I told you when you met us. Clara comes first." Emily looked around the small house. "This is her home. Nothing can ever change that."

Noah had known they were running headlong into a brick wall, that an impasse was at hand. But somehow the breakup threw him like nothing ever had. His first words came from a place of hope. A certainty that if they talked their way through it there might still be a chance.

"Then stay here." He grabbed at anything that might make sense. "I'll live there half the year and here the other half. Whatever it takes."

She shook her head. "That isn't fair. You need a girl who will stand by you, be there for you after practice. Hold you after a hard week and sit front row for every home game." Fresh tears filled her eyes. "I can't be that girl, Noah. You need to go. Find the life you're supposed to live."

"No, Emily." He was on his feet. "If you won't fight for us, I will. There is a way. There has to be."

But no matter how long they talked that night, her answer was the same. It was over. She walked him out long before he was ready to leave. As he was about to say goodbye she came to him instead. Her hands were on his face and in his hair and she was kissing him.

Like she might die if he ever left.

He kissed her, too, holding her like he was clinging to his very life. His lips were on hers, his hands pressing her to himself. Between kisses he looked into her eyes. "Please, don't do this, baby. We can find a way."

But after a few minutes she stepped back. They were both breathing hard, both terrified and sick about what was happening. Emily shook her head. "We can't, Noah." She closed her eyes. "Go. Please, go."

Begging her was out of the question at that point. Noah had been trying to change her mind for the past few hours. And so he did what she asked him to do. He backed down the porch steps and then he walked to his car. He didn't say goodbye. He couldn't. It was the one word he never wanted to say to Emily Andrews, even then.

Noah didn't sleep all that night. He was too busy working out scenarios where he and Emily could stay together. Even if it meant great sacrifice. He would bear any hardship for her. Whatever it took he was willing.

But Emily wasn't. She insisted he needed something more, and nothing was going to change her mind.

For the first few days, Noah was too numb to break down, too devastated to call Emily and beg her again. He avoided her in the cafeteria at dinnertime and took different routes to his classes so they wouldn't meet up.

He could only imagine how upset Clara must've been. She didn't want Emily to end things with Noah any more than she wanted to move to San Diego. But the breakup was done. As tormented as Noah was about Emily's decision, a part of him was angry at her. If she really loved him, wouldn't she have at least tried? If he wanted to split his time between San Diego and Bloomington, what was it to her? She could've given the situation a chance.

Overnight, football became his only life. God and the sport he loved. If Emily wasn't going to try, then he had to let her go. Best to get to San Diego as soon as possible.

So he could move on.

But no matter what he spent his hours doing that weekend, he couldn't get Emily's face out of his mind. He missed her more with every breath. The feeling of her fingers laced between his was forever etched on his soul. Her voice and laugh and the way she looked at him when she was in his arms.

The ache in his heart was a physical presence that Noah couldn't bear. He needed to see her, had to talk sense into her. No one had a love like they did. They needed to try a long-distance relationship before she could give up on the idea.

He'd gone to a different church that Sunday so he wouldn't run into her. He didn't want to have to pretend things were over, pretend he was okay with being broken up. Better to avoid her altogether. But that evening he couldn't wait another minute.

Noah picked up his phone, but before he could place the call, the phone began to ring. He hesitated before he realized what had happened. She was calling him, just when he was about to dial her. His heart beat hard against the wall of his chest. "Hello?"

"Noah. Please . . ." She'd been crying again. He could hear it in her voice. "Please come over."

He was on her front porch ten minutes later. This time she fell into his arms as soon as he walked inside. "I'm sorry." Tears streamed down her face. "I'm so sorry."

And they were kissing, her tears salty on his lips, her arms and hands clinging to him like he might otherwise disappear. He took a step back first and then he got her a tissue. His whole body wanted nothing more than to take her in his arms and kiss her again.

But he couldn't. He shook his head. "What . . . what is this, Emily? You said it was over."

"I know." She dabbed the tissue against her face, her expression a mask of confliction. After a few seconds she caught her breath. "But I can't do this. I miss you too much."

Noah's heart skipped a beat. A ray of hope! "Really?"

The hurt in his soul started to let up. "Me, too. I was calling you tonight. At the same time you called me."

"I have an idea." Emily put her arms around his neck. With her blue eyes looking deep into his own, she told him her plan.

After graduation, she and Clara would take a trip to San Diego. A vacation. While they were there, Emily would look for an occupational center like the one in Bloomington. She and Clara would visit it and then they'd take trips to the beach and the San Diego Zoo and Balboa Island. On his day off Noah could even join them for an afternoon at Balboa Island.

"And maybe by the end of the week, Clara might love it." She lifted her shoulders and let them fall again. "I think it's possible." She took a breath. "I'm sorry how I acted before. Totally selfish. Not to even try. It was . . . it was crazy of me. Breaking up with you like that." She caught a quick breath. "A love like ours is worth fighting for." She spread her fingers over her heart and then moved her hand to his chest. "Us. Right here. This is love." A quick shake of her head. "I'd be crazy to walk away from you and me without at least trying."

Noah was thrilled. Emily's declaration that night was the greatest answer to prayer Noah had ever experienced. The next few days would've been perfect except for one thing. His headache wouldn't quit. The stress of the breakup must have triggered it.

He still had ten days before he had to report to training camp, but rather than think about finishing his classes or where he would live when he got to San Diego, Noah couldn't stop thinking about Dr. Roberts's warning. *Get a second opinion. Your life could depend on it.*

Since he no longer had the neurosurgeon's name and number, Noah got the information from the team physician. As soon as he called, Dr. Porter cleared his schedule. He met with Noah the next morning.

This time there were different tests, assessments that measured Noah's ability to multitask and react to urgent situations. The process gave him a headache, but still he thought he'd done well. Right up until Dr. Porter called him back to his office.

"Your brain is compromised, Noah. The damage shows up everywhere we have the power to look." He held up a few slides and photos. "The scan shows impairment across most of your brain, and your test results were middle of the road. Not where I'd like to see them."

Noah couldn't believe it. "What about the other tests? The NFL doctor cleared me."

"Young man . . ." Dr. Porter narrowed his eyes. "My standards and those of the NFL are very different. Surely you can understand that." He set his elbows on his desk. "I wouldn't subject anyone's brain to what happens in football. Let alone someone with your history."

How could this be happening? God had told him it was okay to play football. He had good plans for Noah, right? Everything Noah had ever wanted was right in front of him. Emily was going to help Clara try to love San Diego and his football career stretched out in front of him like a golden road. The possibilities were endless. A few years in the NFL and he could retire to be an announcer or a coach.

He could stay with the game as long as he lived.

Noah shifted in his seat and leveled his gaze at the doctor. He felt as sharp-minded as he had before the concussions. "Bottom line, Doctor. What are the risks?"

Concern seemed permanently etched in the man's face. He looked at the photos and scans and the folder of test results in front of him. Then he turned to Noah. "What I'm about to tell you isn't based on absolutes. The truth is, there is no way to know how your brain will react to any single hit. You could take another six hits over the next few years and be fine."

"That's all I need to hear." Noah was ready to walk out, ready to start living out the brilliant future in front of him. He moved to rise from his chair.

"I'm not finished." Dr. Porter didn't move. Just waited for Noah to sit back down. "The possibility that all things will be well after another hit is just that. A possibility. There's also a very great chance that a lesser hit than the ones you've taken could disable you, Noah."

"What?" Noah could feel the blood draining from his face. He settled back in his seat. "Why?"

"I told you. Because your brain cells are compromised." The man sighed. "A minor hit could leave you unable to walk and talk and feed yourself." He paused. "A major hit, like one of your previous two, could put you in a vegetative state. For the rest of your life." He hesitated again. "A devastating blow—the kind that typically ends careers—could kill you, Noah. On the spot. Right there on the field."

The words were coming at Noah like so many ruthless tacklers, pushing him back, stopping him from ever getting to the line of scrimmage, keeping him from all he longed to do. The game he had worked for all his life. He fought for clarity. "What are the odds? You said it was possible I could bounce up after a hit and be no worse for it." He crossed his arms and stared at the doctor. "Give me the percentages."

Dr. Porter shook his head. "There's no way to know, one hit to the next. Every time a football player takes a blow to his head, brain cells are damaged. Most of the time that damage doesn't make a long-term impact. Or if it does, it takes a while to show up. It's something a guy can live with." He shrugged. "But when the brain's already suffered a great deal, things are different. Sometimes the consequences become apparent in later years. When players in their fifties don't remember their names. They lose their memory, sometimes years at a time go missing." The information in front of Dr. Porter drew his attention again. "I'd say . . . you're ten times more likely to have devastating consequences from the wrong kind of hit. Ten times more likely than the other guys on the field."

Noah felt the fight leave him. His efforts to gain clearance before the draft had been all-consuming. But he had done it. Now, here, all he could do was sit back and let the numbers have their way with him. Ten times more likely. *Ten times*. He thanked Dr. Porter, collected his copy of the report and headed for the door.

"Ultimately it's up to you," the doctor said before he left. "A lot of guys play with these kinds of odds. They love the game that much." He gave Noah a sad look. "Only you can make that decision."

That weekend Noah kept mostly to himself. He went to the Indiana stadium and sat at the top of the bleachers, staring at the field. The place where he'd had so much success. And so much pain. He lifted his eyes to the cloudy sky overhead. Thunderstorms were forecast for today. Fitting, Noah thought.

Lord, talk to me. What I am supposed to do? You opened the door for me to play in the NFL. You told me You had good plans for me . . . and now this? A thought came to him. He had clearance already. All he had to do was get on the plane, collect his new uniform and his signing bonus and he would be a pro football player. The money sat in an account, ready for him to use as soon as he reported for camp.

"God, was that from You? The fact that I passed those tests?" His whisper hung on the warm afternoon breeze. "Won't You tell me what to do? Please?"

There were no words from heaven, no still, small voice playing inside his soul. But gradually bits of conversations came back to him. Everything said to him over the last month.

I'd get two clearances, if I were you. So the people you

love don't have to bury you early. . . . Get that second opinion, will you? For peace of mind. . . . A minor hit could leave you unable to walk and talk and feed yourself. . . . A major hit could put you in a vegetative state. For the rest of your life. . . . A devastating blow . . . could kill you, Noah. On the spot. Right there on the field.

And of course the statistic that shook Noah to the core: the fact that he was ten times more likely to have terrible consequences from the wrong kind of hit. Ten times.

Noah lifted his face to the sky. And gradually a peace came over him, like he'd never felt before. God hadn't been talking about football. Those weren't the good plans He had for Noah Carter. A smile tugged at his lips. The choice was actually pretty simple. A life on the field, where every day could be his last. Where even if he lived through his time in the NFL, he might not know his name by the time his kids entered high school.

Or a life with Emily Andrews.

Noah felt his smile fill his face. *Thanks, Lord. For making it easy*. On the way home from the field he called Joel Walker. One thing was certain.

His would be the shortest professional football career ever.

18

This time Noah didn't want to wake up. He was just at the good part, the chapter of his story where he gave Emily the greatest gift ever. The gift of life. His life.

But he was wide awake. He rolled over and stared at the off-white apartment ceiling. There was no falling back to sleep now.

He climbed out of bed and looked around the room. The scratchy carpet again, but something was different. What had happened this time? It was the same room, but when Noah looked to the window it was open and warm air drifted in.

Warm air at Christmastime?

He blinked a few times. Indiana was never this mild in December. He drew a deep breath and checked his face in the mirror. "Yikes." He stepped back. His reflection made him catch his breath. He looked terrible. His blond hair was darker, cut short. The lines around his eyes had spread and now there were creases on his forehead and near his mouth.

Whatever was going on with his head, the pain and damage were taking their toll on his face. That had to be it. He heard voices in the next room. Finally, something that made sense. His family was here, where they belonged. Enough of that strange man sitting next to Emily.

Before he left the room he turned back to the bed. If Emily was here, then surely she'd slept in bed with him. Even if he couldn't remember yesterday at least she had been with him, the two of them sleeping next to each other, their legs intertwined.

But her side was still freshly made. Like she hadn't even come to bed. He stared at the empty spot where she should've slept and pieces of his memory were suddenly clear. She hadn't fallen asleep next to him in a long time. Granted, the dates didn't line up. Entire chapters of his story were missing. Like time was slipping away, hours for years.

Still one terrible, tragic constant remained: the love of his life wasn't here with him.

Noah sighed. He went toward the voices in the living room, and fixed a smile on his face. "Hey there!" He said the words before the kids came into view. "Everyone having a good morning?"

That's when he saw them, Aiden and Olivia.

Panic grabbed at him, suffocated him. They weren't little anymore. They weren't even ten and eight. Olivia was on a phone, her legs draped over the arm of the corner chair. Aiden was flipping channels with the TV remote. He barely looked up when Noah entered the room. "Hey." He muttered the word. "Shouldn't preseason ball be on by now?"

Preseason? Noah blinked a few times. His headache was back, stronger with every passing minute. "You mean football?"

Aiden turned his eyes to Noah. "Dad." His tone was a mix of contempt and condescension. "Of course football. It's August."

"Right." It was August? Noah felt his knees begin to tremble. What could he say? When did Aiden get so old? And mean? Noah forced himself to concentrate. His son was waiting for an answer. "The games might start a little later."

"True." Aiden turned off the TV and tossed the remote on the sofa. He leaned back and closed his eyes. "What are we doing today, anyway? A whole day's a long time, you know?"

Olivia looked up from her phone. "A very long time."

"Give me a minute." Noah tried to keep his tone upbeat. "Dad needs a little coffee."

It was true. Coffee would help his headache; at least it used to help. But he needed the time for another reason. So he could study his kids, try to figure out what had happened to them. When had they grown up and become so . . . so different? *God, where has the time gone? I can't take this!*

While the pot brewed, Noah grabbed his phone. It looked different, but the pass code was the same. First thing he did was open the calendar. What was the date? He absolutely had to know at least that detail.

There it was. August 12. Okay, that much lined up with what Aiden said. It was August. But what year? Noah made a few clicks and what he saw was too outrageous to believe. If the year was correct Aiden was fifteen and Olivia was thirteen. His kids weren't kids anymore. They were teenagers.

From his spot in the kitchen, Noah observed them. Olivia wore tight jeans and a skimpy tank top. Part of her stomach was showing—Emily never would've worn something like that. So how could she allow it for their daughter? Olivia's ears were pierced and . . . he looked closer. Yes, she was wearing makeup.

And what was keeping her so busy on the phone?

His attention shifted to Aiden. The boy was an athlete, no doubt. If Aiden was fifteen, then Noah felt sorry for the other guys, the ones who had to defend him on the football or soccer field. Whatever sport he played.

Noah poured a cup of strong coffee. Straight black. A memory hit him and he felt a surge of hope. Maybe his mind was clearing up. "It's Saturday. How about pancakes?"

"Too many carbs." Olivia didn't bother to look up. Just kept her eyes glued to the phone.

"Not that many." Noah still worked to keep his voice upbeat. "Besides, a few carbs never hurt anyone. Not on a Saturday morning."

Aiden shot Olivia a harsh look. "Why do you care? You'll just throw them up an hour from now."

Noah's breathing came faster. What was Aiden saying? Olivia threw up her food? On purpose? There was a name for that condition. What was it? The harder he thought, the more his head pounded. This couldn't be happening.

"That's not funny." Noah returned to the living room and gave Aiden's shoulder a light push. "Don't talk about your sister that way."

Aiden scowled at him. "What are *you* saying?" His laugh was angry. "You already know. You're the one who wanted her checked into some inpatient place."

How was Noah supposed to answer that? He had lost another five years of memories. Of course he didn't remember about Olivia's problem or his own response. But he could feel his heart breaking. His baby girl had an eating disorder. How did that happen? He didn't dare say anything or they'd know the truth.

Dad was losing his mind.

He decided to ignore their rude attitudes and mean glances. Pancakes were on the menu. And like the last time he could remember them being here, he scrambled a few eggs for each of them.

While the pancakes were cooking, Noah looked for syrup. There wasn't any. Fine, he would make his own. Butter, brown sugar, and vanilla. That's all he needed. He pulled up a quick recipe on his phone, and when breakfast was ready he set the table and put the dishes of food in the middle.

"Come eat." Again Noah's tone was kind. Both kids were on their phones now, and neither one responded.

As if they couldn't hear him at all. He raised his voice some. "I said, come eat."

This time Aiden and Olivia looked up. His tone must've told them he meant business, because they both shuffled to the table, still looking at their phones. Noah sat across from them. They started eating without praying, without saying a single thank-you or even pretending to be interested in Noah.

"I have a question." He looked from Aiden to Olivia. "What makes you think you can be on your phones all the time? When I'm sitting right here, trying to talk to you?"

Aiden blinked a few times. "Must be a bad brain day, huh, Dad?" He held up his phone. "You gave them to us. So we'd have something to do when you were busy. Whatever you do."

Noah made a note to check his social media accounts later. That would give him some idea of what he'd been doing. Either way, that last part was pure dagger. His headache was getting worse. What exactly *did* he do with his time these days? Noah didn't have a clue. He turned to his daughter. "So, Olivia . . ." Noah tried to think of more neutral questions. She was still stuck on her phone, still acting like she couldn't hear him. He raised his voice. "Olivia, could you put your phone down, please? I'm trying to talk to you."

"I'm talking to my boyfriend." She sneered at him. "We're in a fight, okay?"

"You're always in a fight." Aiden rolled his eyes and

put his phone down next to his plate. Then he helped himself to four pancakes. "He's the worst kid in middle school, and you're dating him."

Noah felt like he was having an out-of-body experience. Not just now but every time he woke up. Okay, so he needed medical help. His brain was falling apart. But why had Emily allowed their kids to act like this? He needed to find out more about Aiden and Olivia, why they were rude and how come they didn't pray before eating. Why his thirteen-year-old daughter was dating some bad boy.

But first he had to know something more important than any of that.

"Where's your mother?" He aimed the question at Aiden. His son was being more responsive than Olivia. "She's going to miss pancakes."

This time Olivia set down her phone and both kids stared straight at him. Olivia spoke first. "You really think Mom would join us for pancakes? Here? With *you?*" She shook her head, clearly disgusted with him. "Mom has her own Prince Charming now. They're always together."

"Yeah." Aiden twisted up his face. "You're starting to worry me, Dad."

Noah's heart skidded into a crazy fast rhythm. Emily was . . . she was . . . He couldn't finish the thought. *No, God, don't let it be true.* Ice ran through Noah's veins and he stared at his plate. For a long time Noah kept his questions to himself. When breakfast was finished, he showered and shaved. Then he put a bag of sandwiches together, found a blanket, a Frisbee and a football and walked over to the kids.

They were both in their chairs in the living room, back on their phones. "Turn off your phones." Noah used a louder voice this time. He was tired of being ignored. "Do it now."

"Why?" Aiden lowered his phone and glared at Noah. "We can do what we want. That's always how it is at your house."

At your house. The words terrified Noah, but he couldn't let that show. "We're going to the park. Now."

"The park?" Olivia twisted her mouth, a scowl fixed on her forehead. Based on Olivia's look Noah might as well have said they were going to pick through the local dump heap.

"For a picnic." Noah took a step closer. His daughter looked so much like Emily. But this morning she had none of Emily's kindness. Noah aimed his words right at her. "And you're going with us. Because I said so."

Both kids shot him rude looks, but he didn't care. They were too young to drive, so as long as they were here, they were his. He kept his voice stern. "Get in the car. Both of you." Their attitudes were terrible, so Noah upped the stakes. "Oh, and you can't take your phones." He held out his hand. "Give them to me."

"What?" Olivia shrieked. "You can't do that!" She looked like she might burst into tears. "A phone's private property."

"Well, it's my property today." Noah took both phones and put them in a basket on top of the fridge. Then he corralled the kids into his old VW. Older still, apparently.

Fifteen minutes later they were at the park—something that hadn't changed—and Noah spread the blanket out on the grass near the swings. The kids weren't hungry yet, and with no phones they wandered onto the playground. Noah wasn't going to give up. If this was a day with his kids, he was going to make it the best possible.

"Let's have a contest. See who can swing the highest." He walked past them to the swings and took the middle one. "This old man's still pretty strong." That much turned out to be true. Even though the years had disappeared, Noah was still an athlete. His brain was a mess, but his body was fit.

Maybe it was his challenge, or the way he made the contest sound fun. Whatever it was, the kids dropped the worst of their attitudes and joined him, one on either side. In no time they were laughing, all three of them. Pushing their feet to the sky, as high as they could go.

"Come on, Dad," Olivia whined her complaint. "Give us a break. We could never beat you."

"Never." He chuckled. The rush of air in his face, the grove of trees, a hundred shades of green everywhere he looked. Somehow his headache had faded. He was with his children and they were having fun.

Finally.

Whatever had just happened, the three of them felt

like a family again. Only Emily was missing. But Noah didn't want to think about that. Not now. After a few minutes, he slowed his swing a little. He was in good shape, but he couldn't keep going at full speed.

At the same time, Aiden pushed past him. The boy was almost as tall as Noah now, and clearly strong. "Yes! I did it!" He pumped a little higher. "I beat you, Dad."

"You did." Noah chuckled. "I have to admit. My son has me by a yard."

"At least." Aiden sounded proud of himself. His eyes looked alive for the first time today.

On Noah's other side, Olivia slowed down, laughing too hard to push herself. "Uh . . . you make it look so easy!" She grinned at Noah. "I really thought I could do it."

They stayed on the swings a little while longer. Noah forced himself to think of something else. "I know!" He looked from Aiden to Olivia. "Synchronized swinging!"

"What?" Livi couldn't stop smiling. "Synchronized?"

"Definitely." Noah made up the rules as quickly as the words crossed his lips. Aiden would kick his legs up, then Noah, then Olivia last of all. "So it looks like a pattern."

It worked for a while and both kids thought the effort was cool. At least that's what they said. When they finished swinging, Noah ran to the monkey bars. "Fastest time across wins." The bars were high above the ground. Noah had to climb up to reach them. "Aiden, time me."

"I can't." He made a face, but it was more silly than frustrated. "You have our phones, remember?"

"True." Noah thought for a few seconds. "Okay.

Count like this: one-one-thousand, two-one-thousand." Noah pointed at him. "That's the best we can do."

So Aiden counted while Noah moved as fast as he could across the bars and back again.

"Eighteen!" Aiden hurried over and took Noah's place. "I can beat that, easy."

This time Olivia counted, and Aiden turned out to be right. He moved down the bars and back in just sixteen seconds. Olivia wanted a try next.

"Spot me, Daddy. In case I fall." She turned to him, her eyes pleading.

But all Noah could think was that she'd called him Daddy again. His baby girl. His Livi. He was at her side immediately. "I've got you, Livi. Give it a try."

Her expression changed and she looked at him, all the way to the deepest place in his heart. "You called me Livi."

He allowed a light laugh. "I've called you that since you were born."

"Not for a long time." Aiden was listening. He squinted at Noah and a grin tugged at his lips. "I like it."

Olivia's smile filled her whole face. "Me, too." She gripped the bar ahead of her. "Okay, here goes."

She made it from the first one to the next before she fell into Noah's arms. He easily caught her and set her gently down on the mulch that covered the play area. But when her feet touched the ground, she didn't let go. She wrapped her arms around him and held on tight.

After a few seconds she seemed to remember her age

or the situation or the fact that life had changed, and she stepped back. "I've missed you, Dad."

He didn't know what to say. Half of his life was gone. Disappeared. More than half. So he just hugged her again and pointed to their picnic. "Let's eat lunch."

They sat on the blanket and Noah had an idea. "How about we pick a question? Then everyone can answer it." The kids weren't as happy as they'd been at the playground, but they were kind, at least. They clearly wanted this time with him. "I'll go first." Noah thought for a second. "Greatest accomplishment in your life so far."

Aiden leaned back on his elbow. His eyes looked so much lighter than before. "That's easy. League MVP last football season."

Noah wasn't surprised. But the detail was new to him. He nodded. "I'm proud of you, Aiden. I . . . I can't wait to see you play."

"Dad?" Olivia sat cross-legged and stared at him. "You never go to Aiden's games."

There was no way that could be true. He'd started to say so when Aiden spoke up. "That's okay." His smile fell off a little. "You will one day. Right, Dad?"

He didn't go to his son's games? Really? What sort of father was he? Noah hated himself, but again if this was his reality he had to say something. "I will. Definitely."

"Okay." Olivia still sounded carefree. Like the time on the playground had changed her. "My greatest accomplishment. Hmmm." She giggled. "Not the monkey bars, that's for sure."

"What about dance?" Aiden was more interested now, in Noah and his sister. "You're amazing, Liv."

Olivia was a dancer. Like her mother. Suddenly all Noah could see was Emily, the way she'd looked moving across the dance floor in the rehearsal studio at Indiana University. The way Clara had cheered for her and Noah had breathed in the sight of her. Grace personified. Of course Olivia was a dancer.

His daughter clapped her hands and grinned at Aiden. "Yeah, that's it." She lifted vulnerable eyes to Noah. "My solo at the last recital. That was my greatest accomplishment."

"I agree." Noah was taking a chance. He must've been at Olivia's dance recital. Certainly. But he could tell from the look on her face that he hadn't been there.

"Did you ever watch the video, Daddy?" The hurt in his daughter's eyes was palpable.

Seeing the brokenness in Olivia was more painful for Noah than any headache ever could be. "I did." He must have. "You were beautiful, Livi. The best dancer ever. Just like your mother."

The kids seemed uncomfortable with the mention of their mom. Aiden sat up and put his legs out in front of him. "What about you, Dad? What's your greatest accomplishment?"

Noah's answer was easy. "Loving your mother and being a dad to the two of you. In all my life there's never been anything greater than that."

For the next minute, Aiden and Olivia only stared at

him. A lifetime of pain shone in their eyes. Olivia broke the silence first. "Then why did you leave us?"

"Leave you?" Noah shook his head. "Livi, I never left you. I'm right here."

"You know what she means, Dad." Aiden sounded frustrated. "Why'd you move out? We were just babies. I was four years old."

"And I was two." Olivia's eyes welled with tears. "All I ever wanted was my daddy living in the same house as me."

Noah felt his eyes well up. *What kind of man have I become, God? Who am I?* He needed to be alone. He couldn't take the heartbreak of what he was learning. He had walked out on them? All of them? Why would he do that? What could possibly be bad enough to make him move out? He hung his head. No wonder Emily wasn't around.

"I remember something." Aiden was still looking at Noah, still caught up in the moment. "It was the night before you left. You came into my room and sat on my bed. And you told me nothing would change. You'd be there for me, even though you lived in another house." He shook his head. "But that never happened."

"You don't go to Aiden's games or my dance recitals." Olivia dabbed at her eyes. And for a moment Noah could see the little girl she'd once been. Before he ruined everything. Before he became the worst dad ever. She blinked and two tears fell onto her cheeks. "If . . . we're your greatest accomplishment, why didn't you stay, Daddy? Why didn't you keep loving Mommy?"

He had no answers. So he said the only thing he could say. "I'm sorry." His own face was wet now. He held out his arms and Olivia came to him, cuddled up beside him the way she used to do when she was just two. "I'm so sorry."

Aiden didn't have to be asked. He stood and crossed the blanket to Noah and sat close to him on the other side. "I used to wonder if you ever loved us at all."

"I do." Noah put his arm around his son. "I'm so sorry."

The mood stayed sweet between them through lunch and back at Noah's apartment. He understood now. It was all his fault. He had moved out. Somehow he had walked away from the only girl he ever loved. He had left Emily and the kids. And all these years his children had wondered if he ever cared at all. And because of some terrible aftereffect of his concussions, he couldn't remember any of it. A handful of memories in more than a decade. He needed to see a doctor, but then what?

Nothing could give him those years back.

Sometime that evening, Emily came for the kids. Noah gave them their phones, then he hugged them and kissed their heads. Things would be different, he promised. They'd never have to wonder if he loved them. He did. He always had. All of them cried and held on to each other until finally Emily left the car and ran up the sidewalk to Noah's front door.

"Okay. Next Saturday, then?" Noah rubbed his sleeve across his face. "We'll go to the park again?"

Aiden and Olivia both nodded and dried their eyes. Noah opened the door and there she was. His wife, the woman he longed for more than his next breath. She seemed to notice that all of them had been crying, which made the tender moment suddenly awkward. She took the kids and looked at him for a single beat of his heart. "Thanks, Noah."

That was it. Just two words.

He nodded and they were gone. All three of them. This time Noah didn't follow them outside, didn't try to talk Emily into understanding that they were still married. Clearly they were not.

Instead he watched from the window, and then he saw the man. The same one from Aiden's soccer game. And something else. In the shadow of the apartment complex lighting he saw the glint of a diamond on her left ring finger. He couldn't take his eyes off it. "No, God." His words were the most tortured whisper. "What have I done?"

It was true. The guy wasn't just hanging around. He and Emily were either engaged or . . . or married. He watched as the man jumped out of the car and opened the door for Emily and Olivia. The perfect gentleman. Emily's Prince Charming, like the kids had said. And then the guy slid behind the wheel and drove off.

With everything that had ever mattered to Noah.

His greatest accomplishment.

19

Emily was tired of sitting on the swing. The late fall air had gotten colder with the passing of the last storm and she needed to stretch. Still more bad weather was forecast through the morning. She wandered back into the house and looked down the hallway toward their bedroom. The light was off. Noah was obviously asleep.

Like he didn't have a care in the world.

Think of others better than yourself. Wasn't that something Kari Baxter Taylor always talked about? Yet, Noah couldn't see past his own reflection. The social media world was all about his followers, his fame. And a million girls who didn't even know him.

Emily moved into the den, left the lights off, and shut the double doors behind her. It was two in the morning. The last thing she wanted was to wake the kids. There was still more to the story of Noah and her, still pieces she wanted to relive.

Yes, their marriage was dead. But it had been so beautiful once upon a time. What they shared deserved to be remembered.

A requiem for all that was.

Emily crossed the room to the bookcase and pulled a photo album from the middle shelf. Of all the pictures the two of them had taken together, of all the images their followers had oohed and aahed over on social media, there was one picture that would always be her favorite.

She opened the book and there it was. Right at the front. The moonlight through the window was bright enough that she could still see every detail.

It was the photo that had started the whole thing.

Noah had her in his arms and her feet were off the ground. A sunset painted the sky and he was holding her close, face-to-face, the two of them clinging to each other. And next to them was Clara, beaming bigger than life because Noah had made two decisions.

The biggest decisions in all his life.

Holding the album open to that page, Emily sat in the glider chair, the one by the window. She set it in motion, ever so slightly, and let her eyes rest on the photo.

Emily had made her decision. She couldn't live without Noah Carter, so she had to find a way to live with him. If that meant convincing Clara to move to San Diego, then she'd at least try. After Noah took her back, Emily worked every day on her sister, showing her pictures of the beach and talking about how wonderful it would be to have a winter without snow.

Clara was starting to come around, though Emily still wasn't sure how her sister would adjust to any of it. Neither of them had ever been to the West Coast before, for one thing. Usually after Emily talked about visiting the West Coast, Clara would end the conversation with something sweet or sad. "This is home, Emily," she would struggle to say. Or, "Please don't stay in San Diego. I need here. I need you."

The hope was that once Clara managed to get on a plane and actually see California, she'd change her mind. Maybe she wouldn't even want to go back to Indiana. In reality, though, Emily wasn't quite sure. She and Noah began praying about the situation. But Noah was busy. There were physicals and TV interviews and meetings with his agent. Between the draft and the day he was supposed to leave for camp, Emily felt like she barely saw him.

Three days before he was set to leave, Emily was home making dinner for Clara when she got a text from Noah.

Turn on your TV. ESPN.

That was all. Just *Turn on your TV*. Nothing more. *Strange,* she thought. She dried her hands on a towel and did as he asked. And suddenly there he was, standing in front of a dozen microphones with at least that many cameras in his face.

"Hey! Noah." Clara had been at the dining room table doing classwork. She set her pencil down and stared at the TV. "Why?"

"I don't know." Emily took the nearest chair, her eyes fixed on the screen. "Let's listen."

She turned up the volume in time to hear Noah start

talking. Emily's heart raced within her. What was this? What was he doing? She leaned closer.

"I regret to announce, that as of today I am officially retiring from professional football." Noah was the picture of professionalism, a jacket and tie, white buttoned-up shirt. He looked down for a moment and then at the cameras again.

Emily couldn't breathe. She was on her feet. Why was he saying that? Had something happened? "Noah . . ." She uttered his name under her breath and waited, listening.

He was speaking again. "In the course of my physical exam this past week I got a second opinion regarding my previous concussions. Even though I'd been cleared by the NFL, I wanted peace of mind before making such a big commitment. The second doctor cleared me, too, because my results were within the normal range."

Noah didn't smile. This was a very serious matter, clearly. "But he did explain that because of my past injuries I was ten times more likely to be disabled by a hit to the head."

Emily closed her eyes. She couldn't imagine.

"Ten times more likely to end up in a vegetative state after one wrong tackle." Noah paused. "And ten times more likely to die on the field. All from a blow to the head. The sort of thing that is commonplace in football."

He exhaled. "And so I have made a decision to live. Not only that, but to love." The hint of a smile crept onto his face and he looked straight into the camera.

"Emily Andrews, I love you. I'd rather have a lifetime with you than twenty years in the NFL." He paused. "Meet me at the bench by the cafeteria in half an hour." He looked around the room, the picture of professionalism once more. "That's all I have."

Noah walked away from the podium and Joel Walker stepped up. "Mr. Carter is not taking questions at this time. If there is any other development to this story, we'll let you know."

Before his agent could step away from the microphone a reporter yelled out, "What about his signing bonus, five million dollars? What happens to that?"

Emily could see the struggle in Joel's face. "Mr. Carter will return it." He did a curt wave, and walked off in the same direction as Noah.

The station cut back to the studio, where all three *SportsCenter* announcers looked too shocked to speak. Emily understood. She felt the same way. Noah had retired from football? Had that really just happened?

Clara spoke first. "Noah wants . . . to meet you."

She was right. "Thank you, Clara. I need to get ready." Emily smiled at her sister. "You already look perfect."

"I know. Thanks, Emily." Clara beamed. She started putting away her paper, like she understood they had to get to the school. Noah was meeting them.

Emily turned off the stove and covered up the half-done chicken and broccoli. They could eat later. Then she ran to her room and switched into her prettiest pale pink sweater and her darkest jeans. She fixed her hair so it hung straight around her face and touched up her makeup. Whatever Noah was up to, she wanted to look her best. She had a feeling she and Clara wouldn't be the only ones around when they got there.

It took nearly twenty minutes to find a parking spot and walk at Clara's pace to the bench outside the cafeteria where Emily and Noah often met.

Sure enough.

Hundreds of students had gathered around, forming a sea of spectators. Emily would never know why so many of them were interested in Noah's announcement. Easing their way through the crowd, Emily led Clara to the bench. She helped her sister sit and then tried to look over the sea of people for Noah.

Some guy standing nearby yelled for the crowd to back up. "Give the girl room. Don't ruin this."

Emily tried to imagine why Noah had asked her to meet him here, on national television. Even as she wondered, three camera crews hurried over, each of them led by a panicked-looking reporter.

But the students wouldn't let them through the crowd. "She can talk to you later," the loud student shouted. "Everyone stay back."

Emily planned to thank the guy when this was over. Without his help, Noah wouldn't have a place to stand once he got here. Clara tugged on her sleeve and Emily turned to her. The students were noisy, so it was hard to hear.

"What's Noah doing?"

Emily smiled. "I guess we're about to find out."

She watched for him, replaying the ESPN announcement again and again in her mind. Had a first-round draft pick ever retired from the game before taking a single snap? Emily didn't think so. But Noah hadn't told her about the second doctor's warning.

With all that was at stake, with the gravely serious risks, Noah really was choosing life. Emily had a feeling his decision was the hardest Noah had ever made. The truth was still resonating through her, still sending aftershocks across her heart and soul. Noah had retired from football. Nothing about that seemed even a little bit real.

Her mind was still trying to comprehend his announcement when she saw him above the crowd, his blond hair and tan face. From the first moment she spotted him, his eyes were fixed on her alone.

Only her.

Moving with great purpose, Noah stepped through the crowd and made his way closer, all while keeping his gaze on hers. As he finally approached the bench and the clearing where she and Clara sat, Noah began a slow jog, and suddenly Emily was in his arms. He framed her face with his hands and kissed her. Not too long, since they had an audience. But long enough to let her know exactly how he felt about her.

Then he did something she absolutely didn't expect.

He pulled out a small black box and dropped to one knee.

All around them the crowd cheered and cried out,

but Emily couldn't hear anything except Noah. He opened the box, and there in a cushion of velvet shone the prettiest engagement ring Emily had ever seen.

A small round solitaire, surrounded by tiny crushed diamonds on top of a thin gold band. He held the ring up to her. "Emily, I want to spend my life with you. A long life. And I want to love you every minute I draw breath." Tears spilled onto his cheeks, but they did nothing to dim his smile.

She nodded and blinked away her own tears so she could see him better. A few yards beyond them the camera crews moved past the students for a better view. All Emily could see was Noah.

He smiled bigger. "A long time ago you told me you wanted to remember this, the days when we were young." He smiled bigger. "I want to remember these days, too. And I don't ever want them to end." He was still on one knee, still looking at her like she was the only person in sight. "And so I have a question for you."

Her legs felt weak. Was she going to drop to the ground right here? She covered her mouth with her hand as Noah continued.

"Emily Andrews, will you marry me?"

"Yes." She took the ring and Noah was on his feet, pulling her into his arms. "Yes, Noah, a million times yes."

"There's something more." He took another ring from his pocket and held it out to Clara. This ring had three blue stones. With Emily standing next to him, Noah raised his voice so Clara could hear him. "Clara, I would like to be your big brother. Because you're going to live with us for the rest of your life. Because no one loves you more than God and your sister and me." He smiled at Emily. "Right?"

"Right." Emily looked at her sister.

Clara had never seemed happier, like she couldn't begin to believe what had just happened. But she definitely understood. That much was clear. Because she struggled to her feet and in the loudest voice she shouted, "Yes!"

The three of them formed a tight group hug. Then Noah picked up Emily and swung her in his arms. He tilted his head back and shouted, "I'm going to marry Emily Andrews!"

Right at that exact moment, someone snapped the picture.

It was a defining instant, seconds after she had said yes to Noah, and after Clara had agreed to live with them forever.

Like the news would report that night, Noah Carter showed more excitement and emotion in that moment than he'd shown when he was drafted. He had made the right choice, ESPN would say later. Fans from across the country weighed in. Most of them agreed with Noah. Football was a dangerous sport. Better to live and love than to follow a dream that might make both of those things impossible. And so Emily had used the photo to start their first family album.

And Noah had used it for something else.

To start a joint account on Facebook and Twitter. He

chose the only name he could possibly use: @When_We_Were_Young. From the beginning people everywhere clamored to follow them, hanging on any detail Noah posted. It was like the whole world wanted to know about Noah and Emily and Clara. And how a guy like Noah Carter could choose living a regular life with the girl he loved over the thrill and money and fame of the NFL.

News stations and celebrity magazines covered the story, declaring that Noah and Emily were that kind of throwback couple everyone wanted to be. Something normally reserved for the movies.

From the beginning, Noah insisted that the account belonged to both of them. "Whatever I say publicly, I say it with you."

Their numbers soared. Ten thousand followers in the first few days became a hundred thousand by the end of the week. And that was just Facebook. Noah posted Bible verses and funny moments and pictures from all the beautiful times the two of them shared. Sometimes he'd feature Clara, too.

And the followers kept coming.

Long before the wedding, they were contacted by everyone from reality show producers to sponsors. Sponsors most of all. You can make a living off social media, they were told time and again.

At first neither of them was interested. Noah tested for the Bloomington Fire Department and was hired top of his class. Money would be tight, but they would be fine. Noah and Emily sorted through the offers and always they said no. What was the point of selling out to sponsors? No need to hock products in their posts. Nothing real about that.

It was Noah who changed his mind first.

"If people want to pay us for posting, let them." They were on the steps out front of her house. "Maybe more people will find us and be encouraged. You know, to have faith and love better." He paused. "That can only be a good thing, right?"

Emily felt a little cautious, but she agreed for one reason. "We're pointing them to the light."

"Exactly." Noah smiled and took her hand. "Bible verses and pictures of the two of us. People need couples to look up to, Emily. A reason to believe that God is real and . . . love can be this beautiful."

She tilted her head and let herself get lost in his eyes. "No love is as beautiful as ours."

He kissed her forehead. "That'll be our little secret."

Emily stared at the photo for another minute, just taking it in. She remembered exactly what it felt like to be there, the pinks and blues overhead reflecting in his eyes. It was a dream come true.

The most breathtaking beginning.

She turned the page and looked at the pictures that followed. All of them had been used in a post at one time or another. Noah didn't waste anything. The last half of the album contained pictures from their wedding.

They had a full wedding album, of course. But the

candid shots were here, a reminder of the season when Emily said yes. When they both said I do. She stopped at the first picture of them on their wedding day.

She ran her finger over the image of him, young Noah, his blond hair and blue eyes. Muscled shoulders filling out his handsome dark gray suit. The white button-down shirt looked crisp against his tan skin. The black bow tie, a perfect finish.

"What happened to us?" She spoke straight to the photo, as if the younger Noah from those days might hear her and find a way to change things. "It's over. Can you believe it?" The words hurt to say them. "Who could've seen this coming?"

Her eyes shifted to her own image. Her smile was brighter than the sun. "You don't smile like that anymore, Emily." She spoke to herself as she ran her finger over the dress. Even through the plastic of the photo album, Emily could feel the silk and lace of that pretty white gown.

But nothing could touch the look in her eyes. The excitement and expectation, the certainty that Noah Carter would be hers, and she would be his forever and evermore. This had to be true for most divorced couples. If they tried hard enough they could all remember a time when they stood before family and friends to celebrate forever. When getting married was the brightest, most beautiful moment in their lives.

So how did everything fall apart? Especially for Noah and her?

Despite the situation at hand, Emily managed a slight smile as she turned the page. The wedding was stunning. A packed church, his brother and a few teammates serving as groomsmen. And his father as his best man. Emily's bridesmaids were friends from dance, but her maid of honor was Clara. There could've been no one else.

Emily didn't invite her father. He hadn't reached out since her mother's death. Nothing she could do about that. So Emily walked down the aisle by herself. At least it looked that way to people at the wedding. The truth was Emily took that walk with the one who had stood by her all her life.

Her Heavenly Father.

She remembered the vows, remembered promising her life to Noah. When they would talk about their wedding in the years that followed, they would remember every look and nuance of that day.

Emily closed her eyes and she could hear him speaking the words, like he was standing right here in front of her. "Life is short, the days never promised. But I can promise you this." He had been lost completely in her eyes, his fingers wrapped around hers. "I will never let go of your hand, Emily. I will walk beside you through the valleys—the way you walked beside me through mine in college. I will celebrate with you on the mountaintops and I will be the constant you need, the love you deserve, the life both of us want."

Tears filled Emily's eyes. Every word was still etched

on her heart. The look on his face, the sound of his voice. It was all right here, with her still.

The way it always would be.

She remembered her vows, too. How she had looked deep to the place in his heart that was hers alone. "We are never promised tomorrow. You taught me that. But in the days we do have, I promise to stand by you and support you, to cheer you on and believe in you. I promise to stay, Noah. I'll always stay. No matter the season, whatever happens, I will be here. Forever and ever."

Neither of them could remember a thing about the reception that followed. There were finger foods and music and dancing in the church hall. But all either of them could think about was the night to come.

In the week leading up to the wedding, Clara had hit it off with Noah's mother. Though Noah's brother and his family had to fly back to London, Noah's parents stayed at the house with Clara. So Noah and Emily could have a honeymoon.

They spent the first two nights in a bed-and-breakfast on Lake Superior. Emily could still feel the butterflies in her stomach as they left the reception. Just the two of them. They talked about those early days of the honeymoon often. Especially during their first year of marriage.

Emily and Noah were already passionate about each other. Every touch, every glance. Every kiss and embrace. But after coming together during their honeymoon, they felt sorry for other people. Like no one could've had a love as great as theirs. It was better than anything either of them had dreamed.

Noah and her, wrapped in each other's arms, whispering and laughing beneath the sheets, skin to skin.

Emily took a slow deep breath. *Enough*.

This wasn't helping. Images from their honeymoon remained, but she pushed them away. Replaced them with the real Noah Carter. The one moving out in the morning.

When they returned from their honeymoon, they spent a few days with his parents. But as soon as his parents' plane took off, Noah turned his attention to his and Emily's social media. People were dying to know about the wedding. They wanted details, anything Noah could give them.

Yes, Noah. Everything about their Internet presence was always driven by him.

They might've shared the social media accounts, but that didn't mean their fans were dim. Noah did the posting—everyone figured that out from the beginning. And that first week as husband and wife, living at home with Clara, Noah posted enough material to keep their followers busy every day.

"It's good for people," Noah told Emily. "Look." And he'd show her comments from their followers.

> All I want is to be like Noah and Emily Carter #Goals.

> I'm going to church now. I'm doing anything Noah and Emily do. I want their life! #jealous.

Why is the highlight of my day @When_We_Were_Young? #RealGoals.

I want someone to look at me the way Noah looks at Emily. Please, God! #LotsofGoals.

And from there, well, from there it snowballed. Before they celebrated their first anniversary, they were making six figures simply sharing their love story with the world.

Emily flipped back to the album's first page, to the picture she loved so much, and a thought occurred to her. She never could've imagined that this single photo would spark a generation's fascination with Noah and her. She couldn't have dreamed of the avalanche that picture would start. The tsunami of attention. Or that one day that most brilliant moment would represent something neither of them had seen coming.

The beginning of the end.

20

Of all the dreams he'd had lately, this was easily the best. Noah put his arm over his eyes and prayed the night would last forever. Because one thing was certain—here he could spend the rest of his life with Emily.

In the season after she said yes.

His sleep grew deeper and deeper and gradually he could see her again, the way she looked with her eyes all lit up, telling him yes. "Yes, Noah, a million times yes."

That night, when all the commotion and excitement died down, Noah picked up dinner and brought it back to Emily and Clara's house. No television, that was Noah's only request. His announcement and their engagement, everything about his decisions that day—all of it would still be in the news tomorrow.

So that night all he wanted was this. A quiet evening with Emily and Clara.

Over fried chicken and mashed potatoes, Clara suddenly put down her fork and looked at him. Her smile took a few seconds and then filled every part of her face. "This," she said, "is the best . . . day of my whole . . . life."

Her words were slow with fits and starts and sometimes running together, but Noah and Emily understood exactly what she said. Noah reached across the table and took her hand. "It's my best day, too."

"And mine." Emily raised her iced tea.

Clara wasn't done. She looked from Noah to Emily and back again. "I prayed for this. Every day." She looked up, as if God's presence was hovering directly over her. Then with words brimming with hope and gratitude she finished her thought. "Thank You, God. You heard me. You see me!"

It was hard to eat chicken after that. Both Emily and he stood and walked over to Clara. They hugged her and made a circle together. Then they did something that would become a regular occurrence for the three of them.

They prayed.

When Clara went to bed that night, when she was happy in her room, still smiling in her sleep, Noah and Emily returned to the den. Noah started a playlist he'd made especially for that night.

The first song was Adele's "Make You Feel My Love."

"I thought it might be a good night for a dance." Noah held his hand out to her. That pale pink sweater and her baby blue eyes. The electricity when their hands touched and she stepped into his arms.

They had to be careful, especially now. Since they knew it was only a matter of time before they were married. Standing there alone with Emily, Noah was deeply aware of her. Every move she made, the feel of her arms around his shoulders. *Stay focused,* he told himself. *Don't let things get away from you.* He took a deep breath and looked into her eyes. It was important to God that they wait till they were married.

So it was important to him. To both of them.

But as they danced, as their bodies swayed together, a heat began to build that made Noah dizzy with anticipation. Gradually the music stopped and they stood there, lost in the moment, caught up in each other's nearness.

The kiss that happened next still took Noah's breath. It held all the feelings they'd ever had for each other. The longing and waiting, the times when Noah wasn't sure they'd ever be more than friends. Even the breakup that had happened last week.

All of it was there in that single kiss.

It started slow, but after a few minutes, Noah needed a break. "Come on." He took her hand and led her out to the front porch. Spring meant the nights were still cold. He stood next to her and pulled her close to his side. Together they turned their faces to the sky.

"It's beautiful." Emily's breathing was almost back to normal. As if she had needed the break, too. The night was clear, a sliver of the moon hanging off to the side. Every star in the sky seemed to sparkle just for them.

"Think about it." He looked at her. "God's going to let us look at those same stars every night together for the rest of our lives."

She smiled. "Even when we're a hundred."

The air between them grew more serious. Noah

brushed his thumb across her brow. "It'll never be enough. No matter how long we have."

One night a week later they were out front, a blanket over their laps, when Emily took a deep breath. "Can I tell you something?"

"Of course." Noah turned in his chair so he was facing her. "You sound serious."

"I was just thinking, how God works all things to the good for those who love Him."

"My favorite new Bible verse." Noah smiled. "Explain."

"Well, no one would've wanted you to get those concussions. I watched them both happen and"—she met his eyes—"honestly I've never been more scared in my life." She looked up at the sky.

"Me, too." He wasn't being cavalier. "And the good part is?"

Her smile warmed the night. "The good part is this. That we're here. That we're staying in Bloomington." Sincerity shone in her eyes. "I'm sorry about the NFL, Noah. You wanted it so much."

"I did." His voice held the weight of the situation. He leaned back on his hands. "But I want you more. It was my decision."

"I keep thinking how different life would be if you were in San Diego now." Her tone rang with hesitancy. "I told you I'd take Clara to San Diego and I would've. With all my heart I would've done my best to get her out there and try to make her fall in love with California." She shook her head. "But I don't think it would've worked."

Noah thought about that for a long moment. "I know. Clara wants to be here."

"She does." Emily smiled again, a tender look that told him she would always understand the cost Noah had paid to walk away from football and be here with her. To not take the chance with another head injury. "So that's what I've been thinking about. How God works everything out to the good."

Their love story kept playing through Noah's mind, the days of their engagement and as they headed into the summer and their fall wedding. By then their social media platforms were blowing up. The same magazines and news outlets that had reported on Noah's retirement from football covered the explosion of their numbers on Facebook and Twitter. Noah had added an account on Instagram, and that became crazy successful, too.

Everyone wanted a piece of them, the chance to bask in their love so that just maybe a bit of it might rub off. Emily didn't mind back then. In fact, on rainy nights they would sit on the sofa and read the comments left by their followers.

It wasn't long before a famous jeans brand was willing to pay them $50,000 a year if Noah would talk about their jeans once a month. Wear them once a week.

How hard would that be?

Sponsored posts, they were called. And after the jeans they were contacted by other advertisers. Rawlings wanted him to talk about their foam footballs and Sherwin-Williams painted the home where Emily and Clara had grown up. A free paint job and $100,000 for the year—all for the mention of Sherwin-Williams whenever they posted a picture in front of the house.

And on it went.

When their wedding came, a national men's clothing company provided free suits for Noah and the groomsmen—plus enough cash for an extravagant honeymoon. All for a mention and a photo. Noah went along with it easily. They were a light in a dark world. An example. Role models for young people.

Anyway, none of that held even a fraction of his attention when their wedding day finally came. Noah knew he could face consequences for his concussions later in life. He was at higher risk for losing his memory, for one thing. Headaches would be a given.

But even if he forgot everything else, he would remember forever the way Emily looked when she walked down the aisle toward him that day. Just her and the glow of the Holy Spirit around her.

She was a gift from God. The greatest blessing the Lord would ever give him. To think, out of all the guys in the world, Emily Andrews had chosen him.

They honeymooned for a few nights in a bed-and-breakfast and spent the rest of the week in New York City in the Ritz-Carlton on Park Avenue. Best suite in the house. Compliments of the manager, a woman who turned out to be a follower of theirs.

Every morning Noah woke up under those luxurious Ritz-Carlton sheets and looked over at Emily, sleeping like a princess beside him, her blond hair spilling across the pillow. And every morning he prayed the same thing. *Lord, I don't deserve her. Help me to cherish her. Every day for the rest of my life.*

When they got home, after the posts about the Ritz and other moments that highlighted their honeymoon, Noah returned to his job as a paramedic at the Bloomington Fire Department.

By then he worked twenty hours a week at the station, and spent the rest of his time on social media. It was sometime that year that a friend of his commented on their platform.

"Man, you're Internet famous." He chuckled. "Never saw that coming."

Internet famous. It was a term Noah hadn't heard before. But it made sense. By then, Noah was posting two or three times a day, enjoying it more all the time.

One night they were out to dinner with Clara, and Emily looked distant. Distracted, even. Noah reached for her hand. "You okay?"

"Sure." She smiled, but still she didn't seem like herself. "It's just . . . you posted about my burned cookies." She lifted her shoulders and searched his eyes. "Why, Noah? Can't some things be just for us?"

He apologized and tried to register her words as a warning. "I'll be more careful."

And he was. But still sometimes Emily thought his

posts went too far. It was one thing to share about their wedding and where they went on their honeymoon. But she didn't want people knowing about her fears or failures. Some things had to be just for them.

Even still, at that point Emily was on board with the process, believing that good things were coming of their public persona. But Noah felt her concern.

On their first anniversary, he made her a promise. He would keep some things private, of course. And he would be very careful that the posts reflected their lives. And not the other way around. If that ever happened, he made her another promise. He would pull the plug on all things social media.

But he didn't.

With every passing year, their following grew and Noah became more committed to it. So committed that he hadn't seen the troubling signs even when they were right in front of his face. Proof that Emily was pulling away from him, bit by bit. Even though he knew she was disappointed in the time he spent on the computer, he had thousands of people cheering him on. Every day. Every post.

So he didn't let up.

Not until the morning when Emily spoke five painful words over breakfast, words Noah never thought he'd hear.

"I think we're in trouble."

Of course, by then it wasn't just Emily's notion or a concern about what the fans would believe. They really were in trouble. But even still Noah didn't know how to do anything but keep taking pictures and finding Bible verses and encouraging quotes to share. Keep posting and pretending. As if by breathing life into their Internet presence, he might breathe life into their marriage.

When in fact the truth was quite the opposite.

Noah was killing it with his own two hands.

21

The sun wasn't close to coming up yet, but still Kari couldn't sleep. She'd gone from Jessie's room to the sofa, and the sofa back to her bed. All while trying not to wake up Ryan. But now she gave up on sleep altogether. With near-silent movements, she slid out of bed again and made her way to the kitchen. Might as well do something useful. The bills needed paying so she flipped on a light, grabbed the mail folder and sat at the table.

She was forty minutes through the stack of things to pay when she heard something behind her.

Even with her back to him, Kari knew it was Ryan. She could feel him watching her. She finished writing out one more check, slipped it into the envelope, and hesitated. They still hadn't found their way back to the love and deep connection they were familiar with. Every hour drew them closer to the announcement coming Sunday. And the awful reality of the move to Arizona grew.

"Kari." His voice was quiet, but heavy with emotion. "Can you look at me?"

Kari took a quick breath and turned around in her

chair. He was probably here to fix the tension between them. He might apologize again for accepting the position. Beg her to understand. Explain that he was having trouble sleeping, too.

But as soon as their eyes connected, Kari knew she was wrong.

Her husband seemed broken, like something terrible had happened. He held a large manila envelope, and with slow steps he came toward her. "I . . . I found this."

Whatever it was, the impact clearly had been dramatic. Kari stood and crossed the kitchen to meet him. She took the envelope, but never looked away from him. Instead she waited for an explanation.

"Open it." Tears brimmed in his eyes.

Her heart beat harder than before. Whatever the contents, they had rocked Ryan's world. That much was evident. She glanced down and noticed her hands. They were shaking. What was inside? Was it his contract with University of Arizona?

She steadied herself, loosened the fastener at the flap and pulled out a document. The six pages were immediately familiar. Her eyes found the top of the first page. *Elizabeth Baxter's 10 Secrets to a Happy Marriage.* Tears blurred her vision and she blinked them away. This was the list her mother had made before she died. Ten ways her kids might have the type of marriage she and Kari's father had shared.

Right up until cancer took her from them.

Kari crossed the kitchen and returned to the chair at

the table. Ryan followed and took the seat next to her. For more than a minute Kari read her mother's words. The first secret was the most obvious. *Divorce is* not *an option*. Kari blinked a few times. Of course not.

A move to Arizona could never be reason enough for Kari to consider leaving Ryan. Nothing ever would be. Without looking up she reached over and took Ryan's hand. He clung to hers like they'd been apart for weeks.

Kari kept reading. Her mother's next secret was the one Kari had been trying to do. Something she and Emily had texted about earlier.

Marriage is not 50/50.

She scanned the paragraph below.

A happy marriage means putting God first and your spouse second. Period. You, yourself, are no longer on the list of what matters most. It's pretty simple; God has you here to serve one another. Love acted out is serving. Giving 100% of yourself to your spouse.

Kari closed her eyes. Of all the times for Ryan to bring this to her. She was trying to put him first, even if she didn't like the outcome. She looked at him. "Where did you find it?"

"In our closet." He searched her eyes, her heart. "It's a long story. Anyway, I don't know, Kari. I've been thinking about us, and the announcement to the kids." He sighed. "I found this and decided to read your mom's words again. After I did, I thought maybe you'd want to read them, too."

A frustration spread through Kari. Was he trying to show her how wrong she was? That she should be happy for him because that's what the Bible said? But still her mother's words pressed in deep against her soul. How selfish had she been feeling lately? Worried about a move more than the man she married?

She blinked and turned to face Ryan. "I don't know what would've led you to the closet." She lifted the pages a few inches. "Or how you knew what I was feeling." Tears fell onto her cheeks. Her words were strained, her heart breaking. "But this . . . it's exactly what I've been trying to do. Please don't tell me how I'm failing at it."

Confusion lined his forehead. "That's . . . not why I brought it to you."

"What?" Kari shook her head. "I don't understand. And why now, in the middle of the night?"

"It's a crazy story." Still holding her hand, Ryan rested his elbows on his knees, his face closer to hers. "I was sound asleep and something woke me up." He paused. "Or Someone." He looked at the document and then back to Kari. "You weren't in bed, so I got up to look for you. But there was a light on in the closet."

A light? "I didn't leave it on."

"Me, either." He raised both his shoulders, the beginning of a smile at the corners of his lips. "I have no idea. But there—on the floor—was this envelope."

"On the floor of the closet?"

"Yes." He straightened and leaned back. "Kari . . . I spent the last half hour reading it, and praying about everything your mother believed about marriage." His eyes shone with the impact he had apparently experienced. He reached out for the pages. "May I?"

Kari released his hand and gave them over.

"I feel like I was just sitting with your mother." Sadness colored his eyes again. "It made me remember how much I miss her." He looked at the printed pages and seemed to search for a specific section. "Here. Listen to this. It's from your mom's second point. Marriage is not 50/50."

A wave of anticipation came over Kari. Where was Ryan going with this?

He began to read. "'The Bible is very clear about men and women's roles in marriage. The Bible says that the man must love as Christ loved the church, laying down his life for his wife.'" He stopped and looked right at her. All the way to her heart. "I haven't been doing that, Kari. I made the decision about Arizona with almost no discussion." He hesitated. "I assumed it was from God because it came my way. Without any real thought of you."

"Ryan . . ." She could feel her heart softening.

"There's more." He found his place on the page again. "When a man loves like that, when he leads like that, a woman can easily respect him. That marriage will work beautifully, and both husband and wife will win."

He set the document down and took hold of her

hands. "You've respected me from the minute I brought up the possibility of the move." His voice fell, his words colored with obvious pain. "But you were also honest."

She winced. "A little too honest."

"No." He released her hands and picked up the document again. For a long while he stared at it, turning the pages. "Every word your mom wrote. Every bit of wisdom spoke to me tonight." He set the document down and found her eyes again. "I'm wrong, Kari. You have a right to share your thoughts on something like this." He uttered a sad laugh. "I was so excited about the offer I didn't give a whole lot of consideration to the impact on you and the kids. What it would be like leaving our family here in Bloomington."

Kari couldn't believe this was happening. It was the middle of the night and somehow Ryan had found her mother's deepest thoughts on marriage and read them. And now . . . now she could hardly breathe. "I'm willing to move, Ryan." She crossed her arms. A shiver worked its way down her spine. "You know that."

"I do." He leaned forward and touched her face. "You'd do anything for me. Go anywhere." He sighed. "But this time around it's my turn."

The sky was still dark outside, the house still quiet. Kari searched his eyes. "I . . . I'm not sure what you mean."

The resolve in his voice was undeniable. "I'm turning down the job, Kari. We're staying here."

Her heartbeat quickened. What was he saying? She

squeezed Ryan's hand. They weren't moving to Arizona? Was he serious? "But . . ." Her thoughts swirled and she searched for the right words. "You really want this. It'd be huge for you. You said so yourself."

"Yes. All true." Passion rang in his voice. "But did you hear your mom's words? They're in the Bible. In Ephesians. I knew that, of course. But I looked them up before I came down to the kitchen." He relaxed a little, like his decision was already made. "It's not only that I'm *supposed* to lay down my life for you, Kari." He stood and eased her to her feet and into his arms. With their faces inches apart, he lowered his voice to a whisper. "I *want* to."

Suddenly Kari felt terrible. If she hadn't complained, he wouldn't consider turning down the job. "People don't just walk away from a position like this." She put her hand on his cheek and looked deep into his eyes. "I said I'd move, and I mean it."

He shook his head. "No." He smiled. "My mind is made up." He kissed her forehead. "I'll put my résumé in at Indiana and again with Jim Flanigan and the Colts. If God wants me to leave Clear Creek High, it'll be obvious to both of us."

The new truth was hitting her in waves. They weren't moving, weren't walking away from family and friends and all that they knew here in Bloomington. "Ryan." She hung her head. Tears stung her eyes, but she didn't cry. She was too overcome with joy and relief. "Are you sure?"

"Completely." He moved in closer and kissed her lips. "I got carried away. The offer, the idea of heading up a major college program." He was still talking in quiet tones, careful not to wake the kids. "Then I thought about Emily and Noah."

Kari nodded. "They need my mom's wisdom."

"Exactly." Ryan looked deep into her eyes again. "It's easy for me to look at Noah and blame him for making social media more important than his wife and kids." He hesitated. "But social media is his job. And that's when it hit me, there in our room. Reading those ten secrets." He took a long breath. "I was doing the same thing. Making my job more important than you and the kids and the life we've built here."

For all the time Kari had spent thinking about the move and telling the kids they were leaving Bloomington, she had never dreamed the situation might end like this. "I . . . can't believe it."

"God had the final say." He smiled, and for the first time in a few weeks he looked like himself. The Ryan who loved her more than his own life. "God and your mother. Can't beat that." He brushed his knuckles against her cheek. "I sure do miss her."

"Me, too." For a moment neither of them said anything. "I can't believe the envelope was just sitting on the closet floor."

His eyes softened. "Like I was supposed to find it."

"Maybe so." Kari could feel the muscles in her neck and shoulders relax. Everything she'd been dreading wasn't going to happen after all. "You've always loved me, Ryan. With everything in you. But this . . ." Her throat was too tight to finish.

"I know." He kissed her again, longer this time. "This is home. For all of us." He whispered the words near her face. He took her hand. "Let's go to bed. I have a feeling a certain young couple will need us tomorrow."

Kari nodded. "Definitely." She slid her fingers between his and followed him up to their room. She'd never seen tonight ending up like this. But God had done what only He could do. He had worked a miracle in their love and their lives.

Now she could only pray He would do the same for Noah and Emily.

22

Noah sat straight up, gasping for breath. This time his dream had scared him. He had never wanted their social media presence to get the best of him, never imagined it would come between Emily and him.

No way.

He was almost afraid to get out of bed and look out the window. It was summer yesterday, he and the kids had the best day at the park. Now his window was open again, and once more the wind was warm. The way it was yesterday.

Good. He exhaled. Maybe his memory was coming back. He'd lost so much, so many years. It was about time he started tracking with the passing days. So he could make good on his promises. Spend more time with the kids.

Then like he was just realizing the news for the first time, Noah remembered what Aiden and Olivia had told him. He had moved out when they were little. He pictured the strange man driving away with his wife and kids.

And the ring on her left hand.

It's okay, Noah. One step at a time. Lord, help me find my life again.

He had a lot to do, especially assuming this was Sunday. First he wanted a meeting with Emily. She wasn't married yet; at least he didn't think so. The kids hadn't mentioned it. So that meant there was still time.

From the edge of his bed, he could see just a glimpse of the sky out the window. *God, if I can just get her to talk to me.* First, he'd call her and tell her he was sorry. If the social media was in the way, he'd be done with it. Whatever it took. If he had it to do over again, he never would've left. No way.

If only she'd sit down with him, he would go over all the pieces of their past, the beautiful ones he'd been dreaming about and the sad years he'd missed. He'd bring up their dinner dates in the Indiana cafeteria and the times he'd watched her dance. He'd tell her how much he loved Clara and missed her.

And he'd tell her that only she knew what he'd gone through during his concussions. He wouldn't be here today if she hadn't nursed him back to health. He wouldn't have left football for anyone but her, and no one else had ever loved him like she did.

How was it possible? Could he really have walked away? When he still loved her with every breath? When he was dying to hold her?

His phone started to ring, and Noah looked around. As he did, a terrible feeling hit him. The carpet was the same ratty gray, but the walls were a different color. Dark gray paint. What did that mean for him? Had more time passed? He couldn't stand the thought. The phone was still ringing, so he hurried out of bed and found it on the dresser.

"Hello?" Noah was breathing harder than before. He could see the mirror now, and once again he looked different. Older. More lines around his mouth and across his forehead. Gray tinged his sideburns. He closed his eyes and focused on the call.

"It's me." Emily's voice sounded unhappy. "You need to be there at eleven o'clock, Noah. At Clear Creek. It's important to her."

Eleven o'clock. He shook his head, forcing himself to concentrate. "Today?"

"Yes, today." Her tone grew frustrated. "Her graduation is today, Noah . . . don't act like you don't know."

Whose graduation, he wanted to ask. Certainly not Olivia's. She was just swinging beside him at the park, just calling him Daddy and asking him to catch her as she fell. "At Clear Creek High? Is that what you're saying?"

"Where would you expect Olivia's graduation to take place?" She released a pent-up breath. "Just be there, Noah. We're losing her. You know that, right?"

Noah was afraid to say anything. "She's on the phone too much. I know that."

For a few seconds Emily didn't respond. "The phone? You think that's her problem?" A bitter laugh sounded across the line. "She's smoking pot, Noah. Sleeping with some guy from juvenile hall. She's a complete mess."

No. He shook his head and covered his face with his free hand. Not his Olivia. *Livi, sweetie, what happened?* None of this could be true. "I thought she was into dance?"

Emily made an angry sound. "See, this is what I can't stand about you. She's not thirteen. She hasn't danced since you missed her last recital the year she turned fourteen. Remember that?"

Not a bit, he wanted to say. But he didn't want her to think he was crazy. His head was hurting again. "I've . . . I've been a terrible father."

"It's good to hear you admit it." Her words were sharp, her tone even more so. "If only you hadn't promised them you'd be there." She exhaled. "You don't know what it's like to sit in the stands and watch Aiden's games and see him look all over the stadium for you. After every single play."

He had been a terrible, wretched father. How could he have let things get so bad?

She had more to say. "You don't know what it was like to talk to our crying daughter after every dance recital you missed, promising her that yes, Daddy still loved her. He just forgot how to actually be a father."

The pounding in his head was getting worse. Had he been to a doctor in all these years? Was this really his life, missing years at a time? Every word from Emily cut deep. Noah could only figure he hadn't attended his kids' events because his memory was such a mess. He couldn't remember a thing and now his kids had paid the price.

Football had done him in, after all.

Noah changed gears. "So eleven o'clock at the school. I'll see you there." He needed to bring up the idea of a conversation. Now was as good a time as any. "And, Emily, I wonder if the two of us could get something to eat after." He missed her so much. He wanted to feel her in his arms again. "Just the two of us. We really need to talk."

Another sigh. "Noah, Bob and I are throwing the graduation party. You're welcome to come, but clearly this afternoon is not the time for you and me to talk."

"Bob?" He spoke the one-word question before he could stop himself.

"Okay, now I'm actually worried about you." She was definitely running out of patience. "Yes, Bob. My husband." She seemed to let that sink in. "He and I are throwing Olivia's graduation party." This time her tone softened. "Besides, what would you and I talk about? You've let the kids down time and time again. You've hurt them, Noah. I really don't have anything to say to you."

Noah slid to the floor. How could he blame her? He swallowed hard. "I understand. I'll see you there, Emily."

After the call, Noah checked the time. Ten o'clock. He had one hour to get ready and get to the school. He struggled to his feet. Every movement made him feel old. Like a man twice his age. Whatever Olivia thought about him, Noah couldn't change that now. But he would be there this time.

While he brushed his teeth and dressed, and during the entire drive to Clear Creek High, fear stayed right next to him, grabbing at his throat time and again. Olivia was eighteen and dating a thug? She was smoking pot? Noah hated all of this. But what could he do now? It was his fault she was this way. He had ignored his kids and failed them on a hundred levels. Of course she was a mess.

He found Emily in the school gymnasium. Noah ignored the Bob guy standing next to her. He refused to acknowledge the man with more than a brief nod. Bob wasn't Emily's husband. Noah was. He had promised her forever a lifetime ago, and he meant it. He still meant it. "So . . . the ceremony is in here?"

"Yes." She looked him up and down. "You look nice." It wasn't so much a compliment as a statement of relief. "Thank you for putting in the effort."

It was obvious she was making clear just one point. In every way that mattered, Noah had been a terrible father. The absolute worst. And for that he was deeply sorry. But he couldn't talk about that here. Not now. Instead he smiled at her. "Of course." He looked toward the stage. "Where's Olivia? Can we see her before it starts?"

Emily seemed to weigh that. "You can try." She shrugged. "Might make her whole day. That girl would do anything to get your attention."

Again Noah's headache pounded against his skull. The comments just kept coming, all of them telling him the same thing. He walked to the stage and jogged up the stairs, where he was about to go behind the heavy velvet curtain when a tall, handsome young man approached him. Noah squinted. In the dim lighting, he wasn't sure but . . . this had to be Aiden. His boy all grown up.

He got closer and it was obvious. This was definitely Aiden. "Son." Noah did his best not to make the word a question.

"Dad." He looked frustrated. He lowered his voice and glanced over his shoulder. "Why are *you* back here?" He took a step closer. "You're just going to make things worse."

Noah tried to think of something to say. "I . . . I love her, Aiden. It's her graduation."

"Yeah, well." Aiden reached into the back pocket of his black jeans and pulled out a folded envelope. "I wrote this. In case you actually showed up." He handed the letter to Noah. "Just so you have even the slightest idea how I feel about you." His pause held the weight of the world. "How all of us feel."

"Okay." Noah's head pounded in time to his heartbeat. He peered behind the curtain. "So . . . you think I should talk to her later?"

For a long moment Aiden just drilled his eyes into Noah's. "I don't think you should talk to her at all." He gave a single, angry shake of his head. "But that's just me." Without waiting for any response, Aiden started to back up. Then he stopped himself. "I'm sitting with Mom and Bob. Maybe you could find a different spot."

Noah nodded. "Yeah." Did his kids really hate him so much? He didn't want to think about what else he'd done over the years to warrant this. He tried to stay in the moment. His voice sounded like it might break, his heart filled with apology. "Yeah, I'll do that."

Aiden turned to leave.

"Wait." Noah reached for him, but stopped short.

His son turned back around one last time. "I gotta go, Dad." Impatience marked his voice. Not the disrespect of a fifteen-year-old, but the certain disdain of one man to another. "What is it?"

There were a hundred things Noah wanted to say. But only one mattered. "I'm sorry." He shook his head and looked off for a minute, at a past broken in tiny day-size pieces. All that he could recall. "I don't remember everything I did to let you and Olivia down. To hurt you two."

"And Mom," Aiden cut in.

"Yes." Noah locked eyes with Aiden again. "And Mom." He exhaled, dizzy from the pain in his head. "But I'm sorry. I'm just so very sorry." He hesitated. "Please believe me."

He wanted to run to Aiden and take him in his arms, undo all the terrible ways he'd abandoned his son. Build something better. Starting today. Didn't Aiden know? He would walk through fire for his son. Whatever it took. Except Noah hadn't done that at all. He hadn't walked through fire. He had walked out instead. He whispered the words once more. "I'm sorry."

A long pause, then Aiden nodded. "Yeah, Dad." His eyes softened, just enough to give him away. "That much I believe." He gave a final sad look at Noah and then walked off the stage.

A minute passed while Noah stood there, his son's letter in his hands. Gradually he made sense of things the way they were. Aiden's harsh words weren't just because he hated Noah or felt disgust for him. Those things were probably true. But the real reason Aiden felt this way was because he was so hurt. Deeply hurt. The kind of pain that could only be inflicted on a boy by his father.

A father who had walked away when that child was just four years old. Aiden might be grown, he might be a man ready to take on the world. But that little boy still lived inside him. He still wanted nothing more than a daddy who stayed.

Noah had seen all that in Aiden's eyes. And there wasn't a thing he could do about it.

The ceremony passed in a blur. Noah's headache wouldn't let up, but he stayed focused. He watched his little girl step onto the stage, her blond hair short and spiky with pink-dyed tips.

She looked sure of herself, but hard at the same time. Like she'd fought an army of demons to get here. Noah narrowed his eyes and suddenly she wasn't eighteen in a cap and gown. She was his Livi, toddling across the floor to him, arms open wide.

Daddy! . . . Hold me, Daddy.

And he was picking her up and swinging her around

in his arms and thinking how she looked like her mama. And Clara, too. The innocence in her eyes was Clara's. And he was whispering into her ear, "I love you, Livi. . . . Daddy will always be here for you."

But he hadn't kept his promise.

From his dark seat in the back, away from Emily and Bob and Aiden, tears filled his eyes and ran down his cheeks. He had let his baby girl down every way a daddy could. He blinked and the memory disappeared. Instead there she was, eighteen and angry, taking her diploma and moving ahead without smiling or even shaking the principal's hand. Her contempt for school and authority was palpable.

Noah wondered if everyone else in the gym could feel it.

When the ceremony was over, when parents and family members were gathered around their graduates, congratulating them and taking pictures, Noah slipped to the back of the room and grabbed a Styrofoam cup of black coffee. He hung there and watched. Emily and Bob and Aiden approached Olivia, and for the first time that day, he saw the defiance in her eyes let up. She smiled at Emily and hugged her. For a long time. As if the two of them had survived some terrible ordeal. The way soldiers looked when they'd survived a war together.

The sight burned through Noah's heart. He felt the truth hit him like a kick to the stomach. He was the ordeal. He was the war. No getting around that now.

Noah looked up in time to see Bob hug her. Whatever he said, his words must've been kind because they both smiled and hugged again. Bob, the good guy. The one who had taken over Noah's family. The guy who had stepped in when he stepped out.

Stepped up when Noah stepped down.

The weight of it all made it hard for Noah to breathe. Okay, so he'd made the terrible decision to walk out on Emily. But why hadn't he been a better father? What could've made him miss his children's special moments? Was it his aching head? The memory loss? Noah tried to focus.

Next Aiden walked up and hugged Olivia. But it was clear the two weren't close. Or maybe Aiden was disappointed in her. Something was off.

After a few minutes, Olivia pulled away to talk to another student. Noah watched her go. This was his chance to make a move. If he didn't talk to her now, he would lose his opportunity. But she hadn't seen him yet, so she was starting to turn away.

"Olivia!" He cupped his hands around his mouth. "Olivia! Wait."

His voice seemed to startle her. In slow motion she turned and looked at him. For a fraction of an instant he saw his little girl in her eyes. His Livi. But then just as fast it was replaced by anger. An anger that took Noah's breath.

Never mind. Nothing could keep Noah from her now. He walked straight up to her and put his hand on her shoulder. "You did it!" He forced himself to sound excited. Pushed himself to ignore the way Olivia smelled faintly of pot. Just like Emily had said. He looked past the dark circles under her eyes.

"What are you doing?" She brushed his hand from her shoulder.

"Olivia, please." He lowered his voice. "I'm here to support you." He tried to find a smile. "Congratulations." The uncertainty in his tone felt awkward even to him. "I'm proud of you."

She took a step back. "I told Mom I didn't want you to come."

That wasn't what Emily had said. Panic tightened its grip around Noah's throat. What was he supposed to say? "I . . . wanted to be here. I wouldn't miss it." He wanted her to really hear him. The things in his heart. "Look, whatever I've done in the past, I'm sorry. I never . . . ever meant to hurt you."

Her eyes grew darker, meaner. "Well, you did." She shook her head. "It's too late." She lifted her chin and shot her final words like arrows. "Go home, Dad. I'm done here."

Noah tried to follow her. He made every effort to stand nearby with his cup of coffee as Olivia talked with her friends and teachers. If she could see him, she didn't act like it. After half an hour Noah went home. Back to the apartment.

The little box with the same matted carpet where he'd apparently lived since he walked out on his family.

Not until he dropped to the chair by his living room

window did he pull out Aiden's envelope and open it. The letter inside wasn't long, but it was full of rage and pain. Even his printing looked angry.

Noah sighed and remembered the hurt in his son's eyes. Then he started at the top.

Dad,

Mom said you might come to the graduation today. I haven't seen you in almost a year, so I decided to write to you. Just in case we ran into each other.

Olivia and I had a talk the other day. You probably know by now, she's struggling. I'm worried about her. A lot. Anyway she still talks to me.

She told me the other day that every morning she wakes up, looks in the mirror and asks herself two questions. "Why did my dad walk out on me?" and "Why didn't he want me?" Those two questions have shaped her and haunted her and driven her to be the person she is today.

You know what I think? Olivia's the person she is today because she was trying so hard to find answers to those questions. Here's what I told Olivia. When those questions hit, remind yourself of the truth.

Every single time.

Tell yourself that none of this is your fault. It's not her fault or my fault. It's not Mom's fault. The reason we're all such a mess is because of you,

Dad. You're the one who walked out. You're the one who didn't call or show up or care to be close to us. Selfish pride or a crazy need for fame. Whatever the reason, it wasn't our fault. I know that now.

Noah's hands shook so hard he could barely read his son's words. Tears ran down his cheeks, and his head pulsed with pain. It was all really true. He had walked away when they were little and never looked back. For what? For a social media platform? For fame? He rubbed his palm across his eyes so he could see. Then he kept reading.

The hardest part is that every now and then you'd come around. You'd hang out with us at your apartment or take us to the park. And for just the shortest minute, Olivia and I would believe. We would actually believe that you would come to her dance recitals and sit in the bleachers for my games. Not once in five years, but every game. Every season. Every dance performance.

But no, that never happened. Everything you said was a lie, Dad. Every word. Your whole social media garbage. All that was a lie, too. All you cared about was yourself. So now, I have a request. I won't ask for anything from you again. Just this.

Please, Dad, will you get out of our lives for good? Don't make us wonder if and when you'll show up. Don't look at us like we're four and two again and like you might somehow find a way to fix everything. It's broken. Forever. So go. Stay out of our lives so we can find a way to heal.

Because I don't care what the cool kids or the psychologists or every separated parent says. Divorce is hell for kids. That's the way I see it. You cut us to the core when you walked out of our lives.

But you walked. It was your choice. Now, please, shut the door behind you so we can lock it.

Once and for all.

Aiden

Noah was crying hard now. He stared at his son's final words and folded the paper, slipped it back into the envelope. Aiden was right. Noah had ruined everything. His kids would always hate him because of it. Even if he never talked to them again, the awful thoughts would come. Why did he leave? How come he didn't love them enough to stay? And the worst one:

Why didn't he want them?

The questions hung like daggers over Noah's head and one by one they began to fall, cutting him and shattering his heart and soul. He moved to the window and stared at the gray sky. "God, help me!" His voice was barely a whisper. Like he wasn't sure how to do this anymore. "I . . . I need a miracle, Lord." He hung his head. "Look what I've done to my kids." His voice grew louder. "Please, help me!"

There was no response, no great comfort from above.

And of course not. Noah couldn't remember the last time he'd prayed or read his Bible. It only made sense that even the Lord had given up on him. But still he gripped the window frame and prayed. He had no choice. God was his only hope. He was out of options. Noah had no one and no answers for the sort of man he had become.

Aiden's letter had said it all.

23

Emily left the photo album on the sofa and walked to the window in the den. The sun was rising in the distance, casting subtle pinks and yellows across the morning sky. Emily stood there, frozen in place. And while the world around her got lighter, she was consumed with just one wish.

That dawn might never come. So there would never be a time when Noah would climb in his truck and drive away. Noah, who had loved her and Clara so well. Emily closed her eyes.

Clara.

Sweet Sister, how I miss you. Emily blinked back fresh tears. *I miss you every day.*

Emily still had an hour before the kids would be up. If she was going to remember the past, she couldn't stop here. She grabbed a blanket from the sofa and took it to the office. The place where Noah had undone their marriage one post at a time.

The room where she had criticized him and yelled at him more times than she could count. Losing their marriage was both their faults. She could see that now. After

Clara died, Emily didn't want to smile for Noah's camera or pretend everything was okay. She became snappy and mean when Noah talked about their platform or when he shared an encouraging comment from a follower.

They should've taken a break from the Internet back then. She should've told Noah she was too sad to smile for the public. Instead she let a wedge grow between them. Yes, Noah should've been more in tune with her feelings. But why hadn't she taken even a single hour to discuss the situation? With kind words, asking for his understanding?

She could remember a time when their Bible study group talked about the importance of treating each other with kindness and respect. Smiling. Patient voices. That sort of thing. But Emily hadn't heeded Ryan and Kari's wisdom at all.

A memory came back to her. A time after Clara died, when she walked into the kitchen and saw Noah clearing the table, setting up two coffee cups and a bouquet of flowers.

Emily could remember the way everything about the moment grated on her last nerve. "Really, Noah? You're going to do this?" She put her hands on her hips. "We aren't having coffee, so why pretend? It's all so . . . fake."

Just thinking about her harsh tone from that time made her wince. How could she have talked to him like that? Noah Carter, the man she loved?

Emily sighed as she sat down in the desk chair. The

obsession with social media was Noah's fault, for sure. But Emily understood her role in their breakup so much better after staying up all night. The memory of her younger self was so different from the person she'd become. And her attitude and expression and voice had grown almost mean toward him.

With a sadness she couldn't possibly shake, Emily faced the window and covered her legs with the blanket. It was chillier now. That or she was just terrified of the morning. If only it weren't so early, she'd call Kari and beg her for something, anything that might change the outcome of the next few hours.

But Noah's mind was made up.

She stared outside to the world beyond. The sky above the trees. Another breath and then her vision blurred. More memories came. And the beautiful time after their first year of marriage was suddenly real and vibrant and playing out again right in front of her.

After the wedding, Emily started teaching dance at a local studio while Noah continued working part-time as a paramedic for the Bloomington Fire Department. It was a job he loved, and something to fall back on. If the Internet fame ever wore off.

But all the while Noah kept up their social media posts. At least three a day. Photos from breakfast or a coffee date down the street, the two of them walking through downtown Bloomington while Clara was at her occupational school. And their numbers continued to grow.

Then the spring following their third anniversary, Emily began feeling an all-day kind of nausea. One Saturday while Noah was at work, she and Clara drove to the nearest Walgreens. Emily tried to be sly about her real reason for stopping at the store. She filled the cart with a case of water bottles and some Advil for Noah's occasional headaches. Finally she made her way down an unfamiliar aisle and after a quick look she dropped the next item in the cart.

A pregnancy test.

Clara positioned one crutch against the cart and leaned on the other one. Then she removed the box from the cart and stared at it. Like Christmas morning, a smile came over her that left no doubt. Clara understood. Her eyes lifted to Emily's. "Baby? You?"

Emily grinned. "We'll see."

She took the test before Noah got home, only because she didn't really think she was pregnant. A flu bug had been going around Bloomington. Maybe it was that. But moments later, the lines appeared. Two of them.

Since Clara had been with her at the store, Emily brought the results to the living room. Clara was at the table drawing trees. She loved trees. And at the sound of Emily's footsteps, Clara looked up. She saw the white plastic stick in Emily's hand and instantly she was on her feet, leaning against the table so she wouldn't fall.

"Baby? Yes, Emily?" Her words were as exuberant as they were loud. "God, please, baby!"

Emily held up the test, and she could feel the hope

and possibility in her smile. "Yes!" A single laugh came from her, because she still couldn't believe it. "A baby, Clara. We're having a baby!"

Clara grabbed her crutches and came painstakingly around the table. Then she fell into Emily's arms and started to cry. At first Emily thought something was wrong. She pulled back and looked at her sister, and as soon as she did, she knew. Clara was crying tears of happiness. "You and Noah." She blinked a few times and then she laughed, too. "A baby!"

Noah's reaction was just as unforgettable. When he came home that night, Emily and Clara were waiting for him. The plan was for Emily to tell him first. She had the results in her hand ready to show him.

But as soon as he opened the door, Clara blurted out the news. "Baby! Emily has a baby!"

At first Noah dropped his keys and wallet and looked from Clara to Emily and back again. "Clara . . . for real?"

"Yes!" She jumped around, best she could.

Noah wore his dark blue paramedic outfit, his face smeared with ash from whatever calamity he had helped with that day. His eyes found Emily's again and she felt her face light up. She gave him just the slightest nod. "Yes, Noah." She held up the stick. "We're having a baby."

He walked inside, his mouth open. Shock and joy and disbelief filling his expression. "You . . . you're pregnant?" Before she could respond he picked her up. The way he had done when he asked her to marry him. "We're having a baby!"

"Yes!" Clara was still celebrating.

And there in the midst of that moment, a thought occurred to Emily. These really were the days when they were young. When they were becoming a family and showing the world what love looked like. Just like their social media platform claimed. Noah and her, working hard for their family, and then coming home one evening to the news that would change their lives forever. They were going to be parents.

She could feel his arms around her again, smell the mix of his cologne and the smoke from his uniform. She could sense the touch of his face against hers as they kissed. Life was a rare and beautiful gift and Emily knew—she absolutely knew—each chapter in their story would only get more wonderful.

Clara was Emily's greatest cheerleader in the months that followed. Emily was sick day and night for the first trimester and well into the second. She would be on the sofa, curled on her side, a bowl nearby just in case. And her sister would know exactly what she needed.

Even with her crutches, she would hobble into the kitchen and find something to help Emily. A glass of orange juice or a box of crackers. A piece of string cheese. Clara would forgo one of her crutches in her effort to bring Emily what might make her feel better.

One afternoon Clara made her a peanut butter and jelly sandwich. During that pregnancy, PBJs were Emily's favorite. One of the few things Emily could keep down. Clara set it on a pretty tray and added a single plastic flower. Somehow she carried it with one hand and set it down on the coffee table.

Then she nudged Emily awake. "Time to eat." She sounded so sincere, so concerned. "The baby hungry."

Emily struggled to sit up, the nausea practically crippling her. She wasn't hungry, but Clara was right. She needed to eat. Noah was always telling her the same thing. At that point, four months in, she weighed less than before she got pregnant.

Emily looked at Clara and realized something profound. How much she needed her sister. All her life she'd looked after Clara, and now Clara was looking after her. Emily took hold of Clara's hand and lifted it to her own cheek. "You are my best friend, Clara. Do you know that?"

Her sister beamed. "Always and forever."

Emily and Noah decided not to find out the baby's gender. Only Clara seemed to know Emily was carrying a boy. She would walk up to Emily in the kitchen or when they were on the porch and she'd place her hand on Emily's bump. "Sweet baby boy." She would smile and look at Emily. "What his name?"

The two sisters would laugh, because even Clara knew there was no real way of telling yet. Not without a test. But Clara was sure all the same. So when Aiden was born that fall, Clara grinned at Emily and shrugged her shoulders. "I knew."

"Yes." Emily smiled at her sister. "You always know, Clara."

There was no better daddy anywhere than Noah.

From the moment he first held Aiden, he was utterly smitten. That week he asked his boss if he could cut his hours down to twelve a week. By then, their number of followers was at an all-time high. With more followers came more money, more clicks meant more paying sponsors.

"Even if the Internet money dries up completely, I want to work less hours," Noah told her one night when he was holding baby Aiden. "I love being here with you two and Clara." He drew Emily into his arms. "Every hour I'm away, my heart is here with you."

She could still hear him breathing those words against her face. *Every hour I'm away, my heart is here with you.* When had he stopped feeling that way? When had she stopped believing it?

Every now and then, Clara would make her way to Noah when they were all in the living room. Her eyes and smile would light up and she'd look straight into Noah's face. "Forever, right?"

And Noah would take her hand and nod his head. "Forever and ever."

"Daddies don't . . . always . . . leave." She said it all the time after Aiden was born. Almost like a game, where they each knew the script.

"Not this daddy." Noah would put his hand alongside Clara's cheek. "Not ever."

Emily and Noah had talked about Clara's need to repeat it so often. Emily was certain Clara remembered what it was like having her father walk out the door. And so no matter what happened, Clara didn't want that for Emily and Noah. She knew they couldn't take it.

And Clara couldn't, either.

A bit of cold air drifted through the office and Emily shivered again. She tucked the blanket in tight around her legs. Why was it so cold?

It was raining outside again, another thunderstorm headed their way. Fitting, she thought. On a day like this. She closed her eyes and let the rest of the story come.

Aiden was the most delightful baby, the happiest little boy. Since Noah was home more, every morning they got him out of his crib together and took him to the front window so Aiden could see the birdies. By the time he was nine months old he would point outside and flap his elbows. "Tweet, tweet!" he would cry out.

And Noah would kiss Aiden's cheek. "That's right, buddy."

Emily would join in. "Good morning, birdies. Good morning, day." And Aiden would try to say everything she did.

Emily wanted to capture every moment and save it for some far-off day. She couldn't imagine Aiden growing up and getting married. He was theirs and they were his and every morning began a greater adventure than the one before.

When Aiden was one, they would pile in the car and drive to Lower Cascades Park. "Swing, swing," Aiden would cry out, his face the purest picture of happiness.

Clara would come with them and sometimes she would leave one of her crutches on the nearest bench and join them, pushing Aiden in his swing.

It wasn't only laughter and love that marked their every day back then. It was the Lord, too. Noah led them in a prayer every morning and every night. Aiden was always first to say "Amen!" And when Clara and Aiden were asleep, Noah and Emily would read the Bible together.

Sure Noah would find a way to make a social media splash of all of it. But Emily convinced herself she didn't mind. They were being a light to the world, right? Sharing what was good and right and true with a world that desperately needed it. Noah always said that, and Emily tried to believe it.

A post that drew record views was a photo of Clara with Aiden at the bottom of the slide at the park, both of their faces bright with smiles. Noah had captioned it simply, "Sometimes it's the little things."

But after Aiden's first birthday, Emily noticed Clara slowing down some. She seemed more out of breath making her way through the house, more tired than before. A doctor appointment confirmed what Emily had feared.

"Cerebral palsy affects the brain in ways we're still figuring out." The man had been kind, even as Noah and Emily sat there holding a squirming Aiden.

Clara remained perched on the edge of the examination table, her legs hanging over. At the doctor's words she stared at the floor, fear etched in her face.

The doctor went on to explain in the kindest terms that life required a healthy brain. Emily watched Noah clench his jaw. Because of his concussions, the truth was something he knew only too well. With cerebral palsy, neurons began to die much earlier than normal. The net effect was a slowing down, the need for more and more effort to do daily tasks. Seizures were a very real possibility.

Noah seemed to read Emily's mind. He stood and looked at the doctor. "If you don't mind, I'll take Clara to the waiting room. So you and Emily can talk."

With the sweetest look and the gentlest care, Noah helped Clara slip her arms into her crutches. Then he guided her out of the room and shut the door. Aiden stayed with Emily, and settled into her lap. Like even he could sense this was a serious moment.

"I'm sorry." The doctor looked at the door and back at Emily. "I didn't mean to upset her."

Emily nodded. "She understands everything. So . . . yeah." She couldn't wait to get out of the office, to find five minutes by herself so she could break down and grieve the horrible news. But first she needed more information. "What's this mean for Clara? Is there . . . a prognosis?"

The man sighed and shook his head. "People with Clara's condition don't usually live to be thirty."

For a moment Emily thought she might fall off her chair. How come she hadn't known this awful reality before? Why hadn't her mother told her? Later, back at the house when Clara went to her room for a nap, Emily talked about the terrible news with Noah.

"Honey, of course your mom didn't tell you." Noah took her in his arms. "She didn't know she wasn't coming home."

Emily let that sink in. He was right. "Of course she wouldn't tell an eighteen-year-old that her sister wasn't going to live a full life."

"Now wait." Noah's eyes filled with tears. The love in his voice was so vast, so deep it stayed with Emily still. He leaned in closer to her. "Whatever happens, don't you ever—not for one minute—think Clara hasn't lived a full life. No one loves life more than her." He searched her eyes. "And no one has ever been more loved."

It was a truth that kept Emily going even as she watched Clara's energy ebb away. Every few months she noticed how Clara moved more slowly. Three days after Olivia was born a year later, Clara made the switch from crutches to an electric wheelchair.

Emily tried to make the change a positive one. "You'll be faster than me now." She fought the tears in her voice when they came home together. "Aiden can ride with you when we walk to the park."

Clara never seemed sad. Not once in all her life. From her wheelchair that day she only grinned up at Emily. "Aiden is a good boy."

"Yes, he is." Emily stooped down to hug her. "And you're the best aunt our kids could ever have."

Sometimes Clara would move from her wheelchair

to the couch and Emily would position Olivia in her arms. Clara loved the baby girl with everything in her. One night while holding her, Clara looked right at Emily. "I'm glad."

"You're glad?" Emily angled her head. "Glad about baby Olivia?"

Clara's smile was deeper than usual. "Glad to know her."

It was like Clara understood how quickly the end was coming.

One night when Olivia was four weeks old, Clara decided to turn in early. Her wheelchair was in the corner of the room. In the evenings, she didn't like to use it. "I want normal," she would smile at Emily. "Okay?"

"Of course," Emily would tell her. Who but Clara could think there was anything normal about her life? But at least she thought so.

And so on that night she used her crutches as she made her rounds to the people she loved. Olivia was her first stop. Clara shuffled up to the swing where Olivia was sleeping. "Love you, baby." She carefully touched the baby's cheek. "See you later." For a long time Clara just looked at Olivia, like she was memorizing her.

Emily stopped cleaning the counters in the kitchen and studied her. Clara always made a big deal about saying good night. Usually because she was so happy, she didn't want the day to end. This was different. More intentional. Emily dried her hands and kept watching.

Clara moved to Aiden, who was playing with his

Thomas train in the middle of the floor. Noah sat beside him, acting the part of the conductor. The Colts were on TV and suddenly Noah caught Emily's eye across the room. He must've felt it, too. As if he also understood something was different this time.

"Buddy." Clara sat on the footstool near Aiden. "Come here."

Most people couldn't understand Clara. Speech was that difficult for her. But all of them knew exactly what she was saying. Even Aiden. He scrambled to his feet and jumped up on Clara's lap, his blue eyes turned to hers. "Night-night?"

"Yes." Clara kissed his forehead. "For now."

That's what she said to him. *For now*. As soon as Emily heard the words she felt a ripple of fear course through her. What did Clara mean, *For now*? Clara was still looking at Aiden, smoothing his hair with her hand. "Always love Jesus."

Aiden clearly didn't know what that meant. Not yet. But he threw both his hands high in the air. "Praise Jesus!"

"That's right!" Clara set Aiden back down and he scrambled over to his spot near Noah. Usually she would say good night to Noah next. Not this time. She turned and hobbled into the kitchen, right up to Emily. "You are the best. Always the best."

Emily set the dish towel down and held her close. "Clara . . . is everything all right?" She searched her sister's eyes. "You feeling good?"

Clara locked eyes with her and smiled. "Everything . . . perfect."

"Good." Emily brushed her sister's blond hair off her forehead. "Get some sleep, okay? Pray to Jesus."

"Yes." Clara was always smiling. No matter how hard the walk ahead, when she had blisters on her hands from her crutches or when she couldn't keep up with the rest of them, always Clara kept smiling.

But in that moment her smile faded. She put her shaky hand alongside Emily's face. "Thank you, Emily." Her eyes looked damp. "I love you."

The fear running through Emily doubled. "I love you, too. You just need a little rest."

Clara nodded and after a few seconds she turned away and struggled across the room to Noah. By then, Emily had tears in her own eyes. What was this? Why was she so different tonight?

Emily took a step closer and watched Clara put her hand on Noah's shoulder. Her smile was still missing. "You are . . . good."

Aiden played at their feet, unaware that anything was different about that evening. Noah locked eyes with Clara and stood. He glanced at Emily and then turned to Clara again. "Thank you. Only God is good, but thanks." He grinned at her, like he was trying to keep the moment normal. "You going to sleep?"

"Yes." She nodded slowly, with a greater purpose than usual. Then she moved her hand to Noah's wrist, as if they were the only two people in the room.

Emily thought she was going to launch into her routine with him. The one about daddies and forever and ever. But she didn't. Instead she told him she loved him. Then she said just one word.

"Stay." Her eyes didn't look away, didn't break contact with Noah's. That was all, just "stay."

Noah's happy expression fell off. He took Clara in his arms and held her for half a minute. He kissed the top of her head. "I will always stay, Clara. You know that. I won't ever leave."

She nodded and finally her smile was back. But it didn't quite reach her eyes. One more look around the room, one last look at Emily and a grin for Noah. Emily was concerned enough that she helped Clara to her room that night. Helped her brush her teeth and wash her face, change into her pajamas and get into bed.

Emily kissed her cheek and told her she loved her again before saying one last good night and shutting the door. Long after the kids were asleep, she and Noah sat on the front porch talking about Clara's strange behavior.

But it wasn't until the morning that they understood it.

When she wasn't up at seven like usual, Emily opened her door and turned on the light. Right away she knew something was wrong. Clara's legs and arms were sprawled out at unnatural angles and her hair was a mass of tangles around her face.

"Noah!" Emily screamed for him. "Hurry. Come here!"

The kids were still in bed, but Noah was there in a heartbeat. Emily was too busy with Clara to look at him. "Clara! Wake up!" She gave her sister's lifeless body a shake. "Please, Clara. Open your eyes." Panic seized Emily and she started to cry and scream. "No, God . . . not Clara. No!"

That's when she whipped around to see what Noah was doing. He had his phone up and before she could stop herself she shouted at him, "Don't post this! Are you crazy?"

"I'm not." His response was more startled than angry. "I'm calling 9-1-1."

The rest of that morning was a blur of tears and broken hearts and a goodbye that came way too early. Like the doctor had warned them, a seizure had taken Clara in the middle of the night. Emily and Noah talked about how Clara was free of the constraints of her body now, dancing with Jesus. Hugging her mother. But none of it made Emily feel any better.

When she was alone she couldn't stop thinking how Clara had known after all. And in the days and weeks and seasons that followed, suddenly everything she had said to them that night held enough meaning to last a lifetime.

The fact that she was glad she got to meet Olivia, and her wish that Aiden would always love Jesus. Her thank-you for Emily, the way she looked into her eyes and told her she was perfect. Everything was perfect. As if she wanted Emily to know that walking through life together had been the greatest gift a sister could give.

And of course what she had told Noah.

Stay.

Emily's face was wet with tears, the way it always was when she let herself think about Clara's last day. She squinted at the morning sky. It was raining harder now, thunder crashing every minute or so. Emily stood and folded the blanket, then she walked to the window. "You didn't have to thank me, Clara." Her whispered voice broke. "You were never any trouble."

She studied the dark clouds. Trouble was all that remained after Clara died. The meanness in her tone when she snapped at Noah that morning remained. In big and small ways it stayed. No question they were both at fault for what had led to this day.

She checked the time on her phone. Seven o'clock. The kids needed to get up. She didn't want them here when Noah packed his last things and left. They were going to the Taylors' house again. Emily didn't know what else to do.

As much as she was at fault for how she'd treated Noah, in the end, he had completely and fully broken the promise he made to Clara that night. Noah hadn't stayed. He was leaving in a few hours. Which was maybe the only good thing about Clara taking her trip to heaven earlier than Emily would've wanted.

At least she wasn't alive to see this.

24

Noah woke to a sharp knock at the door. He jumped out of bed, pulled on a pair of jeans and a T-shirt, and looked around. The apartment. Same carpet. He massaged his temples. His head was still killing him. The knock came again, louder this time. Who could be here this early? Another two knocks rang through the apartment.

"Hold on." Noah started for the door, then he remembered Aiden's letter. He had fallen asleep holding it. The letter was all he had of his son, so he couldn't lose it. He rushed over to the bed and lifted the comforter and sheets. Where was it? He had slipped it back into the envelope, but it had been with him when he fell asleep. He was positive.

Another two knocks, harder this time.

He would look for the letter later. He hurried to the door and opened it and there . . . there was Aiden. Tall and strong, looking just like Noah back when he first fell in love with Emily.

"Aiden. Come in." Noah watched his son, the way he

nodded and stepped inside. This wasn't the defiant teenager or the angry twenty-year-old. More time had slipped by. "Is everything . . . okay?"

"Yes." Aiden turned kind eyes to him. "I told you I was coming by today."

"Right." Noah grimaced. He literally couldn't remember anything since that afternoon when he read his son's letter. "I guess . . . I lost track of the days."

"Yeah." Aiden patted his arm. "You do that a lot. You need to see a doctor. I've told you."

"You're right. I will." This was the nicest Aiden had been to him since the time at the park that afternoon when he was fifteen.

A few seconds passed while Aiden just stared at him. Not with hatred or disdain, but with love. Real, actual, father-son love. Then in a rush, Aiden was in his arms. The two hugged and held on to each other. Like maybe Aiden had always loved him, after all.

Whatever had happened, Noah must've gotten it together. After reading the letter he must've contacted Aiden and taken him to lunch. Or maybe they'd walked a few laps on the path at the park. Anything to connect.

Yes, that must be it. Noah would've told him all the ways he was sorry and how much he loved him, all of them. And Aiden must've forgiven him. Since then Noah must've been the father he was supposed to be. He stood a little straighter.

Finally.

Aiden was taking a seat at the small kitchen table. He

patted the spot across from him. "Sit down, Dad. We need to talk."

Gladly. Noah hurried over. His son wanted to talk to him! This was just the improvement he had prayed for. Back when he begged God for a miracle. When they were seated opposite each other, Noah gave Aiden a cautious smile. "So . . . you look good. Are you well?"

"I am." Aiden's eyes grew even softer and his voice held an understanding that defied their rocky past. "I graduated from college last year."

Panic slapped Noah in the face. "I . . . I was there, right?"

Aiden hesitated. "No, Dad." He sighed. "I haven't seen you since Olivia's graduation." He leaned back. "I asked you not to contact any of us and . . . well, you haven't. Not me or Olivia . . . or Mom."

Noah felt sick to his stomach. That had to be wrong. The letter had been the saddest thing Noah had ever read. Of course he would've called Aiden and tried to work things out. He covered his face with his hand and pressed his thumb and forefinger into his temples. "That's . . . not possible."

"Dad." Aiden sounded concerned. "I'm telling you the truth."

Noah lowered his trembling hand. His head was pounding and his heart couldn't take much more. Better if it actually stopped beating. At least he wouldn't have moments like this. He stared at his son. "I don't remember things."

"We figured that." Aiden leaned closer, his forearms on the table. "Maybe that's why you check out. Why you didn't come around or keep your promises." Aiden's tone held no condemnation. "Tell me what you remember."

Even the slightest shake of his head hurt. Noah winced. "I was sitting here, reading your letter. The afternoon of Olivia's graduation."

Aiden's eyes grew wide. "You really need help, Dad. Maybe surgery or something."

Noah didn't care about that. He felt pathetic and small as he reached out and took his son's hands. "Please, Aiden. Tell me what I missed."

No question Aiden was taking this seriously. He nodded and drew a deep breath. "A lot. . . . Okay. Let's see." His eyes found someplace near the ceiling. "Olivia went to Cal Berkeley for a year. She moved in with some ex-con and dropped out of school. Came back here and bounced from community college to art school. One relationship to the next and now . . ."

Aiden's voice trailed off. His look gave Noah a sinking feeling. Like however bad things were, they were about to get worse. Noah released his son's hands and sat up straighter. "Tell me."

"I will." A slow breath leaked from Aiden's lips. "Let me tell you about myself first. It's a better story."

Noah's heart raced, echoing through his head and intensifying the pain in his temples. He had no choice but to wait. Besides he could use a little good news. "Okay."

"I played football for Michigan—your old college

rival." Aiden smiled. Whatever grudge he'd held against Noah, it was gone now. "People used to say that was why you didn't go to my games. You wouldn't set foot in Michigan Stadium."

"No." He shook his head. More pain. How come he hadn't asked Aiden what school he was at when they saw each other at Olivia's graduation? How much had he missed over the years? The reality was devastating. "That wasn't it. I would've been at every game, Aiden. I meant to be there."

"I know." A sad smile played on Aiden's lips. "You meant a lot of things, Dad." He crossed his arms. "Anyway, I went to Fellowship of Christian Athletes at Michigan. I was one of the leaders by the time I was a senior."

FCA? Noah had known about them when he was at Indiana. But there hadn't been time to get connected. Not when he spent every spare moment with Emily and Clara. "Are . . . you still involved?"

"In a way." Aiden's eyes lit up some. "I'm a youth pastor now. I help kids at Clear Creek Community. Mom says it's the church you and her and Aunt Clara used to attend."

Yes. Clear Creek. Noah closed his eyes. He'd ruined everything. And still God in all His goodness had spared Aiden. He blinked back a rush of tears and looked long at his son. "So . . . you believe? You and Jesus, you're close?"

"Very much." Aiden's smile reached deep into his eyes. "Mom says it was Aunt Clara's last wish for me.

That I'd love Jesus always." He gave a shake of his head. "Sometimes I can almost feel her praying for me from heaven."

"Yes." Noah sensed the first tears trickle down his face. "That would be her."

"Anyway, my work now is helping teens." His smile dropped off. "A lot of them are from broken homes and, well, I've been there." He paused. "I figure maybe I can help a few of them. So they don't wind up like . . . Olivia."

That was coming, whatever had happened to Olivia. But for now Noah listened to his son. The pain he had caused was something Aiden was using to help other kids. Kids like he was. Back when Noah was busy breaking his son's heart day after day, one missed moment after another.

The tragedy of it all had shaped Aiden. It defined him. And that was more sorrow than Noah could bear.

"One of the reasons I'm here is to look you in the eyes and tell you something that's been weighing on me for a couple years." This time Aiden reached for Noah's hands. "I forgive you, Dad. That day at Olivia's graduation you told me you were sorry."

One of the few moments Noah remembered.

"Dad, I was so filled with hatred . . . so much anger and pain. I couldn't hear it." He let go of Noah's hands and sat back in his chair again. "But I hear it now. I see it in your eyes, and I forgive you. I really do."

It was a gift Noah didn't deserve. Not at all. His tears

came harder as he nodded. "If only . . . I could do things over." The thought hung in the air between them for a minute. Then Noah dragged his palms over his face. He had to compose himself. Aiden had information he desperately needed. "What was I doing? All those times when I wasn't there?"

Aiden shrugged and looked around, like he was trying to find the kindest words to form an answer. "You . . . had a lot of friends. Girls. People you met online."

"Like . . . from a website?" Noah couldn't imagine himself hitting on girls over the Internet.

"Fans mostly." Aiden's shoulders slumped a little. "The ones who used to think you were the perfect husband for Mom. They wanted to be next after you moved out."

Disgust washed over Noah. He shuddered at the picture. "So . . . I spent my time with them? Is that what you're saying?"

"I guess. I mean . . . you've had four or five girlfriends. Some of them had kids, so yeah. You were busy with them."

Noah thought about the handful of days he remembered from the past almost twenty years. Not once had he been with a woman. Always the only one he ever wanted was Emily. He shook his head. "I . . . don't remember them."

"The times you came around to see Olivia and me, you were between relationships. Full of sorrow and promises." Aiden's voice sounded sadder now. Regret for himself and for Noah. "It was the same thing every time."

What could Noah say? "I never . . ." He gritted his teeth and looked directly at his son. "I never loved anyone but your mother. I love her still."

Aiden just stared at him. "She's pretty amazing."

"She is. She always was." Noah could see her again, her pretty face and long blond hair. The way she looked dancing with him in the living room. "I miss her with every breath."

Something in Aiden's expression changed. Like this part was going to be difficult, too. "She's moving. She and Bob." His eyes held a resignation. "I've invited them to church a number of times, but they're not interested. Bob got a transfer to Los Angeles. They leave after New Year's."

Of all the things Aiden had said, this was the craziest. Emily would never leave the kids. If Aiden and Olivia were here in Indiana, then she would be here, too. Regardless of Bob's situation. "I . . . can't believe that. What does Olivia think?"

"That's the other reason I'm here." Aiden drew a deep breath. "Olivia . . . I'm not sure you want to see her."

"I do." Noah moved to the sofa and buried his face in his hands. Then he lowered them and stared at Aiden. "I need to talk to her. Do you know where she is?"

"Dad." Aiden looked fearful now. "I don't know. She's really bad off." He hesitated. "You wouldn't recognize her."

"That's okay." Noah saw his coat on the chair. He

wasn't sure what month it was, but there had to be a reason it was out. He slipped it on and spotted his phone on the counter. A quick check and he knew. It was autumn again. The time of year he used to love so much. Fall, when everything felt crisp and clean and beautiful.

What better time to find Olivia than now?

"Take me to her." He turned to his son. "Please . . . I have to talk to her."

The look on Aiden's face said he didn't think it would make a difference. But he had said it was one of the reasons he was here. So he grabbed his keys and stepped out of the apartment ahead of Noah. "Come on. I'll drive."

Aiden seemed to know exactly where to go. They parked a block down from the Fourth Street overpass and made their way carefully beneath it. The place stunk like body odor and human waste. Garbage and cardboard lean-tos dotted the ground.

They came across a bearded man, thin with most of his teeth missing. His eyes rolled back as he tried to look at them. "Wha's up?" He said the words like they were a celebration. Then he laughed at himself and slapped his knee.

The guy was higher than the freeway overhead.

Aiden didn't waste time. "I'm looking for my sister. Olivia Carter."

A dizzy spell seemed to hit the man. He leaned one way and then the other, but finally he pointed higher up the hill. Near the cement belly of the bridge. "There."

"Thanks." Aiden put his hand on the man's shoulder. "Remember me, Willy? Aiden Carter."

The man squinted, but something changed in his expression. "Pastor Aiden?"

"Right." Aiden looked straight into the man's eyes. "I gave you a ride to the shelter last week." He paused. "They want to help you, Willy. Jesus loves you. We talked about that."

The man looked off at a heap of garbage, his eyes distant. "Jesus. Right."

Noah watched, mesmerized. His son was not just a pastor. He was living out his faith. How amazing that after all Noah had done to harm his son, Aiden had become this kind of man.

"Okay, then." Aiden took a step back. "I'll come back later today. You need detox, man. Be ready."

Willy nodded and turned around. A few steps and he crumpled into a pile of filthy blankets. Like he was overcome at the thought of the shelter, detox and Jesus. From his position on the ground he waved at Aiden. "I'll be here."

Suddenly panic pushed aside the pride in Noah's heart over watching Aiden. What were they doing? He needed to find Olivia. There was no time for this. He started up the hill and Aiden stayed close on his heels. His headache was gone now, Noah wasn't sure why. But his heart beat so fast he expected it to break free from his chest. Why were they looking for Olivia here, beneath an overpass in a homeless camp? There were people passed out under blankets and in makeshift tents. Drug needles lay scattered on the ground. Noah felt like he might pass out. Was his baby girl here somewhere?

He had to find her.

Aiden pushed a large cardboard box aside and then another. But the people beneath them were not Olivia. Then when they reached the third one, Aiden slid the box to the side and there she was, lying on the ground, passed out. Needles were strewn around her.

"Olivia." Aiden took a step closer. "Livi, wake up."

With everything in him Noah didn't want this sad broken person to be his daughter. But it was her. Noah had no doubt. Not because he recognized her skinny, pockmarked face. But because of her matted pale blond hair. The same hair he used to brush after bathtime when she was two.

"Livi!" Noah dropped to his knees beside her. The reality was devastating. How long had she been like this? He stared at the drug paraphernalia lying around her. She was an addict. That was clear now. It was the reason Aiden hadn't wanted him to come today. His poor Livi was here on the streets passed out. It was more than he could take. He put his hand on her shoulder. "Livi, baby, wake up!"

Aiden touched his arm. "Dad . . . she's unconscious."

Noah wasn't going to let that stop him. He inched closer to her. "Olivia." His hand was on her shoulder, shaking her just enough to get a response. "Livi, it's me. Your dad. Wake up."

For the most horrific moment, Noah wondered if she was dead. If the way he had abandoned his little girl had left her on this cold lonely hillside to die.

But then she moved. Not much, just the fingers on her right hand. A groan came from her lips.

"Livi, honey, wake up." Noah lowered his face to hers. He kissed her gray cheek. "We gotta get you out of here. You need help, Livi." He felt for her pulse and when he found it, panic suffocated him. Her heartbeat was slow and weak. "Livi!" He tried to open her eyelids, but she just stared straight ahead. Blank.

Lifeless.

The whole time, Aiden stayed a few steps back and shook his head. "It's too late for her, Dad. She wants this. Her entire life is about her next fix." His voice was louder now, higher-pitched.

Noah looked over his shoulder and there it was, how much Aiden really cared. His son was crying. "She won't leave. I've tried."

This was an emergency. Noah fumbled for his phone. With shaking hands he dialed 9-1-1 and almost instantly someone spoke on the other end. "Nine-one-one, what's your emergency?"

"My daughter." Noah could feel the damp earth leaking through his pants. He was still on his knees, still leaning over Olivia. "She's on the ground beneath the Fourth Street bridge. I think . . . she overdosed on heroin. Please can you send someone?"

The operator promised to send an ambulance. Noah

cradled Olivia's dirty head in his hands. He kissed her forehead and her cheek.

"Livi, wake up!" This time Noah shouted the words. "Wake up, baby. It's your daddy." And in the horror of the moment, Noah remembered something. He was a paramedic! He could help her!

He felt for her pulse again. Nothing. He moved his fingers, changed the position of his hand. *Come on, God, where's her pulse?* Tears spilled from his eyes and his body shook. *No! God, please not Olivia!*

Aiden joined him on the ground now, kneeling at her side. He placed his hand on Noah's back. "Dad . . . is she? Is she gone?"

"No! She's still with us. She has to be!" Noah sprang into action. He straightened Olivia's arms and legs and started chest compressions on her. Everything was coming back to him now, how to work on a patient. How to save a life. If he could help other people surely he could bring back Olivia.

Bent over her, Noah put his face near hers. "Breathe, Livi! Breathe."

But she wasn't responding. He pinched her nose and opened her mouth. Never mind the dried foam around the edges of her lips or her cold skin. Never mind that for other people, death looked this way.

It couldn't happen to Olivia. Not for his little girl.

Eight quick exhales, then Noah pushed on her chest again. One . . . two . . . three . . . four. "Livi, wake up. Baby, I'm here." He was crying and shouting, pleading for her to open her eyes, to draw a breath. "Please, God!" He stood and screamed at the heavens. "Help her! I can't lose her."

Noah dropped to his knees and started the exhalations again. He wasn't sure how long that went on, but suddenly a team of paramedics was standing nearby, moving him aside. They ran tests and checked her pulse.

Aiden was pacing a few feet away. "God, be with my sister. Please, would You breathe life into her? Please, God!"

After a few minutes one of the paramedics turned to him. A guy Noah didn't recognize. He hung his head, walked up and lifted his face to Noah. His eyes held no hope. "I'm sorry." He put his hand on Noah's arm. "She's gone." He sighed and looked back at Olivia's body. "There was nothing we could do."

"No! Not my little girl!" Noah fell to his knees again. This couldn't be happening. He didn't want to live if his daughter was dead. He bent over, his face down amidst the needles and trash. "Livi!" He screamed her name into the mud and garbage around him. "Come back to me, baby!"

But she wasn't coming back. Olivia was dead and all he wanted was to die, too.

Take me back, Father. Back to when Emily still loved me and Aiden was four and Olivia was two. Back to when we were young. Noah couldn't bear to open his eyes, couldn't stand to see his daughter's broken thin lifeless body lying amidst the trash.

This was all his fault. He didn't deserve to live. He buried his face deeper in the dirt. *Take me back, Lord. Take me there or take my life.*

Suddenly something was happening. Noah felt dizzy and sick and like he was falling. But there was nowhere to land. All of life was rushing past, but no one could see him or hear him. "Livi, baby . . . Daddy loves you."

He screamed the words, but they never left his mouth. Whatever this was, he was all by himself. He could no longer hear Aiden crying behind him, no longer feel the rush of interstate traffic overhead. No longer see the flashing lights from the ambulance. He was cold and desperate and alone.

And all around him was nothing but darkness.

25

The pounding was everywhere, throughout his head and heart and soul. Noah turned from one side to the other, tangled up in the trash and debris around him. He couldn't breathe, couldn't sort through the awful truth. Olivia was gone. His baby girl had died and he hadn't had the chance to say goodbye.

He was dead, right? Or at least he thought so. Probably in hell, since that was what he deserved. Grace wasn't for people like him.

But then he felt something smooth and cool. Cloth against his skin. His eyes jerked open and he sat straight up, gasping for breath. It was pouring rain outside. That was the pounding. He felt his knees, but they were dry. Like he hadn't just been kneeling beside his Olivia. And his headache was gone.

But why wasn't she here? What had they done with her body?

His eyes darted around the room, his breathing coming in short gulps and gasps. Where in the world was he? The sheets were wrapped around his legs and torso. Twisted and tight, like they were trying to suffocate him. He was in bed, that's where he was. Right here in bed.

He had to find Olivia, had to know what they did with her. And where was Aiden? He untangled his legs and pushed his feet to the floor. As he did, a shock shot through his body.

The scratchy carpet was gone. This was the wood floor, the one in his bedroom before . . .

He looked around. The walls and windows. The sky outside. This wasn't his apartment!

His heart started to beat faster, and suddenly the truth came into focus. This was his old bedroom! Not the place where he'd lived for the past two decades. This was his *real* room. The one he had shared with Emily before he moved out.

"God . . . what's happening?" He ran to the window. Through the pouring rain he saw the most wonderful sight. His front yard! Just like it had been before he moved away. He put his hands to his head. His hair was full and soft, completely different than it had been just a few minutes ago.

What year was it? Where was Aiden? The two of them had just been together and the paramedics were telling him the news. And Noah was facedown in the dirt because he couldn't bear to look. And he was asking God to give him back the years or take his life. And Livi was gone . . . his Livi was gone.

But now . . .

He ran to the bathroom and looked in the mirror.

What he saw made him grab hard on to the edge of the counter. This wasn't the aging man without a hope, the defeated shell of himself who had destroyed Emily and their children and everything good about their lives.

Noah blinked and stared at his reflection. His fingers made their way over his smooth face. He was young again. The floor was cold beneath his feet and in the bedroom behind him the awful carpet was gone. Definitely this was his home.

So what had happened? He was gasping for breath now, trying to get his mind around it. Was it a miracle? Or maybe this was a dream and he wasn't really home? Was this God's way of showing him what he had lost? He patted his arms and legs. Everything felt real.

But so had the dirt beneath his face a few minutes ago. This must be a dream, that had to be it. None of this could possibly be real. He had missed every chance to love his wife and kids. All of life was behind him.

Or was it?

His heart was beating so hard it echoed through the bathroom. A chill passed over him from his head to his toes.

"What year is it?" Noah whispered the words, his breathing uneven. He ran from his room through the once familiar kitchen and living room to the kids' playroom. "God . . . what are you doing?" The toys were picked up, stacked in bins and on the shelves. Just like they'd been the night before he left home. Aiden's Noah's Ark play set was in the corner, too. And there in the middle of the floor was Olivia's furry rocking horse. All the way he remembered it that long-ago time.

Noah was shaking so bad he almost couldn't move, couldn't take himself to the kids' bedroom. But he had to do it, had to figure out what was happening. With an energy he hadn't felt in decades, he ran to their bedroom.

Their beds were there, Aiden's and Olivia's. Her baby doll and blanket were on her pillow and Aiden's bunny was on his covers. Noah dropped to the edge of his son's bed. His shaking was worse now, but a feeling had taken root in his soul. Something he hadn't felt in longer than he could remember.

The feeling was hope.

His mind tried to make sense of everything that had happened. He was suffering late effects from his concussions. Clearly. His head had been hurting for most of the last twenty years. And huge gaps of time were missing. But when he lay down, when he went to sleep, all he could think about were the good times from their early years.

He clasped his hands. Maybe that's what this was. He was dreaming again. This was the next part of the story, right? The part where he stopped knowing how to love Emily and he rented an apartment? That's what this was.

The day he was going to move out. *Lord, what's happening to me? If this is only a dream, take me out of it. I can't relive it again.*

This was how the house had looked, how the playroom and the kids' bedroom had looked the day before he moved out.

But he was different.

Because now he knew what life looked like three and eleven and sixteen years from this moment. The lonely apartment and scratchy carpet. The pitiful drugstore Christmas tree. Missing his kids' recitals and games. Watching Emily disappear from his life, and knowing how he would have given anything to hold her hand again, to feel her in his arms. To dance with her and kiss her. But none of those terrible thoughts had crossed his mind on *this* day the last time he was here. The day before he left his family. A lifetime ago. If only this weren't a dream. If he had known then what he understood so painfully now, he never would have moved out.

I can't bear to walk out on them again. Please, God . . . take me from this place. I can't bear to—

Noah Carter. A gentle voice stopped his prayer short. *My precious son, don't you know? My mercies are new every morning.*

Noah slid off the bed to the floor. The voice was firm and marked with authority. "Who . . . who said that?" His hands and legs trembled. Where had the voice come from? Now he was hearing things. He looked up and then to the window. He was alone in the kids' bedroom. No one else was in the house.

Then it hit him. "God . . . is that you?"

The voice came again, strong and kind.

Noah . . . I have set before you life and death, blessings and curses . . . now choose life . . . so your children might live.

The words were a Bible verse! It was one Ryan and Kari Taylor had shared at the first Bible study he and Emily attended.

His mercies were new every morning. Each word rang through his soul like a beacon of the brightest light. They played again and again in his mind. *I have set before you life and death, blessings and curses . . . now choose life . . . so your children might live.*

So Olivia wouldn't be lying dead on a trash pile under the interstate.

Noah hurried to his feet. He was still shaking, still barely able to breathe. But he was certain of one thing. The words had come from God. Definitely.

He looked from the door to the window and back again. "I don't know where You are, God. But I hear You."

Maybe everything he'd been through in the last twenty years was all just one terrible nightmare? An aftereffect of his concussions? What if time hadn't marched on, taking his family from him? Destroying them, one year at a time?

Was that what God was trying to tell him?

Noah didn't hesitate. He ran to the living room and looked at the wall. There they were, the photos of Aiden and Olivia. Four and two. And the kitchen . . . Noah ran there next. He opened the refrigerator, and there was his leftover burger from last night.

The one he'd gotten on the way back from the cemetery.

That gave him another idea. He raced back to his bedroom and there on the floor were his work pants. Inside out and crumpled in a heap. The ones he'd worn to see Clara's tombstone. The knees should be muddy. He grabbed them and struggled to turn them right-side out again.

Please let the knees be muddy, please, God.

His hands couldn't move fast enough, but finally he could see the dirt. Mud caked across both knees. He dropped the pants and ran to his closet. It was empty. Nothing here.

He stopped cold.

Of course it was empty. He looked across the room and there were his suitcases. All of them packed full of his clothes. Because today was the day he was moving.

He was here and he was alive and awake. And in an hour he was supposed to pack up his truck and drive to his new home.

The apartment from his nightmare. With the scratchy carpet.

If this was real, if it wasn't too late, then God had done the impossible. And maybe He really had! Noah was breathing faster again. Was this a miracle? Yes, that's what had happened. God had given him a miracle!

He zipped open his suitcase and grabbed a pair of jeans and a thermal shirt. Never in all his life had he gotten dressed so fast. Then at the last minute he grabbed his old blue flannel jacket. Something warm to stop his body from shaking.

Wherever Emily and the kids were, he had to find them. Noah raced down the hall and grabbed his keys from the kitchen counter. But as he did he saw something fall to the floor. A note with Emily's handwriting.

"What's this?" He picked it up and read it.

I took the kids to Ryan and Kari Taylor's house.
Please go. None of us need to see you drive away.

"No!" He shook his head. No, he wasn't driving away. He couldn't ever drive away. Noah dropped the note and it fluttered to the floor as he ran outside to his truck. The rain soaked his hair and back, but he didn't care. "Please, God . . ." He was still shivering as he started the engine. "Please don't let it be too late."

He was a street away from the Taylor house when he remembered God's words. *My mercies are new every morning.* Wasn't that part of a Bible verse? Part of a song. It was something they had sung at church when they used to go.

God's mercies were new every morning, right? The song said so. *Great is thy faithfulness.* Yes, that was it. Noah gripped the steering wheel. He could only hope that on this day, in the minutes to come, God's promises really would be true. That Emily would give him mercy. Because the morning was definitely new. And God was faithful.

If all of this wasn't a dream.

Noah stepped on the gas. In two minutes he was going to see the girl he loved. The one he missed with every fiber in his being, every heartbeat. The one he had almost lost.

His precious Emily.

• • •

EMILY WAS SURE of one thing. Aiden knew what was happening. That was the hardest part. Emily sat with Kari at her kitchen table while the kids played with a bucket of Lincoln Logs on the living room floor. Jana Alayra sang from a video playing on the television. Aiden sang along.

Kari had made coffee for both of them again. Then she handed Emily a document, stapled together. "This is for you."

If it was some marriage Bible study tool, Emily wanted to tell Kari not to bother. It was too late. No matter how much she wished that wasn't true. Emily looked at the front page.

Ten Secrets to a Happy Marriage.

"My mom wrote it before she died." Kari sat down and leaned back in her chair. "Ryan found it last night." She paused. "Just when the two of us needed it most."

"The two of you?" Emily lifted her eyes to Kari. "For your marriage?"

"Yes." Kari took a sip of her coffee. "Just because we lead the group doesn't mean we don't have our moments. Marriage takes work." She smiled, even though a hint of sadness remained in her eyes. "Ryan and I were struggling, thinking more of ourselves than each other." A deep breath. "We're good now. And Emily, you and Noah . . . you can be, too." She hesitated. "No matter how dark things are right now, I have to believe there's still hope."

Emily looked at the top of the first page of the document. The words took her breath. *Divorce is not an option.* The very first point Kari's mother had made. If only that were true for Noah and her. "Thanks." She handed the document back to Kari. "It's too late for this." She could feel herself shutting off. She didn't need this advice. Not now.

"Keep it." Kari slid the pages back to Emily. She didn't seem daunted. "Anyway, Ryan's already at work, but he told me to tell you he's praying for you and Noah. For a miracle. We both are." She let that sink in for a moment. "Even now."

"Noah's probably already gone." Emily hated to kill the mood, but there was no reason to believe a miracle would happen. It was too late.

Another sip of her coffee and Kari looked intently at Emily. "So, you haven't talked to him since he went to bed last night?"

"No." Emily held the warm coffee mug against her face. She was so cold. The rain didn't help. "He just kept sleeping. Like he didn't have a care in the world."

"I hoped that after we texted, he might've woken up. The two of you could've talked things out." Kari wasn't pushing. She was being a friend and a Bible study leader.

Emily got it. She shook her head. "If there was a way I could change all this, I would." She sighed. "I don't know how to live with Noah anymore." Tears stung her eyes. In the near distance lightning flashed in the sky. Another storm. She focused her thoughts. "But last night I didn't sleep at all. Just . . . kept remembering the beautiful moments between us. And it's like even though I can't live with the man he's become . . . I don't know how to live without him, either."

Kari seemed to let that statement sit for a minute. She sipped her coffee and looked right into Emily's eyes. "That's because you're not supposed to." She hesitated. "You know what the Bible says about not letting anything separate a husband and a—"

A screeching sound came from out front. Alarm flashed on Kari's face, and both of them raced toward the front door. The second Kari opened it, Emily gasped. "Noah?"

He had pulled his truck into the Taylors' long driveway and apparently slammed it into park. What was he doing and why was he here? Emily started to breathe faster. There wasn't a single reason why he should be in his truck outside. Not one.

"Go to him." Kari put her hand on Emily's shoulder. "I'll watch the kids."

Emily stepped outside before her heart caught up. Was he trying to punish her, make her watch him drive off to his new life? Or maybe he was here to say goodbye to the kids. Like they needed that. Emily's heart thudded hard against her ribs. Whatever reason Noah had for coming here, Emily wasn't sure she wanted to know. But she had no choice.

Thunder shook the ground and then, in the pouring down rain, Noah got out of the truck and stood there. Just stood there getting drenched, blinking back the water so he could see her. Something was different about him. Emily could tell from the shelter of the Taylors' front porch. "Emily Andrews," Noah shouted above the sound of the rain. "Please. Come here."

And so she did the only thing she could do, the thing she'd done since she was nineteen. She ran to him.

As fast as her body would take her.

26

He couldn't be dreaming because the rain was stinging his eyes and he was standing on the Taylors' gravel driveway. Lightning split the sky a ways off and the thunder rolled. Water was running down his back and chest and into his work boots and it was all very tangible. Not only that, but for the first time in two decades—or maybe the first time since Clara died—Emily wasn't standing far off.

She was running right for him.

"Emily!" He shouted her name, and the closer she came the more he knew that this was real and it was a miracle. He moved toward her, onto the lawn. Then like he'd done at Olivia's side as she died under the overpass, Noah dropped to the ground. Only this time he grabbed at the grass. Handfuls of it. "I'm here, Emily. We're young again!"

Emily had almost reached him, so Noah quickly stood up. He raised both fists in the air. "Look at us!" He shouted at the top of his lungs so she could hear him over the storm. "I asked God to take us back to when we were young, and He did it . . . we're really here!"

She stopped a few feet from him, wiping the rain from her face. "Noah . . . what . . . what happened to you?"

He ran to her and put his arms around her. Their bodies came together wet and scared and panting too hard. "I'm here, Emily." He pressed his face against hers and kissed her cheek, her neck. "I'm never leaving. I love you so much."

Finally he could breathe again. She was life to his bones, health to his lungs and he wasn't ever letting go. She brushed the rain from his eyes. Thunder crashed nearby. "Should we sit in the truck?"

"I don't care." He laughed and let his head fall back. "Thank You for the rain, God. Bring on the storm! Wash away everything that happened last night, every minute of it."

Emily looked scared. Noah's behavior probably made her wonder. "You think I've lost my mind, right?"

"I . . . I'm trying to figure it out."

"I didn't lose it, Emily. I found it!" He lifted her off the ground and spun her around. Then he let her slide back to the grass in front of him. "I have so much to tell you."

"Okay." Clearly she didn't know what had happened to him, but she was here. She wasn't walking away and that was something. Rain poured down her face as lightning hit a few blocks away. "But let's get in the truck."

"Yes! The truck!" Noah laughed out loud. "Whatever you want, Emily. It's yours now and forever!" He let go of her and took her hand. They ran to the truck and Noah opened the door and helped her into the passenger seat. At the same time he caught a glimpse of something that set his heart free. A glimpse of what might be the future. Because the angry girl he'd seen last night was gone. Emily wasn't glaring at him anymore.

She was smiling.

• • •

EMILY HAD NO idea what had happened to Noah, but he was a different man. Completely different.

She was soaking wet, shivering from the cold air outside and the craziness of the moment. Noah climbed in behind the wheel and turned to her. "God did it all, Emily." Water still ran down his face. "He did it in one night. At least I think that's what happened."

He looked like a crazy person, his hair wet and matted to his forehead, the goofy grin on his face. His hands were muddy from the grass he'd pulled out of the Taylors' lawn. And he couldn't stop talking. A hundred miles a minute.

"You're really here. It's the greatest thing in all my life, Emily. I'm here and you're here and we're young again." He wiped his dirty hands on his jeans and took her fingers in his. "I can't believe you're really here."

"Yes." Emily searched his eyes, his face. What had happened? His hugs from a minute ago had been a mix of passion and desperation, as if Noah had come back from the dead—and she was the first person he could take hold of. But his eyes were swollen, too. Like he'd been crying.

"Come here, baby. Let me hold you, please." He practically crawled over the console to take her in his arms. "Don't let go. Don't ever let go."

"Noah." She made a sound more doubt than laugh. "Start at the beginning. What happened?"

He released her and settled back into his seat. Then with a deep breath Noah told her a story she wouldn't have believed if it hadn't been him. He sounded like someone with mental issues. Schizophrenia, maybe. Emily held her breath and prayed that wasn't it. *Exhale,* she reminded herself. She had to hear every detail.

Outside the rain let up some and Emily hung on every word Noah said. The story was unlike anything she'd ever heard. He had been dreaming—lots of dreams. And in each of them he had relived a piece of their love story. What brought them together.

But when he would wake up, he would be older. Years older. His hyper joy settled down. "It took me a few times to realize I wasn't only living in an apartment, I was living there alone and you were married to some guy named Bob." His eyes locked on to hers. "The kids, Emily . . . they were a mess. Worse every time until . . ."

"Until what?" The nightmare sounded horrible. She shivered a little more. "Tell me, Noah. What happened to the kids?"

"The last time, when I woke up, Aiden was at the

door. He was twenty-three, Emily. And he'd found his way back to God."

Tears flooded Emily's eyes. "He was twenty-three? What about Olivia?"

Noah shook his head. Tears came for him, too, and before he could say another word he was crying. Weeping. He covered his face with his hands and when he could finally talk, he said words that struck terror in Emily's heart.

"She died. Of an overdose. Under a bridge outside Bloomington."

"Dear God." Emily's voice fell. She shook her head. "Noah, that's awful."

"It was." He pulled her into his arms again. "The whole thing was awful and real and terrible and . . . and even now . . ." He brushed his damp fingertips against her face, her hair. "Tell me I'm here, that you're real and last night was not. Is this really happening?"

She ached for him, for all he'd been through. Later she wanted to hear the rest of the details. But for now there was something they had to do. "The kids are inside." She opened the car door. "I think they'd both like to see you." Her smile felt easy and natural. The way it hadn't for far too long. "That should answer your question."

"The kids!" Noah was out of the car and around to her side in a flash. He held her hand as they hurried back to the Taylors' front door. Already the sky was clearing, the sun breaking through the clouds.

Noah walked through the door first. "Aiden! Olivia!"

Emily watched Aiden look up. He dropped the Lincoln Logs and jumped to his feet. "Daddy?"

Poor boy. He had been deeply aware that Noah was leaving today. Now the mix of joy and uncertainty was evident in his eyes. Aiden didn't need an invitation. He ran across the room and Noah caught him up in his arms. Once Emily had seen a video compilation of kids whose parents had just returned home from battle.

Their moment of reunion.

It was exactly the same right now for Noah and Aiden. The two clung to each other like they were survivors of the worst possible war. Which they were. Survivors who were here and whole and ready to face life again. The war was behind them.

Emily knew it with everything in her. Today wasn't an ending after all.

It was a beginning.

• • •

NOAH COULDN'T LET go of Aiden. He wasn't playing soccer on the ten-year-old team or giving him rude looks at fifteen. He wasn't an angry twenty-year-old or a man at twenty-three.

Aiden was four. He was four and he was a little boy who loved Bible stories and playing in the park and being anywhere his parents were. He was little and he was here in Noah's arms. In all his life—in the years ahead when

Aiden would grow up with a mommy and daddy at home, Noah would never forget what this felt like.

Right here, the day he decided to stay.

"You're wet, Daddy." Aiden laughed. He looked into Noah's eyes. Playful and happy. Like the child he'd been before last night. The boy he was supposed to be was back.

They were all back.

"I am wet. I know." Noah made a silly face. "It's kind of fun."

"Yeah!" Aiden flashed a silly face of his own. "I love the rain!"

After a minute he set his son down. Aiden continued to cling to Noah's leg.

But now Noah turned his attention to Olivia. His baby girl. She was still sitting on the floor near the creation they'd been building. Sitting there watching Noah, her mouth open.

Olivia couldn't possibly grasp what was happening here. What had almost happened. But somehow she had an understanding. Noah knew it. His baby girl was deep that way. Because she stood up and with steps that got faster and faster, she ran to him.

"Daddy!" And like that she was in his arms.

Like air to his lungs was that single little cry: *Daddy!* He was her daddy again. God had given him a second chance, even when he didn't deserve it. "I'm here, Livi. Daddy's right here." She held him tight around his neck and when she pulled back, she rubbed her nose against his. "Wuv you, Daddy."

"I love you, too, Livi."

In the distance Noah finally spotted Kari Taylor. She was holding a tissue to the corner of one eye. "Looks like you all need to get home and into some dry clothes."

"Yes!" Emily added her laughter to the mix. "As fun as it is to be drenched like this. Home sounds a lot better. Even if I burn the pancakes."

Noah stared at her. There she was, the teasing funny wonderful girl he'd married. His Emily. He looked from her to the kids. "I know! I'll cook the pancakes."

"Yay!" Aiden pumped his fist in the air. "I love when Daddy cooks."

Pancakes. They would forever be part of his terrible night. The dream or whatever it was. But from now on the memories around their favorite Saturday morning breakfast would be happy and wonderful. Noah ran his hand along Livi's back. He looked from her to Aiden. "After we eat, I have a surprise for you." Noah raised his eyebrows. "I don't know about you, but I can hardly wait."

"Me, too!" Aiden jumped around.

"Me, too, Daddy." Olivia was still in his arms, still staring at him like he was her hero. Which he was. Even with all his flaws. All she wanted was for him to stay.

Like Clara had told him her last night on earth.

• • •

THREE HOURS LATER, after fresh clothes and pancakes, Noah ushered them into his truck. "We're going to the best place ever!"

"I can't wait!" From the backseat, Aiden clapped his hands. "It's the best day ever!"

Noah held Emily's hand as they drove. As soon as he pulled into the parking lot Aiden gasped. "I knew it! The best place in the whole world!" He clapped again. "The park!"

For a moment after Noah parked, he only stared at the play area. The same place he'd brought Aiden and Olivia just last night. When they were fifteen and thirteen. Noah pushed the memory from his mind as they walked from the parking lot to the playground. With Aiden and Olivia hurrying ahead, Noah pulled Emily to him. Then he kissed her like he'd longed to do for a lifetime.

Or for one crazy, miraculous night.

The kiss took her by surprise, he could tell. But then she moved in close to him and the kiss became hers. When he took a breath, he whispered against her skin. "Let's dance, Emily."

She laughed and pressed against him, closer still, and the two of them swayed beneath a canopy of branches. As far as Noah was concerned they weren't dancing back from the edge of a deadly, disastrous cliff. Not anymore. They were nineteen and new and in love, dancing across her living room floor. And all of life was ahead of them.

Noah stepped back. "Hey!" He smiled at Emily and then at the kids. "Let's go to the swings."

"Yes!" Aiden was the first to take off, with Livi close behind him. Noah laughed to himself. He had no words for how good he felt, how wonderful it was that his kids were still little. He didn't want this day to ever end. They reached the swing set. "Look at that." Noah ran his hand along the black seat. "They're dry!"

Emily put Olivia in the baby swing, and Noah helped Aiden climb onto one of the three big swings. "I know, Daddy. Let's see who can swing highest."

Just like that his tears started up again. He adjusted his sunglasses, grateful Aiden couldn't see him cry. "Now that . . . is a very good idea, Aiden." He took the middle swing and grinned at Emily. "I bet Mommy wins."

"Mommy always wins." She flashed Noah a flirty look and gave Olivia one more push. Then she took the seat beside their daughter and set her swing in motion.

Soon all four of them were swinging, completely in sync with each other, sunshine on their faces, pushing their legs to the sky as if it wasn't almost the end of the world. As if life hadn't almost come to a sudden crash.

And a thought hit Noah.

Aiden and Olivia would never know the terrible heartache and loss they had been spared. They would never know and he would never tell them. Because God really had set before him life and death, blessings and curses. And after today, Noah would never choose death again. Whenever God gave him the choice he would choose life.

Now and forevermore.

27

Kari didn't get a call from Emily until late that night. God had indeed worked a miracle for the couple, for their whole family. Something about a dream and watching Aiden and Olivia grow up all in one night.

"It's okay," Kari told her. "You and Noah can tell us all about it later."

When the call ended, Kari checked @When_We_Were_Young on Instagram. Noah had added a new post, just an hour ago. It was a meme of a park and a swing set, the sun shining through the branches. There was a Bible verse over the scene. The Scripture was from Deuteronomy 30:19.

> I have set before you life and death, blessings and curses.
> Now choose life, so that you and your children may live.

A smile lifted Kari's mouth and she nodded. "Yes, Noah. That's it." She turned off the computer and found Ryan in the living room. Her sister Ashley had told her about keeping her family off social media for a season. And Kari had liked the idea so much she and Ryan were starting the challenge, too. The kids were at the kitchen table playing Sequence and laughing.

Ryan looked up from a chair in the adjacent family room. "Everything okay?" He lowered his brow, clearly concerned. "What is it?"

They needed privacy for this talk. The kids didn't understand that Noah and Emily had been on the brink of divorce. Kari motioned for him to follow her outside. When they were out back, Kari smiled at Ryan and pointed toward heaven. "He did it. God did it."

"For us?" He looped his arms around her waist and drew her close. "Definitely."

"Yes." She laughed. "For us. But for Noah and Emily, too."

Ryan's eyes lit up. "Are you serious?"

"I am." Kari's heart soared with joy. She felt the sparkle in her eyes. "Wait till you hear what happened."

And as she told Ryan the story—or at least the part she knew—she felt a surge of hope and faith that by now was a regular part of her existence. Because this was the second miracle God had worked in their midst—all in one day. And if Kari knew anything about life and the God they loved, this much was true.

It wouldn't be the last.

• • •

AIDEN LAY IN bed that night long after his mommy and daddy had prayed and tucked them in. He couldn't stop thinking about the one thing that mattered most of all.

The storm was over. Everything was okay.

Which meant God had answered him. Aiden smiled in the dark. "Thank You, God," he whispered out loud. "You kept Daddy home today."

God had listened. He had done something special to Daddy's heart. Aiden could tell because tonight Daddy said amen after the nighttime prayer.

All on his own.

Something else. At the Taylors' house Daddy had told them he wasn't leaving. Over and over again he told both of them. Olivia didn't understand. She was too little. But Aiden was old and it made sense to him.

Still Aiden didn't know for sure it was true until they were at the park. That's when he turned around and saw Daddy and Mommy kissing. Aiden smiled in the dark. It meant Daddy wasn't ever going to move away. He was staying right here.

Where he belonged.

• • •

EMILY HAD BEEN trying to grasp all that had happened, how God could have worked such a miracle. Noah was a completely different person. All he wanted the rest of his life was to love her and the kids. It was enough to make Emily wonder if this time she was the one dreaming.

That night when the kids were in bed, Noah led her to their room. The place where they hadn't loved each other for longer than Emily could remember. He took her in his arms and held her face in his hands. "Emily . . . I will never, ever do something to harm you again." He kissed her with a passion that made her dizzy.

"Wait." She wanted to kiss him, wanted to fall back into their bed with him and show him how much she still wanted him. But she had something to tell him first. They were both breathing faster, the anticipation there for both of them.

He searched her eyes. "What is it, Emily?" Concern flashed on his face. "Is it too soon?"

"No." She laughed and this time she kissed him. "Not soon enough." She released a quiet laugh. But just as quickly she felt her smile fade. "I have to tell you something, Noah." She ran her thumb gently along his cheekbone. "The struggle between us, it wasn't just you."

"It was all me, Emily." He rushed ahead, running his hands down her arms. "Don't say another word. This was my fault."

She let him finish. Then she shook her head. "God showed me. I changed, Noah." The sting of tears hit her. "I was mean and short with you. I lost my patience and stopped trying to talk things out."

"Emily . . ."

"I mean it." She wanted him to truly grasp this. "It was you, but it was me, too. Kari gave me a list of things her mom taught her, ways to make a marriage work." She looked into his eyes and let herself get lost in the depths of his love. "Maybe we can read it together."

"We will." He looked like he was hanging on every word she said. "There's nothing more important in all the world."

All she wanted was to kiss him. But she needed to finish. "I'm sorry, Noah. For how I treated you." She blinked and felt a tear roll onto her cheek. "I'm so sorry."

"It's behind us now. We're both sorry." He came in slowly, desire dark in his eyes. "Now we can move on."

Their kiss took Emily back to the first time they'd come together this way, depth and emotion and a desperate kind of love. A oneness Emily couldn't live without. The kiss grew, and in a different kind of dance, they moved to their bed and for the next hour they proved to each other just how much they'd missed this, how very much they had when they were together. Not just their beautiful, physical love but something more.

The certainty of forever.

• • •

A WEEK HAD passed since his crazy night of horrible dreams. Seven days since he and Emily had been back together—heart, mind, body and soul. They had celebrated their eighth anniversary and these had been some of the best days of Noah's life.

But there was still something he had to do before they could turn the page, before they could start living out the next chapter of their lives. He thought about how he was going to do it, what he was going to say.

That first night he'd simply posted the Bible verse

from Deuteronomy. Every day since then he'd let that last post sit there. He hadn't been near the computer. Now it was Saturday morning and it was time. Noah got up as quietly as he could, but next to him Emily stirred.

She blinked her pretty eyes open and looked at him. "Mmm . . . where are you going?"

"I have to take care of something." He leaned over her and kissed her. However long God might give them together, he knew one thing—he couldn't get enough of her.

She smiled at him. Whatever he was feeling, he could see in her expression the feeling was mutual. She'd proven that a number of times this past week.

He stepped out of bed and looked deep into her eyes. "I'll be right back."

Then with all the purpose he'd ever felt in his entire life, he walked to the den and turned on the computer. He started with Facebook. A few clicks and he was staring at the question.

Do you want to delete the page @When_We_Were_Young?

Noah didn't hesitate. He clicked the yes button and then signed off. Instagram was next. He went through the same steps and then he did it again for Twitter. Each time he clicked yes. In five minutes he erased every bit of their Internet presence. All of it was gone. He turned off the computer and took a deep breath.

Freedom coursed through his veins. He felt perfectly wonderful. No more living in the virtual world. The one he had here and now was far too beautiful. Noah wouldn't do anything to threaten that ever again. *I'm back, Lord. Back when we were young.*

The morning sun was coming up over the distant trees. Noah looked out the window and for a moment he thought about Clara. She would be happy. He was making good on his promise. This daddy wasn't leaving. He was staying.

Now and forevermore.

ELIZABETH BAXTER'S 10 SECRETS TO A HAPPY MARRIAGE

1. Keep God first
   - By loving God more than your spouse, you will always be humble enough to love your spouse more than humanly possible. This makes for a beautiful marriage.
   - *Matthew 6:33—But seek first the kingdom of God and His righteousness, and all these things will be added to you.*

2. Divorce is not an option
   - From the beginning, remove the word "divorce" from your vocabulary. People do not look for a door where one does not exist.
   - *Mark 10:9—Therefore what God has joined together, let no man separate.*

3. Marriage is not 50/50
   - There will be days when one of you falls short. Make it your goal to give 100 percent every day. That way you're both covered. Every day, forever!

- *Colossians 3:23—Whatever you do, work at it with all your heart, as working for the Lord.*

4. Know your spouse's love language
   - People speak love in different ways. Gifts, acts of service, words of affirmation, physical touch, intentional time. Figure out how to speak to each other so that the love between you will grow.
   - *Romans 12:9—Love must be sincere.*

5. Expect the best of each other, be patient, and forgive easily
   - Attitude is everything in marriage. Look for ways to humbly be kind to your spouse. Keep short accounts. Don't worry about being right.
   - *Ephesians 4:2—Be patient, bearing with one another in love.*
   - *Colossians 3:13—Bear with each other and forgive one another . . . forgive as the Lord forgave you.*

6. Keep dating
   - Your marriage must be a priority. Seek God first, then your spouse. Never stop dating and pursuing each other. Value and celebrate your love.
   - *Song of Solomon 3:2—I must seek the one my soul loves.*

7. Build each other up
   - Kind words are free. Look for ways to encourage each other. Every day.
   - *1 Thessalonians 5:11—Therefore encourage one another and build each other up.*

8. Laugh often
    - Find reasons to be silly. Smile and be light-hearted. You'll laugh about it later, so make up your mind to laugh about it today.
    - *Proverbs 17:22—A cheerful heart is good medicine.*

9. Live within your means
    - Couples who get in debt stay stressed. Living within your means can be great fun. Take walks. Play board games. Visit your park. Clip coupons.
    - *Hebrews 13:5—Keep your lives free from the love of money and be content with what you have.*

10. Fix yourself, not your spouse
    - Work to be kinder and gentler. Be the person your spouse married. Listen well. Be intentional.
    - *Matthew 7:3—Why do you look at the speck of sawdust in your brother's eye and pay no attention to the plank in your own eye?*

ACKNOWLEDGMENTS

No book comes together without a great deal of teamwork, passion and determination. That was definitely true for *When We Were Young*!

First, a special thanks to my amazing publisher, Beth Adams, and the team at Howard Books. Also to the team at Simon & Schuster—Carolyn Reidy and the rest of the gifted people who bring my books to all of you! I think often of our times together in New York and the way your collective creative brilliance always becomes a game changer. You clearly desire to raise the bar at every turn. Thank you for that. It's an honor to work with you!

This book is so very special because of the incredible talents of my editor, Becky Nesbitt. Becky, you have known me since my kids were little. Since the Baxters began. How many authors actually look forward to the editing process? With you, it is a dream. And always you find ways to make my book better. Over and over and over again. Thank you for that! I am the most blessed author for the privilege of working with you.

Also thanks to my design team—Kyle and Kelsey Kupecky—whose unmatched talent in the industry is recognized from Los Angeles to New York. Very simply you are the best in the business! My website, social media, video trailers and newsletter along with so many other aspects of my touring and writing are top of the book business because of you two. Thank you for working your own dreams around mine. I love you and I thank God for you every single day.

A huge thanks to my sisters, Tricia and Susan, along with my mom, who give their whole hearts to helping me love my readers. Tricia as my executive assistant for the past decade, and Susan, for many years, as the president of my Facebook Online Book Club and Team KK. And, Mom, thank you for being Queen of the Readers. Anyone who has ever sent me an email and received a response from you is blessed indeed. All three of you are so special to me. I love you and I thank God for each of you!

Thanks also to Tyler for joining with me to write screenplays and books that—for now—the readers don't even know about. You are such a gifted writer, Ty. I can't wait to see your work on the shelves and on the big screen. Maybe one day soon! Love you so much!

Also, thank you to my office assistant, Aurora Galvin. You create space for me to write! This storytelling wouldn't be possible without you.

I'm grateful, also, to my Team KK members, who use social media to tell the world about my upcoming releases and who hang out on my Facebook page answering reader questions. I appreciate each of you so much. May God bless you for your service to the work of Life-Changing Fiction™.

There is a final stage in writing a book. The galley pages come to me, and I send them to a team of five of my most special reader friends. My niece Shannon Fairley, Hope Painter, Donna Keene, Renette Steele, and Zac Weikal. You are wonderful! It always amazes me the things you catch at the final hour. Thank you for loving my work, and thanks for your availability to read my books first and fast.

Also, my books only happen with the help of my family, especially my amazing husband, Donald. Honey, thank you for your spiritual wisdom and leadership in our home, and thanks for talking through books like this one from the outline to the editing. The countless ways you help me when I'm on deadline make all the difference. I love you!

And over all this, is a man who has believed in my career for two decades, my amazing agent, Rick Christian of Alive Literary Agency. From the beginning, Rick, you've told me to dream big, set my sights high. Movies, TV series, worldwide reach. All for God and through Him. You imagined it all, you prayed for it to be. You believed. While I write, you work behind the scenes on film projects and my work with Liberty University, the Baxter family TV series and details regarding every book I've ever written. You are brilliant and driven, compassionate and dedicated. I used to dream of having you as my agent. Now I'm the only author who does. God is amazing. Thank you, Rick, and thank you for praying for me and my family. That most of all.

Finally, my greatest thanks to God Almighty, who is First and Last and all things in between. I write for You, through You and because of You. Thank you with my whole being.

Dear Reader Friend,

My youngest son, Austin, is the one most likely to pull me aside and show me the new songs he loves. That was the case one humid summer day when he showed me a John Mayer ballad called "Never on the Day You Leave."

I listened to it again and again, and it occurred to me that the lyrics were spot-on. It's never on the day you leave that you know just how sad a breakup will be. How devastating a divorce. And like that, a story began to take shape in my heart.

What if a man could see where the sad and empty years would take him after he walked out on his wife? What if a woman could remember all the reasons she'd said "I do," and in the process become desperate to make things work?

All in one night?

My whole life I've been a fan of Charles Dickens. Which is why every Christmas our family gathers to watch *Scrooge*, the musical with Albert Finney. It was my father's favorite, and it is mine. And always I think what a gift Scrooge is given. The chance to see what has been, what truly is and what might be—in a single, life-changing night.

For that reason, *When We Were Young* is one of my favorite books I've ever written. This story is a gift from God—I truly believe that. And so if this book has touched your heart, the way it has touched mine, I beg you to pass it on. Buy another copy and donate it to your local library. Give a dozen of them as Christmas gifts this year.

For some people, *When We Were Young* will save their marriage. It will cause people to consider the consequences down the road, and not just the trouble of today. Others will read it and experience a healed relationship with a parent or sibling or friend. Maybe a restored faith in God.

What could be more important than that?

As with many of my other books, this novel gave you the chance to spend a little time with our favorite family—the Baxters. And now you have had the chance to watch the first season of *The Baxters* on TV. Something I only dreamed about back when God gave me these very special characters. The series is expected to become one of the most beloved of all time. I know you'll be watching.

You'll find the Baxters again in my upcoming book, *Two Weeks,* which features Landon and Ashley Baxter Blake's son Cole, and an unforgettable story of love, sacrifice and life's inevitable goodbyes. I know you'll love it, like I do. I'm grateful you're sharing in the journey!

Excessive use of social media is a problem today. Not just for young people, but for all of us. Still, in limited amounts it can be used for the good. It is my goal that you leave uplifted and encouraged after hanging out a few minutes on my Facebook, Twitter, or Instagram. But it's also my hope that you spend far more time with real people, doing real things. Be more concerned with living your life than documenting it. More determined to connect with family and friends than compare yourself to them.

Honestly, the best way to connect with me is through my newsletter. Every week or so I send out an email that includes a few paragraphs from my heart, something you cannot get anywhere else. A few words to give you a greater sense of peace and hope. To help you live with a deeper faith and more intentional love toward family and friends.

Also, my newsletter is the only place you can receive updates about the Baxters TV series, other movies based on my books, and my contest winners. I choose a few of my newsletter readers each week to win an autographed book. Visit my website, KarenKingsbury.com, to sign up! Like so many others, you can be among my closest reader friends, the ones who get my newsletter.

Until next time . . . I'm praying for you.

Love you all!

THE BAXTER FAMILY: YESTERDAY AND TODAY

For some of you, this is not your first time with the Baxter family. You began with the book *Redemption,* when the Baxters were introduced. But for many of you, this is your first time to see the Baxter family in one of my novels. Yes, you could go back and read more than twenty books on these most-loved characters. The list of Baxter titles—in order—is at the beginning of this book. But you don't have to read those to read this one. In fact, there will be other Baxter books coming in the next few years. These books are a collection, and can be read in any order.

If you wish, you can begin right here.

Whether you've known the Baxters for years or are just meeting them now, here's a quick summary of the family, their kids, and their ages. Also, because these characters are fictional, I've taken some liberty with their ages. Let's just assume these are their current ages.

Now, let me introduce you to—or remind you of—the Baxter family:

• • •

THE BAXTERS BEGAN in Bloomington, Indiana, and the family still lives there today.

The Baxter house is on ten acres outside of town, with a winding creek that runs through the backyard. It has a wraparound porch and a pretty view and the memories of a lifetime. The house was built by John and Elizabeth Baxter. They raised their children here. Today it is owned by one of their daughters—Ashley—and her husband, Landon Blake. It is still the place where the extended Baxter family gathers for special celebrations.

• • •

JOHN BAXTER: John is the patriarch of the Baxter family. Formerly an emergency room doctor and professor of medicine at Indiana University, he's now retired. John's first wife, Elizabeth, died long ago from a recurrence of cancer. Years later, John remarried Elaine, and the two live in Bloomington.

• • •

DAYNE MATTHEWS, 43: Dayne is the oldest son of John and Elizabeth. Dayne was born out of wedlock and given up for adoption at birth. His adoptive parents died in a small plane crash when he was 18. Years later, Dayne became a very visible and popular movie star. At age 30, he hired an attorney to find his birth parents—John and

Elizabeth Baxter. He had a moment with Elizabeth in the hospital before she died, and years later he connected with the rest of his biological family. Dayne is married to Katy, 41. The couple has three children: Sophie, 8; Egan, 6; and Blaise, 4. They are very much part of the Baxter family, and they split time between Los Angeles and Bloomington.

• • •

BROOKE BAXTER WEST, 41: Brooke is a pediatrician in Bloomington, married to Peter West, 41, also a doctor. The couple has two daughters: Maddie, 20, and Hayley, 17. The family experienced a tragedy when Hayley suffered a drowning accident at age 4. She recovered miraculously, but still has disabilities caused by the incident.

• • •

KARI BAXTER TAYLOR, 39: Kari is a designer, married to Ryan Taylor, 41, football coach at Clear Creek High School. The couple has three children: Jessie, 17; RJ, 11; and Annie, 8. Kari had a crush on Ryan when the two were in middle school. They dated through college, and then broke up over a misunderstanding. Kari married a man she met in college, Tim Jacobs, but some years into their marriage he had an affair. The infidelity resulted in his murder at the hands of a stalker. The tragedy devastated Kari, who was pregnant at the time with their first child, Jessie. Ryan came back into her life around the same time, and years later he and Kari married. They live in Bloomington.

• • •

ASHLEY BAXTER BLAKE, 37: Ashley is the former black sheep of the Baxter family, married to Landon Blake, 37, who is now captain of the Bloomington Fire Department. The couple has four children: Cole, 17; Amy, 12; Devin, 10; and Janessa, 6. As a young single mom, Ashley was jaded against God and her family when she reconnected with her firefighter friend Landon, who had secretly always loved her. Eventually Ashley and Landon married, and Landon adopted Cole. Together, the couple had two children—Devin and Janessa. Between those children, they lost a baby girl, Sarah Marie, at birth to anencephaly. Amy, Ashley's niece, came to live with them a few years ago after Amy's parents, Erin Baxter Hogan and Sam Hogan, and Amy's three sisters, were killed in a horrific car accident. Amy was the only survivor. Ashley and Landon and their family live in Bloomington, in the old Baxter house, where Ashley and her siblings were raised. Ashley still paints and is successful in selling her work in local boutiques.

• • •

LUKE BAXTER, 35: Luke is a lawyer, married to Reagan Baxter, 35, a blogger. The couple has three children: Tommy, 15; Malin, 10; and Johnny, 6. Luke met Reagan in college. They experienced a major separation early on, after having Tommy out of wedlock. Eventually the two married, though they could not have more children. Malin and Johnny are both adopted.

• • •

IN ADDITION TO the Baxters, this book will revisit the Flanigan family. The Flanigans have been friends with the Baxters for many years. So much so that I previously wrote four books about their only daughter and oldest child—Bailey Flanigan. For the purpose of this book and those that might follow, here are the names and ages of the Flanigans:

Jim and Jenny Flanigan, both 46. Jim is a football coach for the Indianapolis Colts, and Jenny is a freelance writer who works from home. Bailey, 24, is married to Brandon Paul, 27, and they have one child, a daughter, Hannah Jennifer, almost 1. Bailey and Brandon were once actors in Hollywood—Brandon, very well known. Today they run the Christian Kids Theater in downtown Bloomington. Bailey's brothers are Connor, 21, a student at Liberty University; Shawn and Justin, both age 18 and seniors at Clear Creek High; BJ (James), 17, a junior in high school; and Ricky, 15, a freshman.

In addition, Flanigan family friend Cody Coleman has resurfaced in recent books. Cody lived with the Flanigans when he was in high school and had a long-standing crush on the family daughter, Bailey. But all that changed when Brandon Paul entered the picture. Even before the relationship between Brandon and Bailey got serious, Cody began to have feelings for Bailey's former college roommate, Andi Ellison. Over the following years, Andi and Cody shared two failed engagements. Now, though, the two are married and may appear in future storylines.

ONE CHANCE FOUNDATION

The Kingsbury family is passionate about seeing orphans all over the world brought home to their forever families. As a result, Karen created a charitable group called the One Chance Foundation.

This foundation was inspired by the memory of her father, Ted C. Kingsbury. Ted always said, "Life is not a dress rehearsal. We have one chance to love, one chance to truly live!"

Karen often tells her reader friends, "You have one chance to write the story of your life!"™ Now, with Karen's One Chance Foundation, readers can join her in the belief that all of us have one chance to make a difference in the lives of orphans.

In the Bible, James 1:27 says people with pure and faultless religion look after orphans. The One Chance Foundation was created with that truth in mind.

If you are interested in giving to Karen's One Chance Foundation and having your dedication printed in one of Karen's upcoming novels, visit www.KarenKingsbury.com. Below are dedications from some of Karen's reader friends who have contributed to the One Chance Foundation:

- Time stood still when we were young . . . Never forget! —Love, Chacha
- Stephanie, Rachel & Nathan—We love you to the moon & back! Love, Mer & Paudre
- Dear Denise, All your life you've faced challenges of spina bifida!! You have shown all who know you a faith that surpasses understanding. I love you! MaryDale
- Mom, Thank you for all of your love and support! Merry Christmas! Mark and Susan
- To Kingston Painter, a true champion for Christ! Keep shining your light for Jesus! Love, Karen and the team at Life-Changing Fiction™
- Josh & Abbie, we wish you much love, happiness and forever joy! Love, Mom & Mike
- Kylie + Caroline: I love you both infinity to the power of infinity! Love, Mama
- Thanks for being a great mom and an amazing grandma. Vanessa
- To my amazing husband, Greg, & my beautiful son, Zayden, without you I would be lost. Love always, Keena (Mommy) 2018
- Michael, you are "awesome"! You have been through so much & always have a smile on your face. Love you forever, Mom (Kim O'Connell)

- Thankful that Donna and Lee became "we" and for twenty-five years with my sweetest friend!
- You are the heart of our family, we love you, Meemaw (Amy Huckaby). Love from Your Grandchildren
- In loving memory of Hunter Kyle & Tiffany, my beautiful grandchildren who went to be with the Lord too soon. My love forever, will see you again! Love, Grandma
- My Dearest Caroline, I would be lost without you, I love you more and more every day. Your loving husband, Christopher
- In memory of my twin brother, Tony Clements. I cherish all the years of fun and friendship. I'll miss you forever. Love, Tonya
- Ali & Johnny, my gifts from God! Autumn, Wade & Zach, also. I Love You All, dearly! Mom (Andrea)
- In memory of Mum & Dad, Christine & Jim Robertson. Until we meet again. Love, Graeme, Sharon & Trevor
- To my soul mate & best friend, Vern. Happy Anniversary!! Thirty-one years and counting . . . I love you more! Taunia
- Dearest Robert, I praise God for second chances & for the sixteen glorious years together. Each time I

walk Walter & Molly in our orchard I am reminded of God's love for us, your love for God & our love for each other. This love was displayed in our wedding bands & in our marriage. In our wedding vows we made a covenant to God & each other & that was never broken. Thank you. Love, Lou

- To my husband and children (Greg, Tristan, Camille & Braydon). Thank you for being a blessing in my life. Love, Mom (Jen Ashfeld)
- Thank you, Momma, for the godly example of the Proverbs 31 woman you are. I love you! —Christi Taylor
- Thanks, Mom, for sharing your love of these books with me. Mya's next. Love, Angela
- Lody, Scoob, Twister & Bridger Bear, U R My Life!! Forever a Smile, Always a Laugh! Love, Mom
- To Ron & Ann White—the best parents. To Jamie Cochrane—the best son. Love you all, Jennifer/Mom
- To the One Chance Foundation with love, Sheree Nickleston
- Amy, What joy to see the way you embrace God's plan for your family. We are blessed! I love you, Mama
- To the dear, wonderful Heather Tuller (Isaiah 6:8). Love, Flynt and Flynt C

- Valerie and Meredith . . . we are so very proud of both of you! Love, Mom and Dad
- To the One Chance Foundation with love, Josephine Siaumau
- In loving memory of my precious son, Douglas Pruitt, who now lives in heaven. I will love you forever. I miss you so very much. Love, Mom (Judy Roberts)
- With love to our seven grand-blessings who fill life with joy . . . Nana & Poppy Holman
- Jacki—I'm glad you're my Karen Kingsbury "sister." Love you! Tammy Augustine
- In memory of my husband, Danny. When We Were Young you captured my heart. Love, Lisa Cromwell
- Charlene DJ Kroeker, forever 21. Jesus Your All, Beautiful, Spunky & Adventurous. Jared Mc, your "keeper." We love & miss you. Your K & M Families
- To Barb Tuttle: Even without meeting face-to-face, you became God's precious prayer angel to me! Blessings, Jan Miller
- To Daphne Bynum: Your ever-loving support is a tribute to your steadfastness in the Lord. You've blessed my life! Love, Jan Miller
- Missing my Sis—Lois Meyers (Who I always shared my KK books with!) Love, Brenda Brown

- Dear Melissa, Thank you for being my wife. I could not ask for more. Love, Jason
- Happy Birthday, Carol! My lifelong, devoted friend! With love, Sharon
- In loving memory of Mickey Hamilton, the Lord picked you just for me—Love, Stefanie
- We love you, Mom, aka A'ma! You're the best! Love, Sue, Steph, Jensen, Mia & Sav
- To Kim, my forever friend. You are a treasure to me. Love, Ginger. Proverbs 18:24
- To Kristen, an amazing wife and mother! Love, David and Kadence Brock
- Leah Hardwick, Your heart for orphans & underprivileged kids is amazing! Love, Mom & Dad
- Carden, Jacob, Laney, Lincoln, Brek & Holli, Grandma loves you!!! Love, Jackie Hollevoet
- To my greatest blessings. My son, daughter and four grandchildren. Love Always, Mom, Grandma Judy Resley
- Happy Birthday, Stacey! We appreciate you! Love, Your Redheads and Grandbaby
- Nathania, you are a blessing and we love you. Happy fourteenth birthday from Mom & Dad
- To Team KK—It is a joy to have each of you on the team! You all are simply the best team an author

could have!! Love, Karen & Susan and the team at Life-Changing Fiction™

- Thanks, Sharon Borst, for sharing God's love in your special ways. You are loved!
- Thank you for always being there for us! We could always count on you & Dad to love & support us. That means so much. Lots of Love, Jodi
- To the One Chance Foundation with love, Bethany Taylor

WHEN WE WERE YOUNG

KAREN KINGSBURY

1. What did you like most about Emily? What did Noah like about her?
2. How did you feel about Noah? How did Emily feel about him? Give an example.
3. Do you know any couples like Noah and Emily? How do couples like these inspire you?
4. Did Noah and Emily's early love remind you of yours, or that of someone you know? Talk about their early love. Talk about your love story. Or the love story of someone you know.
5. How important was faith to Noah and Emily's relationship?
6. What did you like most about Clara? Tell about a special-needs person you know.
7. Explain how sometimes a special-needs person seems to understand life and love and faith more than people without special needs. Talk about someone like this.
8. How have you seen social media used for the good? Give an example.
9. Give an example of how social media has been used for the bad. Talk about this.
10. Are you aware of "Internet famous" couples? How do you think this type of life might be hard on a marriage?

11. What are the spiritual and relational dangers of posting your life every day on social media?
12. How important is a Bible study support group for married people? What about single people? Explain.
13. Have you or has someone you know walked out on a relationship and regretted it later? Talk about that.
14. The real loss of a broken relationship only happens later. Especially with marriage. Talk about how you can't know the extent of loss on the day you leave, but only years later.
15. Noah was given a very great gift—the ability to see how the future might play out after he leaves his family. How would this gift have helped you or someone you know?
16. At the same time, Emily received the gift of reflection, remembering the details and years that had first brought Noah and her together. How could the gift of memory help you or someone you love?
17. Ryan and Kari Baxter Taylor had the gift of powerful words from Kari's mother, Elizabeth Baxter. What was something that spoke to you from *Elizabeth Baxter's 10 Secrets to a Happy Marriage*?
18. What is hardest on a relationship—differences or pride? How can faith in God help these problems? Explain your answer.

19. What does it mean to put the other person first in your marriage or relationships? Give an example.

20. How did you feel about the final scene in *When We Were Young*? What action did this book make you want to take in your marriage or relationship with someone you love—a sibling, parent, friend, et cetera?

Pass this book on.
Give it to a cashier.
Leave it at a bus stop.
Donate it to a school.
A book is only life-changing if it's being read.
—Karen Kingsbury